MANIPULATED BY A KILLER

"I know that I sure as hell didn't write that letter to you, but circumstantial evidence points to me," Reed said. "Maybe whoever sent it wants you to think I'm the person who wrote it."

"But why?"

"To get me in trouble."

Ella rose to her feet but quickly realized her mistake. Reed didn't move out of her way, so only inches separated her body from his. She felt his heat, smelled his sweat, heard his in-drawn breath when his leg accidentally brushed against hers. Or had it been accidental?

"Why—why would someone want to get you in trouble?"

"If I get in big enough trouble, I go back to the pen." Did Reed sway slightly toward her or did she lean into him? Only a hairbreadth separated them now. "Whoever really killed Junior Blalock doesn't want me to stay free, doesn't want me snooping around trying to find out the truth."

For a split second, she thought he was going to kiss her. She froze to the spot, unable to move, unable to breathe. *You don't want him to kiss you, do you?* The shock of realizing that yes, she did want him to kiss her, motivated her self-preservation instincts. Maybe Reed Conway fascinated her in a way no other man ever had. Maybe the aura of danger and machismo that was such an intrinsic part of him aroused some primitive female need within her. But she was an intelligent, cautious woman who knew better than to succumb to baser instincts. . . .

Books by Beverly Barton

AFTER DARK

EVERY MOVE SHE MAKES

WHAT SHE DOESN'T KNOW

THE FIFTH VICTIM

THE LAST TO DIE

AS GOOD AS DEAD

KILLING HER SOFTLY

CLOSE ENOUGH TO KILL

Published by Zebra Books

Beverly Barton

EVERY MOVE SHE MAKES

ZEBRA BOOKS
KENSINGTON PUBLISHING CORP.
http://www.zebrabooks.com

ZEBRA BOOKS are published by

Kensington Publishing Corp.
850 Third Avenue
New York, NY 10022

All Kensington titles, imprints and distributed lines are available at special quantity discounts for bulk purchases for sales
promotion, premiums, fund-raising, educational or institutional
use.

Special book excerpts or customized printings can also be
created to fit specific needs. For details, write or phone the
office of the Kensington Special Sales Manager: Kensington
Publishing Corp., 850 Third Avenue, New York, NY 10022.
Attn. Special Sales Department. Phone: 1-800-221-2647.

First Printing: September 2003
10

Printed in the United States of America

*To my daughter, Badiema Beaver Waldrep,
and my son, Brant Beaver, who have filled
my life with joy and given me countless
reasons to be a very proud mother*

Chapter 1

He had been waiting fifteen years for this day and nothing—absolutely nothing—was going to ruin it for him. Not the guard's smart-ass farewell comment. Not the drizzling rain. And not the fear that clutched his stomach like a giant fist. If he made a mistake and broke their rules, they'd send him back here to Donaldson. He had to play it smart, be careful, and make sure he didn't get caught doing anything illegal. But come hell or high water, when he got home he was going to prove a few things to some people, starting with Webb Porter, the man he held responsible for ruining his life.

As a prisoner, he had proven to *them* that he could be a model inmate, a reformed character who was remorseful for his past sins. If he hadn't messed up so badly those first couple of years, he'd have been out of this place long before now. But at eighteen, he'd been a stupid punk, filled with hatred and rage. The hatred and rage were still inside him, but he had learned to keep them under control. Channeled properly, strong emotions could work to his benefit.

When he'd finally wised up, he would have done anything for a chance at being paroled. The only thing that had kept him sane and made him fight to survive under intolerable conditions was the dream of freedom.

Once he returned home, he would take things one day at a time. Wouldn't make any waves. Wouldn't ruffle any feathers. At least not right away. He had been waiting fifteen years; he could wait a little longer. But no matter what he had to do or who he had to hurt in the process, he intended to reclaim the life that had been taken from him. He had come to this prison as an eighteen-year-old convicted murderer, who, only months before his arrest, had been a star athlete with the world by the tail and a bright future. He had paid his debt to society, had served his time for being convicted of slitting his bastard of a stepfather's throat. Now he was free. Free to go home. Free to unearth the truth. Free to make sure the guilty paid as dearly for their crimes as they had made him pay.

But first things first. Reed Conway grinned as he marched out of Donaldson Correctional Facility, head held high, shoulders squared, backbone ramrod straight. When he got back to Spring Creek, he wanted to eat his fill of his mama's fried chicken and peach cobbler. He wanted to guzzle down a six-pack of ice-cold beer with his cousin Briley Joe and have some fun, the way they had when they'd been teenagers. And he wanted to get laid. Just about any willing woman would do just fine.

"I wish it weren't raining." Judy Conway wiped the foggy window, her circular motions creating a small clearing in the car's hazy windshield. "I wanted today to be perfect for Reed's homecoming. The sun should be shining."

"Don't worry about the weather, Mama," Regina said as she reached out and clasped her mother's hand. "Reed won't care. And a little rain couldn't possibly spoil this day. We've been waiting an awfully long time for him to come home to us."

Judy squeezed Regina's hand. "It's going to be so hard for him. He was just a boy when he went in that awful place. He grew from a boy to a man inside the walls of that prison. I can't help wondering if it'll be possible for him to adjust to living in the outside world."

"Don't be so pessimistic."

"I'm trying to be realistic." Judy caught a glimpse of two men walking in the rain straight toward the car. Her heartbeat accelerated. The shorter man, with his black umbrella held high, barely kept step with the taller one, who was all but running. "It's them. Look, honey. Mark has Reed with him."

Mark Leamon's father, Milton Leamon, had been Reed's attorney, and when the elder Mr. Leamon had passed away five years ago, his son, fresh out of law school, had taken over his father's practice in Spring Creek. And Regina had gone to work for him three years ago, when he'd decided to add a legal assistant to the small firm.

Judy grabbed the handle and swung open the car door. Sitting in the backseat, Regina mimicked her mother's moves. They jumped out of the Lincoln and stood side by side. Regina held a floral umbrella over her mother's head, but the closer her son came toward her, the harder it was for Judy to stay put. She left the umbrella's protection and raced toward Reed, disregarding the drenching rain. He increased his pace and they met at the edge of the roadway, mother and son, soaked to the skin. A broad smile spread across Judy's face. Tears trickled from her eyes and mixed with the raindrops on her cheeks.

"Reed!" She grabbed him, wrapping her arms securely around her firstborn, the son of her first husband, who had died in a bloody war halfway around the world only weeks before Reed was born nearly thirty-three years ago.

His strong arms encompassed her in a celebratory bear hug and they clung to each other. Finally Reed grabbed his mother's shoulders and stared into her face. She gazed back at him, at the handsome features so like Jimmy Conway's. Reed had always been his father's son—in looks, talent, and temperament. But his smile was hers. Same straight, white teeth. Same wide, full mouth. *Thank you God,* she prayed silently. *Thank you for letting me see my son smile again.*

"I'm coming home with you, Mama." Reed spoke with emotion in his voice, but she knew he wouldn't cry. Neither tears of happiness nor tears of sorrow. She hadn't seen her son cry since he'd been a small boy. So strong and brave and in control.

Since early childhood, he'd been her little man. And when she'd made the horrific mistake of marrying Junior Blalock, Reed had become her protector. Her former husband's brutal ways had forced Reed to grow up too fast, to take on adult burdens when he'd been just a boy. She blamed herself for what had happened. She always would.

"Reed?" Regina laid her open palm on her brother's shoulder.

Grabbing his mother's hand, Reed turned to face Regina. "Hey, kid. How's it going?"

"Y'all can talk on the way home," Mark Leamon said, as he tried to hold his large black umbrella over mother and son. "In case y'all haven't noticed, it's raining."

Reed laughed. The sound wrapped around Judy's heart and filled her with a mother's joy.

"Mark's right," Regina said. "Even with the umbrellas, we're getting drenched out here."

"You sit up front with Mark," Judy said. "I want Reed all to myself on the way home."

Within seconds, they were inside Mark's black Lincoln Town Car, leaving the Donaldson Correctional Facility in Bessemer, Alabama, and heading toward home. Home to Spring Creek in the northern part of the state.

Regina turned sideways in her seat so that she could carry on a conversation with the backseat occupants.

"You wouldn't believe what-all Mama's done this week getting ready for your homecoming." Regina settled her gaze on her brother. "Ever since Mark told us that you'd been granted a parole, we've been getting a room ready for you and Mama's bought you some new clothes and—"

"Leave a little something for a surprise," Judy said teasingly.

"Mama, I told you not to go to any trouble." Reed held Judy's hand in his firm grip. "I kind of want to get a place of my own eventually, and Briley Joe has already offered to let me move into the room over the garage. I know you have only two bedrooms at your place."

"We've fixed up the room off the back porch for you," Judy said. "It was just storage, and I kept my sewing machine in there. Even if you decide to move later on, I want you to have your own room while you're with me."

"I offered to take the storage room," Regina said. "But Mama wouldn't hear of it. She said the last thing you'd want would be to put me out of my bedroom."

"Mama's right," Reed told her. "I don't want my coming home to cause any problems for you or Mama."

But my homecoming is going to stir up a hornet's nest and that's for sure. Judy heard Reed's unspoken comment inside her head, as surely as if he had spoken aloud. No matter what her son had professed to the parole board, she knew in her heart that Reed had neither forgotten the past nor forgiven the people he held responsible for convicting him of Junior's murder. It was only a matter of time before Reed locked horns with Webb Porter, and when he did, all hell would break loose. She couldn't bear to think about what might happen to Reed—and to Webb.

* * *

Webb Porter rose from the bed, picked up his clothes off the chair, and headed toward the bathroom.

"Sugar, are you leaving already?" Sierra asked him.

He paused, glanced over his shoulder, and smiled at the redhead lying naked on black satin sheets in the middle of the black wrought-iron bed.

"Sorry, but we're having a little family dinner party tonight and it's a good hour and a half drive back to Spring Creek."

Whimpering, Sierra pouted playfully. Webb chuckled, then went into the bathroom, hung his clothes on a hook attached to the back of the door, and turned on the sink faucets, letting the warm water flow. As he lathered his genital area, he recalled the enjoyment he'd just shared with his Huntsville mistress. At fifty-eight, he wasn't quite the stud he'd once been, but he still wanted sex on a regular basis. Over the years, he'd had several mistresses, some lasting for years. Currently he had two. One was here in Huntsville, less than two hours from home, but still far enough away that his comings and goings went unnoticed. He'd met Sierra Camp at a campaign rally when he'd run for senator the first time. She was a childless divorcée in her early forties who wasn't looking for a husband. Sierra was an independent woman who required nothing in the way of financial support from him. They got together occasionally, whenever he came home to Alabama.

His D.C. mistress was another matter altogether. He provided Cheri with a car and an apartment. He visited her regularly, two times a week when he was in Washington, and she gave him whatever his heart desired. She was young—younger than his own daughter—and wild and fun. And sometimes she wore him out, made him feel old. If she didn't give the best damn blow jobs he'd ever had, he would have already traded her in on an older model. Someone smarter and classier. Someone more like Sierra.

Webb dressed hurriedly but took time to make sure his tie was straight and his hair was neatly combed. He prided himself on his thick mane of salt-and-pepper hair.

When he emerged from the bathroom, Sierra, who had donned a short black silk robe, met him with open arms.

"Give me a good-bye kiss," she said.

Webb wrapped his arms around her waist, then dropped his hands to cup her buttocks. She laughed. He covered her lips with his, and when she sighed, he thrust his tongue inside her mouth. Then he ended the heated kiss quickly, swatted her behind, and nodded toward the door.

"Walk me out," he suggested.

She laced her arm through his and went with him down the hall, through her kitchen, and to the back door. He always parked in her garage, came in through the back door and exited the same way.

"Any chance you'll make it back up this way next week?" Sierra asked as she ran her hand down the front of his shirt, pausing at his belt buckle.

"I don't know if I'll still be in Alabama," he told her. "I'll give you a call in a few days, when I know my plans."

"You do that. And if I'm free, we'll make some plans of our own."

Webb nodded, then went into the garage, got in his Mercedes, and waited for her to hit the door opener. He took his sunglasses from where he'd stuck them behind the sun visor and slipped them on. He gave himself a quick inspection glance in the inside rearview mirror and smiled at his reflection.

"You should feel guilty, you horny old bastard," he said aloud. "What if Ella ever found out about your affairs? What would your daughter think of you then?"

Ella had been the joy of his life since the moment he

and Carolyn had adopted her. She'd been two weeks old. He'd taken one look at her and immediately fallen in love with her. He had never loved anyone the way he loved his little girl. Ella idolized him, and by God, he wanted it to stay that way. He kept his affairs out of town, not only to protect his wife from ugly rumors, but to hide the truth about his less-than-perfect marriage from his daughter.

When the garage door lifted, Webb waved goodbye to Sierra, put the car in reverse, and backed out of the driveway. Checking his watch, he groaned. He'd be cutting it close to get home in time to shower, shave, and change clothes before Carolyn's little family dinner party tonight. He'd have to think of some excuse for why he'd been delayed in Huntsville. It didn't matter how feeble the excuse; Carolyn never questioned his explanations. He figured she suspected the truth but preferred to look the other way and pretend they actually had a good marriage. That was what Ella believed. That her parents adored each other. Perpetuating that lie was as much his fault as Carolyn's. He should have ended their marriage years ago. But it was too late now. Divorce would ruin his political career, and it would break Ella's heart. He didn't dare risk doing either. Other than Ella, his career was all he had.

As usual, Carolyn Porter's dinner party was a huge success. With Bessie's delicious meal combined with Carolyn's sparkling personality, every event in the Porter home seemed to come off without a hitch. Even Webb's late arrival hadn't seemed to disturb his wife in the least. It never ceased to amaze Ella how kind and considerate of each other her parents were. She envied them their abiding love. She hoped that one day she would share that kind of commitment with a man. Being a woman, she recognized the look of love in her mother's eyes whenever her father came into a room. And she couldn't imagine a man more attentive to his wife than her father.

When Dan reached between them on the Duncan Phyfe sofa and slipped her hand into his, Ella tensed, but when he gazed at her adoringly, she managed to smile at him. She'd been dating Dan Gilmore on and off for nearly a year now. Friends and acquaintances were making bets on just when the two would tie the knot. She liked Dan and enjoyed his company, but she simply couldn't imagine spending the rest of her life with him. Actually, she couldn't imagine the two of them ever making love. Dan wanted her, and he'd made it perfectly clear that he was more than ready for a sexual relationship. She'd been putting him off for months now, but how much longer could she expect him to wait?

"I didn't want to ruin a perfectly lovely meal, so I didn't bring up the subject while we were eating," Jeff Henry Carlisle said, "but it's a subject that needs discussing."

Ella glanced at her uncle, a small, dapper man with huge blue eyes and a round, cherubic face. His thinning brown hair and neatly groomed mustache were edged with gray. Although Aunt Cybil's husband could on occasion be a pompous jackass, she loved him dearly and overlooked his many faults. He'd been like a second father to her all her life. Growing up, she'd spent as much time next door at Uncle Jeff Henry and Aunt Cybil's as she had at home. She thought it tragic that they didn't have any children, considering the way they both doted on her.

"Whatever are you talking about, brother?" Carolyn asked.

Jeff Henry cringed, but Carolyn didn't seem to notice. Ella wondered how it was possible that her mother seemed totally unaware that her brother-in-law despised her using the affectionate term *brother* when she spoke to him. Even a blind person could sense how utterly besotted Jeff Henry was with his sister-in-law. When she'd been sixteen, Ella had realized that her uncle was in love with her mother, and she had thought his affection for her mother a tragic thing for him—and for Aunt Cybil.

"I'm referring to the fact that Reed Conway was released from prison today," Jeff Henry said.

All the color drained from Carolyn's face. Ella started to rise and go to her mother, but before she did, her father, who sat in the brocade armchair beside Carolyn's wheelchair, reached over and clasped his wife's hand.

"Are you all right, my dear?" Webb asked.

"Yes, I'm quite all right." Carolyn brought Webb's hand to her mouth, kissed him tenderly, and held his hand to her side. "I already knew about Reed's parole, but I'd almost forgotten that he was being released today. I'm sure Judy is very happy to have her son home with her after all these years."

"Of course she's ecstatic about his release," Jeff Henry said. "But I am not the least bit pleased that a convicted murderer is going to be living in our peaceful little town. I think they should have thrown away the key when they locked that good-for-nothing boy up. That's what's wrong with this country. Murderers being set free. Crime rates rising. If I were running things I'd—"

"Stuff it, will you?" Cybil Carlisle's voice held a sharp edge as she chastised her husband. "We all know your views on what you'd do if you were God. You'd put us all back into the mid-nineteenth century. You'd restore slavery, wife beating and—"

"Cybil, must you be so unkind?" Carolyn's silvery-gray eyes glared at her sister.

"I've never laid a hand on you," Jeff Henry said, his face suffusing with color. "And Lord knows I've had reason to."

"This is neither the time nor the place for the two of

you to air your differences." Webb's voice rose slightly, his tone cautioning his in-laws.

"Of course, you're quite right," Jeff Henry agreed. "Please forgive us." His gaze settled on Carolyn.

"I, for one, am eager to see the bad boy return." Grinning, Cybil ran her hand through her short, dark hair. "If I recall correctly, Reed Conway was a damn good-looking hunk. And sexy as hell. And no doubt after fifteen years in the pen, he's horny as hell and aching to get laid."

"Cybil!" Carolyn's normally soft voice screeched with disapproval. "Must you be so vulgar? Especially in front of Ella."

"Good God, Ella is thirty years old," Cybil said. "If she doesn't know about the birds and the bees by now, it's high time she was learning."

"You had too much wine with dinner." Jeff Henry rose from the sofa, offered his hand to his wife, and gave her a stern look. "We should go home. I think we've worn out our welcome tonight."

Cybil laughed—a loose, silly laugh that indicated she had indeed become inebriated. She looked up at her husband, then lifted her hand to his. He gently assisted her to her feet, and after more apologies, he guided Cybil out of the living room and into the foyer.

"Perhaps you should help Jeff Henry," Carolyn said to her husband.

Webb nodded. "Sorry that the evening ended on such a sour note, Dan. I'm sure you realize that Cybil isn't always so unpleasant. She's a wonderful woman, but she simply can't handle alcohol."

Talk about trying to put a pretty face on something, Ella thought. Her father was indeed the consummate politician, capable of putting a positive spin on any occurrence. Why he even bothered trying to defend Aunt Cybil she didn't know. After all, it wasn't as if Dan hadn't been born and raised in Spring Creek. He'd heard all the whispered little rumors about Cybil Walker Carlisle's penchant for men and liquor. As much as she loved her aunt, Ella hadn't turned a blind eye to the woman's weaknesses. More than once, her mother had been horribly shamed by Cybil's misadventures. If the two sisters didn't resemble each other almost enough to be twins, no one would ever believe that the highly moral, genteel Carolyn was related to the wild, immoral Cybil.

"Every family has their little differences of opinions," Dan said diplomatically.

"Thanks for being so understanding," Webb said. "I'd better go see if Jeff Henry needs a hand." Webb excused himself to follow his in-laws.

Dan turned his attention to Carolyn as he stood. "Mrs. Porter, dinner was lovely as always. Thank you for inviting me."

"You must come back often," Carolyn said. "We're quite fond of you, you know."

"And I'm quite fond of y'all," Dan replied.

Oh, Mother, please don't speak for me. Don't give Dan the impression that I care more for him than I do. I know you'd love to have him as a son-in-law, but you shouldn't wish for me anything less than what you and Daddy have.

"Walk me out, darling?" Dan offered his hand to Ella.

"Certainly." She ignored his hand as she rose to her feet without any assistance.

As they headed into the foyer, Ella heard her mother ringing for her nurse, Viola. When they reached the front door, which Webb had left wide open on his hasty departure, Dan pulled Ella into his arms. She went willingly, not knowing how to disengage herself without hurting his feelings. He was a sweet man and she was quite fond of him, but she didn't love him.

When his lips sought hers, she gave herself over to the moment. Sweet and tender. If only she could love Dan, it would make her mother so happy. She responded to him, enjoying the warmth of his embrace and the genuine affection of his kiss. He lifted his head and gazed into her eyes.

"Dinner and a movie Friday night?" he asked.

"Uh . . . yes. Sure. I'd love to see the new Meg Ryan movie."

"Sweet dreams," Dan said. "Dream of me."

Ella smiled. When Dan was halfway down the sidewalk, he turned and waved. She kept on smiling. Then she closed the door and sighed. She was thirty years old and no raving beauty. There wasn't a horde of eligible men beating a path to her door. So why wasn't she thrilled to have a great guy like Dan courting her, a guy so obviously interested in a permanent relationship?

Because he didn't create butterflies in her stomach. Because she wanted a kiss to be more than pleasant. Because the thought of making love with Dan didn't excite her.

Unbidden, her Aunt Cybil's comments echoed inside her head: *Reed Conway was a damn good-looking hunk. And sexy as hell. And no doubt after fifteen years in the pen, he's horny as hell and aching to get laid.* A flush warmed Ella's cheeks. She remembered Reed Conway. They had traveled in different circles as teenagers and she'd been almost sixteen when he'd gone to prison, but anyone who'd ever known Reed would never forget him.

And Ella in particular had a good reason to remember the son of her aunt and uncle's housekeeper. When they had been growing up, she and Reed hadn't exchanged more than a dozen words. She had run into him occasionally when he'd been with his mother at the Carlisles' house, but for the most part, he had ignored her. And after politely saying hello to him on those occasions, she had tried to ignore him. But she often found herself watching the town's bad boy, who, by the age of seventeen, had gained himself quite a reputation as a star athlete and a hell-raiser. Considering that they had barely known each other, she'd been utterly surprised when she had received a letter from Reed only a few months after he'd been sent to prison.

> *I'm going to think about you while I'm in here. Dream about you. See those big brown eyes of yours following me, looking at me with such hunger. You didn't think I saw you staring at me, but I did. And I knew what you were thinking . . . what you wanted. And baby, I'm just the guy who can give you what you want. When I get out of here, I'm going to look you up. Until then I'm going to think of you while I jerk off.*

Although her parents had taken that first letter and the one that followed away from her and destroyed them, she'd never forgotten what he had written to her. Even after her father explained to her that Reed had written those letters because he hated Webb and would use any method to harass him, Ella had been unable to erase those crude yet erotic words from her mind.

Reed Conway had been released on parole today. Would he look her up as he'd said he would in the letters he'd written all those years ago? *Get a grip, Ella,* she cautioned herself. *Reed wrote those letters to torment your father, not because he had any personal interest in you. You don't have anything to worry about. He's not going to bother you. He probably doesn't even remember you.*

Chapter 2

His mama's house wasn't much to look at, but it was home. And anywhere *outside,* even a two-bedroom, one-bath shack, had a prison cell beat six ways from Sunday. He hated knowing that his mother and sister had spent the past fifteen years here. When he'd been eighteen, one of the reasons that he had wanted to make it big, to be a success, was so that he could take care of his mother and Regina and give them a better life. But he had failed them both and left them to fend for themselves. If he had things to do over again, would he—could he—do anything different?

When they'd first arrived at the house this afternoon, he'd noticed the repairs that had been made on the place. New paint on the inside and out gave the structure a decent appearance. Inside, homemade covers for the threadbare sofa and chairs, and handmade quilts used as bed coverlets added a touch of hominess to an otherwise drab house. And his mother kept her home as spotlessly clean as she did the Carlisle mansion. Damn! After all these years, she was still slaving away as the housekeeper to people who weren't fit to kiss her feet. He intended to find a way to change things, to move his family out of the white-trash area of Spring Creek. Once he settled some old scores and set the record straight, he'd find a job outside Spring Creek and take his mother and sister with him.

Strange how he felt confined sitting here in his mama's living room. A restlessness stirred inside him, a need to run free like an untamed animal. Every once in a while Briley Joe would nod toward the door, a hint that he wanted them to be on their way. But Reed couldn't bring himself to cut short his homecoming party. Mama had fixed all his favorite foods. Regina had hung a "welcome home" banner, edged with yellow ribbons, over the double doorway leading from the living room into the kitchen. And his sister had used balloons here and there to add a festive touch. Summer flowers from the beds that lined the walkway graced the center of the old wooden kitchen table.

"That was a fine meal, Mrs. Conway." Mark Leamon smiled warmly at Judy as he stood. "I appreciate your inviting me to join your family celebration."

"After all you've done to help Reed, it was the least I could do," Judy replied. She glanced at her daughter and added, "You know you're always welcome here. Isn't that right, Regina?"

Regina smiled shyly as color flushed her pale cheeks. "Of course. But Mark already knows that. This isn't the first time he's had dinner with us."

Reed couldn't help noticing the way his little sister looked at Mark Leamon. The way a woman looks at a man she cares about, a man she loves. Even though Regina was nearly twenty-six, he'd continued thinking of her as that same scared little girl who'd run into his arms screaming when she escaped from Junior Blalock's clutches. Although she had visited him when he'd been in prison, he'd never really looked beyond those big blue eyes and sweet smile to see the attractive young woman she had become. Maybe big brothers didn't like to think of their little sisters as adults, as sexual women who would want to be with a man.

Regina was a knockout. The kind of girl men would always look at a second time. A mane of golden-blond hair hugged her shoulders. She was tall and curvy. China doll beautiful. How was it that Mark hadn't picked up on the signals Regina was putting out? Unless he was the densest guy in the universe, it was only a matter of time until he figured out that she was his for the taking.

Reed knew he'd have to do something about the situation before that happened. It was clear as glass. His little sister had the hots for her boss. Poor girl, didn't she realize that she'd set her sights a little high? Mark was a member of the upper echelons of local society. He was, after all, related to Senator Porter. A first cousin once removed. He might offer Regina a hot affair, but when the time came for Mark to choose a wife, he'd pick one of his own kind.

It wasn't that he disliked Mark. The exact opposite was true. The guy had done everything in his power to help Reed, even agreeing to work with him to unearth more facts about Junior Blalock's murder and to do what he could to get the case reopened. Mark was one of only a handful of people who actually believed that Reed hadn't killed his stepfather. Sometimes he wondered if his mother really believed he was innocent.

Reed lifted the iced-tea glass to his lips and took a hefty swig, then stood and shook hands with Mark. "Once I get settled in, I'll be in touch and we can start the ball rolling."

Judy gave Reed a curious stare but didn't question his comment—not then. When Regina walked Mark to the front door, Reed leaned down and whispered to his mother, "You need to put a stop to that before Mark realizes how easily he could have her."

Judy shushed Reed, then countered with a question as she stood. "Just what are you and Mark up to?"

Reed draped his arm around Judy's shoulder. "Don't

worry your pretty head about me. I promise that I'm going to keep out of trouble."

Judy glared at him as if she doubted his word. But then again, what reason did she have to trust him? He had always promised to stay out of trouble, but somehow he'd managed to break that vow time and again.

Reed studied his mother. How was it possible that a fifty-year-old woman who'd lived such a hard life could still be so attractive? White streaked her naturally light-blond hair, which she wore chin-length and curled about her heart-shaped face. She was slender and leggy and probably didn't outweigh Regina by more than ten pounds.

"Hey, Reed, how about we head out?" Briley Joe scooted back the kitchen chair and stood to his full six feet.

Reed glanced at his cousin and grinned. "Yeah, sure. In a few minutes."

"Time's a-wasting, buddy boy. Home and hearth will still be here in the morning."

"Are you going out tonight?" Judy asked, a note of concern in her voice and a look of disapproval on her face.

"I just want to show the boy a good time, Aunt Judy." Briley flashed her his irresistible-to-all-females smile. "A few drinks, a few laughs."

Briley Joe clamped his big hand down on Reed's shoulder. His nails retained a trace of grease stain under the tips. Briley Joe owned Conway's Garage, where he was the chief mechanic. It was where Reed would start work tomorrow; no one else in town would employ him. He was determined to support himself and not be a financial burden on his mother and sister, not even for a few weeks.

"You can save that smile for someone who doesn't know you the way I do," Judy said to her nephew; then she lowered her voice so that only Reed and Briley Joe could hear her. "Reed's not a boy anymore. He doesn't need my permission to go out honky-tonking with you. But you know as well as I do that he'll be in violation of his parole if he's caught in a bar."

"Ain't gonna happen," Briley Joe said. "The bars are full of ex-cons and don't nobody care, least of all the cops."

"Mama, we're not—" Reed started to explain.

"At least stay long enough to tell your sister good night." Judy nodded to the front door, which could be seen plainly from the kitchen.

Mark ruffled Regina's hair the way an adult would caress a child. "Why don't you stay home tomorrow and spend some time with Reed? Consider it a paid holiday."

"Oh, Mark, that's so nice of you. I'd love to—"

"She'll be at work promptly at nine," Judy said, emerging from the kitchen to stand, hands on hips, in the middle of the living room. "This family doesn't take charity of any kind. It was nice of you to offer, but Regina works eight hours for eight hours' pay."

Damn it, Mama, Reed wanted to shout. *Can't you just once put aside your pride?* Giving a valuable, hardworking employee the day off with pay wasn't exactly charity. Judy Conway had a blind spot when it came to accepting anything for free. She always had been a proud woman—too proud to accept anything from anyone. Even when she'd had to send her kids to bed hungry, she had refused any kind of government assistance. And when other kids ate hot lunches at school, Judy had refused free lunches for Reed and Regina, instead packing peanut-butter-and-jelly sandwiches every day and somehow scraping together enough money for them to buy a half-pint of milk. To this day, Reed hated peanut butter. *We'll make do* had been Judy's credo. Apparently it still was.

"I didn't mean to offend." Mark looked down at his feet, obviously a bit embarrassed by Judy's response to what he had probably thought of as nothing more than a kind offer. "Whatever Regina wants." Mark opened the door, but before he left he lifted his gaze, nodded to Reed, and then said, "Thank you again, Mrs. Conway, for your hospitality."

When Mark walked onto the porch, Regina all but ran after him. Her voice carried from outside, making it easy to hear her comments.

"Mark, I'm sorry about Mama. You have to understand that she—"

"It's all right," Mark said. "I might not understand your mother, but I admire her. She's a fine woman. And if you decide to take the day off—"

"I'd better not. I don't want to upset Mama. Besides, Reed and I will have plenty of time together now that he's home. Oh, Mark, I just can't thank you enough for everything you've done to help him."

Feeling like a voyeur, Reed put his arm around his mother's waist. "Why don't I help you clean up the dishes before Briley Joe and I leave?"

She nodded, glanced quickly at the open front door, and then headed for the kitchen. Briley Joe already had the back door open and was waiting impatiently.

Judy turned to Reed. "Mark is a fine young man as well as a very good lawyer. Regina's lucky to be working for him. She has a bright future. And yes, I know she thinks she's in love with him and he has no idea how she feels. But I do not for one minute believe he'd ever take advantage of her."

"Good God, Mama, who are you kidding? He's a man, isn't he? She's a beautiful woman who's nuts about him."

"If Mark ever realizes how Regina feels about him, he could discover that he has similar feelings for her. It's not beyond the realm of possibility that he could ask her to marry him."

"The way Regina's father asked you to marry him?" The minute the words were out of his mouth, he wished them back. In all the years since Regina had been born, they had never once spoken about the circumstances surrounding her birth. He'd been only seven, but he'd known his mother wasn't married. The kids at school had made ugly comments about Judy, and he'd come home with a bloody nose more than once for defending his mother's honor.

Judy slapped him, a resounding strike across his cheek. In all his life, she'd never slapped him. But never before had he ever deserved it more.

"Mama . . . God, I'm sorry. I didn't mean—"

"Why don't you and Briley Joe just leave? Now." Judy gathered up dirty dishes from the table and stacked them on the counter.

"Come on, cuz." Briley Joe nodded toward their escape route.

"I had no right to say what I did." Reed's hand hovered over his mother's shoulder. "I just don't want to see Regina get hurt."

"You go on out and have a good time tonight," Judy said, her voice soft and lightly laced with emotion. "I'll leave the back porch light on for you." She wiped her hands off on a dishcloth and turned to face Reed. Her eyes were dry. All her tears were lodged in her heart. He knew his mother. She was as tough as nails, as strong as steel. "You have your key, don't you?"

"Yeah, I've got my key." He leaned over and kissed her cheek. "I'll holler at Regina before we go."

By the time he'd said goodbye to his sister, Reed heard Briley Joe racing the motor of his Ford pickup. With a final wave, he headed out the back door. Well, he'd eaten his mama's home cooking, so that meant one down and two to go—a six-pack and a willing woman were next on his agenda.

When Reed hopped into the truck, Briley Joe squealed the tires as he raced out of the gravel drive and onto the road leading into town.

"Hell, man, I thought we'd never get out of there." Briley Joe shoved his foot down on the accelerator, sending the old truck into greased-lightning speed.

"After fifteen years without a woman, you've got to be dying for some hot pussy."

Reed laughed, the sound mixing with the warm summer wind blowing in through the open windows. Leave it to Briley Joe to hit the nail on the head. Reed laughed again, louder. Damn, but it was good to be free.

Ella stood outside her mother's bedroom door. She had never been allowed entrance into Carolyn's inner sanctum without knocking first and asking permission. She'd been taught respect for other people's privacy from early childhood. As a little girl she'd felt privileged when she'd been allowed to bring some of her toys to her mother's suite and play quietly on the floor. Often Carolyn had read to her, and later they'd shared a meal together, just the two of them.

Viola was always nearby. Then and now. If not in the room with them, then hovering just beyond the door to her connecting room. Of course, Ella understood the necessity of having her mother's nurse close at hand. Viola had joined the household before Ella's adoption, so her presence in the mansion actually predated Ella's. Sometimes she felt guilty for wishing she could have her mother all to herself, especially when she thought about how dependent her mother was on Viola. Carolyn's spine had been severely damaged after a dreadful horseback riding accident, leaving her paralyzed from the waist down. Only daily exercises, seen to by the devoted Viola, keep atrophy from claiming Carolyn's leg muscles.

Aunt Cybil had upset her mother this evening. It wasn't the first time and certainly wouldn't be the last. As much as she loved her mother, her loyalties were divided. She didn't approve of her aunt's drinking or of the way she occasionally treated Uncle Jeff Henry so cruelly. But Ella loved her mother's younger sister because Aunt Cybil adored her so unabashedly. Her aunt had been the one who'd bought her her first bra; the one who'd explained about menstruation; the person she'd turned to when she wanted to know the facts of life. Often Ella felt as if she had two mothers, each performing different functions in her life. Carolyn was her moral center, the one who taught her good manners and lectured her on the art of being a lady. But it was Cybil who had made mud pies with her and pushed her high into the sky on her backyard swing and taught her how to drive a car.

Whenever a family evening ended badly, Ella knew that it was her job to console her mother, while it was her father's job—when he was in town—to help Uncle Jeff Henry control Cybil. How was it possible, Ella wondered for the millionth time, that two sisters whose physical appearances were almost identical could have personalities that were poles apart?

She lifted her hand and knocked. Viola opened the door, her expression void of any emotion.

"She's been waiting for you," Viola said. "I've changed her into her gown and helped her into bed. I don't know why she puts up with it. Family or no family—"

"Why don't you go on to bed, Viola? I'll stay with Mother until Daddy returns."

Her mother's nurse huffed. "Very well, Miss Ella. But if you need me—"

"I'll call you if I need you."

Viola plodded over to Carolyn's bed, fluffed the pillows around her, and asked if she needed anything. Ella watched how caring and attentive the nurse was, and once again she chastised herself for disliking the woman. Viola Mull looked like Mrs. Potato Head, with thin legs and a rotund body. She kept her gray hair cut in a short, straight bob that made her head look as round as her figure.

"Ella, darling, is that you?" Carolyn's voice contained just a hint of weakness, as if she was exceedingly weary.

"Yes, Mother."

"Come sit with me." Carolyn patted the bed. "Talk to me until your father comes home."

Wearing pale-yellow satin pajamas, Carolyn sat perched in the middle of the massive, canopied mahogany four-poster with white lace trailing down the posts and pooling on the hardwood floor beneath. Pristine white sheets edged with lace perfectly matched the white down coverlet that lay folded at the foot of the bed. White pillows, stacked three deep, rested behind Carolyn's thin body.

"Let my hair down for me and brush it, would you?" Carolyn smiled at Ella. Ever since she'd been a child, Ella would do anything to be rewarded with one of her mother's smiles. She had spent a lifetime trying to please Carolyn, hoping that in some small way she could repay this lovely woman for having adopted her and giving her a family and a life that others could only dream of having.

Ella went into the adjoining all-white bathroom and gathered up her mother's silver brush and comb along with the matching hand mirror. When she sat down on the side of the bed, she laid the items in her lap, then scooted up in the bed so that she sat beside Carolyn. Brushing her mother's hair had become a ceremony over the years, and to this day she loved the feeling of closeness this simple act generated between them. One at a time, Ella loosened the pins that held Carolyn's hair in the loose bun. When she removed the last pin, her mother's shimmery black hair fell down her back, stopping just inches above her waist. Only a few strands of gray glistened when the lamplight struck Carolyn just right.

Ella began brushing, slowly, carefully, making sure she didn't pull too hard and cause Carolyn any discomfort. As she had so many times before, Ella marveled at her mother's beauty: alabaster skin, silky black hair, and striking silver-gray eyes. How often had Ella wished this woman were her biological mother? If she were, then maybe Ella would be prettier. Even though people often mentioned that she actually resembled both her parents, Ella found it hard to believe that she looked anything like the stunning Carolyn. She did have the same color hair, but there the resemblance ended. Carolyn was thin and petite, classically beautiful, and feminine in an old-fashioned, ladylike way.

Ella sighed as she continued brushing her mother's hair. When she finished the task—one hundred strokes—she held up the mirror so that Carolyn could inspect herself.

"Lovely, darling. Thank you." Carolyn leaned over and kissed Ella's cheek. "You're such a good daughter. I'm going to miss having you here with me when you and Dan get married."

Ella tensed. She'd been dreading this conversation. As a child her parents had chosen her playmates, and as a teenager they often had picked her dates. She was well aware of the fact that Dan Gilmore's parents were part of the old-money set in Spring Creek—people whose ancestors had been a part of this town since before the War Between the States. Carolyn had telephoned Dan's mother shortly after Dan's divorce had become final last year and insisted on getting their *children* together.

"Mother . . . I . . . I don't think Dan and I will be getting married."

"Has that young rascal not even hinted about marriage?"

"He's hinted, but . . . I don't love Dan."

Carolyn lifted her eyebrows and rounded her mouth as she sighed. "I see. And is there someone else?"

"No, there's no one else."

"Dan is quite a catch, you know. If you let him get away, some other lucky girl will be wearing his ring by this time next year. His mother has told me that he wants to get married again. His son needs a mother, and a man in his position needs a suitable wife.''

''And I'm suitable?''

''Of course you are.'' Carolyn laughed softly. ''You have all the right credentials. You're bright and charming and very successful. And you're Webb Porter's daughter—and my only child.''

Never once had her mother ever told her that she was pretty. She knew she wasn't, but didn't mothers lie to their little girls and tell even the ugliest duckling that she was the fairest of them all? Carolyn had told her she was smart, clever, charming, loyal, devoted, and even sweet, but never pretty.

''I don't want to marry a man just because he finds me suitable.''

Carolyn took Ella's hands in hers and rested them in her lap atop the spotless white sheets. ''People marry for many different reasons. I'm sure Dan loves you. Why wouldn't he? But Ella, my dear child, you're already thirty and you've never been exactly popular with men. It's not as if there's some white knight out there waiting to sweep you off your feet.''

''Daddy swept you off your feet, didn't he?''

Carolyn's smile wavered ever so slightly. ''Yes, of course he did. But love like Webb's and mine doesn't happen for everyone. What we share is very rare. Naturally, I wish you could find someone like your father, but—''

''But girls like me don't end up with hunks like Daddy, do they?''

''Eleanor Grace Porter! What a thing to say.'' Carolyn couldn't keep the stern look on her face and soon burst into soft giggles. ''Webb is a hunk, isn't he?''

Ella hugged her mother. ''Yes, he is.''

''What are my two girls giggling about?'' Webb stood in the doorway, a wide smile on his face.

''Let's not tell him,'' Carolyn said. ''The man's ego is already the size of Texas.''

"Girl talk," Ella said. "Nothing that concerns you."

Ella kissed her mother, retrieved the silver items from atop the coverlet, and placed them on the bedside table. She paused as she approached her father.

He wrapped his arm around her shoulders and led her out into the hall. "Good night, princess."

Ella kissed his cheek. "Is Aunt Cybil all right?"

His smile vanished. "Cybil is her own worst enemy. She's miserable and she tries to make everyone around her miserable."

"I think it would be terribly sad to be married to someone who was in love with someone else."

Webb tapped her affectionately on the nose. "You're too smart for your own good, young lady. You always were."

"Mother wants me to marry Dan."

"And what do you want?"

"I want the kind of love you and Mother have—real love."

"If you want real love, then don't marry Dan Gilmore."

"Do you mean that, Daddy? Even if—"

He laid his index finger over her lips. "You wait for the real thing. For that can't-wait-to-see-him, can't-live-without-him, want-to-be-with-him-forever kind of love."

Ella hugged Webb fiercely. "I love you, Daddy."

"And I love you, princess."

Reed Conway was back in Spring Creek. Paroled today. The bad boy had returned and was sure to stir up trouble. Big trouble. He was the type who'd be damned and determined to prove his innocence. That couldn't happen—not now; not ever. There had to be a way to put him back where he belonged—behind bars—before he asked too many questions. Before he dug too deep. If he didn't live up to the conditions of his parole, if he committed a crime, even some minor infraction of the law, he could be sent back to Donaldson. *Think. Think. How can I see to it that Reed makes a fatal mistake? Something serious enough to revoke his parole. He can't be allowed to stay in Spring Creek long enough to unearth any long-buried secrets.*

Chapter 3

She had told him her name was Ivy Sims. She'd been
divorced twice and was presently between boyfriends.
Her only kid, a fifteen-year-old boy, lived with her first
husband in Mobile. She was too friendly, too chatty,
and very obviously interested in more than sharing a
drink at Desperado's. She'd been skimming her red,
claw-like fingernails up and down his arm for the past
five minutes, and a couple of times she had none too
subtly eyed his crotch. He'd had a hard-on since the
minute he got a whiff of her cheap perfume—something she'd probably bought at the Dollar Store. If he
had his pick of women, Ivy wouldn't be his number-one
choice. She was probably a good ten years older than
he was, and every year showed on her darkly tanned
face. The deep age lines of a lifetime smoker edged the
corners of her mouth and eyes. And although she had
nice, big breasts, she had no hips and a flat ass. But
right now, Ivy looked damned good. Like a delicious,
greasy hamburger would look to a starving man. She
wasn't prime rib, but horse meat would do if a man was

hungry enough. And Reed was hungry. Hell, he was famished.

"Briley Joe told me you just got out of the pen. Is that right, honey?" Ivy's full, red lips widened in a sensual smile.

"That's right. Just got out today." Reed lifted his bottle and downed the last drops of his fourth beer.

"You sure do look good for a man who's been behind bars." She wrapped her hand around the hard, bulging biceps of his right arm. "You must have spent a lot of time in the prison gym."

"I take it that you don't care that I've been in Donaldson for the past fifteen years, convicted of murder."

"Who'd you kill? Or are you one of those guys who was innocent and did time for a crime you didn't commit?" She chuckled teasingly.

"Yeah, that's me, all right, an innocent man. They sent me away because a jury said I slit my stepfather's throat."

"I had a stepfather," she said. "Mean son of a bitch. I thought about slitting his throat a time or two, but my old lady divorced him before I ever worked up the courage."

"Want another drink?" he asked.

"I think I've had enough for now. Want to dance?"

"Thought you'd never ask." He eased off the bar stool, then helped her to her feet and slid his arm around her waist.

When they reached the crowded dance floor, she turned into his embrace and plastered her body against his. His sex tightened painfully. Ivy's little outfit didn't leave much to the imagination. Her short skirt showed off a pair of long, skinny legs, and her cropped top hugged her boobs and exposed her midriff. She was pressed so snugly against him that he could barely breath. They moved awkwardly together, their bodies' rhythms slower than the shit-kicking music the live band played.

Ivy nuzzled the side of his neck, then whispered in his ear, "Just how horny are you, honey? Your prick feels like it's made out of iron."

"Horny enough to fuck you for a week and still be hard as a rock," he admitted.

She laughed, the sound grating oddly on his nerves. It was a throaty, rough laugh—a vulgar laugh coming from a vulgar woman. Ivy Sims was exactly what he needed tonight. He slid his hand between them and covered one breast. Her nipple jutted into his palm. He kneaded the round, soft flesh covered by nothing but her stretchy black top.

"My apartment isn't far from here," she told him. "We can be there in ten minutes."

"What are we waiting for?"

She grabbed his hand and led him off the dance floor and through the horde of hell-raisers and fun-seekers that frequented Desperado's. Reed caught a glimpse of Briley Joe sitting at a table with a cute little brunette. His cousin grinned and nodded. In high school, he and Briley Joe had shared the details of their sexual escapades, each always trying to out-boast the other.

The warm, humid night air hit him the minute they went outside. He took a deep, sobering breath. He wasn't drunk, but he wasn't completely sober either. He hadn't had a beer in fifteen years, and four in a row had given him a slight buzz. Reed draped his arm around Ivy's hips, then lowered his hand to clutch the right cheek of her butt. She giggled again. By the way she reacted to his pawing, he figured she was almost as eager to get laid as he was.

"Here's my car." She rummaged inside the tiny shoulder bag she carried and pulled out a key chain. "You want to drive?"

"Naw, you drive." He caressed her butt. "I'd rather concentrate on other things."

She unlocked the car, pulled out of his arms, and shoved him inside and onto the front seat. She raced around the hood and got in on the driver's side. "You keep your hands to yourself while I'm driving," she told him. "We don't want to wind up in a ditch instead of my big old comfortable bed, now do we?"

"I'll keep my hands off you, but it won't be easy." He needed a woman so badly right now that he would gladly screw a three-toed sloth as long as it had tits and a cunt. And Ivy was certainly a few notches above rock bottom.

By the time they reached her apartment, a brick duplex on a tree-lined street on the south side of Spring Creek, Reed had decided that Ivy was downright gorgeous. Hell, he'd always liked blondes, hadn't he? Even bleached blondes with dark roots.

Ivy's hands trembled as she unlocked her front door. Reed stood directly behind her, his erection pulsing against her rear end. His muscular arms circled her. One hand covered a breast and the other crept up her skirt and eased between her legs. She shivered with anticipation. She was already hot and wet and throbbing.

She flung open the door. Reed shoved her inside and slammed the door behind them. She'd left a lamp burning in the bedroom, and only that dim glow and the illumination from the nearby streetlight kept the living room from being totally dark. The minute she dropped her shoulder bag on the sofa, Reed reached out and tugged on her cropped top. She lifted her arms and let him remove the garment. He tossed it on the floor and grasped both of her breasts. She groaned in response to the pressure of his big hands as his fingers dug into her flesh.

"Take it easy," she told him.

His touch gentled immediately. His thumbs skimmed over her nipples. She sighed. Then he lowered his head and took one peak into his mouth and suckled. She tossed back her head and moaned with pleasure. He slid his hand between her legs and pushed upward until he reached his goal. After slipping his fingers inside her bikini panties, he rubbed her nub until she closed her legs and held his hand in place. He worked his fingers over her slippery folds and inserted them up and into her.

Reed's movements were rough and crude. But she had to remember how long it had been since he'd been with a woman. The last time he'd made love, he'd been a kid, a teenager.

Ivy unzipped Reed's jeans, reached inside, and slipped her hand under his briefs. He groaned deep in his throat when she encircled his shaft and withdrew him gently.

"God, Ivy, I can't wait any longer." He grabbed her and flung her onto the sofa.

She lifted her hips, jerked off her panties, and spread her legs. "Come on, big boy."

"It's been a long time for me. I'm out of practice." He pulled a condom out of his pocket, ripped open the packet, and slid the rubber over his erect penis.

"It's all right, honey," she said. "I'll be gentle with you."

Her teasing laughter turned to gasping sighs when he thrust into her. God, he was big. Big and hard and pumping into her like a jackhammer. If he didn't slow down, he'd be finished before—

A animalistic cry of completion moaned from deep within him as he climaxed. Convulsions of release racked his body.

He slumped over to her side, easing part of his weight off her. "I'm sorry. I know you didn't come."

"It's all right," she said, and meant it. She'd never seen a guy more in need.

"Give me another chance and I promise I'll do it right next time." He used his fingers to comfort and entice her. "What do you say?"

"Why don't you stay all night?"

"I was hoping you'd say that."

* * *

Ella arrived at her office promptly at eight o'clock. She liked to get in earlier, but when her father was in town, she stayed home to have breakfast with him. Ordinarily she grabbed a cup of coffee and a biscuit and ate on her drive from their home on East First Street to the courthouse in the center of the town square. Her mother seldom woke before ten, and then Viola usually served Carolyn breakfast in bed. So, this morning she'd had her father all to herself. There was no one she loved and admired more than Webb Porter, and she thought herself fortunate to be his daughter. Despite the fact that they didn't share the same genes, they were remarkably alike. In her case, nurture definitely won out over nature. She was a true Porter in every sense of the word. Her father had told her so many times. The fact that they thought alike on so many issues and had similar traits and habits seemed to delight her father as much as it did her. They were as close as any parent and child could be. She knew without a doubt that she was the joy of Webb Porter's life. There was nothing he wouldn't do for her.

Ella laid her briefcase down atop her large antique oak desk. Her father had sat behind this very desk when he'd served as a circuit court judge, before his election to the U.S. Senate ten years ago. When she'd been elected last year, he had told her that she was carrying on a family tradition. Webb had been a local district attorney and then a judge. His father before him had been a congressman, and his grandfather the lieutenant governor.

After removing her jacket and hanging it over the back of her chair, Ella sat down in the tufted-backed oxblood leather swivel chair. Her mind instantly wandered back to something her father had said during breakfast.

"If that man contacts you, I want to know about it

immediately," Webb had told her. "He swore revenge against me, and I wouldn't put it past him to come after you in order to hurt me."

"Daddy, do you really think Reed Conway is a danger to our family?"

"I think he very well could be. If he's bent on getting back at me, then it's possible that he'll go after the people I love. So I want you to promise me to be careful and notify me if he approaches you, either in person or with a phone call."

Ella shivered. A sense of foreboding echoed inside her. Did she truly have something to worry about where Reed Conway was concerned? Was her father being overly cautious? Would Reed actually jeopardize his parole in order to seek revenge? If anything happened to a member of her family, Reed would be the first person the police would question. She really hadn't known Reed, except to recognize him as Judy Blalock's son. Judy Conway. After her second husband had been murdered, she'd legally changed her name back to Conway.

And of course, Ella had known Reed as the star of Spring Creek High's football team. He'd been the guy every girl wanted and every parent feared. He'd had a reputation as a stud, and even when she'd been fifteen, she had understood why girls were drawn to him like moths to a flame. He'd been big and ruggedly good-looking and possessed a cocky smile that made you think he'd been up to no good. And from what she'd heard, he usually had been up to no good.

A knock on the door brought Ella back from her memories. "Yes?"

"It's me, Miss Ella," a gentle masculine voice said. "I've come to fix your lights."

"Come on in, Roy."

One of the flourescent light fixtures overhead had burned out yesterday and she'd had her secretary, Kelly, request a maintenance man to replace the bulb. Roy

Moses, with a tool belt hanging below his jelly-belly tummy, just above his hips, entered the room carrying a ladder. He smiled and nodded, his squinty brown eyes, greeting her with his usual appreciative glance. Roy was a few years older than she, a bit slow-witted, and one of the sweetest guys she'd ever known. He wore his white-blond hair cropped short, which made his full face look perfectly round, like a pale pink ball.

"Good morning, Miss Ella. How are you today?"

"I'm fine, Roy. And you?"

"Fine as frog hair." He chuckled, the sound a series of deep, slow haw-haw-haws.

"That's good." Ella had known Roy most of her life. He had a sister who was a nurse and a brother who was a fireman. Roy's IQ score identified him as borderline retarded, but he was a hard worker who held down two part-time jobs. He wasn't a member of the regular maintenance staff, but was employed as a part-time janitor who did odd jobs at the courthouse—a position Webb Porter had insisted be created for him. His other position was at Conway's Garage, where he washed and waxed cars and did odd jobs.

"Don't want to disturb you none," Roy said as he set up the ladder beneath the fluorescent ceiling fixture.

"You aren't disturbing me. Go ahead and do your job."

"You look real pretty this morning, Miss Ella."

"Thank you." Every time he saw her, Roy told her how pretty she looked. She suspected he had an innocent crush on her.

"Did you hear the news?" Roy began climbing the ladder.

"What news is that?" Ella unsnapped her briefcase.

"That Reed Conway is out of prison."

"Oh, that. Yes. I'm sure everyone in Spring Creek is aware that he was released on parole yesterday."

"I liked Reed." Roy inspected the light fixture. "I'll have to take this down and go get another one."

"You liked Reed Conway? I didn't realize that you'd actually known him."

"Sure, I knew him. He was my friend. My brother Tommy played football with Reed and he used to come to our house sometimes. He was always nice to me. He never made fun of me the way some of Tommy's other friends did. And he'd let me toss around the football with him and Tommy." Roy chuckled his good-natured haw-haw-haw. "Reed used to call me 'my buddy Roy Boy.' "

"I didn't really know him," Ella said.

"You would have liked him. Everybody liked Reed. I couldn't believe it when they sent him away to prison. Anybody who knew him knew he wouldn't have killed nobody. Not Reed."

"Sometimes even good people do bad things."

"I know Reed's stepdaddy was a bad man, but if Reed killed him, he didn't mean to." Roy removed the burned-out light fixture and climbed down the ladder with it. "I'm going to be working with Reed."

"What?"

"Over at the garage," Roy said. "Briley Joe gave Reed a job. He said wouldn't nobody else in town give Reed a job. I can't hardly wait to see Reed again. He's supposed to start work today. I'll bet he'll call me Roy Boy. Sure will be good to have a buddy again."

Roy carried the light fixture with him as he left Ella's office. She stared at the metal ladder he'd left behind. In the years since Roy had been working at the courthouse, Ella had found him to be a remarkably good judge of character. It was as if he had some strange sixth sense that allowed him a special insight into human nature. How was it that he could be so wrong about Reed Conway? The man was a murderer. He'd been tried and convicted. Her father had been the prosecuting district attorney, and there hadn't been a doubt in Webb Porter's mind that Reed Conway had viciously slit his stepfather's throat. Even his own mother had been forced to testify that she'd witnessed a brutal fight between a drunken Junior and a furious Reed. Junior Blalock had tried to rape Regina Conway, who'd been only eleven at the time. If Reed had killed Junior while defending his sister, he wouldn't have been prosecuted for murder, but Reed had caught the man later, after the fact, while Junior had been unconscious. Reed had cut his throat from ear to ear.

I want to wrap my hands around your soft white neck and then move them down your bare shoulders and over your sweet breasts.

Ella shook her head to dislodge the memory, to erase the words that were forever etched in her mind. Words Reed had written to her from prison. Two love letters that had been both frightening and titillating to the sixteen-year-old Ella. Harassing letters that had infuriated her father and prompted him to take legal action to end Reed's letter writing.

She hoped she could avoid seeing Reed Conway. But what if her father was right and the man sought her out? Heaven help him if he did threaten or harass her in any way. Webb Porter would have the man's head on a platter.

Reed woke slowly, languidly, lying facedown, the smell of cheap perfume on his pillow. He opened his eyes and glanced at the other side of the bed. *Empty.* He listened. *Silence.* Where was Ivy? When he lifted his head to look at the alarm clock on the bedside table, he saw the note propped up against the lamp.

Gone to work. Last night was great. Let's do it again soon. She'd underlined *soon* three times.

Reed grinned. He couldn't remember the last time he'd felt so good. Ivy was an all-right kind of woman. She'd been understanding about his lack of patience and expertise. Hell, he was rusty at sex. In the pen, he'd warned off potential rapists. It had helped that he'd been big and surly even as a teenager. And those first few years, he hadn't given a damn about how much trouble he got into or whether he killed somebody protecting himself. For the past fifteen years, he'd found his sexual pleasure in the palm of his own hand. Fucking a woman beat the hell out of just dreaming about fucking one.

Reed climbed out of bed and stalked off to the bathroom. He peered at himself in the mirror over the sink. His eyes were bloodshot and he badly needed a shave. And he had a silly grin on his face. The grin of a man who'd spent the night screwing a most obliging woman. Ivy wasn't the girl of his dreams, but she'd been mighty accommodating.

He pawed his chin, testing the scratchiness of his beard stubble. Ivy hadn't complained about the stubble. She hadn't complained about anything. Any other woman would have kicked his butt out of her bed and demanded that he shave. He'd just bet that Ella Porter didn't let a man even kiss her unless he was clean-shaven. Ella Porter, Webb's darling daughter. He'd barely known the girl. Other than seeing her a few times over the years at the Carlisle house, their paths had never crossed. So why was it that she'd been the girl he had thought about while he was in prison? Why was it that she'd been the fantasy of more than one wet dream? Was it because he'd written her those damn crude love letters? The only reason he'd written them was because he'd known they'd piss off Webb. Fifteen years ago, he'd have done just about anything to hurt Webb. And he'd found out right quick that the best way to get to the high-and-mighty Mr. Porter was through his beloved little girl.

Reed took a quick shower, then reluctantly put on the clothes he'd worn the night before. He bundled his briefs into a wad and stuffed them in his jeans back pocket. Before leaving Ivy's apartment, he checked for her phone number and memorized it. He just might ask her for a repeat of last night's highly satisfactory performance.

He showed up at Conway's Garage two hours late for his first morning on the job. But Briley Joe just grinned at him and patted him on the back.

"Ain't nothing like good pussy, is there? I'll bet Ivy taught you a trick or two, didn't she? As I recall, the lady knows how to please."

"She sure as hell pleased me."

"She's not first-class, but you had to start somewhere. You can work off some of your frustration with her and then move on to something better."

"Is that your subtle way of trying to tell me that you've got something better?" Reed knew Briley Joe was the sort who liked to brag about his sexual conquests. In that sense, his cousin was as immature as he'd been at eighteen.

"Yeah, I'm getting some from one of the classiest broads in town. If I told you, you wouldn't believe me."

"So, tell me and let me be duly impressed."

"Talking kind of fancy, aren't you? You haven't let that college degree you earned in the pen go to your head, have you?"

"That college degree didn't do me a damn bit of good getting a job on the outside, did it?" It stuck in his craw that the only job he could get was as a grease monkey in his cousin's garage. Reed clamped his hand down on Briley Joe's shoulder and grinned. "So who's this classy broad you're screwing?"

"Cybil Carlisle."

"You're kidding."

"Yep. I'm getting all I want from Jeff Henry Carlisle's wife. Can you believe it? And I'm here to tell you that she's one wild woman."

"You're playing a dangerous game, cuz," Reed said. "If Jeff Henry ever finds out, you're as good as dead."

"That Pillsbury Doughboy wouldn't dirty his lily white hands on me."

"You're right about that, but he wouldn't think twice about hiring somebody to beat the shit out of you, and if that didn't stop you fooling around with his wife—"

"Nobody knows. You're the only person I've told. She warned me that if I opened my big mouth about her to anybody, she'd cut me off."

"Damn it, man, she's Webb Porter's sister-in-law. She was a *Walker* before she got married. Her family's been one of the ruling clans in this state for the past two hundred years. Why would she risk her reputation and your life to have an affair with you?"

"Because Cybil Carlisle likes to walk on the wild side. And I can tell you that there's nothing better than a lady who wants to get down and dirty with a bad boy. You ought to try it sometime. Maybe with that niece of hers. I'll bet Miss Ella Porter has never forgotten those hot letters you wrote her."

"I'd like to forget those letters, and I'm sure she has forgotten them. From what my mother tells me, Judge Porter is good woman—a real lady. If I even said hello to her, she'd run scared."

"You won't know until you give it a try. Who knows, she might not run."

"Ella was never my type. And God knows I wasn't her type back then, and I'm sure as hell not her type now."

"Okay, so the judge doesn't crank your motor. She's not the only class act in town. Look around. I'm sure you'll find somebody who suits you."

"I'll stick with Ivy and her type for the time being," Reed said. "A good, uncomplicated fuck is all I want from a woman right now. My main focus is on finding out exactly who killed Junior Blalock and let me take the fall. Mark Leamon believes in me and he's going to help me try to prove my innocence."

"You ever think that Aunt Judy might have done it?"

"No! Mama would never have let me go to prison for a crime she'd committed."

"Yeah, you're probably right. Aunt Judy would do

just about anything for you and Regina." When Briley Joe removed his ball cap and scratched his head, curly brown locks fell across his forehead. The rest of his shoulder-length hair had been pulled back into a short ponytail. "Man, where can you start? The police didn't find no evidence against anybody but you. And we know you didn't kill Junior. So who did? Who else besides you, Aunt Judy, and Regina had a reason to want to see Junior dead?"

"I don't know for sure," Reed said. "But I've made out a list of possible suspects, and Webb Porter's name is at the top of that list."

Chapter 4

Ella removed her robe, hung it in the closet, and collapsed happily in the swivel desk chair. What a day! Presiding over a case fraught with emotion always got to her. She tried to not allow her own personal feelings on the matter affect her, but she found that she was only human and couldn't completely divorce herself from her own sensitivity on certain issues. Had Clyde Kilpatrick committed suicide, or had his death been a tragic accident? The insurance company said suicide. The family said accident. From today's evidence, she had reached a tentative decision. But would the jury come to the same conclusion that she had? Even though it meant Clyde's two children would not see a dime of his insurance money, the facts plainly showed that the man had killed himself. He'd left a note forgiving his wife for her infidelity, but also stating that he didn't want to live without her. The damning evidence had come from the ballistics expert, who had explained the trajectory of the bullet that entered Clyde's body, saying that it was highly unlikely, if not impossible, for an accident to have been the cause.

Ella kicked off her two-inch gray heels, wriggled her toes, and lifted her stocking feet up to rest on her desk. The heel of her foot accidently brushed against a white envelope, sending it sailing off the desk and onto the floor. Grunting, she leaned over and picked up the legal-size envelope. Her name was typed across the front. Only her name. Eleanor Porter. Odd, she didn't remember this particular bit of correspondence being on her desk earlier today. She'd eaten lunch at her desk around twelve-thirty—a salad she'd ordered from the Oakwood Bar and Grill across the street from the courthouse.

She flipped the letter over and noticed it was still sealed. Undoubtedly someone had hand-delivered the message. But who? Kelly had already left for the day, so she couldn't ask her until tomorrow. Ella pulled a brass letter opener from the pencil holder that was part of the gold-monogrammed leather desk set Uncle Jeff Henry had given her when she'd been elected circuit judge last year. After slicing open the envelope, she reached inside and pulled out the single-page missive. She unfolded the white stationery and read.

Ella, sweet Ella, I dream of you at night and wake in a cold sweat. Aroused and wanting you. Desperately. You were meant to be mine. I have made plans for us. Delicious plans. Long, hot nights together. Naked. Going at each other like a couple of wild animals. Monkey fucking. You can't even begin to imagine all the things I want to do to you. All the things I long for you to do to me. When the time is right, I'll come for you. I will not allow anyone to stand between us. Not ever again. I'll make you turn against your evil family. When you choose me, it will break your father's heart. And that is only the beginning of my revenge.

Ella swallowed hard. Dear God! Who would have sent her such a thing?

The letter was typewritten. Actually, it looked as if it

had been composed on a computer and printed from a laser printer. There were several laser printers at the courthouse and one at the public library. And several copy shops provided laser printers for use by their customers. Unless there were fingerprints on the envelope or the plain white paper, there was probably no way to trace the letter.

Was this a prank? Dan Gilmore certainly hadn't penned the heated love letter. Did she have a secret admirer out there somewhere? Was someone stalking her, watching her without her being aware of his presence? A chill raced up her spine. She'd heard of women being stalked by ex-lovers or ex-husbands, and celebrities being harassed by crazed fans. But she had no "ex" anything. And she certainly wasn't famous. However, she was a well-known figure in the community, in all of Bryant County for that matter.

Ella Porter, you aren't the type of woman that men become obsessed with and you know it. No one would ever . . . Oh, dear Lord, no! Years ago, Reed Conway had written her two letters very similar to this one. Until her father had seen to it that he couldn't send any more. And Reed Conway had been released from prison yesterday. Was it possible that he had written her this crude love letter? Yes, of course it was possible. If the man still blamed her father for his imprisonment, then he might be trying to get to her father through her. He'd done it once before; why not now?

Daddy would be furious. He would confront Reed and accuse him of harassing her. Even though she couldn't be sure the letter had come from Reed, there would be no doubt in her father's mind. He would condemn Reed without benefit of hard evidence. The police would be called in and the story might leak to the media, and her mother would find out and become terribly upset. Ella could well remember the hullabaloo that went on in the Porter household when Reed had written to her from prison. She didn't want a repeat of those nerve-racking days.

The letter can't hurt you, she reminded herself. *It's only a bunch of words.* If Reed had written it, he had done it solely to get a rise out of Webb Porter. If she didn't show anyone the letter, then Reed wouldn't have accomplished his goal. Surely, if he realized she had ignored the silly piece of trash, he wouldn't bother writing another.

Ella removed a key chain from her pocket and unlocked the bottom drawer of her desk. After pulling out the drawer, she lifted and opened her gray leather purse, then stuffed the letter back into the envelope. She slid the envelope into her purse behind her wallet and closed her purse. The best thing to do was forget about the message and hope that would be the end of it. But she wouldn't destroy the letter. Not yet.

She didn't want to involve her father or the local authorities unless it was absolutely necessary. She wasn't a sixteen-year-old innocent. She was a grown woman, a thirty-year-old circuit court judge. She could certainly handle this situation without help. She would find Reed Conway and confront him with the letter, then warn him that if he knew what was good for him, he'd leave her alone.

Jeff Henry Carlisle sipped tea from a Moss Rose Haviland china cup. The silver tea service that Judy Conway had placed on his intricately carved mahogany desk in the study had been in his family for six generations. The desk itself had come overland from Virginia and then down the Tennessee River to Alabama before the War Between the States, as a wedding present for one of his ancestresses. Of all the fine rooms in his home, he thought he loved this one best. His own private domain, filled with beloved treasures, both family heirlooms and items he had acquired at estate sales and out-of-the-way antique shops. There were even a few items he had picked up on his and Cybil's trips to Europe. Unfortunately, his wife didn't give two hoots about the things that were precious to him. "A bunch of old junk," she'd once said of the priceless antiques that adorned each of the twelve rooms in their home. All the rooms, that is, except her bedroom. She had decorated that room in a garish nineteen-twenties art deco style that made him feel nauseated every time he entered her private quarters.

His wife might physically resemble her older sister, but that was where the similarities ended. Carolyn was a lady, through and through. Genteel, in the way Jeff Henry's mother had been. A gentleman never used a curse word in her presence, because it would shock and offend her. Carolyn was a fragile flower to be cherished and protected from the harsh realities of the world. Ah, dear, sweet Carolyn. He had loved her madly when they'd been young, but she had thought of him only as a friend. She had wanted no one but Webb Porter. And what Carolyn wanted, Carolyn got. Who could deny such a woman anything?

He supposed that, in a way, he was still in love with Carolyn. But it was a pure love, untainted by anything physical. His love for her was a noble thing, much like that of the knights of old for their fair damsels. Carolyn was a part of his heart. That would have to be enough. She was devoted to Webb and would never leave him.

Jeff Henry sighed as he picked up one of Judy's home-made oatmeal cookies. He knew he shouldn't be nibbling, but he'd smelled the cookies baking when he passed the kitchen a half hour ago. In the past few years, he'd acquired a bit of a paunch, but a few extra pounds didn't hurt a man's appearance the way it did a woman's. Some people might consider him vain, but he wasn't. He simply prided himself on his appearance. Cybil told him that his factitiousness drove her crazy.

Well, truth be told, everything about his wife drove

him crazy. It hadn't always been that way. Not in the beginning. When they had first married, she'd tried to please him. He'd been convinced that she actually cared for him.

"I did my best to be like Carolyn," she'd told him. "I knew I wasn't your first choice. I tried, damn it. I tried so hard, but it was never enough. I'm not Carolyn and you've never let me forget it."

He'd made a serious mistake marrying Cybil, but he dealt with things the best he could. He turned a blind eye to her indiscretions. At least she had tried to be discreet about her numerous affairs; he was thankful for that much. The Carlisles didn't believe in divorce. There had never been a divorce in the family, and he most certainly had no intention of breaking that tradition. Perhaps once he would have considered it, if Carolyn had been free. Poor Carolyn, married to a man who didn't deserve her, a man who made a mockery of their marriage. But she was happy in her delusional state, and he would do anything—absolutely anything—to make sure nothing and no one ever ruined that happiness for her.

"Mr. Carlisle?" A woman's voice broke into his thoughts.

He glanced at the open pocket doors leading into the hallway and saw Judy Conway standing there. An attractive woman, if you liked the sexual, earthy type. "Yes, what is it?"

"I'm leaving for the day," she said. "Dinner is prepared. The roast and vegetables are in the oven and the salad is in the refrigerator. Will you need anything else before I go?"

"Has Mrs. Carlisle come home?"

"No, sir, she hasn't."

"Hmm . . ."

"I'll be going now—"

"Yes. Certainly." He waved his hand in a gesture of

dismissal. "I'm sure you're eager to go home and spend some time with your son."

"Yes, sir."

"I do hope you understand why I couldn't recommend that any of my friends give Reed a job. I realize you were disappointed when I refused, but in all good conscience—"

"I understand." The tension in her voice said that although she might understand, she didn't forgive. "Reed has a job with his cousin Briley Joe."

"At the garage?"

"Yes. It's honest work. Not quite what I'd hoped for, considering Reed has a college degree. But it was the only job he could find. No one would help him except family."

Judy's gaze didn't quite meet Jeff Henry's. Her reluctance to look him directly in the eye bothered him. He liked Judy and had a certain amount of respect for the woman. He thought she had always regarded him highly, and he valued her opinion of him. A man should be respected and liked by his employees. That had been his father's opinion and his grandfather's before him. For generations the Carlisles had been benevolent employers.

"Once Reed proves himself, I could be persuaded to reconsider and perhaps help him find more suitable employment. If he stays out of trouble for, let's say, a year, we'll discuss my helping him."

Judy smiled, but the effort seemed false, as if she had forced herself to respond in a positive manner.

"Thank you, Mr. Carlisle. I'm sure Reed will stay out of trouble. He knows how much is at stake."

"I wish him well. Personally, you know that I always thought he should have been rewarded for killing Junior Blalock instead of having been sent to prison."

"Reed didn't kill Junior. He was innocent."

"Yes. Yes, of course. I'm sure, being his mother, that's what you'd like to believe."

Judy laid her clutched fist over her heart. "It's what I know. In here."

Jeff Henry cleared his throat. "You have a good night, you hear? I'll see you in the morning."

"Yes, sir." She turned and disappeared down the hallway.

Did Judy still truly believe that her son hadn't killed her second husband? If so, that meant Reed was still professing his innocence. Merciful goodness. Jeff Henry hoped that didn't mean Reed was going to stir up trouble. It just wouldn't do for the past to be revisited. If that happened, there was no telling who might wind up getting hurt.

No doubt by now she had found the letter that had been placed on her desk while her secretary had been down the hall on an errand. How had Ella reacted when she'd read the letter? Had she been shocked? Had she known immediately who'd written it? Was she at this very minute showing it to her father?

A self-satisfied smile curled moist lips. Ella was such a predictable creature. She would run to Webb and cry for her daddy's help. *Some nasty man sent me this vulgar letter. Do something about it immediately.*

Of course, one letter wouldn't be enough. There would have to be others. And a few untraceable phone calls—some heavy breathing. One step at a time, building slowly to the point when Webb would know his daughter's life was at stake. It would actually be fun to watch the senator sweat.

Nothing meant more to Webb Porter than his precious daughter. He loved her more than anything on earth. More than he'd ever loved his wife. Far more than any of his mistresses. The easiest way to get Webb's undivided attention was to harass his only child. And that was all it would be at first—just harassment. But later . . .

* * *

Ella drove past Conway's garage, which was situated on the corner of West Fifth and Lafayette. Not exactly on her way home, but only a couple of blocks out of her way. She slowed her Jaguar, and with her eyes shaded by sunglasses, she inspected the scene. Two cars were at the pumps, filling up with gas. One of the two large garage doors gaped open to reveal the greasy, cluttered maintenance and repair shop. She caught a glimpse of Briley Joe through the glass front of the building. He was talking to someone she assumed was a customer. Reed's cousin wore his brown hair shoulder-length and pulled back in a short ponytail. She'd never seen the man wearing anything except jeans, as he did today, and he'd topped off his redneck ensemble with a white T-shirt emblazoned with a colorful emblem of some sort.

She didn't see Reed anywhere. No need to stop. She'd have to wait and catch him at work another day. Then, just as she started to increase the car's speed, she caught a glimpse of a tall, muscular man emerging from a car that he'd just backed out of the garage. She instantly knew he was Reed Conway. He was older, bigger. His once-pale ash blond hair was now a dirty blond, almost light brown. Ella's heartbeat accelerated. Her stomach muscles knotted painfully.

There he is. Stop and talk to him. Confront him with the letter and demand that he leave you alone.

She drove on by, her hands trembling, her nerves rioting. The Jag picked up speed as Ella cruised up West Fifth Street, passing rows of houses, many in ramshackle ruins, others in various states of repair and renovation. Anybody who was *someone* in this town lived on the east end, but the middle-class version of nouveau riche was restoring the houses on the west end, some now rivaling the stately old homes that had been kept up generation after generation across town.

Coward! You're running away. You don't have the guts to face him and tell him what you think of him . . . how you feel about his explicit, threatening love letter. Love letter? No, it was smut, pure and simple. But it had implied a threat, hadn't it? Just as those two letters he'd written years ago had done.

Ella turned off West Fifth, made the block, and headed back toward the garage. She was not going to run to her father. She was not going to let her mother find out about the letter, knowing how much it would disturb her. She, Ella Porter, was going to handle this little problem herself. Now!

Mustering every ounce of courage she possessed, Ella whipped her Jag off the street and onto the Conway Garage parking area. She killed the engine, snatched the keys from the ignition, and held them tightly in her hand as she took a deep, fortifying breath. When she stepped out of the car onto the pavement, she found her legs wobbly and her heartbeat thundered in her ears. She snapped open her shoulder bag, eyed the white envelope tucked inside, and then dropped her keys on top of her wallet before closing her purse.

You can do this. You will *do this. After all, what can he do to you in broad daylight, with witnesses all around?*

Squaring her shoulders and tilting her chin, she took several tentative steps and then stopped dead still. Reed Conway turned abruptly as he wiped his soiled hands on a dirty orange rag and looked right at her. She'd never forgotten those ice-cold blue eyes of his. The few times she'd run into him at her aunt and uncle's house, he'd always stared at her. Never smiled; never spoke. Just glared at her with those incredible sky blue eyes.

But he can't see your eyes, she reminded herself, *not with your sunglasses on. He can't look into your eyes and know what you're thinking. He can't see the fear . . . the disgust . . . or the curiosity.* She'd always been curious about Reed, always wondered what it would be like to find out first-hand just what it was about him that had fascinated the girls and intimidated the boys.

Without realizing what she was doing, Ella surveyed him from head to toe. A good six-three. Broad shoulders. Big arms. Biceps bulging, plainly visible, bared by his sleeveless blue-and-white tank top. He was surprisingly tan. He must have served on an outdoor work crew while he was in prison, she surmised. His thick tawny hair curled about his neck and ears. He needed a haircut. His long, thin sideburns met the brown stubble that covered his face. Obviously the man hadn't shaved this morning. The stonewashed jeans hugged his lower body. Ella swallowed hard.

Reed Conway was the sexiest man she'd ever seen, bar none. A lazy, raw sensuality oozed from his pores.

He continued staring at her, as if he were gauging her worth as a desirable woman. She was unaccustomed to men taking stock of her physical assets. Men appreciated her for her intelligence, her warm and caring personality, and her social status. She was no great beauty—a fact that disappointed her mother. But Carolyn assured her that being beautiful was often more a curse than a blessing. So why was Reed looking at her as if he found her attractive? Did he know who she was? Had he recognized her and was only toying with her?

Enough of this! she told herself. *You didn't come here to fall victim to Reed's obvious charms. Nor did you come here to have him ogle you.* Marching across the space that separated them, Ella kept reminding herself of who she was and why she was here. *Show him the letter and tell him you're giving him fair warning that sending another letter would be useless, that you're not going to show the damn thing to your father.*

Reed watched the woman as she approached him. Classy. Well-dressed in a simple gray pinstriped suit and pale gray blouse. Even her gray leather shoes and shoulder bag matched. And she was driving a Jag. A rich, classy broad. That's what Briley Joe would call her. Shiny black hair, secured in a loose bun at the nape of her neck. Pale olive skin. Smooth and creamy. Even on a hot day like today, she looked cool. What was someone like *her* doing here? He glanced past her and eyed her car. He'd thought she might have a flat tire, but that didn't seem to be the case. Maybe a little car trouble?

When she stopped directly in front of him, he flashed her his I'd-like-to-strip-you-naked-and-screw-you-right-here-and-now smile.

She didn't return the smile. Okay, so she wasn't interested. No big deal.

"What can I do for you?" he asked.

"You're Reed Conway, aren't you?"

She knew him? Was she someone from his past? An old girlfriend? He'd managed to lay several Spring Creek debutantes when he was in high school. But not this one. If he'd ever gotten in her pants, he'd remember her.

"Who wants to know?" He gave her a once-over, concentrating on the area from breasts to knees. Giving a lady that kind of sexual appraisal had a way of separating the women from the girls, as well as the available from the unavailable. Besides, he enjoyed looking. She had nice tits—big, but not too big. A small waist. And wide hips. Not today's fashionable figure, but still the kind that gave a guy a woody.

She removed her sunglasses and held them tightly in her left hand. A hand without rings. Short, neatly manicured nails with clear polish. Not flashy. Not married. Not engaged.

He took a good look at her face, but didn't instantly recognize her. Had he known her? She was pretty. Not beautiful the way his mother and sister were, but alluring in an almost exotic way. Full lips, glazed with a colorless sheen. A square face, a well-defined nose, and a pair of large, striking, dark eyes—eyes so brown they appeared almost black.

She stared at him, her gaze boring into him and her lips slightly parted. Suddenly he remembered those eyes. Other things about her had changed. She'd lost weight, grown an inch or two taller, and now possessed an air of confidence that had been lacking in the young girl who'd watched him with those remarkable black eyes.

"Ella Porter, my, how you've changed." He grinned when a look of shock drained the color from her face.

"So have you, Mr. Conway."

"Why so formal, Ella? Call me Reed."

"Mr. Conway, I have a reason for coming here, and it isn't so that we can get to know each other on a first-name basis."

"Then I take it you didn't stop by to welcome me home on behalf of the Porter family." He sensed the tension in her tighten, and he couldn't help enjoying being able to irritate her so easily.

"I received a rather disturbing letter today."

She snapped open her small gray shoulder bag. That was when he noticed her hands were trembling. She was scared. Scared of him. *Son of a bitch!* She jerked a white envelope from her purse and held it between them as if it were a weapon that would hold him at bay.

"Bad news?" he asked flippantly.

"Bad news for you," she replied, shaking the envelope in his face. "I'm not going to run to my father with this. Do you hear me, Mr. Conway? Writing me vulgar, harassing letters isn't going to upset my father, because he won't see this letter or any future letters. You're wasting you time trying to get to my father through me."

"So you received a vulgar, harassing letter today and you immediately assumed it was from me?"

"Are you denying that you sent this?" She flapped the envelope in his face again.

He grabbed her wrist. She gasped. The fear in her eyes gave him an odd sense of pleasure, but it was a pleasure mixed with pain. "Stop waving that damn thing in my face." She twisted her wrist, trying to free it from his grip, but he held fast. She glared at him, the fear in her eyes turning to anger. Ah, he liked the anger much more than the fear. "I'm not denying anything. Nor am I admitting to anything."

"I hardly expected you to admit it," she said, glancing from his face to her wrist. "Will you please let go of me?"

"All in good time, Miss Ella." Tugging on her wrist, he practically dragged her toward the side door of the garage. "But first, I think you and I need to have a little private talk."

Chapter 5

Reed hauled Ella into the garage. She protested verbally and struggled against his overpowering strength. What had she been thinking, coming here and confronting him this way? The man was a convicted murderer!

"Let go of me this instant or you'll be sorry."

He ignored her, damn him! He pulled her inside a windowless room that possessed only two pieces of furniture: a cheap "Kmart special" swivel chair and an old metal desk piled high with books, magazines, and papers. A small air conditioner hummed and rattled in a hole cut out of the concrete wall. With wide eyes and mouth agape, Briley Joe shot out of the chair.

"We need to use your office for a few minutes," Reed said.

Briley Joe shut his mouth and stared at them, grinning at first and then grimacing when he apparently recognized Ella. "You do know who she is, don't you?"

"Yeah, I know who she is."

"Have you lost your mind, manhandling Webb Porter's daughter?"

"If he doesn't let me go, I'll have him arrested," Ella said.

"Hey, cuz, let her go. You can always find another woman. You don't want to wind up back in the pen over a piece of ass."

"A piece of—how *dare* you!" Ella glared at Briley Joe. Did that imbecile think Reed had dragged her into the garage office for a little *slap and tickle*? Her heart nearly thumped out of her chest. Unbidden thoughts swirled through her mind. She started to protest such Neander-thal treatment once again, but before she could do more than open her mouth, Reed shoved her down in the chair that Briley Joe had recently vacated. She gasped aloud as her bottom hit the seat, which was still warm from Briley Joe's body heat.

"Close the door on your way out," Reed told his cousin, who left immediately and quietly closed the door behind him.

"I don't know what you think this little scene will accomplish, Mr. Conway, but I hope it's worth it to you because I can assure you that it's going to cost you dearly." Ella used her authoritarian judicial voice, the same commanding tone she used in the courtroom.

Reed settled his backside onto the edge of the desk, reached out, and spun around the chair she sat in so that she was forced to face him. Resting his hands on the chair's armrests on either side of her hips, he leaned forward, getting close enough so that she could feel his breath on her face. Startled by his nearness, she blinked several times.

"You certainly grew up nice, Miss Ella." He raked his gaze over her face and down her throat, stopping at her breasts, then retraced his visual journey until their eyes met. "Real nice."

"Is this step two in your plan to sexually harass me so that my father will come after you?" Keeping her gaze locked with his, she refused to let him know how much he intimidated her. He was a big man, powerfully built, and surrounded by an undeniable aura of danger.

"You've got me all wrong," he said, grinning. "Besides, it seems to me, if anybody's doing any harassing, it's you."

"Me?" She wanted to knock that cocky smile off his face. Her hands balled into fists, crushing the white envelope in the process. She prided herself on her even-tempered disposition. But this man had enraged her so easily that she felt shocked at her irrational reaction to him.

"Yeah, you. I was here at work, minding my own business, being a law-abiding citizen, when you showed up and started tossing out accusations, accusing me of something I didn't do. I figure that could be called harassment."

"Are you denying that you sent this to me?" She held up the letter she still clutched in her fist and waved it around, all but slapping him in the face with it.

He peered at her over the edge of the envelope, which rested just below the bridge of his nose. "The vulgar, harassing letter? Nope. I don't know anything about it, except what you've told me."

He continued staring at her. Those incredible blue eyes hypnotized her. She couldn't help wondering how many other women had been caught and held by the mesmerizing coldness in Reed Conway's eyes. She swallowed. *Get hold of yourself, Eleanor Porter. He's just a man, like any other man. He puts his pants on one leg at a time, right?* Yeah, sure. She couldn't kid herself. Reed might put his pants on in the same way other men did, but he wasn't like other men. He never had been. Not at eighteen. Not now. He had been a star athlete headed for the University of Alabama on a football scholarship when he'd killed his stepfather. He'd had a bad boy reputation with girls and women alike when he'd been Bryant County's teenage heartthrob and the bane of concerned parents' lives. She remembered accidentally overhearing her uncle Jeff Henry make an off-color comment about Reed all those years ago.

"That boy's got a man-sized ego because he's bigger and better on the football field than anybody else. And the ladies seem to think what he's got between his legs is bigger and better, too."

She could still hear her uncle's and her father's macho chuckles, each in his own way both condeming and envying the boy from the wrong side of the tracks who had been destined for football superstardom.

And now Reed was different because he was a convicted murderer who had served fifteen years in prison. What had those years done to him? Losing everything— his freedom and the promise of a rich and famous future—must have embittered him. He had sworn revenge, hadn't he? Against her father. But he had also sworn something else.

He had sworn he was innocent.

But that wasn't possible. He'd been given a fair trial and was found guilty by a jury of his peers. Not only her father, but everyone in town knew he was guilty. He had to be guilty. All the evidence pointed directly to him. He had admitted beating his stepfather until he was unconscious. The knife used to slit Junior Blalock's throat had belonged to Reed, and only his fingerprints had been found on it.

"If you didn't send me this letter, then who did?" Ella asked. "Who else would have a reason to send me something like this? The content is very similar to those two letters you wrote to me. . . ."

"I shouldn't have written those letters to you."

Ella lowered the hand that held the scrunched envelope. She didn't know if she moved closer or if Reed did, but suddenly they were nose to nose. A wave of dizziness forced her to blink and then refocus her vision so that she looked away, over his shoulder toward the dingy white wall behind him.

"I was wild with anger when I first got to Donaldson,"

he said, his voice low, even, and unbelievably calm. "I lashed out at everyone and everything. I hated your father and I wrote those letters to you to get a rise out of him. It was a stupid mistake. One I've regretted for a long time."

He sounded so sincere that she almost believed him. Dear Lord, she wanted to believe him. She wanted to reach out and stroke his beard-stubbled cheek and tell him that she truly believed he regretted his past sins. She clenched her fist tightly at her side so that she didn't respond physically, didn't allow her own unchecked emotions to get her into trouble. As a small child, her spontaneous, emotional actions had worried her mother terribly, so she'd learned to curb those tendencies in order to please Carolyn.

"I'd like to believe you," Ella said, proud that her voice didn't tremble even though she was shaking like a leaf inside. "But it seems too much of a coincidence that the day after you're released from prison, I receive a letter very similar to the two you sent me fifteen years ago."

"Maybe it's not a coincidence," Reed suggested. He released the chair arms and rose to his full, imposing height.

Ella tilted her head and stared up at him. "What are you implying?"

"I know that I sure as hell didn't write that letter to you, but circumstantial evidence points to me. Maybe whoever sent it wants you to think I'm the person who wrote it."

"But why?"

"To get me in trouble."

Ella rose to her feet but quickly realized her mistake. Reed didn't move out of her way, so only inches separated her body from his. She felt his heat, smelled his sweat, heard his indrawn breath when his leg accidentally brushed against hers. Or had it been accidental?

"Why—why would someone want to get you in trouble?"

"If I get in big enough trouble, I go back to the pen." Did Reed sway slightly toward her or did she lean into him? Only a hairbreadth separated them now. "Whoever really killed Junior Blalock doesn't want me to stay free, doesn't want me snooping around trying to find out the truth."

For a split second, she thought he was going to kiss her. She froze to the spot, unable to move, unable to breathe. *You don't want him to kiss you, do you?* She realized that yes, she did want him to kiss her, and the shock of it motivated her self-preservation instincts. Maybe Reed Conway fascinated her in a way no other man ever had. Maybe the aura of danger and machismo that was such an intrinsic part of him aroused some primitive female needs within her. But she was an intelligent, cautious woman who knew better than to succumb to baser instincts.

Ella eased around Reed, unavoidably brushing against him as she passed. He made no move to restrain her. Instead, he followed her to the door, reached around her, grabbed the knob, and opened the door. His big, hairy arm looped around her waist. She was painfully aware of what their close proximity might look like to anyone who could see them. It would never do to have someone catch her practically in Reed Conway's arms.

"I'll give you the benefit of the doubt this time," she told him. "If you say you didn't write this letter"—she glanced at the letter she still gripped tightly in her hand—"then I'll take your word for it. But if I receive another, I won't be able to dismiss it so easily. Do I make myself clear, Mr. Conway?"

He grinned. *Damn him!* "Yes, Miss Ella, you make yourself perfectly clear. But you're talking to the wrong man."

A heated flush crept up her neck and colored her

cheeks. "Just stay away from me ... and from my family."

"It will be my pleasure."

Ella practically ran from him, her footsteps clicking against the concrete floor of the garage as she made her hasty escape. She didn't slow her pace until she reached her car; then, breathless with uncertainty and heightened senses, she halted long enough to get control of herself before she slid behind the wheel. Prompted by an urgent need to run, to get far away from Reed as fast as she could, Ella inserted the key into the ignition and started the engine. As she zoomed the Jag out into the street, the tires squealed loudly. When she dared a glance in her rearview mirror, she saw a smiling Reed Conway standing in the doorway, waving good-bye.

"Now, there, my man, is one fine piece of ass," Briley Joe said as he walked up beside Reed. "Got class written all over her."

"Yeah, she's a class act, all right." Reed shook his head and laughed. "She's scared shitless of me. And I don't think it's just because I'm a convicted murderer."

"You think the judge has got the hots for you, cuz?"

"I think she's scared of me. That's all."

"Yeah, but wouldn't you like to know what it feels like to make it with one of her kind?"

"Not much chance of that." Reed shrugged. "Women like Miss Ella are too high class for the likes of you and me."

"That's where you're wrong," Briley Joe snickered.

Reed glanced at his cousin and noted the self-satisfied grin on his face. "Don't compare Ella with her aunt."

"Some high-class dames like to get their hands dirty—real dirty." Briley Joe hooked his lean fingers over Reed's shoulder. "Even if you don't think she's anything like her aunt, who knows? Judge Porter might get real turned on just thinking about jumping in the sack with an ex-con."

* * *

Ever the dutiful daughter, Ella called and left a message with Bessie to let her mother know she'd be home a little later than usual. She'd been driving around for the past half hour asking herself what the hell had happened between her and Reed Conway. She had stopped by the garage to confront him about the letter she'd received and came away badly shaken and halfway convinced that the man hadn't sent her the letter.

You're an idiot, she scolded herself as she turned left on Tallulah Street. She needed someone to talk to about what had happened and about her confused emotions. She certainly couldn't run home and confess to her mother that she'd gotten all hot and bothered over Reed Conway. Carolyn was apt to have heart failure just at the thought that Ella might have spoken to the man. And if she even mentioned Reed's name to her father, he was liable to take gun in hand and go after him. No, this situation called for the sympathetic ear of a friend.

She parked her Jag in the driveway beside the restored Victorian house at 508 Tallulah Street. Ella's best friend since childhood, Heather Marshall, had recently returned to Spring Creek after an absence of five years, and the two had picked up right where they'd left off. Of course, during that five years when Heather had lived in Mobile, they'd phoned each other on a regular basis and had visited twice a year. Ella had been Heather's maid of honor when she married Lance Singleton. She'd sat by Heather's hospital bed when she suffered a miscarriage. And she'd offered support during Heather's ugly divorce ten months ago.

Ella stood on the flower-lined brick walkway in front of the house that had belonged to Heather's grandmother and had gradually fallen into disrepair after the old lady's death ten years ago. Heather had spent a small fortune restoring the place, and now the facade boasted its original Victorian colors: pink, cream, and green.

Working on the house had, according to Heather, saved her sanity after her divorce. Luckily, Heather had inherited enough money that she didn't have to work unless she wanted to, and Heather definitely preferred a life of leisure.

Thinking about how different she and Heather were, how different they had always been, Ella rang the doorbell. Even as children, they'd been exact opposites in appearance and temperament. Ella waited. No one came to the door. She rang the bell again. No response. Heather was home. Her black Corvette was parked in the driveway. Ella tried the bell one final time, then gave up and walked off the porch. She'd try the back door. When she made her way around the side of the house and opened the gate that led into the enclosed backyard, she heard water splashing. Of course. Why hadn't she realized that Heather would be in the pool?

Ella marched across the patio and reached the side of the pool just as Heather emerged, water dripping from her tall, slender body, which was clad in a thong and nothing else. Now, as always, Ella envied her friend's almost boyish physique. No matter how much Heather ate—and she had a ravenous appetite—she remained pencil-skinny. But whenever Ella had mentioned this fact to her best buddy, Heather had informed Ella that with boobs like hers, she didn't need to envy anyone.

"Hey, girlfriend, what are you doing here?" Heather reached for a large white towel resting on the wicker chaise longue a couple of feet away, then picked up the towel and ran the terry cloth over her freckled arms and legs. Four sets of gold hoops in Heather's ears and two gold toe rings glistened in the sunlight. A quarter-sized tattoo of a red heart stood out plainly on Heather's tanning-bed-tawny buttock.

"I need an understanding friend to tell me that I haven't completely lost my mind." Ella rubbed her forehead with the tips of her fingers, trying unsuccessfully to ease the headache that had hit her moments after leaving Conway's Garage.

Heather tossed the damp towel onto the tiled patio floor, picked up a short, see-through robe, and slipped into the hot pink fishnet garment. "The ever sane and sensible Judge Eleanor Porter thinks she might have lost her mind. I'm shocked. Sit down"—Heather pointed to the wicker chair to her left—"and tell Auntie Heather all about it."

Ella sat, sighed, and closed her eyes. "You cannot repeat what I'm about to say to another living soul."

Heather plopped down on the chaise longue. "Oh, boy, this must be good. Tell me it has something to do with a man."

Ella's eyes popped open and she gazed at her friend with a startled expression. Maybe this was a bad idea. Heather was bound to get a great deal of pleasure from Ella's admission. After all, Heather had always been the wild one, dating bad boys and even marrying one. On the other hand, Ella had always been the sensible one, dating only upstanding men who had received the stamp of approval from her mother.

"My God, it *is* about a man." Heather twisted around on the chaise and faced Ella. "Surely not Dan Gilmore. The guy is as dull as dishwater."

"No, it's not about Dan." Ella hesitated. Her heartbeat accelerated. "It's about Reed Conway."

"Reed Conway?" Heather's mouth dropped open. "Reed Conway who was sent to prison for murdering his stepfather?"

Ella nodded.

Heather scooted to the edge of the chaise and leaned forward toward Ella. "I take it that you've seen him since he was released from prison yesterday. Come on"—Heather motioned a hurry-up wave with her fingers—"confess. How did you happen to run into Reed and—"

"I didn't run into him," Ella said. "I—I stopped by Conway's Garage to see him." She opened her purse, jerked out the letter, removed it from the envelope, and handed it to Heather. "I found this lying on my desk this afternoon."

Heather took the letter, scanned it quickly, and let out a long, low whistle. "Hmm ... This must have reminded you of those two letters Reed wrote to you way back when. So, you think he wrote this letter?"

"That's what I thought."

"You went to see Reed about this letter?" Heather stuffed the letter back into the envelope and returned it to Ella. "Why on earth didn't you just call Frank Nelson? Checking into something like this is a job for our police chief. I cannot believe you actually confronted Reed. I'd have been scared spitless to accuse him to his face."

"I didn't want Daddy to find out and go ballistic or for Mother to get all upset, so I thought that if I handled the problem myself—"

"What did Reed say? Mercy, Ella, what did he do?"

"He denied writing the letter."

"Of course he did. You didn't think he'd admit to doing it, did you?"

Ella sighed. "After speaking to Reed, I'm not so sure he wrote the letter."

"Uh-oh."

"What does that mean?" Ella asked.

"It means something else went on between you and Reed, didn't it? Something besides a confrontation over that letter."

Ella nodded. She twined her fingers together and nervously rubbed her thumb over the palm of the opposite hand. "I can't explain what happened. It was like heat lightning. For just a split second, I thought he was going to kiss me."

"You're kidding me." Heather reached out and grabbed Ella by the shoulders. "Now, you listen to me, girlfriend—stay away from Reed Conway. The guy is trouble with a capital *T*. Whatever game he's playing with you is a dangerous one. He's got to know that the best form of revenge against your father is by using you."

"Don't you think I know that? But it doesn't change the fact that I . . . responded to him. I wanted him to kiss me. I actually hoped he would kiss me."

"Shit!"

Reed rang the doorbell, then banged on the door. Ever since sweet Miss Ella Porter had left the garage, he'd been walking around with a hard-on. What kind of fool did that make him? He had wanted to lift her onto the desk in Briley Joe's office, strip off her panties, part her legs, and ram himself into her. When she'd stared at him with those big brown eyes, it had taken all his will power not to grab her and kiss her. And if he hadn't read her wrong, he figured that she would have let him. Kiss her, that is. Not screw her.

Reed knocked again. The door swung open and Ivy Sims's mouth spread into a wide grin.

"Well, hello there, sugar. You're early. I just got out of the shower."

Reed visually raked her body from neck to knees. The short floral robe hung open just enough to reveal her thighs and parted above the belt to give him a glimpse of the inner curve of her breasts. Reed pushed her backward, came into the apartment, and shoved the door closed with his foot. Then without saying a word, he grabbed Ivy, thrust his tongue into her mouth, and lifted her up by her butt. She quickly wrapped her legs around his hips as he carried her through the living room and straight to her bedroom. She giggled when he tossed her onto the bed. He unzipped his jeans; then pulled a small square packet from his pocket. She squirmed and held out her arms when he opened her robe. He parted the fly of his briefs and freed his sex, then donned the condom hurriedly. Ivy cried out with pleasure when he impaled her.

He drove into her like a madman, all the while with his eyes tightly shut. The woman beneath him wasn't the one he wanted, but he could pretend she was, couldn't he?

Chapter 6

Expecting a call from Heather, Ella answered the phone on the third ring. "Hello?"

Silence. Complete quiet. Eerie nothingness. Ella's hand tightened on the telephone receiver as she said, "Hello. Is anyone there?"

Breathing. Deep, heavy breathing. Sensual panting. Just like the two unknown calls she had received yesterday.

"If you have something to say to me, say it. Otherwise, do not call me again!" Ella slammed down the receiver. When she lifted her hand, she noticed the slight tremble. *Stop this!* She tightened her hands into fists and plopped them down atop her desk.

Phone calls cannot hurt you, she reminded herself. *Whoever is on the other end of the line is harassing you, trying to upset you.* The caller had not done anything to warrant the fear that grew steadily within her. Ever since she'd received the letter three days ago, she had argued with herself over Reed Conway's involvement. Was he or was he not the guilty party behind the letter and the phone calls? He was, of course, the most obvious suspect, but that alone could not condemn him. But if not Reed, then who? She had read through her files, studying every case over which she had presided since she'd become a circuit court judge. Had a disgruntled felon felt unjustly convicted? Not one of the men or women whom she'd sentenced to prison had threatened her or made any comments about injustice or revenge.

A light tapping outside her office door brought her back from her thoughts. "Yes?" Ella's heartbeat roared in her ears. Where was Kelly? Why wasn't she running interference for her?

The door cracked open slightly and Roy Moses stuck his head in and smiled at her. "Morning, Miss Ella."

She breathed a sigh of relief. "Good morning, Roy." Ella checked her watch and realized that it wasn't quite eight. Kelly wouldn't arrive until eight-thirty.

"I was sweeping up along the hall and saw something lying outside your door." Roy lifted his meaty hand and held out a white envelope. "It's got your name on it."

Ella sucked in a deep breath as anxiety swept through her like a tidal wave. Don't let it be another letter from *him.* "Please, bring it on in." She stood and walked toward the door to meet Roy.

"You sure do look pretty this morning." Roy held out the envelope.

"Thank you." Ella forced a smile, then grasped the envelope. She noticed that her name was typewritten, as on the first letter. Her stomach did a nervous flip-flop.

"You have a good day." Roy plodded toward the door.

"You, too," Ella called after him. The moment he closed the door, she picked up the letter opener from her desk and sliced open the envelope. Willing herself to be calm, she eased the single page of unlined paper from its casing. As she spread open the folded missive, she prayed that it wasn't what she thought it was.

Have you been thinking of me? I've been thinking about you. Bad thoughts. Dirty thoughts. Thoughts that would make you cream your pants.

Ella stopped reading. It was from him! Another sexually explicit, harassing letter. A crude, threatening love letter just like the one she'd received three days ago. Just like the two Reed had sent her from prison fifteen years ago.

This had to stop. She couldn't continue ignoring the matter. Three heavy-breathing phone calls and two menacing letters. She'd thought she could handle the situation without involving anyone else, but she'd been wrong.

Ella picked up the telephone receiver, dialed the familiar number, and waited.

"Porter residence," the housekeeper said.

"Bessie, this is Ella. Is my father there?"

"Yes, ma'am. He's in the library."

"I'd like to speak to him, please."

"Certainly."

The moment she entered Callahan's, Ella saw her father at the bar. She lifted her hand and waved. Smiling, he returned the gesture, then motioned for her to join him. Making her way through the crowd of waiting customers in the entrance foyer, she moved steadily toward the bar. The moment she approached him, Webb grabbed her and hugged her.

"I can't think of anything nicer than your inviting me to lunch," Webb said, then winked. "Unless it would be inviting me to your wedding."

"Now, Daddy."

"You know how much your mother likes Dan. She's been after me to remind you that he'd make a great husband and father." Webb ran his hands down her arms and then grasped her wrist. "Sit. Our table should be ready soon. What can I order for you?"

"Perrier with lemon." She took the bar stool next to her father. "Thanks for meeting me on such short notice. I hope Mother didn't mind my taking you away from the house. I know how much she treasures your days at home with her."

Webb's smile faltered. "I realize your mother thinks I neglect her, but—"

"She understands how busy you are and how important your career is to you."

"Your mother's life hasn't been easy. We've both done the best we could with the hand fate dealt us." Webb lifted his bourbon to his lips and downed the last drops, then ordered another when he asked the bartender to bring Ella's bottled water. "You mustn't worry. I told Carolyn that you'd invited me to lunch and she was delighted. You do know that your mother adores you."

Ella sighed. "Yes, of course, I know." There were times when Carolyn's actions proved without a doubt that she did indeed adore her only child. But sometimes Ella sensed just a little envy coming from her mother. She understood that Carolyn often felt left out of the numerous activities Ella enjoyed with Webb. Things like tennis and golf and swimming. And being so acutely aware of her mother's discontent broke Ella's heart and made her all the more determined to be a good and loving daughter. There was nothing she wanted more than for her mother to be able to walk again. It had been her fondest dream since childhood.

"So, to what do I owe this honor?" Webb asked. "I know that you often eat lunch in your office, so why take the time today to have lunch with your old man?"

The bartender set Ella's Perrier in front of her and then placed Webb's second glass of bourbon on the bar. Ella lifted her drink and took a sip.

"Before I tell you anything, I want you to promise

me that you aren't going to lose your temper and rush out of here half-cocked."

Webb eyed her curiously. "Well, you've intrigued me, princess. I can't imagine what you could say that would have that effect on me."

Callahan's hostess approached them. "Your table is ready, Senator Porter."

Within minutes they were seated at the best table in the restaurant. Webb ordered for both of them, the way he'd done since Ella was a child. Even though she wanted to remind him that she was thirty now and not six, she didn't protest. One of the things she loved about her father was the fact that he never changed. He was her rock, her support, her friend, and her hero. She had always worshiped the ground Webb Porter walked on.

"I promise not to lose my temper, so feel free to share this upsetting news with me. It isn't something about Cybil, is it? If it is, I hope we can keep it from your mother. You know how she gets upset over her sister's antics."

"No, Daddy, it isn't about Aunt Cybil." Ella laid her purse on the table, opened it, and withdrew two white envelopes, both wrinkled from having been crushed in her hand. "I received one of these three days ago and the other this morning. And I've had three phone calls when the person on the other end didn't do anything except breathe heavy." She handed the letters to her father.

Webb removed the first letter from the envelope and read it slowly and thoroughly. His face darkened with rage, but he didn't say a word. Then he read the second letter. His breathing quickened.

"If you received one of these letters three days ago, why didn't you tell me then?" Webb slipped the letters inside his coat pocket.

"I thought . . . well, I hoped that it would just be the one letter."

"You realize who sent these, don't you?" He tapped his jacket, where the letters rested inside his pocket. "But if he thinks he can get away with harassing my daughter, he'd better think again." Webb's voice grew louder with each word he spoke. "I'll put his ass back in prison where he belongs."

"Daddy, you can't be one hundred percent sure it's—"

"Of course it's Reed Conway. Who else could it be?"

Patrons seated nearby turned their heads to stare at Webb. Ella reached across the table and laid her hand over her father's big fist. "Calm down. People are staring."

Webb glanced around at the curious faces. Placing a fake politician's smile on his face, he nodded at several acquaintances, then opened his tight fist and clutched Ella's hand.

"If that man ever comes near you, I'll kill him!" Webb spoke in a low but deadly serious voice.

"I was afraid you would react this way. That's why I hesitated to tell you."

With a large serving tray hoisted on one hand, their waitress paused by the side of the table. Webb released Ella's hand and offered the waitress a smile.

"Please let me know if you need anything else, Senator Porter."

"I'll surely do that."

The minute the waitress served the food and went on to take the order at another table, Webb lifted his steak knife and cut into the thick T-bone. Blood oozed from the rare meat.

"You leave everything to me," he said. "After lunch, I'm going straight to Frank Nelson's office. Reed Conway won't be bothering you again."

Ella eyed her filet mignon. "You have no proof that Reed sent those letters. Without proof, what can Frank do?"

"First of all, he can have these letters tested for fingerprints other than yours and mine. And in the meantime, he can put the fear of God into that boy. Let him know that we won't tolerate such behavior from him."

"Daddy, Reed's fingerprints will be on the first letter," Ella said reluctantly. Although she didn't want to explain how Reed's fingerprints came to be on the letter, she had no choice but to tell her father the truth. She wasn't going to allow her silence to condemn a possibly innocent man.

"How do you know his fingerprints are on the first letter?" Webb asked. He glared at her, his dark eyes narrowing.

"I confronted Reed with the letter the day I received it."

"You what?"

"Lower your voice. People are staring again."

"To hell with people staring!" Webb dropped his knife and fork onto his plate. The metal clanged against the china. "Are you telling me that you—"

"He swore to me that he didn't do it—that he didn't write the letter. And strange as it may sound to you, I think I believe him."

"Little girl, you stay away from the likes of Reed Conway. Do you hear me? I thought you had better sense than to go anywhere near him. Don't you know that he'd like nothing better than to hurt you in order to get to me?"

"Yes, of course, I'm aware of your past history with him and the fact that he swore revenge against you and—"

"Promise me that you'll never go anywhere near him again."

"But Daddy—"

"Dammit, promise me."

"I—I promise."

* * *

By now Ella would have received the second letter. No doubt that was the reason she had been seen having lunch with her father at Callahan's. She had run to her daddy. Ella was so predictable. Using her was almost too easy. Webb's next stop would be at Frank Nelson's office.

Laughter filled the room. Self-satisfied laughter. Making Webb miserable was such a pleasure. It was past time that the senator suffered for his sins. And nothing made Webb Porter suffer more than to think his precious daughter was in danger.

Ella wasn't in any real danger. Not now. Not yet. One did what one had to do to survive, to protect one's self. And to get a little sweet revenge.

A short walk across the room to the computer on the desk. A few clicks and the screen opened to the word processing program. One more message, similar to the others, and then it would be time to up the ante, raise the stakes, unnerve the senator's daughter to a greater degree.

"I want you to go over to where he's working at his cousin's garage and warn him to stay away from my family—my daughter in particular."

Frank Nelson watched Webb Porter, his father's old friend, as he paced the floor. The man was more agitated than he'd ever seen him. There was a sense of desperation in Webb that Frank didn't think he'd ever seen. But when it came to Ella, Webb was a typical father. Only he was a father who possessed a great deal of power and influence.

"I can give him an unofficial warning, but that's all I can do unless we can come up with some proof that he's the one harassing Ella," Frank explained.

"Of course he's the one."

"I agree. He probably is, but without proof—"

"That boy was trouble fifteen years ago and he's even more trouble now." Webb forked his fingers through his silver hair. "His mother didn't deserve the problems he created for her."

"Yes, sir, I agree. Judy Conway is a good woman. God knows what she's gone through over the years."

Webb cleared his throat. "Yes, well, Judy's almost a member of the family, you know. She's been with Jeff Henry and Cybil for ages."

Frank tapped the envelopes lying on his desk. "Webb, you leave these letters with me and I'll drive over to Conway's later on today and have a talk with Reed."

"Thanks, Frank. I knew I could count on you."

Judy said her good-byes to Carolyn Porter and slipped away quietly while Viola lifted the crippled woman into her arms and carried her back to her bed. Judy closed the door behind her. She both pitied and envied Carolyn, as she was sure almost everyone in town did. The poor thing had been an invalid for over thirty years. Judy made a point of not coming to the Porter house unless she had no other choice. There was too much bad blood between their families. But occasionally, like today, Jeff Henry would insist that Judy drop by with some of her homemade bread, since he knew Carolyn loved it so. She had intended to simply leave the bread in the kitchen with Bessie, but the housekeeper had been out shopping and Viola had answered the door-bell's ring. Carolyn had inquired who their visitor was and then insisted that Judy come up for a visit.

"I get out rarely," Carolyn had said. "Especially not in this hot weather. It's such a delight to have a visitor. Come, sit and chat with me awhile."

The woman was Webb Porter's wife, and that very fact made Judy uncomfortable in her presence. But she had stayed twenty minutes. As usual, Carolyn was charming. A true Southern lady. But as usual, Judy felt an underlying tension in Webb's wife.

The moment Judy started down the back staircase, she met Webb. Her heart leaped to her throat. She had prayed she wouldn't run into him. What would she say? How should she act?

"Judy?"

"Hello, Webb."

"What are you doing here?" he asked.

"Jeff Henry sent me over with some homemade bread for Carolyn. He's aware that it's a favorite of hers."

Webb stopped his ascent. Judy continued down the stairs. When she passed him, he reached out for her, but dropped his hand to his side before actually touching her.

"I'd like to talk to you," he said.

"I don't think we have anything to talk about."

"Please, give me a few minutes of your time."

She forced herself to look him squarely in the eye, but regretted the action when he stared at her pleadingly. *Don't let him get to you,* she cautioned herself. *Webb Porter knows how to charm a lady. But this man is your son's enemy and don't you forget it.*

"What do you want to talk to me about?" she asked.

"Would you come downstairs with me? We can talk in my study."

"We can talk in the kitchen, on my way out," she told him.

"If that's what you prefer."

"It is."

He followed her down the back stairs and into the kitchen. She paused by the door. "What is it?"

"Ella has received three disturbing phone calls and two obscene, threatening letters since Reed was paroled."

Judy gasped. "Are you saying that you think Reed made those phone calls and sent those letters?"

"Yes, that's exactly what I think."

"You're wrong. Dead wrong. Just like you were wrong about him slitting Junior's throat fifteen years ago."

"You're Reed's mother. I'd expect you to defend him."

"And you're the man who prosecuted him for murder. I'd expect you to suspect him. But I'm telling you that all Reed wants is a second chance. He's not going to do anything to mess up his parole."

"I hope you're right. But I think you should caution Reed to stay away from Ella."

"Stay away from . . . Are you saying that Reed's been bothering Ella?"

"They made contact and it upset Ella."

"What do you mean they made contact?"

"After she received the first letter, Ella confronted Reed."

"Ah, I see." Judy tilted her chin and glared at Webb. "If you're so worried about Reed contaminating Ella, then perhaps you should tell your daughter to stay away from my son."

Judy left hurriedly while Webb Porter stood there, mouth agape. She closed the door quietly behind her and ran from the back porch and down the brick sidewalk. Her head throbbed. Her heart raced. Damn Webb Porter. Damn him to hell and back.

Webb didn't move for several minutes after Judy Conway's hasty departure. He hadn't meant to upset her, but he should have known that it would be useless to ask her to warn Reed to stay away from Ella. Judy had been Reed's staunchest defender during his trial, and whatever goodwill there had been between Webb and her before then had come to an end when Reed had been convicted of Junior's murder.

He would never forget the night she came to him, pleading for him to have the police search elsewhere for her dead husband's killer.

"Someone else killed Junior," she had said. "I swear to you that Reed didn't slit his throat. He beat him to within an inch of his life, yes, but he didn't come back later while Junior was unconscious and murder him."

Webb had wanted to help her. More than she would ever know. But how could he, when all the evidence pointed clearly to Reed? Webb had despised Junior Blalock almost as much as Reed had. He'd never understood what Judy had seen in that white trash drunkard. He realized how hard it had been for her trying to raise two children on her own, but marrying Junior had only added to her troubles, not relieved them. Of course, Junior had been a good-looking devil and had possessed a certain amount of crude charm. But he'd been a sleaze—a wife beater and a child molester. Webb cringed at the thought of that slimy bastard touching sweet little Regina. If back then Webb had ever suspected that Junior had tried to rape Regina, he wasn't sure what he would have done to the man. *You would have killed him,* a nagging inner voice said.

"Yes, I would have killed him," Webb said aloud.

The intercom buzzer sounded. "Webb? If you're there, dear, would you please come upstairs. I haven't seen you since breakfast this morning."

Webb froze to the spot. There had been a time, long ago, when he had loved the sound of Carolyn's voice: soft, sultry, and honey-coated Southern. But that had been a lifetime ago. Now, the sound irritated the hell out of him. There were times when he couldn't bear even being in the same room with her. She was clinging and whiny and needy, so very needy. He had loved her once, but that, too, had been a lifetime ago. He pitied her. He had stayed married to her out of duty and obligation. Carolyn knew why he stayed, but she didn't seem to mind why he remained her husband, just as long as she could be, now and forever, Mrs. Webb Porter. She claimed to love him, and in her own way, perhaps she did.

They both loved Ella, the one good thing in their lives. But how many times had the truth about Ella's bloodlines haunted him? How often had he wondered exactly how Carolyn would feel about Ella if she knew the truth about their adopted child? If his wife knew about Ella's true parentage, would she hate their daughter? But there was no reason for Carolyn to ever know the truth. And no reason for Ella ever to learn about her biological mother and father. Her adoption had been private—handled by the Porters' family lawyer, Milton Leamon, Webb's cousin. And thankfully, Ella had never asked any questions about her natural parents.

"Webb? Webb?" Carolyn called again and again.

With slumped shoulders, he left the kitchen and headed up the back stairs. When he reached Carolyn's closed door, he hesitated, then knocked. Viola opened the door. The woman glared at him. She had the look of an army sergeant. Hard as nails, tough through and through. Viola could be unpleasant and aggravating, but she was devoted to Carolyn. He didn't know what they would have done without the woman these past thirty-one years.

"Please come in, Mr. Porter." Viola moved out of his way. "Miss Carolyn is quite eager to see you."

Viola walked past him, leaving him alone with his wife. Carolyn sat propped up in the bed, pillows surrounding her. She was still a lovely woman. He tried his best to be devoted and caring. Occasionally he even shared her bed. But Carolyn's paralysis kept her from fully enjoying sex, so their intimate moments together lacked any real satisfaction for either of them. If he loved her, it would have been different. But he didn't love her. He hadn't loved his wife in over thirty years. If he ever confessed that to anyone, they would assume it was because of her condition. But they would be wrong.

"Darling, there you are. What kept you so long? Viola heard you speaking to Judy Conway on the stairs. Has Judy gone?"

"Yes, she's gone."

"Such a sweet woman."

"Yes."

Carolyn patted the bed. "Come sit with me."

Webb crossed the room and perched on the edge of the bed. "Have you had a good day?"

"As good as most. What about you? Did you enjoy your lunch with Ella?"

How did he answer that question truthfully without divulging the truth about the harassing letters Ella had received? Telling Carolyn would only upset her. "I always enjoy time with our daughter."

"We have every reason to be proud of her, don't we?"

"Yes, we do. We've done a fine job with her. You've been a good mother."

"Thank you, Webb. It's nice to know that I'm not a failure at everything."

"Carolyn, please . . ."

"Yes, of course, no need to ruin a perfectly pleasant visit with an unpleasant subject."

"Will you be joining us for dinner tonight?" Webb asked.

"Yes, certainly . . . if you're going to be home. You haven't made other plans, have you?"

"No."

"Webb?"

"Hmm?"

"What were you and Judy talking about?"

Webb noted the hint of jealousy in Carolyn's voice. She had been insanely jealous when they'd first married—a trait that had driven him crazy. Back then, she'd had no reason to be jealous. He'd been a faithful husband. She was still a jealous wife, but she controlled the emotion and hid her feelings quite well. He knew she suspected him of infidelity, but it was a taboo subject between them.

"I asked her about Reed," Webb said.

"Ah, yes, of course. What else would the two of you

have to discuss except her son? I assume he still hates you as much as he did when he first went to prison."

"Yes, I assume he does."

"Let's hope he doesn't make good on the threats he made back then." Carolyn reached for Webb's hand. Reluctantly, he accepted her gentle touch. "I couldn't bear it if anything happened to you. Or to Ella. You and our daughter are my life. You do know that, don't you?"

"Yes, Carolyn, I know." He leaned over and kissed her soft cheek. "You mustn't worry, dear. I'll make sure that Reed Conway isn't a threat to me or to Ella."

"What will you do if he . . . ?"

Webb laid his index finger over her parted lips. "Hush now. Don't fret. Just know that I'll do whatever it takes to keep Reed from disrupting our lives."

Chapter 7

When he heard a car screech to a halt outside the garage, Reed looked up from under the hood of the Pontiac Grand Prix a customer had dropped off to have the air filter changed. A 1957 Thunderbird convertible was a beautiful machine, a classic. And the lady who emerged from behind the wheel was herself a classic beauty. He would have known her anywhere. Remarkably, she'd changed very little in fifteen years. How old was she now? In her late forties, but she didn't look a day over thirty-five. At least not at a distance. Petite but with curves in all the right places. Her shapely body filled out a pair of red capri pants, and her full breasts strained against the red-and-white cotton halter top. Her thick, black hair had been cut in the latest short fashion. A pair of large fourteen-karat gold hoops dangled from her ears. As she approached the garage entrance, she lowered her sunglasses and peered over the rims at Reed. When she recognized him, she threw up her hand and waved.

"Hi, there, Reed." Cybil Carlisle bestowed one of her thousand-watt smiles on him. "Welcome home."

"Hello, Mrs. Carlisle."

Before Cybil could advance their conversation, Briley Joe opened the door to the office and came outside to greet their customer.

"Afternoon, Mrs. Carlisle." Briley Joe appraised her obvious physical assets, skimming her from top to bottom. A smug, I've-had-some-of-that-and-it-was-good grin spread across his face.

Her smile broadened when she turned her attention to Briley Joe. "I'm glad you're here. I need to talk to you about tuning up my engine."

"Come on into my office and let's discuss your problem."

Briley Joe held open the door for Cybil, who slunk past him and into the cool air-conditioned interior. Before he followed her inside, he paused, glanced over his shoulder, and winked at Reed.

Reed laughed, then shook his head. Hell, that Briley Joe was a hound dog. Screwing around with Jeff Henry Carlisle's wife wasn't the smartest thing his cousin had ever done. He could understand the fascination, but no piece of ass was worth risking your life. Enraged husbands shot their wives' lovers every day of the week. And a guy as rich as Jeff Henry was the type to hire somebody else to do the dirty work while keeping his own hands clean.

Personally, Reed had never liked Jeff Henry. Too much of a snob, and a fancy-pants to boot. Reed hated that his mother still worked as the Carlisles' housekeeper. She'd been with the family since he was a little boy. He could well remember the times he'd stood sulking in the kitchen, warned by his mother to stay out of sight and be quiet, that Mr. Jeff Henry didn't like being bothered by children. But he'd soon learned that one child in particular had free rein in the Carlisle household. The little princess, Ella Porter. Not only had she been allowed to play in any room of the house, she'd often sat in Jeff Henry's lap and drunk lemonade while

Reed peered around the corner. In the beginning he had envied Ella, and later on, after his sister, Regina, was born, he had disliked Ella intensely. He had somehow gotten the notion in his head that Jeff Henry was Regina's father, and that being the fact, he wondered why Jeff Henry didn't hold Regina in his lap, read stories to her, and let her have the run of his home. Of course, by the time he was twelve, he realized that his mother's employer probably wasn't his sister's father after all. When he was twelve, just a few days before she married Junior Blalock, his mother had kissed Webb Porter. Reed had seen them there in the Carlisles' garden. He might have been just a kid, but he knew the difference between a passionate embrace and a friendly hug. In a rather loud voice, Webb had asked Judy not to marry Junior. But before Reed had gotten close enough to hear his mother's soft response, Ella had come running from the Porters' backyard, calling for her father.

As a teenager, Reed had asked his mother who Regina's father was, and she'd told him it was none of his business. She'd denied that either Jeff Henry or Webb Porter was the man who'd gotten her pregnant. Giving birth to an illegitimate child had to have been torment for his mother, who was by anyone's standards a good, decent woman. Having an abortion would have been out of the question for her. She was the religious type who believed that life began at conception.

Sweat dripped off Reed's chin, trickled down his back, and dampened his stained cotton T-shirt. Being a mechanic was dirty work, especially on a hot summer day in a local garage in a one-horse town like Spring Creek. But hot, dirty, and tired, Reed felt great. He was free and that was all that mattered. For now. He didn't want to spend the rest of his life in this job, or even in this town. But he couldn't make plans for the future until he'd come to terms with the past. And that meant finding out who really killed Junior, so he could clear his name.

And just what are you willing to risk in order to accomplish that goal? he asked himself. *One false move on your part and you'll be back in the slammer. You touch one hair on Princess Ella's head and Webb Porter will serve your balls up on a silver platter.*

He had compiled a list of suspects—people with reason to want Junior Blalock dead. People other than himself and his mother. Jeff Henry Carlisle and Webb Porter topped that list. They were his main targets, despite the fact that Mark Leamon assured him time and again that neither man was capable of murder or of allowing an innocent teenage boy to spend half his life in prison.

Reed wiped his hands, mixing sweat and grease on the dingy rag. He heard a faint sound coming from inside the office. Giggles? Throaty giggles. His imagination kicked into overdrive. Images of his cousin and Cybil Carlisle flashed through his mind, followed quickly by unwelcome thoughts of Ella. He had to stop thinking about the senator's daughter. No good would come of having her on his mind. She was forbidden fruit.

A loud thump jarred Reed from his musings. Something had either fallen onto the floor inside the office or had hit the wall. Three days ago he'd had Ella all alone in the same ten-foot-square area where Briley Joe no doubt was, at this very moment, getting from Cybil what Reed wanted from Ella. Suddenly Reed's sex hardened. He cursed himself for a fool.

"You've missed me a lot, haven't you?" Briley Joe grabbed her hands when she tried to unzip his jeans. "You ought to come around more often. If you did, you wouldn't be so horny now."

"I thought you liked me horny." She tried again to grasp the tab on his zipper, but he clutched her hands, brought them up, and flattened them against his chest.

"I like you any way I can get you. You know that." His cunning grin created dimples in his cheeks. "But it might be fun to spend more than thirty minutes together some time. What do you think?"

She glared at him. Damn the man! Why did he have to talk? She wasn't interested in conversation. Surely he knew there was only one reason she came to him. She didn't want love or romance or even friendship. She wanted the same thing from this Neanderthal grease monkey that she'd wanted from the other, less desirable men she'd used over the years. She wanted a quick tumble to relieve sexual tension. And she wanted her ever-loving husband to know that she was getting laid by a white trash stud.

"I think it's time for more action and less talk," Cybil told him. "If we stay in here too long, Reed's going to wonder what's going on." She didn't like the smug look on Briley Joe's face, or the way his lips curved into a tentative smile. "Damn you, he knows, doesn't he? You told him!"

"Reed knows how to keep his mouth shut."

"He'd better." Over the years she'd made certain that her numerous indiscretions hadn't become a public scandal. People might speculate about her morals, but her infidelity was nothing more than unsubstantiated rumors. Only her family knew she was a tramp. Her saccharine, holier-than-thou sister, Carolyn, her not-so-saintly brother-in-law, Webb, and, of course, her beloved husband. Jeff Henry hated her now. But his hatred was preferable to his indifference. At least he felt something for her. There had been a time when she had desperately wanted his love, but she'd finally realized that her husband could love only one woman. *And that woman wasn't her!* Jeff Henry had worshiped the ground Carolyn walked on since they'd been children. When she married Webb, she'd broken Jeff Henry's heart. And when he had realized that the marriage was going to last, he had asked Cybil to marry him. And like a young fool, she'd said yes. In less than six months, she'd realized that she was nothing more than a substitute for the real thing. And Jeff Henry quickly learned that his wife was no carbon copy of her older sister.

The feel of Briley Joe's callused hands skimming across her midriff reminded Cybil of where she was and whom she was with. She pressed herself against him, rubbing her mound over his erection. Her body throbbed with need. It had been nearly a year since she'd had sex with her husband—his choice, not hers. Even if they despised each other, they could still satisfy their basic needs in their marital bed. She was willing; Jeff Henry was not. She couldn't help wondering if he got his jollies by sitting at Carolyn's bedside, reading romantic poetry to the poor invalid.

If her husband loved her, if he shared her bed, if he wasn't in love with her sister, she wouldn't have to seek solace elsewhere. Years ago she'd been stupid enough to think that if she screwed around, Jeff Henry would care, that he'd take notice of her. He'd taken notice all right, but not because he cared.

"You're going to wind up in big trouble if you keep messing around with trash," Jeff Henry had told her. "If you don't catch some vile disease, sooner or later one of your redneck lovers will beat the hell out of you."

He'd been right on one count. And the beating had come sooner, not later. Fifteen years ago, she'd had an ugly little affair with Junior Blalock and wound up bloody and bruised. That sorry bastard had loved inflicting pain. How Judy had stayed married to him, Cybil would never know. He'd been pretty good in the sack, but a little too rough even for Cybil's crude tastes. When Jeff Henry had arrived at the emergency room that long-ago night, he'd been livid. To this day she didn't know with whom he'd been the most angry, Junior or her. But it hadn't been her own husband who'd gone to see Junior and issued him a warning. It had been her sister's husband, good old Webb. He'd always been dear and kind to her. They understood each other. In an odd sort of way, Webb and she were two of a kind. Both were trapped in loveless marriages, and both hid a life-altering secret.

Briley Joe raised her halter top, then lifted her breasts as if he were weighing them and lowered his mouth to one tight nipple. Excitement spiraled through her, sending waves of awareness from her breasts to the depths of her femininity. Tingling sensation clutched her pelvic muscles and released a preliminary shot of moisture.

He rammed his hand between her thighs and clutched her mound, fondling her through the thin cotton of her capri pants and bikini panties. "I want to hear you tell me how much you want it."

She grabbed him by the buttocks. "Are you going to fuck me or are you going to talk all day?"

That shut him up. He dragged her pants and panties down and off with a quick jerk, then swiped the side of the desk clean with a backward lash of his hand. Stacks of papers and an array of magazines landed haphazardly over the concrete floor. With his gaze focused on her face, Briley Joe lifted her up on the table, spread her legs apart, and unzipped his jeans. His sex sprang free. Big. Hard. Ready. Cybil licked her lips.

"You're a real bitch, lady. But then you know that, don't you?" Briley Joe thrust into her.

Cybil bit her bottom lip to keep from crying out with pleasure from the feel of him inside her. She had needed this so much. To be with a man.

"God, baby, you're hot and dripping wet." Briley Joe pumped into her several times. Sweat dampened his flushed face. His nostrils flared.

They went at each other like a couple of animals. Wild. Coarse. Snarling. Cybil climaxed first. Every nerve in her body experienced the intense orgasm. She kissed him, drowning her cry inside his ravaging mouth. But when he came only seconds later, he tossed back his head and groaned, the sound reverberating inside the small room. When she tried to pull away from him, he restrained her, remaining inside her as the aftershocks rippled through them. He spread kisses across the side of her face, then up and down her neck.

"That was so good," he whispered in her ear. "So good." He caressed her cheek with the back of his hand.

Let me go, she thought. *Don't be sweet and romantic. It's not what I want. You know that, dammit. Haven't I told you repeatedly that sex is all I want from you?*

She pulled away from him, dislodging him from inside her. He didn't protest, just stepped back to give her room to maneuver. Although she tried not to look at him while she slid off the desk and gathered up her clothes, she couldn't help catching a glimpse of him in her peripheral vision. His penis hung limp and damp, but still large enough to be impressive. Sometime during their mating, she had partly ripped open his shirt. Perspiration glistened on his hairy chest. He was muscular and tan, almost as hairy as an ape. And no matter how much he scrubbed his hands, there was always a hint of grease under his nails. He was the antithesis of her purebred, pale-skinned, gentlemanly husband.

Damn, she had to get out of here before she asked for more. She didn't dare stay longer. People might question why Cybil Carlisle was at Conway's Garage for more than thirty minutes. After all, whatever problems she had with her car wouldn't require her to converse with the garage's owner for an hour or more. She probably shouldn't have come here. She'd had sex with him in this office only once before today. Another time when she'd been pissed at Jeff Henry and needed a little TLC. Usually, she met her lovers in out-of-the-way places where they were unlikely to be detected. But sometimes she dared risking discovery. Times like today, when a part of her wished the whole damn town knew what she'd been doing with Briley Joe Conway on the dingy desk in his grimy little office.

Cybil wiped herself with her bikini panties, tossed them into the wastebasket, then hurriedly pulled on her pants and straightened her halter top. "I've got to run."

"When will I see you again?" Briley Joe asked.

"I'll be in touch, sweetie."

She blew him a kiss, then opened the door and headed straight for her parked car. Reed Conway was staring at her. She could feel him watching her every move. She wondered how Briley Joe would feel about sharing her with his cousin? Reed was a bit young for her, but by doing some swift calculations in her head, she figured out he was nearly thirty-three. Fifteen years her junior. So who cared? But Reed was Judy's son, and she didn't want to do anything to upset Judy. The poor woman had experienced more than her share of misery over the years. Reed was a sweet temptation, but she'd leave him alone. For Judy's sake. Besides, she already had as much he-man as she could handle with Briley Joe.

Once inside her T-bird, Cybil opened her purse and removed a small hand mirror. She cringed when she looked at herself. Briley Joe's marauding mouth had pretty well erased most of her makeup, and his roaming fingers had mussed her hair. She looked like she'd just had sex.

Cybil grinned. A sad little giggle erupted from her throat. Would Jeff Henry even notice her when she went home? And if he did, would he give a damn that she'd been with another man . . . again?

Reed slammed the hood on the Grand Prix, pulled a rag from his back pocket, and wiped his hands. He glanced at the closed office door, then pivoted his head to watch Cybil Carlisle whip her T-bird onto the street. Was she actually going home to her husband looking like that? The man would have to be either blind or a fool not to realize what she'd been up to.

Suddenly Reed tensed. A police car turned off from the main road and pulled to a stop in the parking area to the side of the garage. *Don't imagine the worst,* he cautioned himself. After all, Briley Joe had a contract with the city to work on all local government vehicles. The man who stepped out of the car was a tall, skinny guy with auburn hair who sported a neatly trimmed reddish-brown beard and mustache. Spit-and-polished, as if he'd just stepped out of a bandbox. The man's shoes, uniform, and hat were immaculate. Even in the summertime Southern heat, he was barely perspiring. He looked to be about Reed's age, maybe a few years older. Their gazes met and held. The policeman threw up a hand and motioned to Reed with his index finger. Reed sighed. He'd been summoned.

As he approached the officer and got a better look at the guy's face, Reed recognized him. Frank Nelson. They had been friendly rivals back in high school. Frank had been captain of the basketball team and his daddy had been the county sheriff. Reed had heard that Frank was now the local police chief. That meant Frank probably wasn't stopping by to welcome him home. No, he'd bet his last dime that somebody had sicced the chief of police on him. But who? And why?

Give yourself three guesses and the first two don't count. Who, other than Webb Porter, could snap his fingers and make the local law jump?

"How are you doing, Reed?" Frank asked as he stopped a couple of feet away.

Reed stuffed the dirty orange rag into the back pocket of his jeans. He noticed that tiny perspiration beads dotted Frank's forehead. So, the guy did sweat after all. "I *was* doing just fine."

Frank removed a neatly folded white handkerchief from his pants pocket, snapped it open, and wiped his moist forehead. "Have you been writing any letters lately?"

"Nope. Can't say that I have." So that was what this

little visit was all about. Miss Ella had called in the law. He had misjudged her. He'd figured she might give him a break. Of course, this wasn't the first time he'd been wrong about somebody, and it probably wouldn't be the last.

"Judge Porter has received two rather nasty letters since you were released from Donaldson. Letters a lot like the ones you wrote her when you were in prison. Odd coincidence, don't you think?"

"Yeah. A really odd coincidence. But that's all it is." *Don't lose your temper,* Reed warned himself. *Do not say or do anything that will antagonize the law. You don't want to screw up your parole.*

"So, you're saying you didn't write those letters and you haven't made any phone calls to the judge?" Frank dabbed at his neck with the handkerchief.

"When she received the first letter and came here waving it under my nose, I told Judge Porter that I didn't write it. And now I'm telling you that I didn't."

"Well, I'd sure like to believe you, Reed, but . . ."

"Do you have any evidence that I wrote the letters or that I made any phone calls?"

"Huh? Well, no, but Senator Porter—"

Reed snorted. "So, Senator Porter sent you here to put the fear of God into me, did he? You go back to the senator and tell him that I don't scare so easy."

"You'd be smart not to cross Webb Porter. You mess with his daughter and he'll cut out your heart and feed it to the buzzards."

"If I wanted to mess with his daughter, I wouldn't waste my time writing letters to her."

"Dammit, Reed, that smart mouth of yours is going to get you in trouble." Frank heaved his thin shoulders as he let out a long, low, disgusted sigh. "You stay the hell away from Ella Porter if you know what's good for you."

"I'll keep your advice in mind."

"Consider yourself warned."

Reed grinned. He had a way of intimidating other men and he knew it. Maybe it was his size. At six-three and two-thirty, he wasn't the biggest guy around, so maybe his give-a-shit attitude had more to do with it than his size. He'd stared down tougher sons of bitches than Frank Nelson every day he'd been in the pen.

Frank broke eye contact first, snapped around, and marched off, back to the police car. Just as Frank drove off, Briley Joe came outside and walked over to Reed.

"What'd he want here?"

"He wanted to give me some advice?"

"About what?"

"About how much trouble I'll be in if I don't stop messing with Ella Porter."

Briley Joe's eyes widened. He snickered as he elbowed Reed in the ribs. "I didn't know you'd been messing with her."

"I haven't," Reed said. "Not yet."

Chapter 8

Dan Gilmore walked Ella to her front door. She supposed she could at least ask him to come in for a few
minutes. After the concert in the park, he had hinted
that he'd like for her to go home with him. No, he had
actually done more than hint. He'd all but asked her
to spend the night with him.

"Don't you think it's time we move our relationship
to the next level?" he'd asked. "We've been dating on
and off for nearly a year now and—"

"And you think it's time for us to have sex."

He'd stammered a bit at that point, then told her
he cared for her and that his long-term goal for their
relationship was marriage. However, he didn't want to
rush into wedded bliss. Not after his disastrous first
marriage.

"I like our relationship the way it is," she'd said. "I'm
sorry, Dan, but I'm not quite ready for the next step."

Coward! She chided herself now that the date was over
and he'd brought her home without a word of protest.
*You should have told him that you'll never be ready to move
to the next step with him. You should have said, "I like you*

a lot, but I don't love you and I have no intention of having sex with you—not now or in the future."

Ella removed her key from her purse. Dan slipped his arm around her waist. *Go ahead and kiss him good night and get it over with,* she told herself. *He's expecting it.*

He pulled her close and covered her mouth with his. She tried her best to respond, but she did little more than simply allow him to kiss her. A part of her wished that she could feel something sexual, some spark of arousal. Marrying Dan would make her parents very happy, especially her mother. But just because she was thirty and eligible and men weren't lined up at her door, it didn't mean she was so desperate that she would commit herself to a lifelong relationship with a man she didn't love. Not even a man her mother considered an ideal catch.

Dan ended the kiss, then grasped her hand in his. "Dinner tomorrow night?"

Say no! End this thing here and now. Put both of you out of your misery. "Sure. Dinner tomorrow night will be fine."

"Pick you up at six?"

"Mm . . ." Forcing a smile, she nodded.

He returned the smile, released her hand, and stood at her side, waiting. "Would you like for me to unlock the door for you?" He glanced at the key ring she clutched in her left hand.

"Oh, no, thank you. You go on. I can let myself in."

She watched him walk down the sidewalk to his car. When he got behind the wheel of his Lexus, he waved farewell before he closed the door. With her strained smile still in place, she waved back at him. The moment his car disappeared down the street, she shoved her key ring back into her purse, went down the steps, and made her way around the side of the house. She opened the garden gate and entered the backyard.

She felt restless, oddly dissatisfied and just a bit melancholy. The night was warm, with a soft, slightly humid summer breeze. The sky was clear, revealing a three-quarter moon and an abundance of stars. A lush garden surrounded her. Wisteria clung along the fence row and trailed up the latticework arbor that served as an entryway, leading from the brick patio to the stepping-stone walkway that ended at the Victorian-style gazebo. A variety of plants flanked the path: aster, begonia, day lily, geranium, hydrangea, nasturtium, and rhododendron. Lots of pinks and lavenders in various shades and repeated geometric shapes. Symmetry. A profusion of exploding color.

Victorian lampposts, glimmering with electric lights, added a park-like atmosphere to the private garden. Her parents' home had been built in the early 1900s by her father's grandparents after the original family house burned to the ground. But it had been her grand-mother, the first Eleanor Porter, who had been the gardener in the family and had planned and executed the design of the backyard garden in the late thirties, shortly after her marriage.

Ella sighed. This was a night for romance: for lovers to stroll arm-in-arm, to sit together in the swing in the gazebo and share kisses. A night to strip off their clothes and skinny-dip in the pool; to lie beneath the stars and make love until the moon faded and a new day was born.

Ella sighed. She was such a romantic fool. There was no Prince Charming waiting to sweep her off her feet. There was no gallant, old-fashioned Southern gentle-man longing to pay court to her. The only man in her life was Dan Gilmore. A nice, ordinary guy. A guy who bored her to tears.

The air was heavy with the scent of flowers. She breathed deeply, savoring the smells. Ella stepped inside the gazebo, then reached out and gave the white wicker swing a gentle push. She watched it move back and forth for several minutes before she sat down and closed her eyes. This was her very favorite place in the whole world. Happy memories had been created here. Sitting in the swing for hours and talking with her father, the two of them discussing a variety of issues. Sometimes disagreeing, but more often than not, being in total agreement. And there were memories from her childhood, cuddled in the swing beside Aunt Cybil on springtime afternoons while her aunt read fairy tales to her. Spending time all alone in this very spot, relaxing, resting, escaping from the real world that existed outside the fenced walls of the Porter estate.

Daydreaming, fantasizing, pretending. Within the sanctuary of the gazebo, she could, for a few fleeting moments, be anyone she wanted to be, go anywhere she wanted to go, do anything she wanted to do. She could be thin and beautiful. She could be wild and free. A dream lover would come to her and share her life, giving her everything she needed from a man. Passion and excitement, love beyond all reason—an only-you, forever-after kind of love.

A noise caught her attention. Her eyelids flew open. She glanced all around the gazebo and saw nothing. Squirrels? Birds? The wind in the treetops? She listened, but heard only the nighttime stillness. The faint, melodious drone of summer insects; the humid breeze whispering through the greenery; the trickle of water in the fountain.

Ella undid the top three pearl buttons on her dress and spread the garment apart so that the breeze could reach her warm skin. She closed her eyes and caressed her neck with her fingertips. Her flesh was hot and damp to the touch. She allowed her fingers to journey downward to the V between her breasts, then she dipped her index finger into the crevice. And all the while, she thought of a man's hands on her body, of a man's fingers exploring. Big hands, strong hands. Muscular arms. Holding her, claiming her.

She heard the noise again. Footsteps? Was it possible

that her father had returned from Birmingham early? No, he would have telephoned if his plans for a weekend golf trip with his campaign manager had changed. Perhaps Viola had come outside for a breath of fresh air. No, it was unlikely that Viola would have left Carolyn alone at this time of night. And the housekeeper didn't live in. So, whoever or whatever was out there was an intruder.

Ella's heartbeat accelerated. A rush of adrenalin pumped through her body. There really wasn't anything to fear. The crime rate in Spring Creek was reassuringly low. And the sound she heard might be coming from a dog or a cat that had made its way through one of the openings in the ten-foot-high shrubbery that lined the far side of the garden. Scanning the area a second time, Ella hoped to see an animal padding about on four feet. Her gaze stopped at the red maple tree a good fifteen feet away from the gazebo. A dark form stood near the tree. A human form. Ella stifled a scream, locking it in her throat. The figure moved. Tall, wide-shouldered, long-legged. A man. A large man.

Ella ordered her legs to move. *Stand. Run.* The order was ignored. She sat frozen to the spot, her gaze riveted to the menacing hulk coming slowly but steadily her way. Finally her body cooperated and she rose to her feet. Moisture coated the palms of her hands. A shiver of apprehension rippled down her spine.

He emerged from the dark corner into the light cast by a lamppost several feet away. Instinctively Ella lifted her hand to her mouth as she gasped aloud. Recognition came, then a wave of relief, quickly followed by a new and even greater surge of fear.

Reed Conway!

He halted halfway between the maple tree and the gazebo, his stance proud and utterly masculine. She couldn't see his eyes there in the shadows, but she sensed his heated glare. An aura of pure masculine power and danger emanated from him and quickly trapped Ella with its virile potency.

Run. Scream. Issue him a warning. Her mind rattled off a series of choices. *For pity's sake, do something!*

But all she seemed capable of doing was waiting, frozen like a statue in the center of the gazebo. Reed walked with a sauntering strut, easy and sure. Confident. As if he were a man who feared nothing. She should ask him what he was doing here on private property. She should order him to leave immediately.

She did neither.

He continued his leisurely march toward her, becoming larger and more threatening with each step he took. Then suddenly he stopped just short of the gazebo entrance and looked directly at her. Their gazes locked instantly. Every muscle in her body tensed. Every nerve rioted. A hundred crazed butterflies fluttered wildly in her belly. She and Reed stared at each other for what seemed like an eternity. Even in the dimly lit garden she could make out the crystal coolness of his incredibly blue eyes.

She couldn't bear one more minute of the sizzling awareness that radiated between them, so she ended the all-consuming deadlocked gaze that connected them. The moment she glanced away, he entered the gazebo. Instinctively she moved away from him until the backs of her legs encountered the swing.

Although the night was warm, damp with Southern moisture, she felt the heat of his big body—a heat that intensified as he drew closer. She sucked in a deep, aroused breath. He loomed over her, a good five or six inches taller than her five-foot-nine height. And even though she was not a small woman, the breadth of his shoulders and chest dwarfed her. Everything feminine within her reacted to his raw masculinity. Her mind tried to caution her, tired to override her body's undeniable attraction to this primitive male. But in all her thirty years, Ella had never experienced such fierce longing.

It was irrational, ridiculous and unsuitable. Reed Conway was the last man on earth who should ignite such extreme emotions within her.

"All alone tonight, Miss Ella?" he asked, his voice smoky-dark and deep.

A discernible shudder quivered through her from head to toe. The corners of Reed's wide mouth lifted slightly. Damn the man, he knew that he both frightened and intrigued her, and that knowledge gave him a power over her that she did not want him to possess. When she took a long, steadying breath, his gaze left her face to watch the undulation of her chest as her breasts rose and fell. A hot flush of embarrassment crept up her neck and onto her face. She thanked the Lord that it was nighttime and the lighting in the garden was soft and dim.

"What are you doing here?" she asked. "You're trespassing on private property and that's against the law."

His grin widened. He took the final step that brought their bodies into alignment, only a hairbreadth separating them.

"I came to see you."

Lord, help me! She shut her eyes for just a moment, long enough to block out that hungry look in his eyes. *You imagined that look,* she told herself. *Reed didn't come here to seduce you. And even if he did, you're too smart to let that happen. This man is a convicted murderer. He's dangerous. Like a wild animal that's been let out of a cage. Tell him to go away. Tell him to leave you alone.*

"I don't want you here, Mr. Conway." Her voice sounded shaky, even to her own ears. "Leave now and I won't—"

"Tell your daddy." Reed chuckled, a oddly mirthless sound. "There's something you should know, Miss Ella—I'm not afraid of your daddy."

"Then you're a fool. If my father knew you were here, alone with me, harassing me this way, he'd—"

Reed grabbed her by the shoulders. She cried out,

uncertain what he would do next. His fingers dug into her soft flesh beneath the thin barrier of cotton. She winced with a twinge of pain, and the moment she did, he loosened his hold. Her eyes lifted to meet his stare, and for one endless moment, she thought her heart stopped beating.

"I hear you got another letter," he said. "And some phone calls, too."

"Yes." She could barely get the word past the lump in her throat. Her heart had lodged there.

"And you went straight to your daddy, didn't you?"

Reed slid one hand across her shoulder, then quickly grabbed her by the nape of her neck. She swallowed hard.

"Yes. I'd told you that if you sent me another letter, you would leave me no choice but to tell my father."

He drew her closer, forcing her to face him, their noses almost touching. "And I told you that I didn't write any letters to you. But you didn't believe me, did you?"

"I wanted to believe you."

"You told Webb and he sicced Frank Nelson on me."

"Let me go." Fear began to override the desire she felt. "Release me now or I'll scream."

"Do you think I came here to hurt you?"

He pivoted his head just enough to align his cheek to hers, then rubbed his stubble-rough skin against her smooth flesh. Ella went weak in the knees. He nuzzled her neck with his nose, then brought his lips up to her ear. When she quivered, she knew he could feel the trembling. Would he recognize it as a sign of fear or arousal? For the life of her, she wasn't sure which it was.

"You're afraid of me, aren't you?" he whispered. "You should be afraid. I'm dangerous to you, Miss Ella. I could ruin your life."

The feminine core of her body reacted in a purely physical way to the nearness of an overpowering male, a male whose body was pressing against hers. Clenching and unclenching, her intimate folds flooded with sexual moisture. A tingling sensation radiated upward and outward.

"If you hurt me, my father—"

He pressed his index finger over her mouth. She gasped. He explored her upper lip, then circled to pay equal homage to her lower lip. His touch was gentle and seductive. With sudden, amazing clarity, Ella realized that Reed Conway wasn't going to attack her, that he had no intention of physically harming her. He was playing a game with her. A frightening sexual game.

"If you didn't write the letters or make the phone calls, then you have nothing to worry about," she said breathlessly. "You can't get in trouble for something you didn't do."

He lifted his head and looked her squarely in the eye. "Are you really that naive? Lady, I just spent fifteen years in Donaldson for a murder I didn't commit. So don't tell me that I can't get in trouble for something I didn't do."

"I'm sorry." The moment the words came out of her mouth, she wished them back. Now he'd think she believed him, believed that he was innocent. But she didn't believe it. Or did she?

He released his hold on the nape of her neck. His hand at her shoulder eased downward, along her arm to her hand. He entwined his fingers with hers and placed his thumb against her palm. She barely silenced the gasp that sprang to her lips when his thumb repeatedly circled the center of her palm in a maddeningly slow and titillating motion.

"I'm sorry, too," he said. Then he moved away from her, took a long, hard look, and walked away, back into the night from which he'd come.

Ella stood alone in the gazebo for quite some time. Confused and unnerved. And aroused to the point of aching. She had to avoid any future confrontations with

Reed Conway. No matter what, she had to make sure he didn't come near her again.

Carolyn sat by the window and watched Reed Conway walk away from Ella. If he hadn't left when he did, she would have been forced to call the police. What was he doing here? What had he said to her daughter? And why hadn't Ella run from him? Surely she hadn't invited him here. To anyone seeing the two of them together, they appeared to be lovers meeting for a late-night tryst. But Carolyn knew better. Reed Conway was scum. Ella would never lower herself to become involved with a man like that.

Some women were fascinated by that type, by the bad boys of the world. God knew the chest-beating, white trash type appealed to her sister. But Ella was a better person than Cybil. Carolyn had raised her daughter to be a lady. Surely Ella would never shame the family the way Cybil had. But better to be safe than sorry.

Should she mention to Ella that she'd seen her with Reed? Should she call Webb and inform him? Of course, if she phoned Webb at his Birmingham hotel, God only knew who might answer. Some woman he'd picked up at the country club or some girl he had met in the hotel bar? If she knew her husband—and she did—he wasn't spending the night alone. The first time she'd found out that Webb had been unfaithful, it had broken her heart, but over the years her heart had hardened. Webb couldn't hurt her anymore.

Carolyn decided to wait and see if Ella would mention Reed Conway's late-night visit. If her daughter had nothing to hide, then surely she would tell her. As for informing Webb, there would be time enough for that later, if necessary.

"Are you ready for bed now, Miss Carolyn?" Viola asked.

Carolyn glanced up at her devoted companion and smiled. "Yes, I'm quite tired."

Viola looked out the window and then at Carolyn. "I see your daughter is back from her date."

"Yes, she's been back for a while."

"Do you think she'll marry Mr. Gilmore?"

"If I have anything to say about it, she will. Dan's a good catch. He'd make a suitable husband. I don't understand why Ella isn't more grateful to have him interested in her. It's not as if my daughter could have any man she wanted. Dan appreciates all her good qualities. He married a beautiful young girl for love the first time. My guess is that this time he wants compatibility and companionship with a sensible, intelligent woman."

"You'd think with her receiving those awful letters and getting those phone calls, she'd be turning to Mr. Gilmore for comfort and understanding."

"She has her father to protect her and comfort her," Carolyn said. "No other man could live up to Webb in Ella's estimation."

Viola clasped Carolyn's wheelchair, turned it around, and pushed it toward the bed. As Viola reached out to assist her patient, Carolyn grabbed her hand. "Don't forget that as far as Webb and Ella are concerned, I don't know about the letters and phone calls. They haven't told me because they want to spare me the worry. Aren't I fortunate to have a husband and a child who care so much about my peace of mind?"

Chapter 9

Ella slipped off her sunglasses and dropped them in the side pouch of her shoulder bag. She opened the car door, lifted her coffee mug from the holder, and stepped out into the courthouse's parking area. She had an assigned space right outside the north entrance to the old building that had housed the seat of Bryant County government for over a century. She remembered that during her childhood her family had petitioned to restore the structure, which had been erected in the late 1890s instead of tearing it down and replacing it with something more modern. Wholeheartedly, Ella agreed with the vast majority of local citizens—the courthouse on the town square was what kept Spring Creek alive when so many small towns had died slow, painful deaths as big malls stole customers from downtown businesses.

After walking up the side steps, she entered the long hallway that led to the elevator. Usually she took the stairs, but this morning, she was running late and she'd awakened with a splitting headache. The headache had slowed her down—that and the fact that she hadn't slept well in several nights. Not since her confrontation with Reed Conway in her garden. She had tried to put the man and their unnerving meeting out of her mind, but the harder she tried not to think about Reed, the more she thought about him.

Ella punched the elevator's "Up" button. When the doors swung open, she entered and was grateful that she had a few moments of privacy before facing the day. Jury selection in an attempted-murder trial would begin this morning. The case had been postponed once because the defendant had tried to commit suicide. All the components for a media-sensation trial were there: a wife accused of hiring a hit man to murder her husband; the wife a socially prominent woman; and the husband a renowned physician. The case had been moved to her court from another county.

The elevator opened and Ella emerged. When she glanced down the corridor and saw her office door open, she made a beeline in that direction. Her heart beat a fraction faster as her mind cautioned her not to jump to conclusions. There were all sorts of reasons why her locked door might be wide open. It was possible that Kelly had arrived early this morning—possible, but not probable.

The moment she reached the doorway and saw Roy Moses standing in the middle of her office, she sighed with relief. But that relief was short-lived, dying the moment she noticed the white envelope clutched in his hand.

"Good morning, Miss Ella." Roy smiled warmly.

"Is there a problem in here?" she asked. "Did maintenance send you up here?"

"No, ma'am. But Kelly told me yesterday to bring up a box of computer paper and a new cartridge for your printer first thing this morning." Roy's gaze settled on the items he had placed on her desk.

"Thank you." Ella eyed the envelope Roy held.

"What have you got there in your hand?" she asked

as she rounded the side of her desk and placed her thermal mug on top of her felt blotter.

Roy held out the letter. "Oh, yeah, I was about to forget. When I came in I found this on the floor. Just like last time. It's got your name on it."

Ella hesitated. She was afraid this innocent-looking four-by-nine-inch envelope concealed another vulgar, threatening love letter. If it did, she would have no choice but to take some action in the matter. And the last thing she wanted was to find a reason to involve Reed Conway in her life. A part of her longed to believe that he hadn't written the other two letters, that he'd been telling her the truth when he had said he hadn't made those breathy phone calls.

"Don't you want it?" Roy asked, waving the missive in front of her. "It's yours. It's got your name on it." He held it down and pointed to the typed letters. "See?" He pointed to the two words. "Ella Porter."

Ella grabbed the envelope from him, and when she noted the surprised look in his kind eyes, she forced a smile. "Sorry, Roy, I didn't mean to be so grabby. It's just that I'm running late this morning. I have a headache, I haven't had my coffee, and—"

"You want me to go get you some aspirin?"

"Oh, no, thank you. I appreciate the offer, but I have some in my purse."

"If you need anything, Miss Ella, just call downstairs and ask for me. You know I'd do anything for you."

Ella dropped the envelope beside her coffee mug, then reached out and patted Roy on the shoulder. "I know. Thank you. Now you'd better get back downstairs or Mr. Hibbett will be looking for you."

Roy headed for the door, then paused before leaving. "Sure hope your headache gets better."

The minute Roy left, Ella slumped down in her swivel chair, lifted her mug to her lips, and sipped on the black coffee. She suspected that if the letter contained what she thought it did, her headache would only get worse.

Using her letter opener, she ripped across the top of the envelope, then pulled out the single page of stationery. After unfolding the paper, she scanned the message.

> *There is no escape from me. I am a part of you, as you are a part of me. You may tell yourself that you do not want what I can give you, but you're lying to yourself. You want—*

Ella gasped at the explicit wording. This had to stop! She couldn't go on reading these filthy messages and allowing her imagination to run wild. Despite how revolting she found the communique, she couldn't stop herself from thinking of Reed, of him doing the things to her that were printed in the letters. She despised herself for becoming sexually aroused, for allowing Reed to become her fantasy lover.

Ella returned the letter to the envelope and stuffed it in her purse; then she flipped through her Roladex file until she found Mark Leamon's number. She dialed and waited. Regina Conway answered the phone. Ella hesitated.

"Yes, Regina, this is Judge Porter. I'd like to speak to Mark, please."

"Just one moment, Judge Porter."

Ella took another sip of coffee while she waited for Mark to pick up on the other end.

"Ella?" Mark asked.

"Yes."

"What a pleasant surprise. We haven't talked in ages. Is there something I can do for you?"

"Yes, you can have lunch with me today."

"I'd love to, but is there some reason for the invitation?"

"I want to talk to you about Reed Conway." Ella

waited for a response, and when Mark remained silent, she went on. "I'm sure Reed has mentioned to you that since his release from prison, I've received a couple of rather harassing love letters as well as some breathy phone calls. I received a third letter this morning."

"Reed did tell me. And he assured me that he knows nothing about either the phone calls or the letters. I believe him, Ella. If you knew Reed the way I do, you'd believe him, too."

"Meet me for lunch today at Callahan's. Twelve noon. And convince me that Reed is innocent."

Regina stood in the open doorway and stared at Mark Leamon as he hung up the telephone. She'd heard Mark's end of the conversation. Ella Porter had called about Reed. Had she received another one of those letters or another odd phone call? Was Judge Porter going to bring charges against Reed and try to have him sent back to prison? If Reed violated his parole, their mother would be heartbroken. Regina wanted to believe in her brother's innocence as deeply and profoundly as their mother did, and she hated the fact that there was even a shred of doubt in her mind.

She had come to terms with Junior Blalock's murder and truly believed that, despite his rage that horrible night, Reed hadn't slit Junior's throat. But if Reed didn't kill Junior, then who did? Sometimes Regina wondered if perhaps she had done it herself and blocked out the memory. She'd wanted Junior dead. She had hated him enough to kill him.

Don't think about that night! Dear God, she didn't want to remember. Regina turned on unsteady legs and made her way back to her desk as memories of that night washed over her: Junior's drunken breath as he kissed her, as he rammed his tongue into her mouth; the feel of his rough, dirty hands pinching and prodding; the vile, filthy things he'd said to her and tried to do to her. She'd been lying beneath him, her clothes tattered, her body bruised, his penis seeking entrance, when Reed ripped Junior away from her and beat him within an inch of his life.

Reed had saved her. Afterward she hadn't cared whether or not her brother had killed Junior. She'd been so glad their stepfather was dead. Guilty or innocent, Reed had paid for that crime with fifteen years of his life. But she and her mother hadn't gotten off scot-free. The whole town had learned about what happened that night. All the sordid details of their private lives had come out during the trial. To this day she often felt people's pity as they glanced at her and whispered in hushed tones. She hated being known as the girl whose stepfather had tried to rape her—the girl whose brother had killed that stepfather. Only after years of therapy, paid for by her mother's employer, Cybil Carlisle, had Regina been able to live a somewhat normal life. She'd gone to college on a scholarship and gotten a job as Mark's secretary while she worked toward her degree as a paralegal. And in all these years since Junior's murder, she hadn't been with a man, hadn't even dated.

But she wanted to date, wanted to love and be loved, wanted to marry and have children. She had thought those things could never be hers, but that was before she realized, quite recently, that she was very much in love with her boss. Mark Leamon was a good man. Kind, considerate, and highly respected by friends and foes alike. But no matter how much she loved him, Mark was out of her league. She was the daughter of a housekeeper. Mark was the son of a lawyer, the grandson of a lawyer, and cousin to a U.S. senator. And he saw her only as his assistant, as a friend.

"Regina?"

She jumped and gasped simultaneously when Mark spoke to her. He stood in front of her desk, a concerned look on his face.

"Sorry, I didn't mean to startle you."

"I'm all right," she assured him. "My mind was a million miles away. Did you need something?"

"Since Cara is still home sick, I've been depending on you far too much for secretarial duties, haven't I?"

Mark smiled at her and her stomach flip-flopped. She loved the way he smiled, the way he laughed, the way he talked. If she were totally honest, she supposed she'd have to admit that she loved everything about Mark. "You know I don't mind."

"You're a trooper. I don't know what I'd do without you." Mark glanced at his wristwatch. "I'm due in court in fifteen minutes; otherwise, I'd take care of this myself, but—"

"Just name it and I'll be glad to take care of it for you."

"Give Heather a call and tell her that I need to change our lunch date from today until tomorrow."

"Certainly."

"I'm meeting Ella for lunch," Mark said.

"I overheard your part of the conversation," Regina admitted. "She wants to talk to you about Reed, doesn't she?"

"She's received another letter."

"You don't believe that Reed is sending those letters to her, do you?"

"No, I don't think he is." Mark shrugged. "But it looks bad for him, even without any concrete evidence against him. What I'm hoping is that I can convince Ella somebody is trying to frame Reed, the same way they did fifteen years ago."

"The real murderer?"

"That would be my guess. Somebody doesn't want Reed walking around a free man. Somebody is afraid he'll unearth the truth and reveal the identity of the person who killed Junior."

"Then Reed is in danger, isn't he?"

"Yes, he is. And so is Ella, if someone is harassing her to get Reed in trouble."

"If anyone can convince Judge Porter that Reed is innocent, you can. You're the best lawyer in the whole state."

Mark grinned. "You wouldn't be prejudiced, now, would you? After all, I am your boss."

"Boss or no boss, my opinion would be the same."

He checked his watch again. "I have to leave now if I'm going to make it on time." With briefcase in hand, Mark headed toward the door, then stopped and glanced over his shoulder. "Call the florist and order some flowers for Heather, with a note of apology."

Regina nodded and faked a smile. Mark returned her smile, then left hurriedly. Heather Marshall! The redheaded divorcée had stirred up all the bachelors in Spring Creek since her return, but Regina had never imagined that Heather was Mark's type. He was studious and serious-minded and rather dull by most women's standards, whereas Heather was flighty and frivolous and just a bit wild. Maybe opposites did attract. This was their third lunch date in two weeks.

Regina sighed. Why couldn't Mark look at her and see a desirable woman? She knew she was pretty. And people said she was a sweet, likable girl. Did Mark look at her and see, as everyone else in town did, that poor, pathetic little creature who'd been attacked by Junior Blalock? Did he think of her only as the daughter of the Carlisles' housekeeper and the sister of a convicted murderer?

"I'm so pleased that you felt up to having lunch out here on the patio." Jeff Henry gazed at Carolyn, uncaring that she or Viola could see the love in his eyes. His feelings for his wife's sister were no secret to anyone, least of all to Carolyn herself. Thirty-four years ago he had begged her to marry him, only a few weeks before

Webb had proposed. Then later on, he had pleaded with her not to marry Webb. But she had loved that handsome rogue and had stayed with him all these years, despite his numerous infidelities.

"It is such a lovely day, isn't it?" Carolyn sighed contentedly as she glanced around the garden area. "You know how I look forward to your lunching with me every Monday and every Thursday. Webb is seldom home and Ella is always so busy now that she's a judge." Carolyn held out her hand across the table. "Whatever would I do without you, brother?"

He reached out and clasped her hand in his. Small, slender, and soft. A lady's hand. He caressed her, his thumb running across the tips of her neatly manicured nails. Webb's large diamond and matching wedding band on the third finger of her left hand glistened in the afternoon sunlight.

"You'll never be without me, my darling. I look forward to our lunches as much, if not more, than you do."

Sitting several feet away at the edge of the patio, her needlepoint in her lap, Viola cleared her throat. "If you don't think you'll need me for a while, I'll go to the kitchen and join Bessie for a bite of lunch."

With a dismissive wave, Carolyn said, "By all means, go have lunch. I'll be just fine here with my dear friend."

Her dear friend. That's all he'd ever been. All he would ever be. But it was enough. To simply sit here with her. To hear her voice, her laugh. To feel her hand in his. To look at her, so lovely, almost untouched by time. As beautiful now as she'd been at twenty.

"Take me out to the gazebo and read to me." Carolyn glanced at the hardback book lying on the table beside Jeff Henry's place mat. "There's such a nice breeze today. Much cooler than yesterday. But I'm afraid it's going to rain later."

"I brought along my copy of *Wuthering Heights.* I know it's one of your favorites." He scooted back his chair

and rose, then lifted the book and rounded the table.
"I'll read to you until either you grow weary or the rain
sets in. We don't want you getting wet and catching
cold."

He placed the book in her lap, then withdrew her
wheelchair from the table and pushed her from the
patio to the walkway. When they reached the gazebo,
he lifted her into his arms, carried her inside, and placed
her on the wicker chaise longue. She leaned her head
back on the cushion and closed her eyes, then held out
the book to him. He took the book, sat in the swing,
and opened to page one.

"Is Webb due to return home today?" he asked.

Carolyn's eyelids lifted. She sighed. "He telephoned
yesterday to say he was staying on in Birmingham until
tomorrow. I do wish he'd come on home."

"You miss him when he's away, don't you?" Why
was he torturing himself talking to Carolyn about her
husband? He supposed it was because Webb Porter was
a reality—one that he could not ignore. And if being
with Webb was what made Carolyn happy, then he
wanted Webb to be here with her.

"Yes, of course I miss him, but I think he should be
here keeping watch over Ella."

"You're concerned about Reed Conway being
released from prison, aren't you? Surely the man
wouldn't be foolish enough to . . ." He knew Carolyn
too well not to recognize that look of concern on her
face. Something had happened that she hadn't shared
with him. He laid the book down on the swing, leaned
forward, and captured her gaze with his. "Tell me what
has you so worried."

"I don't want Webb or Ella to know that I know."

"Know what?" Jeff Henry realized that Carolyn must
have somehow learned about those damn letters and
phone calls that Ella had received. But who would have
told her? Who else but Viola? The woman was fiercely
loyal to Carolyn and was the only person who would

have dared to go against Webb's wishes to keep the worrisome news from her.

"I know about the letters and the phone calls," Carolyn admitted. "Reed Conway is harassing Ella and there doesn't seem to be a thing anyone can do about it. They have no proof. But I'm concerned that the man will do something to actually harm Ella. I—I . . ." Carolyn gasped. A lone tear trickled from the corner of her right eye. She brushed it away with her fingertips.

Jeff Henry sprang out of the swing, dropped to his knees beside the chaise, and cradled Carolyn's face with his hands. "My darling, what is it? Has something else happened?"

"I saw him. Reed Conway was here in this gazebo on Friday night, with Ella."

"No! That man has gone too far, actually setting foot on private property. Ella called the police didn't she?" Jeff Henry took his hands from Carolyn's face and smoothed them down her shoulders in a comforting gesture before he released her.

"She didn't call the police and she hasn't mentioned the incident to anyone," Carolyn said. "I don't know what was going on, but to someone who didn't know them, didn't know the circumstances, it would have appeared that they were two lovers having a clandestine meeting."

"My word, you don't mean it." Jeff Henry shook his head. He refused to believe that their sweet Ella would have anything to do with that rascal Conway. "Ella wouldn't give a man like that the time of day."

"I'm sure you're right. I think Reed frightens her, but it's possible that she's more concerned with what Webb might do to the man than what Reed might do to her. And I tend to feel the same way. But Jeff Henry"— Carolyn grabbed his hand and brought it to her chest, clinging nervously—"I'm so afraid of what Reed Conway might do in order to get revenge against Webb.

The man belongs in prison. He's dangerous to everyone I love.''

"Now, now, dear heart.'' Jeff Henry patted her shoulder affectionately. "You mustn't upset yourself this way. When Webb returns, I'll speak to him. We'll find a way to control Reed, even if it means having his parole revoked and returning him to prison.''

Carolyn sighed deeply and gazed at Jeff Henry with such genuine gratitude that it was all he could do to stop himself from kissing her. He longed to press his lips to hers, to take her in his arms and profess his undying love.

"I knew I could count on you to help me.'' As she squeezed his hand, she leaned forward and pressed a featherlight kiss on his cheek.

Chapter 10

Callahan's buzzed with the drone of the lunchtime crowd that descended on the restaurant between eleven and two every weekday. Located in the heart of downtown Spring Creek, the restored building, once a drugstore from the early thirties through the mid-eighties, was ideally located to accommodate all the local businesses as well as the courthouse employees and the horde of lawyers whose offices spread out over the small town. Their only competition were two drive-through fast food places and a small sandwich shop. If one conducted a business lunch in town, Callahan's was the only real choice.

When Ella arrived, the hostess led her to a semiprivate back booth, where Mark Leamon waited. She slid onto the seat, adjusted her skirt and dropped her bag down beside her.

"I ordered their raspberry tea for both of us," Mark said, nodding toward the tall frosted glasses of flavored tea sitting on decorative paper coasters.

"Thanks." Ella lifted her glass and took a sip. "Delicious."

Before she had a chance to begin a conversation, their waiter appeared. "Are you folks ready to order?"

Ella glanced first at her unopened menu and then across the table at Mark, who asked, "Do you need a minute?"

"No." She shook her head. "I'd like the spicy chicken salad."

The waiter jotted down her order. "And you, sir?"

"The sirloin sandwich," Mark said. "With fries and onion rings."

The moment the waiter left them, Ella surveyed Mark's stocky physique. "Not worried about your weight, are you? Men are so lucky. If a woman is ten pounds over the norm, she worries herself sick about not being attractive."

"If you're referring to yourself, cousin, I don't think you need worry about your figure."

"Hm . . . mm. Well, I suppose we could spend our entire lunch indulging in idle chitchat, but that wouldn't solve our immediate problem, would it?"

Mark groaned. "I fully believe in Reed Conway's innocence. I think he was wrongfully convicted of his stepfather's murder, and I know he isn't the person harassing you."

"You sound awfully confident." Ella reached down, snapped open her purse, and removed a white envelope. "Take a look at this. It's just like the other two I received last week, which my father took to Frank Nelson. And all three letters are very similar to the ones Reed Conway wrote to me when he was first sent to prison."

Ella handed Mark the envelope. He opened it, took out the letter, and read it quickly, then refolded it and placed it back in the envelope. "Steamy stuff. And admittedly rather unnerving."

"Yes, steamy and unnerving, to say the least."

"Ella, if I hadn't gotten to know Reed so well since I became his lawyer when Father died, I might think him capable of being the author of that trash. But the man I know, the Reed Conway who has struggled to be a model prisoner for the past ten years, would never resort to harassing you or anyone else."

"You sound very confident." Ella picked up the letter from where Mark had laid it on the table and put it back in her purse. "My father believes Reed is simply making good on his threats, that he's trying to torment me because he knows that's the surest way to hurt my father."

"Reed doesn't want to hurt anyone," Mark assured her. "He wants to find out who really killed Junior Blalock. He wants to clear his name. But first and foremost he wants to stay out of prison. He knows that if he breaks the law, his parole will be revoked. He's not stupid enough to risk losing his freedom simply to annoy Webb."

"I want to believe you, but . . . Reed frightens me. I've seen him twice since he's been home and both times I . . . well, I walked away from each encounter feeling as if I'd been threatened."

The waiter interrupted long enough to place a container of freshly baked yeast rolls on the table. In the interim, Mark drank half a glass of tea and while glancing around the restaurant, Ella caught a glimpse of her aunt Cybil at the bar. Her initial reaction was to check on her aunt, try to persuade her not to drink, and then, if necessary, call Uncle Jeff Henry. But Cybil was with friends—a couple of ladies from the local historical society—so that meant she might have a mixed drink before lunch, but she wouldn't get soused. Aunt Cybil had an uncanny ability to save her binges for times when she was either alone or with family. Ella groaned silently.

"Reed can be very intimidating," Mark said. "You must remember that he has survived fifteen years in prison. He's tough and hard. Very hard. And unemotional. But he's no run-of-the-mill ex-con."

Mark regained her attention with his comments, so her mind reversed gears and put concerns about her aunt temporarily on the back burner. "Telling me how intimidating and tough Reed is doesn't ease my fears. If anything, the exact opposite is true."

"Are you aware of the fact that he gained a college degree while serving time in Donaldson? He had already started working toward his master's degree when he was released. He is a man who has prepared for a future on the outside. Why would he risk everything he's worked so hard to achieve just to annoy Webb? I'm telling you, the man isn't looking for vengeance."

"I had no idea he'd acquired a degree," Ella said, completely surprised by this unexpected information. She'd never thought of Reed as the academic type, only the physical type. But except for what others had told her about the man, she really didn't know Reed. "If that's true, then why is he working in his cousin's garage as a mechanic?"

Mark snorted. "Because he isn't the type to let his mother and sister support him. He was determined to have a job of some kind when he was released from prison, and not one person in this prejudiced town would hire him."

"Then why didn't he go somewhere else—Birmingham or Huntsville, where no one knows him?"

"His family is here and so is his past. Reed's not likely to find Junior's killer in Huntsville or Birmingham."

"Okay, let's say I believe you, that I believe Reed didn't write the letters to me or make the phone calls." She had to admit to herself that Mark was quite convincing. But then again, she'd come to this lunch meeting wanting to be convinced. For some inexplicable reason—perhaps a reason too fundamental for her to accept—she needed to believe that Reed Conway was innocent of murder and innocent of harassment. "If Reed is innocent, then who could be harassing me and why?"

The waiter brought their orders, placing Ella's in front of her and then setting down Mark's. "Is there anything else y'all need?"

Ella shook her head. Mark said, "No, thank you. We're fine." Ella lifted her fork from where it rested on her white linen napkin.

"There are several possibilities," Mark told her as he uncapped the ketchup bottle. "First, perhaps someone who's gone through your court in the past year has decided to harass you." Mark tapped the bottle and ketchup poured onto his plate between the fries and the onion rings. "Second, you could have a lovesick suitor with a very dirty mind." Mark dipped a long, thick fry into the ketchup. "Or third, someone is trying to frame Reed, trying to implicate him in the harassment."

Ella used her fork to mix the honey-mustard dressing thoroughly through her salad. "And why would anyone want to do such a thing?"

Mark ate his french fry and then dipped another. "Someone who wants Reed back in prison. Someone who can't afford for the real truth about Junior Blalock's murder to come out."

"The killer," Ella heard herself say; then suddenly she realized she had all but confessed to Mark that she, too, believed that Reed was innocent. "I mean, if Reed isn't the real killer."

"Something tells me that you know he's not, that your gut instincts tell you that although he may intimidate you, might even frighten you a little, he isn't a murderer."

"If I get any more letters or any more phone calls, my family won't rest until—"

"Then don't tell Webb about this third letter. Don't play this game with Junior's real killer. If you don't cooperate with what he or she is trying to accomplish, then it'll stop."

"How can you be so sure?"

"My bet is this person's goal is to get Reed in trouble—enough trouble to have his parole revoked—so if this scheme of harassing you doesn't work, there'll be no need to keep it up.''

"Let's say your scenario is correct, then what's to stop this person from escalating the harassment? Maybe he or she has more in mind than just letters and phone calls.''

"Ella, I don't think you're in any danger,'' Mark said. "After all, whoever's doing this has no reason to harm you. Reed is the target, not you.''

"Do you think Reed's life is in danger?'' *And just why should you care?* she asked herself. *Reed Conway is nothing to you. Nothing except an annoyance. A seductive nightmare that won't go away.*

"I believe that somewhere out there in our safe little town is a killer who got away with murder fifteen years ago and has no intention of letting Reed unearth the truth about who really murdered Junior and why. Yes, Reed's in danger. And you might well be the one person who can help him.''

At six-thirty Ella parked her Jag in front of The Cozy Corner, a bookstore that also sold speciality gifts and greeting cards and boasted the only gourmet coffee bar in town. She went inside the shop to find a new paperback to read tonight. She desperately needed something—anything—to take her mind off Reed Conway. She had to stop wondering about his guilt or innocence. She couldn't continue allowing herself to worry that her father might have helped convict an innocent man.

"Ella!''

The moment she heard someone calling her name, she scanned the area from which the voice had come. The coffee bar. There sat Heather, and at her side was a rather attractive man. Although Ella thought he looked familiar, she didn't immediately recognize him. Heather merely waved but didn't invite Ella to join her. Just as well. She didn't want to intrude when Heather was making a new conquest. And since her recent divorce, those new conquests seemed to be a weekly if not daily event.

When she passed the greeting cards section on her way to the paperback fiction aisle, Ella noticed her aunt Cybil. She hadn't gotten a chance to say hello at Callahan's earlier today because by the time she had finished her lunch with Mark, her aunt had already left. Ella altered her path just enough to stop and speak.

"Hello, Aunt Cybil. How are you this evening?"

"Ella, how nice to see you. I wish you'd make time for us to get together some time soon. I miss our tennis games." Cybil's smile was weak and rather melancholy.

She adored her aunt, despite Cybil's gradual descent into alcoholism. Because her mother had been confined to a wheelchair all Ella's life, her aunt had been the one who'd taken her shopping for clothes and school supplies, the one who had taught her to play tennis and to swim. In many ways, Cybil had been as much of a mother to her as Carolyn had been.

"Why don't we go to the movies together next weekend?" Ella suggested. "We'll find ourselves a lighthearted romantic comedy to see. Then we'll go somewhere and pig out on hot fudge sundaes."

"Oh, darling girl, don't you know that all romances are comedies. In real life and in the movies. We're all a bunch of silly fools when it comes to love." When Cybil took an unsteady step toward her, Ella realized that her aunt was tipsy. Strange how sober Cybil could talk when she couldn't walk a straight line.

"You didn't drive yourself here, did you?" If so, Ella had every intention of taking Cybil's keys away from her and escorting her home.

"Lord, no. Jeff Henry brought me. He's parked up the street. He's such a meany. He wouldn't let me come down here by myself to pick up a birthday card for Sue Ellen Ricks, and he knows Sue Ellen always sends me a card. Every year. Without fail."

"Did you find her a nice card?" Ella glanced at the large, pink card that Cybil clutched to her chest.

"Quite lovely. See?" She held the card out for Ella's perusal.

"Would you like for me to walk you outside to meet Uncle Jeff Henry after you pay for the card?"

"Nonsense, darling girl. I'm perfectly capable of finding my way back to Jeff Henry's Cadillac. The way y'all treat me, you'd think I'm as much of an invalid as Carolyn is. And you know that's not true. It's just that sometimes I drink a little too much."

"I don't mind walking you—"

"Are you meeting someone for coffee?" Cybil deftly changed the subject. "I noticed Heather had a good-looking young man with her. That's what you need. I would so like to see you in love. You need a man of your own. Someone to love you as much as you love him."

"I'm dating Dan Gilmore and he's a very nice man."

"Dan Gilmore. Yuck." Cybil giggled. "No . . . niece of mine . . . would be in love with that stuffed shirt."

"I didn't say I was in love with him."

"Good. I'd hate to think of you wasting your love and your life on a man who would never appreciate you." Cybil leaned over and kissed Ella's cheek. "My precious, precious little Ella."

Ella returned the kiss and took her aunt's arm. Cybil pulled free and walked away, stopping at the end of the check-out line. If only there were some way she could help her aunt. Everyone in the family had tried to help her, but to no avail. Cybil had always been a social drinker, but only in the past few years had her drinking become a problem. And those bouts of drunkenness, which used to occur about once a month, were now happening at least once a week, and occasionally more often.

She knew Cybil was unhappy with her life. Her aunt had never worked outside the home and she only dabbled in charity work. When she'd been younger, she had been a debutante. Now, Cybil belonged to all the social clubs in the area, but her membership in most of the organizations had lapsed. Her marriage to Jeff Henry seemed to be a farce, which often made Ella wonder why the two had ever married. They seemed totally unsuited. When Ella had asked her father about it, he'd said that Jeff Henry had wed the closest thing to Carolyn he could find. And he believed that, at one time, Cybil might have actually loved Jeff Henry.

Their marriage had produced no children, and Ella didn't know whether they had decided to remain childless, or one of them was incapable of having children. All her life, her aunt and uncle had doted on her, and it was obvious they both loved children. Perhaps they should have adopted, the way her own parents had when they found out that Carolyn could never have a child of her own.

Ella kept an eye on her aunt until she went through the check-out line and out the front door. No doubt Uncle Jeff Henry was watching for her. Despite all his faults and flaws, he did try his best to take care of Cybil. He was endlessly patient and caring.

Ella found the paperback fiction section quickly and began scanning the stacks. Maybe a science fiction or fantasy novel, something that would whisk her out of this world and take her a million miles away from her problems. She certainly didn't want a mystery or suspense and definitely not a romance. Nothing that would make her think about Reed.

Just as she lifted Anne McCaffrey's latest novel from the shelves, a shiver of foreboding rippled along her nerve endings—an odd sensation of awareness. Trying not to be obvious about her curiosity, she glanced around in every direction and didn't see anyone nearby. *My imagination must be working overtime.* She tried to ignore the uneasy feeling inside her.

She decided to buy the book and head for home,

but when she passed the nonfiction aisle, she caught a glimpse of someone in her peripheral vision. Stopping dead still, she turned her head slowly and took a closer look. There stood Reed Conway between the two tall shelves of nonfiction reading. He had undoubtedly come straight from the garage. He still wore stained jeans and a soiled white T-shirt. A day's growth of beard only added to the raw masculinity that oozed from every pore in his big, hard body.

Run. Run now, before he sees you. Before he catches you staring at him. You're a fool if you linger, if you speak to him.

As if sensing her presence the way she had his, Reed lifted his head and stared directly at her. "Hello, Miss Ella."

Her heart beat wildly, sounding an erratic rat-a-tat-tat that she could hear inside her head. She almost screamed at him to leave her alone, but of course, she didn't say a word. All the man had done was speak to her. But his gaze touched her, caressed her, fondled her. It was invisible, yet potent. With only the mesmerizing glare from his ice-cold blue eyes, Reed captured her and held her immobile. He replaced the book he'd been flipping through and turned to face Ella again. With her chest rising and falling as her breathing grew harsh and heavy, an anxious anticipation soaring through her, Ella watched while he moved toward her. Slowly, deliberately, he zeroed in on her as a powerful animal would slink toward its helpless prey.

When he was almost upon her, she caught her breath and held it. *Calm down. There is nothing he can do to you here, in a public place.* But she was lying to herself and she knew it. He had already done something to her. With nothing more than a look, he had violated the privacy of her mind and body.

Reed stopped when he was within a foot of her and glanced at the book she held against her chest as if it were a lifeline. "Planning on spending the evening reading?"

"Yes." She barely managed to get the word past the lump in her throat. It was fear, excitement, and sexual awareness—a hard knot of combined emotions.

"What's the matter with that guy you're seeing?" Reed asked. "If you were my woman, I'd keep you too busy to read at night."

A shiver zinged through her, from toes to fingers. An image of just what Reed and she would be doing together filled her mind—a living-color spectacle of naked arms and legs, tangled sheets, damp bodies, erotic whisperings.

"But I'm not your woman, am I?" *Don't just leave it with that kind of statement,* she warned herself. *You practically asked him if he considered you his woman.* "I don't belong to anyone. I'm my own woman."

"I'm glad you're not wearing some other man's brand."

She gasped, startled by the audacity of his bold statement. "Is that your idea of a relationship, Mr. Conway? Burning your brand into as many women as possible?"

He grinned at her then, and heaven help her, she found that she was as susceptible to that sexy smile as any other woman. Her body reacted, tingling and pulsating. Damn it all, Reed Conway was lethal.

"A man only brands the woman he wants to claim as his personal property."

Reed took that final step that brought them together, so close that she could see the silver specks in his blue eyes and the thin white scar that bisected his lower lip right in the middle.

Ella swallowed. Willing herself to remain in control, to give this annoying man absolutely no power over her, she offered him a fragile smile. "I received another letter this morning. Just like the other two."

His self-confident grin faded quickly. "Then I suppose I can expect another visit from Frank Nelson, another warning."

"I haven't mentioned the letter to anyone except Mark Leamon. He's convinced that someone else is writing the letters and making the phone calls in order to incriminate you. He thinks someone wants you back in prison before you discover the identity of Junior Blalock's real killer.''

Reed's breath fanned her face as he gazed into her eyes. Her breath caught in her throat. "And what do you think?'' he asked.

"I—I don't know. What Mark says makes sense, but—''

"But it's easier to believe that I'm guilty, isn't it?''

"No. I'd like to believe that you're innocent.'' *Idiot,* she chided herself. Why had she made such an admission to him? Now he would know what sort of effect he had on her.

"Believe it, because it's true. I didn't kill Junior Blalock.''

He touched her then. He skimmed her cheek with the back of his hand. A faint, gentle graze of rough against soft. She sucked in her breath.

"Hey, you two, want to join us for coffee?'' Heather's voice destroyed the intimacy between Ella and Reed.

Ella jumped. Reed took several backward steps, away from Ella. But for just a moment, their gazes remained linked and a silent message was exchanged—a mutual understanding of monumental importance. Something was happening between them, something neither of them understood but neither could resist. Their accidental meeting tonight would not be the end of it. There was more to come. Much more.

"I was just leaving,'' Reed said. "Nice to have seen you, Judge Porter.''

Rendered speechless by Reed's cool, casual courtesy, she nodded and didn't allow her gaze to linger on him as he walked away.

"Did I run him off?'' Heather asked. "I didn't mean to put an end to your little rendezvous.''

"You didn't put an end to anything,'' Ella lied. "We just ran into each other by accident. I think you embarrassed Reed by asking us to join y'all for coffee, as if we were a couple."

"Ella, Ella, Ella. This is me you're talking to. Your best buddy. Your confidante," Heather reminded her. "I saw the way you two were looking at each other. Girlfriend, you're playing with fire."

"Will you please lower your voice, or do you want everyone in here to hear you?"

"Sorry." Heather wrapped her arm through Ella's. "Want me to ditch tall, dark, and handsome? If you need somebody to talk to—"

Ella laughed. "Go enjoy tall, dark and handsome. I'm going to buy this book"—she held the sci-fi novel up for inspection—"then head for home, where I plan to take a nice, long bubble bath and read until I fall asleep."

"To each their own," Heather said. "You go to bed with a good book and I'll go to bed with a good man. Or at least I hope he's good."

"You're scandalous."

"And you're horny."

"Heather!"

"Believe me, if Reed Conway looked at me the way he looked at you tonight, I'd be dragging him off to the nearest bed."

"You might enjoy living dangerously, but I don't. Remember, you're the one who warned me that Reed Conway is trouble with a capital *T*. And I'm the girl who avoids trouble."

"Yeah, I know. But Ella, honey, you just don't know what you're missing."

Chapter 11

Webb would have preferred to be just about anywhere today than in Spring Park for the annual Fourth of July celebration. With each passing year, he dreaded these public appearances with his happy little family. But the lieutenant governor was here, as were U.S. Congressman Conners, state legislators, and Spring Creek's mayor. And so, the Porter family was in attendance for a command performance. Carolyn didn't make many political appearances with him, and people understood that her physical handicap prevented her from being the full-time supportive wife Webb needed. But over the years, Ella had become her mother's substitute, always available to wave and smile and even give stump speeches.

Carolyn seemed to have no trouble at all playing the part of loving wife whenever called upon to make an appearance. Perhaps inside that fantasy world she had created and lived in, their marriage was the perfect love match they presented to the world and to their daughter. But in reality, he had stopped loving Carolyn before her accident over thirty years ago and he suspected that some time in the past decade she had not only ceased loving him, but had learned to hate him. He couldn't blame her, of course. She had every right to hate him. But heaven help him, what was he supposed to do? He was tied to a woman he didn't love, forced to remain in a marriage that had for all intents and purposes ended long ago. He had a right to some happiness, didn't he? He had worked diligently to keep his infidelities discreet. He never wanted to hurt Carolyn or to disappoint Ella. His daughter idolized him, and he wanted to keep it that way. He wasn't sure what he'd do if she ever discovered her idol had feet of clay.

Webb put his phony politician's smile in place as he pushed Carolyn's wheelchair across the lush green lawn of the park. He headed directly toward the family's picnic table, adorned with a shiny new canopy donated by the Porter and Carlisle families. He waved, nodded, and spoke to everyone he saw. Four different men stopped him to shake hands and shoot the breeze. Two were merely voters, but every vote counted. One was a wealthy supporter whom he dare not ignore. And the other was a longtime acquaintance whom Webb was genuinely glad to see.

A country-and-western band played shit-kicking music from the raised podium in the middle of park. In a clearing across the circular road that surrounded the park, on the north side, a display of Medieval swordplay was in progress, while on the south side, representatives of the Cherokee Nation performed tribal dances. Food venders circled the outer boundaries like an old-time wagon train preparing to fight off an attack. Rows of booths in front of and behind the center podium housed the arts and crafts. Inside a huge, colorful tent near the spring-fed pond, local artists displayed their paintings and sculptures.

Jeff Henry, resplendent in his white slacks and short-sleeved white linen shirt set off by a pair of mustard yellow suspenders, beamed with pleasure the moment he caught sight of Carolyn. Poor old fool, Webb thought. Pining away for a woman who has never loved him and never will. Actually, Webb wasn't sure that Carolyn was capable of loving anyone except herself. He supposed that, in her own fashion, she did love Ella, although there were times when he caught a glimpse of pure jealousy coming from her when he was too attentive to their daughter. Carolyn resented anyone Webb loved. And he loved Ella more than anyone on earth. She was, after all, the very best of him.

"Ella, darling girl, I'm so glad you've finally arrived." Cybil draped her arm over her niece's shoulder. "We've been here thirty minutes and I'm already bored to death. Let's go see if we can find something fun to do, like ogle a half-naked hunk in the dunking booth or pig out on some delicious homemade fudge."

"Ella, if you go off with your aunt Cybil, please keep track of the time," Carolyn cautioned. "Don't forget that we have to be on the podium with your daddy at two o'clock. And if Dan isn't here by noon, call him and remind him he's invited to join us."

"Yes, Mother." Without a backward glance, Ella ran off with Cybil, the two of them giggling like schoolgirls as they disappeared into the huge crowd milling about in the park.

As he'd watched Ella and Cybil leaving, Webb's gaze had lingered on the two women. Despite Cybil's many flaws—and God knew she had plenty—Webb thanked the good Lord every day that Cybil had always been a part of his daughter's life. There were many similarities in the two women, but the resemblances were so subtle that he doubted anyone else noticed. Perhaps only Jeff Henry. Whereas Cybil was petite, as was Carolyn, Ella was tall and big-boned. But the shiny black hair, the peaches-and-cream light-olive skin, and the bold and beautiful smile were identical. And their genuine, heartfelt laughter sounded the same—so unlike Carolyn, who seldom laughed and whose smile seemed a sad parody of the real thing.

"Webb, I'm simply dying of thirst," Carolyn said. "Would you be so good as to get me some lemonade. I think I'll perish if I have to wait until lunchtime."

"Certainly." As Webb patted her on the shoulder, he glanced at Jeff Henry. "Would you like some lemonade, too?"

"Yes, thank you kindly. And don't you worry about Carolyn while you're gone. I'll keep her entertained." Jeff Henry sat on the edge of the concrete bench facing Carolyn.

"I never worry about my wife when she's with you," Webb said, then made a hasty retreat.

He found the lines at all the food and drink vendors too long. Although he could have pulled rank and gone behind the scenes to be waited on, he knew his image as one of the people would be tarnished if he did something so crass. He had an image to uphold, especially in his hometown.

Suddenly Webb noticed Judy Conway and her daughter, Regina, in the line beside him. Judy was the kind of woman that men looked at twice, and not because she did anything to draw attention to herself. She'd been born with dainty features, big blue eyes, and a mane of glorious blond hair. Her daughter was a replica of her, except that her features were larger and more sharply defined. His encounters with Judy had been difficult for both of them over the years, especially since he had prosecuted Reed for murder. Usually he had a difficult time looking Judy directly in the eye. He would never forget the night she came to him, begging for his help to save her son, offering him anything he wanted. God knows he'd been tempted to take her up on her offer, but he respected Judy far too much—then and now. He didn't think she had ever forgiven him for believing Reed guilty of killing his stepfather.

She must have noticed that Webb was staring at her, because she turned and looked at him, their gazes connecting and holding for a split second before she glanced away again. Of all the women he'd known over the years—and he'd known more than his share—no woman had ever fascinated him the way Judy did. He had loved her once, long ago. If Carolyn hadn't been crippled in that damned accident, if he had been able to obtain a divorce when he'd first realized Carolyn was not the woman he'd thought she was, then both his life and Judy's would be different now. Judy would be his wife instead of his sister-in-law's housekeeper. Reed would be his stepson instead of his enemy. And Regina would be his daughter.

But Ella would not be a part of his life. Would he, if he could, trade one life for the other? One daughter for another? God, he'd made so many mistakes—too many ever to rectify in one lifetime.

"Nice to see you and your daughter enjoying the Fourth of July celebration," Webb said directly to Judy, certain she would know he was speaking to her and be unable to ignore him in front of all these people.

Judy glared at him. "This Independence Day is special for my family. My son is home, where he should be."

"I'm glad for you." Webb turned his attention to Regina, who simply stared at him, apparently surprised that Senator Webb Porter would be talking to her mother in such a friendly manner. "Regina, I haven't seen you in quite some time. You've certainly grown up to be a lovely young woman."

"Thank you," Regina replied nervously.

"I understand you're a paralegal for Mark Leamon." Webb moved forward toward the concession window as the line progressed.

Regina nodded. "Mark has encouraged me to go back to school and become a lawyer."

"Is that right? I think it's a brilliant idea. Are you returning to school soon?"

"No, I'm afraid I'll have to save up the money first." Regina followed her mother as she made her way closer and closer to the window.

"Ah, yes, the money." Webb glanced at Judy and the two exchanged a brief, meaningful stare. "Perhaps you can get a scholarship of some sort. Why don't you let me look into it for you?"

Regina eased out of line and took a tentative step toward Webb. "Oh, Senator Porter, that would be wonderful. But is that even possible?"

Judy clamped her hand down on her daughter's shoulder and drew her back into the line. "My daughter won't accept any handouts, but she's a smart girl, and if there's scholarship money out there that she'd qualify to receive, then your help would be appreciated."

"I'll make a few phone calls and see what I can come up with." Webb found himself next in line. He took one final look at mother and daughter—two beautiful women, both of whom might have been his—then smiled broadly at the cashier and ordered two large lemonades and an extra-large root beer.

When Reed met his mother and sister halfway in the middle of the park, he took the tray of drinks out of Judy's hands. He'd seen her in the concession line talking to Webb Porter, and it had taken all his willpower not to storm over there and demand that the senator leave his mother and sister alone. There had been something going on between his mother and Webb Porter once, back when he'd been just a kid, and the very thought that the man had ever touched his mother sickened him. He'd be damned if he'd let that son of a bitch come sniffing around his little sister.

Regina needed a husband, a man who would love her, marry her, and teach her that sex was a wondrous pleasure and not a dirty, cruel attack on a helpless victim. He didn't know for a fact that Regina was still a virgin, but he was ninety-nine percent sure. His mother had told him that Regina had never dated and that, although the years of therapy with the psychiatrist had helped her tremendously, Regina hadn't been able to share a normal relationship with a man. Maybe he'd been wrong to dismiss the notion of Regina and Mark Leamon as a couple. He had no right to pass judgement on Mark, who was a good man, or to burden his sister with his own feelings of inferiority. Who could tell? Maybe it was possible for two people from different social classes actually to be right for each other.

"Mama, we need to talk," Reed said.

"I'll take these sandwiches on over to our table and Briley Joe and I can get everything set up," Regina said. "But don't keep us waiting too long."

The moment Regina was out of earshot, Reed confronted Judy. "What was going on with Webb Porter?"

"Nothing," Judy said. "He spoke to me and I spoke to him."

"I saw him talking to Regina. Hell, Mama, that old scoundrel was flirting with Regina. You need to set him straight or I will."

Judy huffed loudly. "Don't be ridiculous. Webb wasn't flirting with your sister. He was being friendly. That's all."

"Are you telling me that you didn't notice the way he was looking at her?"

"He was looking at her the way he would look at Ella."

"He was looking at her as if he couldn't get enough, as if he'd never seen her before in his life."

Judy laid her hand on Reed's arm. "Webb Porter would never do anything to harm Regina. Take my word for it."

"The way I took your word when you promised me that Junior Blalock would be a good stepdaddy to Regina and me?"

"Oh, Reed." Judy bit down on her bottom lip.

"Damn, Mama, I'm sorry." Holding the tray of drinks in one hand, Reed slipped his other arm around Judy's shoulders. "I didn't mean to say that to you. It's just . . . I can't bear the thought of Webb trying to pull anything with Regina.''

''Webb isn't interested in your sister that way,'' Judy said. ''Don't you ever tell her that I told you this, but . . . Webb saw to it that she got a scholarship to college, and he put in a good word with Mark to help her get her job with him. And I suspect that although Cybil wrote the checks that paid for Regina's psychiatrist, Webb was the one who provided the money.''

''And why would Webb Porter go out of his way to do those things for your daughter—for my sister?''

''Maybe Webb felt partially responsible for your being sent to prison. Maybe it was his way of trying to help your family. Despite what happened between the two of you, Webb is a good man.''

''No, he's not, Mama, and you know it. That man doesn't do anything unless there's something in it for him.''

Judy shook her head sadly. When Reed noticed the sheen of tears in his mother's eyes, he dropped the subject immediately. He seemed to have a knack for saying the wrong thing and hurting her, which was the last thing on earth he wanted to do.

Reed walked Judy to their picnic table, where Regina and Briley Joe had arranged napkins and plastic utensils atop the red-and-white checked paper tablecloth. He set the tray of iced drinks on the table and then took a long, hard look at his sister. She was, in almost every way, her mother's daughter. If she resembled the man who had fathered her, it had to be in very subtle ways. He searched again in his sister's face for any resemblance to Webb Porter and saw none. But was it possible that he was Regina's father? That might explain his interest in her, other than the obvious lascivious reasons that first came to mind.

More than once over the years, while he'd been struggling to survive in prison, Reed had played out countless scenarios in his mind. Who had slit Junior Blalock's throat? And why? If Webb Porter had been involved with his mother, then Webb might have wanted to eliminate Junior. Or if Webb was Regina's father and he'd found out that Junior had tried to rape her, then he might have killed the man. God knew that he himself had been angry enough with Junior to have murdered him, and if his mother hadn't dragged him off that drunken bastard, he probably would have beaten him to death. But no matter what the evidence at his trial had shown, he had not gone back later and slit Junior's throat. Someone else had—someone who obviously hated Junior enough to murder him in cold blood. And someone who didn't mind framing an innocent eighteen-year-old boy for the crime.

Mark Leamon scanned the area where picnickers had spread quilts on the ground in front of the podium and were eating barbecue while listening to a series of country bands and regional singers. He wondered where Regina was in this huge crowd. She had mentioned that her mother hoped Reed would come with them to the annual Fourth of July festival in the park, so he knew Regina would be here. He had thought about asking Regina to attend this event with him, but every time he'd just about worked up the courage to ask her for a date, he lost his nerve at the last minute. He'd never been a ladies' man. In high school he'd been considered a bookworm and a nerd. But since graduating from law school and taking over his father's practice, he'd improved his image. He was still short and stocky, with nondescript brown hair and eyes and a rather ordinary-looking face. However, he dressed for success, drove a pricey car, and had learned that most women liked a man with money.

A lot of men here today would envy him having Heather Marshall on his arm. She was a sexy redhead who dressed in a way that turned men's heads. They'd had several dates since her return to Spring Creek, but he was no more interested in a long-term relationship with her than she was with him.

"I see her," Heather said.

"You see who?"

"Your little assistant, Regina Conway." Heather grinned broadly. "She's to your left, all the way back there near the pond. She's sitting with her family."

"Thank you for pointing her out to me. It's nice to know she came out today and is enjoying herself with her family." Mark's gaze focused on the table where Regina sat. She was laughing at something her cousin Briley Joe said. Mark sighed. He loved listening to Regina laugh. Unfortunately, it was something she seldom did. She was such a quiet, serious young woman. But sweet. Oh, so sweet.

"You were looking for her, weren't you?" Heather lifted one eyebrow in a don't-lie-to-me gesture.

"Now, why would I be looking for another woman when I'm with you?"

"Don't kid a kidder, old pal." Heather glanced in every direction, obviously searching for someone herself.

"Okay, I was looking for Regina. She doesn't have much of a social life and I'm glad she decided to do something fun for a change. She works too hard and doesn't play enough. Actually, I don't think she plays at all." Mark lifted his arm and draped it around Heather's bare shoulder. "So, who are you looking for?"

"Me?" Her gaze settled on the Porter table. "I'm looking for Ella, of course."

Mark's gaze followed Heather's. He chuckled. "Yeah, sure."

"What? You don't believe me?"

"I believe you were looking for Ella all right, but only to see if Dan Gilmore was with her. I don't see why you don't level with Ella about your feelings for Dan. After all, you two are best friends, aren't you?"

"Ella's not the problem. She isn't in love with Dan."

"How do you know?"

"She told me she wasn't. I felt so guilty because I was relieved. You know what I'd said to her about Dan? I told her I thought he was as dull as dishwater."

Mark guffawed. "Well, he is, isn't he?"

"Yes, he is," Heather admitted. "But I've been in love with that guy since I was in pigtails and he was the one boy in town I could never get to notice me. When he married that mealymouthed Greer Swain, I figured I'd lost him forever."

"But now he's free again."

"Yeah, he's free and still not the least bit interested in me." Heather wrapped her arm around Mark's waist. "Come on. Let's go say hello to the Conway family."

"I'm not sure we should intrude."

"Look here, if you're interested in that girl, then go after her. How's she supposed to know you're interested if you don't show her?"

"I don't know how she'd react if she thought I wanted to date her," Mark said. "You know something about her history, don't you?"

"I know that her bastard stepfather tried to rape her when she was a kid. Half the state of Alabama knows that."

"Regina doesn't date."

"What? You're kidding. You mean she has never had a date?" Heather asked. "And she's how old, nearly thirty?"

"She'll be twenty-six in November."

"Uh-oh. If she's got so many hangups that she doesn't even date, then you'd have your work cut out for you even getting a kiss from her. Are you sure you care enough about her to go the distance?"

"If I thought that someday Regina could love me, then yeah, I'd be willing to go the distance. I'd be willing to do just about anything. But—"

"No buts about it." Heather tightened her hold

around Mark's waist. "Just come along with Auntie Heather and follow my lead. We're fixing to find out if Miss Conway is interested in her boss."

"And how to you intend to do that?"

"Watch and find out."

"Wherever did Cybil get off to?" Carolyn asked.

"I think she went to the restroom," Ella whispered to her mother. "You know how long those lines are."

"She's probably off drinking somewhere," Carolyn said. "How Jeff Henry endures what she puts him through, I'll never know. We've all tried to talk her into getting help, but she ignores us." Carolyn reached over and patted Ella's arm. "Dear, I wish you'd speak to her. She's so fond of you, she just might listen to your advice."

"Mother, I've spoken to her numerous times. You know that. Until Aunt Cybil wants help, there's not much any of us can do except be there to pick up the pieces every time she falls apart."

"I'm beginning to think we're doing her a disservice cleaning up her messes, but it's the only way to keep her from shaming the whole family." Carolyn wadded the napkin in her hand, her fingers nervously tightening the cloth more and more. "But it would be terrible for your father's career if the media were to pick up on the fact that his sister-in-law is a lush."

"It's only a matter of time, since just about everyone in Spring Creek knows," Ella said. "Besides, I'm not so sure it would harm Daddy's career. Having addiction problems seems to be in fashion these days, as does infidelity and lying."

"Why, Eleanor Porter, when did you become such a cynic?"

"Since I've matured some and begun seeing the world as it really is instead of the way I'd like for it to be."

"Oh, that makes me sad. My little girl has lost her rose-colored glasses."

Ella leaned down and hugged her mother. As always, Carolyn's small body stiffened, but she lifted her hand and patted Ella on the back with restrained affection. Not once in her life had her mother wrapped her in her arms with motherly abandon and lavished a show of love on her. Of course, she'd never seen her mother overly affectionate with anyone, not even her father. But Webb was different. Boisterous, gregarious, and demonstrative, her father had more than made up for her mother's restraint. And Aunt Cybil, high-strung, nervous, and overly emotional, had always given her bear hugs. And when Ella had been a child, she'd covered her face with kisses. Even Uncle Jeff Henry had the capacity to offer big hugs and an occasional kiss on the forehead or cheek.

As if on cue, her uncle appeared, dressed in his elaborate Confederate general's costume. He looked so authentic, you would think he'd traveled through time, straight from the early 1860s. Ella thought once again, as she had so often, that Jeff Henry Carlisle had been born in the wrong century. He's missed his mark by a good hundred years or more.

"The reinactment is set for three-thirty," Jeff Henry said. "The troops are setting up the cannons and bringing in the horses over on the west side of the park." He removed a white linen handkerchief from his pocket and wiped the perspiration from his face. "This costume is hot, but if I didn't get dressed early, I'd have to miss part of Webb's speech."

"You look very dashing," Ella said.

"Why, thank you, my dear."

"Jeff Henry always looks dashing," Carolyn said. "It's because he's a gentleman and gentlemen always take pride in their appearance. My papa always looked like he'd stepped out of a bandbox."

"I wish I'd known Grandfather Walker."

"Mr. John was quite a gentleman," Jeff Henry said. "I thought highly of him. When I was just a boy, he took me under his wing. I suppose he took pity on me because I'd lost my own father when I was only five, and although Mother did her best, Mr. John, having been one of my father's associates, saw that I needed a strong masculine influence in my life."

Ella smiled as her uncle recounted bygone days. She'd heard this particular story numerous times, but she listened attentively out of respect, and because reminiscences about Grandfather Walker seemed to give both her mother and her uncle great pleasure.

While Jeff Henry continued to drone on and on, delightfully entertaining Carolyn, Webb approached them, laughing happily. Her father was in his element when he was working the crowd.

"Carolyn, you haven't seen the local art work, yet," Webb said. "Why don't we go over to the artists' tent and have a look. I'd like to buy something to show my support. You have such a keen eye, I'm sure you'll choose the perfect item. Something I can display in my Spring Creek office."

Carolyn beamed, so obviously thrilled by her husband's attention. A tremor of emotion showed on her face for a fraction of a second. "What a good idea. I'd love to choose something for you." She glanced from Ella to Jeff Henry. "Would y'all like to go with us?"

"Too damn hot in those tents for me in this getup," Jeff Henry said. "I'll save the art tent for when I've changed back into my street clothes."

"You two go on," Ella said. "I have an idea how to cool off Uncle Jeff Henry."

"Indeed? And just what would that be?" Jeff Henry inquired. "A dip in the pond?"

Ella slipped her arm through her uncle's. "I thought a nice, long walk in the park's garden area, where there are a lot of shade trees, might be just the thing."

"Well, y'all be sure to finish up your walk before time

for Webb's speech," Carolyn reminded them as her husband wheeled her away toward the art tent.

Jeff Henry took the lead, escorting Ella through the throng of celebrators, many of them in shorts, tank tops, and flip-flops.

"Some people just don't care how they look," Jeff Henry said. "Of course the white trash element in our society is noted for a lack of good taste, but it's the appearance of the children of some of our friends that bothers me greatly."

"Teenagers want to look like their peers," Ella said. "When you're sixteen, being different is a fate worse than death."

"Hmm . . . I suppose you're right."

Jeff Henry's Civil War apparel, regal bearing, and snobbish attitude set him apart from the vast majority of people in the park.

But he didn't mind at all. Actually, Ella felt certain that he enjoyed it, that he reveled in it. No doubt about it—her uncle thought himself superior to just about everyone. Others despised him for this offensive trait, but somehow Ella found it rather endearing—an odd quirk that made him unique. It wasn't as if he actually harmed anyone other than himself with his antiquated notions of class differences.

The east end of the park had long been a garden area, and several of the local ladies' clubs in various Bryant County towns had made the Sarah Rogers Garden their pet project. A recently laid stone walkway circled around and about the various flower beds and led into the wooded section, where huge trees, some well over a hundred years old, towered into the sky.

"Ella, my brilliant niece, a walk through the garden was an inspired idea," Jeff Henry said. "It is much cooler over here and a great deal less crowded."

Only a dozen or so people meandered through the garden area, where beauty and quiet prevailed. Most people were too involved in the riot of events taking place all over the park to be bothered with seeking out a tranquil, soothing atmosphere. The tall, thick-leaved trees blocked out a great deal of the afternoon summer sun. All sorts of secluded nooks and crannies offered privacy for those seeking it.

Ella glanced to her left and saw, half-hidden behind a tree, a pair of lovers embracing. Kissing. Even at a distance, she could tell they were young, no more than twenty. The couple apparently couldn't keep their hands off each other.

"Disgusting display," Jeff Henry said. "There is a time and a place for everything, and that sort of behavior should be confined to behind closed doors."

"They're young and in love," Ella said. "Don't you remember what that was like?"

Jeff Henry harrumphed. "Of course I remember. When I was their age, I was madly in love with your mother. But never would I . . . would we have carried on like those two are doing. I respected your mother far too much to have manhandled her that way, especially in a public place."

"Why don't we give them their privacy?" Ella suggested. "The bridge over the pond isn't far and there are benches where we can sit down for a bit."

"Don't let us lose track of time. Carolyn would be upset if we missed Webb's speech."

Carolyn. Always Carolyn. Poor Uncle Jeff Henry. But the person Ella truly pitied was her aunt Cybil. What would it be like to be married to a man you knew was in love with your sister?

The bridge came into view—a wooden arch over the narrow backwaters of the pond that extended from the park into the woods and down to the nearby creek. As they approached the bridge, Ella caught a glimpse of someone in the wooded area, a flash of flesh among all the lush greenery. Another set of young lovers, Ella thought. Perhaps she could distract her uncle enough so that he wouldn't notice. But when they stepped onto the bridge, Ella heard the couple. Grunting, moaning, panting. *Damn!* What were they doing, having sex? It sure sounded that way.

She had to turn Uncle Jeff Henry around before he noticed. "Why don't we head back to—"

"My God!" Jeff Henry's cheeks flushed scarlet. "Is there no shame? Those two are—"

Before she could stop him, her uncle dashed across the bridge, his Civil War saber thumping against his hip. She hurried after him, uncertain what he might say or do. At this point she wasn't sure whether she was more concerned about the couple, who were still oblivious to being watched, or her uncle, primed and ready for an attack.

Suddenly, Jeff Henry stopped, frozen to the spot. All color drained from his face. Ella came up beside him and started to speak, but before a word formed on her lips, she saw that her uncle was hypnotized by the sight. The man in the woods had the woman backed up against a tree, her skirt lifted enough to reveal her slender thighs. He had his hands under her skirt, cupping her buttocks as he pumped into her. Ella's mouth dropped open.

The woman cried out in the throes of orgasm. Ella forced herself to look away. When she glanced at her uncle, she noted the fine mist covering his eyes. Without saying a word, he turned and walked away.

Ella stood there, unable to believe what had just transpired. She glanced back at the couple just as the man reached his climax. How could this have happened? Ella asked herself.

The man was Briley Joe Conway. And the woman was Cybil Carlisle.

The moment Ella started to turn and run, to find her uncle and comfort him, she saw a lone figure on the pathway coming toward her. Her heart skipped a beat when she recognized him. He had obviously witnessed the couple screwing like crazy, just as she and her uncle had. Why, of all the people on earth, did she have to see Reed Conway at this precise moment?

Her gaze met and locked with Reed's. She couldn't read the expression on his face. He neither smiled nor frowned. And his cold blue eyes simply stared at her. No sympathy. No understanding. No judgment. No condemnation.

Ella turned and ran as if the demons of hell were on her heels. Breathless, stunned, and panic-stricken, she caught up with her uncle, who sat slumped on a bench at the entrance to the Sarah Rogers Garden. She sat down beside him.

He didn't look at her. "We will never speak of this again." His voice quivered ever so slightly.

"Uncle Jeff Henry." She grabbed his hand and squeezed it.

"I've known about Cybil's indiscretions for years. What I cannot understand is why she chooses the dregs of the earth to copulate with—brainless men with hard bodies who rut with her like animals. She had an affair with Junior Blalock, you know." Jeff Henry turned his head, leaned over, and vomited on the lush, green grass.

Ella stuck her fist into her mouth to stop the cry of pain that erupted from deep within her.

Chapter 12

"Hello, Miss Ella," Roy Moses said, holding out a pair of bright-red balloons. "I bought these for you."

"Oh, Roy, how sweet of you." She accepted his offering. The helium-filled balloons floated high above her head. In her peripheral vision, she saw her uncle, shoulders squared, chin up, head held high as he marched across the park toward her parents.

"Are you having a good time, Miss Ella?" Roy asked.

"Yes, of course. How about you?" Was she having a good time? Hardly. She had just witnessed Uncle Jeff Henry's ultimate humiliation. And so had Reed Conway. Would that man spread the word all over town that his cousin was having sex with Cybil Carlisle? Maybe she should have stayed, confronted him, and warned him to keep his mouth shut. But what good would it do to warn a man like that?

"I'm having a great time," Roy told her. "I've eaten hot dogs and cotton candy and bought myself all sorts of goodies. But when I saw the balloons, I thought about you. I remember your saying how much you like balloons."

"When did I tell you that?"

"When your daddy sent you that big bunch of balloons on your birthday. You got all excited. And you told me that you loved balloons, that you liked them as much as you liked flowers."

"Oh, Roy, I can't believe you remembered."

"Would you like for me to buy you an Orange Crush? They're mighty tasty on a hot day like today."

"Thank you, but I'm afraid I won't have time right now. My father's fixing to give a speech." She pointed to the podium and noticed her father wheeling her mother up the handicap ramp and onto the platform. "I'm supposed to be up there with him and my mother."

"Then I'll buy you one later. Will that be all right?"

Roy gazed at her with such hope in his eyes that she couldn't bring herself to reject him. She patted his shoulder. "That will be just fine."

She rushed to join her parents, but when she passed her uncle, who stood front and center at the base of the podium, she paused at his side. Without giving her actions a thought, she leaned over and kissed him on the cheek.

"I love you, Uncle Jeff Henry," she said.

He swallowed hard. "I love you, too, darling girl."

Ella thought her heart would break in two. He had used the endearment her aunt Cybil used exclusively for her. What must be going through his mind right now? How did he feel? Did he want to choke her aunt? Kill the man she'd been with?

She had an affair with Junior Blalock, you know. No, Ella hadn't known. Her aunt Cybil had been involved with Junior Blalock. And Uncle Jeff Henry had known. Was it possible that her uncle had killed Junior? Was he capable of that kind of jealousy? Perhaps not, but he was the type who would do anything to prevent scandal from touching his family's good name.

And what about Aunt Cybil? Was she capable of murdering a man in cold blood? Was it possible that she had killed her lover?

Stop this idiotic thinking! Reed Conway killed his stepfather. He was tried and convicted. *Ah, but you have your doubts about his guilt, don't you?*

The voice over the loudspeaker said, "And with Senator Porter today are his charming wife, Carolyn, and his daughter, Judge Eleanor Porter."

The announcer's introduction spurred Ella into action. She took the podium steps two at a time and rushed to her father's side. He wrapped one arm around her waist, then lifted the other and waved at the cheering crowd.

Once the politicians finished their speeches, the dance band returned to the podium and couples began congregating on the makeshift dance floor set up to the side of the raised dais. Tapping her foot to the strumming guitar beat, Regina stood on the sidelines and watched. The band's lead singer crooned out his own rendition of a she-done-him-wrong song. Regina's gaze followed every move Mark Leamon and Heather Marshall made as they swayed to the music. She barely knew Heather, but she hated the woman. Hated her for being in Mark's arms.

"Want to dance, little sister?" Reed came up behind her and curved his hand over her shoulder.

She glanced back at him and smiled. "Sure, but I have to warn you that I'm not much of a dancer. I didn't go to any of my school dances."

Reed led her onto the dance floor, took her into his arms, and said, "Just follow my lead. I'm a bit rusty myself, although a new lady friend of mine has been giving me some practice lessons lately."

"Is this lady friend someone I'd know?" Regina asked.

"Nope. She's not the kind of woman you'd associate with."

"Ah, I see."

"So, I've brought you up to date on my love life, how about filling me in on yours?"

"You didn't tell me anything about your love life. And I'm sure I don't want to know." Regina giggled, relaxing in her brother's strong, comforting arms. "As for my love life, it's nonexistent."

"You should have gone to all those school dances. You should have had boys lined up at the front door. And you should be married to some good guy right now. You've let what happened with Junior close you off from life. That's so wrong. As long as you keep the world at arm's length, then Junior still has power over you—far more power than he had that night."

If anyone else had dared to talk to her about Junior and that night the way Reed just had, she would have run from them. But Reed, more than anyone, knew what had happened and how close Junior had come to raping her. For all intents and purposes, he had raped her. He'd done everything short of penetrating her. He had violated her with his hands and his mouth. He had stolen her innocence. He had made her afraid of men. All men. Except Reed, who had rescued her. And Mark, with whom she had unwittingly fallen in love.

"I don't want to be the way I am," Regina said. "I spent years in therapy, as you well know. But I've never been able to stop thinking that every man I come in contact with knows about what Junior did and judges me by that night and by the trial."

"Mark knows everything about that night, and he certainly doesn't judge you in that way."

"Mark is different."

"You like him, don't you?" Reed asked, a knowing grin on his face. "You like him a lot."

Regina smiled shyly, reluctant to admit, even to her big brother, just how much she really did like Mark Leamon. "Yes, I do. But he's not interested in me."

"What makes you think that?"

"Well, he's not here with me today, is he? He's not dancing with me right now."

"That can be easily remedied."

Before Regina realized what was happening, Reed danced her around several other couples, making a bee-line straight for Mark and Heather. The minute the two couples came up side by side, Reed released Regina, tapped Mark on the shoulder, and suggested they change partners. Regina was mortified.

"Sure thing," Heather said and didn't hesitate to go straight into Reed's open arms.

Standing on the dance floor staring at each other, Mark and Regina shuffled their feet and smiled self-consciously at each other.

"Would you like to dance?" Mark finally asked.

Regina simply nodded agreement and took a tentative step forward. Mark slipped his arm around her, loosely, nonthreateningly, and they began dancing.

"You look beautiful today," Mark said. "That yellow sundress is very becoming."

"Thank you; it's new. I've never worn it before." *I bought this dress especially for you. To impress you. To make you see me as a woman and not just your paralegal.*

Gradually, indiscernibly, Mark drew her closer and closer, until their bodies were almost touching. Regina gazed into his eyes, and for a brief moment she thought she saw genuine affection—definitely something more than just friendship. Was she imagining things, or was it truly possible that Mark felt something for her, something similar to what she felt for him?

"I suppose you've known Heather Marshall for years," Regina said.

"Heather? Heavens, yes. Since we were toddlers." Mark pulled Regina up against him, brushed his cheek against hers, and held her with tender possessiveness. "Heather and I are just buddies. That's all we've ever been and all we'll ever be."

"Really?" Regina's breath caught in her throat. Happiness swelled up inside her. She wanted to jump and shout with joy.

"Actually, there isn't anyone special in my life right now," Mark told her. "But I'd like for there to be."

"You would?" Regina dared to gaze straight at him.

"What about you, Regina, are you looking for someone special?"

"Yes, I am."

"Maybe we'll both find what we're looking for. Soon."

"Maybe we will." Regina felt almost giddy, and the feeling was unlike anything she'd ever experienced. A part of her wanted to grab Mark and say, "Here I am. Take me. I'm yours." But the sensible, pragmatic Regina preached caution. *Wait. Don't rush. Take the time you need. Loving Mark is one thing. Making love with him will be something else altogether.*

Heather draped her arms around Reed's neck and pressed up against him. "So, tell me, bad boy, was that little maneuver planned to get your sister in Mark's arms or me into yours?"

Reed chuckled. Heather was a brazen hussy. He'd always liked the type. "What do you think?"

"I think you were definitely looking out for your little sister's interests and not your own."

"You're smart as well as sexy."

Heather laughed. "So, how's it feel being back home?"

"It feels good."

"Yeah, I guess it does. I never thought I'd move back to this one-horse town, but after a marriage that was something like a prison sentence, I couldn't wait to get free and come home."

"Bad marriage?"

"The worst. He ran around on me and he beat me."

"Must have been rough."

"Not nearly as rough as what you went through,"

Heather said. "I hear prison life is pretty bad, especially for good-looking young guys."

Reed smirked. "The first few years were the worst, but I'm a big boy and it didn't take me long to learn how to take care of myself."

"Ella tells me that you're still claiming your innocence and are determined to find Junior Blalock's real killer."

Reed's gaze met Heather's point-blank. "Now, why would you break Ella's confidence and mention anything to me about your private conversations with her, especially concerning me?" Reed chuckled. "You know all about the letters and the phone calls, don't you?"

"So, you're smart as well as sexy, huh?" Heather took the lead and began backing Reed across the dance floor. "Ella is my best friend. We don't have too many secrets from each other."

"So tell me, Ella's best friend, just what does Judge Porter think of me?"

"Who says she thinks about you?"

"Does she?"

Heather glanced over Reed's shoulder, then inclined her head as if indicating he should take a look. He pivoted her, reversing their positions. The couple next to them danced without touching, the woman stiff in the man's arms, as if she didn't want to be there. Before he could deflect his gaze, Ella Porter caught him staring at her. Her eyes rounded in surprise, and when she noticed the woman in Reed's arms, her expression hardened and she looked away, back at her partner.

"Ella is a truly decent person and a good woman," Heather said.

"Why tell me about her sterling qualities?"

"Because I'm warning you, Reed Conway. If you hurt her, if you break her heart or cause her one moment of pain, I'll come after you and rip out your heart."

Reed nodded as he thumped his tongue against the roof of his mouth. "You're the second person to make that specific threat."

"I assume the senator has already warned you."

"What I want to know is why you think I could ever break Ella's heart."

"You're a man. She's a woman. Things happen."

"Yes, ma'am, they surely do."

Reed waltzed Heather around, past the couple next to them, all the while watching Ella for a reaction. He'd just about given up on her glancing his way again, when suddenly she looked right at him. Heaven help him, he wanted that woman. And unless he was badly mistaken, she wanted him.

"If it's marriage you want, then let's do it," Dan said. "We'll pick out a ring, set a date, and let Carolyn plan the wedding of the decade."

"Why would you suddenly want to get married?" Ella stared at him as if he'd lost his mind. "I thought you just wanted us to sleep together for now and think about marriage in the future."

Dan glanced around at the other couples on the dance floor, and she realized he was checking to see if anyone was listening to their conversation. If he loved her, he wouldn't care if the whole world heard him declaring his intentions, now would he?

"Carolyn mentioned that with a lady like you, marriage was the next logical step," Dan said. "And after giving it some thought, I agree with her." He pulled Ella closer and whispered, "Your mother explained that you were still a . . . er . . . a virgin and that's why you were skittish about—"

"My mother told you that I've never had sex before?" Ella forced her voice to remain calm and low.

"Was she wrong?" Dan asked. "Aren't you a—"

"Does it matter to you?"

"Well, I had assumed that at your age you would have been with someone, at some time in the past. But I must admit, thinking I'd be the first certainly is appealing."

Ella stopped moving, right there on the dance floor, with people all around them. And one person in particular. Reed Conway seemed terribly interested in what she was doing.

"Let's get one thing straight," Ella said in an angry whisper. "You're not going to be the first or the twenty-first. I'm not going to have sex with you. Now or ever. And I'm not going to marry you."

"Ella, please . . . You're making a scene. People are staring at us."

"Let them stare!" Her voice grew just a tad louder.

Dan grasped her wrist and jerked, but she pulled free. "I don't know what's gotten into you lately. I thought—"

"You thought I'd happily marry you even though you don't love me and I don't love you. Well, think again."

Ella stormed off the dance floor, leaving poor Dan to wipe the egg off his face. Had her mother really led him to believe that she was some pathetic old maid who'd never been with a man and had no hope of ever marrying someone who loved her? Did her mother think that she'd honestly be grateful that Dan was willing to offer marriage?

Within minutes, she found herself surrounded by people milling around in the park. Somewhere in the distance she heard Dan calling her name. She had to get out of this crowd, had to get away from everyone, especially Dan Gilmore. Fleeing the festivities, she didn't pay much attention to where she was going. All that mattered was that she find a quiet spot to collect her thoughts and come to terms with the outrage she felt. Her white sandals clipped softly on the pavement as she crossed the road.

"What are you waiting for?" Heather asked.

"You think I should follow her?" All Reed needed

was one word of encouragement from Ella's best friend and he'd run after Ella.

"She's going to need a big, strong shoulder to cry on. Why not yours?"

Reed looked pointedly at Heather. "I'm an ex-con bad boy from the wrong side of the tracks. Why would you trust your friend with me?"

"Did I say I trusted you?" Smiling, Heather gave him a gentle shove. "Junior Blalock deserved killing, so if you did it, you did the world a service. And I just happen to think that what Ella needs right now is a bad boy. A real bad boy. She's had one too many gentlemen pushed on her by her mama."

"You're something else, Heather Marshall."

"Yeah, I know."

Reed kissed her cheek, then turned and rushed through the crowd. He followed Ella's path, barely keeping up with her. A couple of times, he lost sight of her, but the minute she crossed the road, he knew where she was headed. Back to the garden. Back to the wooded area where she'd accidently come across her aunt and Briley Joe going at it like a couple of wild things.

She didn't slow her stride until she crossed the bridge. She stopped running then and stood with her back to him, her shoulders slightly stooped, as she caught her breath. He soon realized that she had no idea he was following her. The area was empty, with not another soul in sight. Over the loudspeakers, Reed heard an announcement, the voice barely discernable from a third of a mile away. The country music had stopped and now the mournful wail of a Muddy Waters blues tune, sung by a local artist, cried out in heartfelt pain. The distinct sounds of harmonica, bass, and guitar blended together as background music for the soulful rendition of "You're Gonna Miss Me."

Reed sneaked up behind her. Something told him that if he announced his presence too soon, she'd bolt and run. When he was only a few feet away from her, she undoubtedly sensed his presence. She whirled around and faced him, her eyes wide with surprise, her mouth opening on an indrawn gasp.

"Are you all right?" Reed asked. "I noticed you and your boyfriend had an argument. You ran off the dance floor, so—"

"Go away. Leave me alone." There was a stricken look in her big brown eyes, like that of a trapped animal afraid for its life.

"You don't really want to be alone right now, do you? Wouldn't you like somebody to give you a little tender loving care?"

"I don't know what you think happened between Dan and me or why you'd assume I might want anything from you, but you've got this all wrong."

Reed took several tentative steps toward her. She took just as many steps backward, away from him. He grinned. Suddenly, the look in her eyes changed from fear to provocation, as if she were daring him to come after her. Well, he'd always been a man who couldn't resist a dare. He moved forward; she eased backward. He wondered if she realized that, unless she changed direction, she was backing up right into a tree. He advanced. She retreated.

"Damn it, why won't you leave me alone?!" she screamed, the words a plea.

"You don't really want me to leave you alone, now, do you?"

He backed her up against the tree. Her breathing quickened. Her gaze flashed right and left, seeking an escape route. There was none. He placed his hands on either side of her head, his palms resting on the tree trunk as he leaned toward her. His chest brushed her breasts. Her gaze connected with his.

"Your aunt has a taste for danger. She likes walking on the wild side. What about you, Miss Ella? Are you looking for some excitement?"

"No . . . no." She trembled.

"I think you're curious," he said. "You'd like to know what it feels like to have a bad boy back you up against a tree and lift your skirt and—"

"Shut up! Shut up!" Ella covered her ears with her hands.

Reed pressed closer, aligning their bodies. Ella was tall enough so that he didn't have to stoop over to reach her mouth or to position his erection against her mound. And he had a stiff one all right. He was as hard as a rock and he hadn't even touched her.

"I want to be your bad boy." His breath mingled with hers. "I want to run my hands up under that pretty red skirt you're wearing and cup your butt in my hands. I want to kiss you until you're breathless and then I want to put my mouth on your breasts. I want to hear you say my name and beg me to take you. Here. Now."

Ella swallowed hard. "I hate you!"

"Do you? You hate me for making you feel the way you do, don't you? For making you want to act on your sexual fantasies. And don't tell me that you haven't been fantasizing about us making love. I can see it in your eyes every time you look at me."

She closed her eyes and dropped her hands from her ears. "If there's one shred of decency in you, you'll go away and leave me alone."

"Ah, but that's the problem, Miss Ella." He nuzzled her neck. She keened softly. "There's no disgrace in admitting that you want me, that you've thought about our being together like this. God knows I've thought about it. I can't seem to get you out of my mind."

She opened her eyes. He stared at her, wanting her as he had never wanted anything in his life. She was temptation personified. He had no right even to touch her, and yet his body told him that this woman belonged to him, that she was meant to be his. If he kissed her, if he allowed himself to touch her, to caress her, would he be able to stop? He honestly didn't know.

His lips swooped down over hers, fast and furious,

but with as much restraint as he could muster. She tried to turn her face, to end the kiss. He kept his mouth tightly on hers. She struggled, inclining right and left, then she shoved against his chest and stopped his attack. They glared at each other for an endless moment, both of them breathless and undeniably aroused.

He kissed her again. Softer. With as much gentleness as he could manage. She didn't struggle, didn't fight him, didn't try to turn away from him. He teased her mouth with sweet kisses, tender nips, and moist, seductive swipes of his tongue. When she sighed with pleasure, he took advantage and dipped his tongue into her mouth. She responded to his blatant invasion, returning his kiss with equal fervor.

They both gave themselves over completely to the moment. Hot. Wild. Free. Consumed with a raging hunger. He devoured; she reciprocated. And when it wasn't enough, when passion demanded more, Ella lifted her hands to encircle his neck. Her fingers threaded through the long hair at the nape of his neck.

He pressed his erection against the apex between her thighs, showing her that he wanted her in the most basic way a man can want a woman. She rubbed herself against him, her movements sensual and alluring. He lifted his left hand, grabbed the back of her neck, and held her head in place, securing her mouth to his. Although he didn't think she was going anywhere, he wanted to make sure. He ached with the need to take her, to open her up and lose himself in her sweet body. He placed his right hand on her hip and caressed her through the fine cotton material of her skirt. Her body was round and full. A woman's body. A man's greatest temptation. He eased his hand down her thigh. His fingers ate the material, bunching it up, drawing it higher and higher, so that he was able to slide his hand beneath and stroke the smooth flesh of her outer thigh.

He lifted his mouth from hers and looked at her flushed face. She whimpered. He raked his cheek across hers, then nibbled on her earlobe. "You do like danger, don't you, babe?"

She shuddered, alive with desire. Needing and wanting. Probably hurting in the same way he was.

He kissed her neck—quick, nibbling kisses—then covered her collarbone with the same attention. His mouth sought and found her pebble-hard nipple straining against her bra and the bodice of her sleeveless red blouse. When he encompassed the peak with his lips and sucked through the material, she flung back her head and moaned.

"Tell me you want me," he said.

"I want you." The words tumbled out in a breathy sigh.

"Say my name," he demanded.

"Reed." She clung to him, her mouth seeking his again. "I want you, Reed."

He inserted two fingers beneath the leg-band of her panties. Just as he skimmed over the triangle of curls, a noise rumbled inside his head. He felt Ella tense. Laughter. The laughter of children. Dammit, not now! But the sound grew louder and mingled with voices.

"Ah, babe, someone's coming this way." He withdrew his hand from her panties, smoothed her skirt over her legs, and garnering all the willpower he possessed, separated his body from hers.

Ella took a deep breath. Her eyelids fluttered and her breasts rose and fell with labored breaths. She was still as aroused as he, still aching for fulfillment.

Within minutes, two women and a gang of preteen boys and girls came into view just across the bridge. Ella wiped her mouth with the back of her hand and tried to move away from Reed. He grabbed her wrist, halting her withdrawal.

"When can I see you again? Tonight?" To his own ears he sounded as if he were pleading. Hell, maybe he was. If she wanted him down on his knees, he'd go there, if that's what it took.

"No," she told him, her gaze jerking to and fro, checking to see if they had been noticed.

"When?"

"I don't know." She pulled free.

"You don't want things to end like this. I know you don't. Sooner or later, we're going to finish what we started here today."

"No." She shook her head. "We can't."

Ella hurried away from Reed, leaving him there in the Sarah Rogers Garden all alone, with the hard-on from hell.

Chapter 13

"I do wish you could get away for a few days and come with us," Webb said as he spread orange marmalade on his toast. "This will be the first time you haven't gone to the beach with us. It won't be the same without you."

"You know Ella can't just up and leave," Carolyn said. "Not now that she's a judge. We've offered to postpone our annual trip this summer and she wouldn't hear of it."

"I don't like the idea of leaving her here in Spring Creek. Not with Reed Conway out of prison. There's no way to know what that man might do. I think we should change our plans, postpone our trip and stay here."

Ella set her china cup on the saucer. This morning was a rare occasion. Seldom did her mother come to the table for breakfast. Customarily, Viola served breakfast to Carolyn in bed. But this morning was special—the first day of her family's annual Gulf Shores vacation. Her family owned a house right on the beach.

"I'd think you two would be looking forward to some

time alone together. You could make this a very romantic vacation."

"She's right, you know." Carolyn reached for Webb's hand. "It's been ages since the two of us had any time alone."

He caught Carolyn's hand in his, but glanced at Ella. "With the Halls and Donnells spending a week at the beach the same time we are, I doubt we'll have much time to ourselves. You know how Kit Hall and Pattie Donnell love to monopolize your mother's time."

"And if I know Jim Donnell and Trey Hall, they'll have you off deep-sea fishing by the second day we're there." Carolyn glanced meaningfully at Ella. "Pattie Donnell is bringing her two grandchildren with her. Jim Jr.'s two little girls. If you'd just give Dan some encouragement, I could have a grandchild one day soon."

"Mother, please, I don't want to discuss Dan. Not again. I've told you and Daddy that Dan and I have agreed to end things. We're having a farewell lunch today."

"For the life of me, I don't understand you, Eleanor. Fine young men like Dan don't come along every day of the week." Carolyn munched on a bite of toast. "It could be ages before someone half as suitable shows an interest in you."

"Carolyn, really," Webb said. "Ella's a fantastic catch for some lucky man. And I dare say that we'll never think anyone is quite good enough for her, but if she doesn't love Dan, then—"

"She could learn to love him." Carolyn glared at her husband.

"I would think you'd want more than that for her. I certainly do."

Ella let out a long, low whistle. Her parents turned their heads and stared at her. "Hey, I'm sitting right here. Don't talk to each other as if I'm not."

"Sorry, honey," Webb said.

"Will you two stop worrying? I'm fine. I'm a big girl who can take care of herself and make all her own decisions. So, what I want is for my mother and father to go to their beach house and spend a relaxing week together. A romantic week."

Before either Webb or Carolyn could reply, Bessie entered the breakfast room with a long, white florist's box in her hands. She cleared her throat.

"I found this lying on the back doorstep," Bessie said. "There's a card attached with Miss Ella's name on it."

"My, my, flowers on a Friday morning. Someone is obviously trying to patch things up." Carolyn eyed the box curiously.

"I don't understand why the florist didn't ring the doorbell and deliver them to the front door," Webb said.

"What do you want me to do with 'em?" Bessie asked.

"Give them to Miss Ella, of course." Carolyn sighed and rolled her eyes heavenward, an expression of exasperation over the hired help's lack of astuteness.

Bessie had been with the Porter house for four years now, ever since her aunt, Maisie Clark, retired at the age of seventy, and still she lacked the proper attitude for a servant. "Maisie knew her place," Ella had heard her mother say more than once. "But Bessie is much too fresh. She acts as if she thinks she's our equal." And it was a real bone of contention between Carolyn and Bessie that Bessie refused to live in as her aunt had done.

"Yes, ma'am." Bessie dumped the box on the table in front of Ella, right beside her plate of scrambled eggs and bacon.

The moment the housekeeper disappeared into the kitchen, Carolyn said, "Webb, we simply must find someone to replace that woman. She's totally unsuited to being a servant."

"Now, we've been through this before," Webb said. "Bessie is good at her job. She keeps this house spotless and she runs things like a well-oiled machine. She's a good cook, too. Almost as good as Maisie was. Just because she doesn't bow and scrape enough to suit you doesn't mean we need to replace her."

"She doesn't bow and scrape at all." Carolyn huffed.

Ella untied the red ribbon from around the white box, laid the ribbon on the table, and lifted the lid. "How beautiful." Red roses. Not her favorite, but beautiful all the same.

"That's odd. There isn't a florist label on the box," Ella said. "Our three local florists usually attach an identification sticker when they deliver flowers."

"Check for a card," Carolyn said. "The florist label may be on the card. I'm sure Dan used The Flower Box."

Yes, Ella thought. Of course Dan would use only The Flower Box, since it was the florist everyone in their social circle used. She wished Dan hadn't sent flowers. If he'd thought roses would soften her heart and make her more inclined to give their relationship a second chance, then he was wrong. He shouldn't have wasted his money.

What if they're not from Dan?

Ella's heartbeat accelerated. When she lifted the card from the box top, her hand trembled. Reed wouldn't send her flowers, would he? He didn't seem to be the romantic type. If they were from Reed, how would she ever explain to her parents? She could hardly say, "I almost made love with Reed in the woods at the park yesterday." She'd gotten very little sleep last night. Actually, she had been afraid to fall asleep, afraid she'd dream of Reed.

Dear God, what had she been thinking yesterday to have allowed things to get so out of hand? That was just the problem—she hadn't been thinking. She'd been feeling. The emotions Reed aroused in her were unlike anything she'd ever known. A hunger so great that she would have risked discovery, right there in the Sarah

Rogers Garden. She would have let Reed make love to her in the same way his cousin had made love to her aunt Cybil. But that kind of mating wasn't lovemaking. It was nothing more than screwing to release sexual tension.

"Aren't you going to read the card?" Carolyn asked.

"Huh? Oh, yes, of course." The small envelope in which the card was encased had her name typed on it. But there was no florist's label. She lifted the card out of the envelope and began to read aloud.

"Red roses for the sexiest woman in town. And a surprise to keep you guessing. This time, there's no harm. Next time—be prepared."

"What the hell kind of message is that?" Webb shoved back his chair, stood, and rounded the table. He grabbed the card out of Ella's hand. "The damn thing is typed."

"I don't understand," Carolyn said. "Why would Dan—"

"Hell, woman, don't be dense," Webb roared. "Dan Gilmore didn't send these."

Ella's hand hovered over the lovely flowers. A dozen perfect long-stemmed roses. Suddenly something slithered over the roses, weaving in and out around the stems. Ella gasped. What on earth?

"Daddy, I—I think there's something in this box." Her pulse drummed maddingly inside her head.

Webb grabbed the box away from her and dumped the contents onto the breakfast room floor. The roses fell apart, scattering across the hardwood surface. A green snake wriggled about at Webb's feet.

Carolyn screamed. Ella jumped out of her chair.

"God damn it!" Webb eyed the scaly creature, then reached down and picked it up.

"Webb, be careful!" Carolyn cried.

"It's nothing but a harmless garden snake," he

explained, then left the room, carrying the squirming serpent with him.

"This is Reed Conway's doing," Carolyn said. "I was afraid he wouldn't stop with letters and phone calls."

Ella whirled around and stared at her mother. "How did you find out about the letters and . . . Daddy and I didn't want you to know. Who told you?"

Carolyn glanced into her lap, averting direct eye contact.

"Viola somehow found out and told you, didn't she," Ella said. "She knew we didn't want you to worry."

Carolyn held out her hand beseechingly. "You mustn't be angry with Viola. You know I depend on her to keep me abreast of everything. She's been my most loyal confidante all these years. She understood that I had a right to know my daughter was being threatened."

"No one has actually threatened me. Harassed me, yes. Threatened me, no."

"What do you call sending someone a snake?" Carolyn glanced toward the closed door leading into the kitchen. "There's simply no way that Webb and I can go off to the Gulf and leave you here alone."

"No, Mother, y'all are not staying here. You look forward to this trip every year. I will not let you cancel your plans because of a stupid garden snake."

"A garden snake this time," Carolyn said. "But what about next time. He said this time, no harm. Next time—be prepared."

"This could have been someone's idea of a sick joke," Ella said. "It may have nothing to do with the letters and phone calls."

Webb stomped into the room. "I thought we'd agreed not to tell your mother about—"

"She didn't tell me," Carolyn explained. "I already knew."

"Viola." Webb groaned.

"We can't go to the Gulf now, Webb."

"I agree."

"No!" Ella flung out her arms, the palms of her hands open, in a gesture of exasperation. "Letters, phone calls, and a harmless garden snake aren't going to hurt me. I refuse to allow the person who is harassing me to scare me."

"The person who is harassing you?" Carolyn inquired. "You can't mean you think it's anyone other than Reed Conway."

"I don't know who it is, but we have no proof that it's Reed." Ella didn't dare say more, couldn't defend Reed and risk her parents' displeasure. *Displeasure? Get real, Ella. Outrage would be more like it.*

"He went a little too far with the prank he pulled today," Webb said. "Frank Nelson should be able to track down the florist those"—Webb eyed the flowers in the floor—"roses came from and find out if they have a record of who purchased them."

"Unless they're stolen," Carolyn said.

"What?" Webb and Ella piped in unison.

"Reed Conway killed a man. You don't honestly think that stealing flowers would be beneath him, do you?"

"I'm calling Frank," Webb said.

Ella laced her arm through her father's. "The flowers were probably purchased at Food Express or another grocery store. If that's the case, there won't be any record of who purchased them. So, go ahead and call Frank, but after you do that, put this problem in his hands. I insist that you and mother get in the car this morning and head for the Gulf as planned. I'll be perfectly all right here for a week without y'all. Aunt Cybil and Uncle Jeff Henry are right next door, and if I get lonely I'll spend a few nights with Heather."

Carolyn frowned. "Oh, dear. I suppose you're right. It's just that I shudder to think what might happen while we're gone."

"Nothing is going to happen. And if by some chance it does, I'll contact Frank immediately." Ella knew what this week at their family's cottage meant to her mother. Over the years, it had become an annual ritual.

"Maybe I'll pay Reed Conway a visit before we leave," Webb said.

"No, Daddy, don't do that. You'll lose your temper and there's no telling what might happen. You and Reed might come to blows. You don't want to go on vacation with a black eye, do you?"

"Someone needs to warn that man again." Webb clenched his hands into fists.

"If Reed needs warning again, let Frank do it. After all, it's his job." Ella patted her father's forearm. "Besides, how many times can Reed be given a warning when there's no proof that he's behind the harassment."

"We'll get the proof," Webb said. "And when we do, Reed will be heading straight back to prison."

"That's exactly where he belongs," Carolyn said.

Was Reed the person harassing her? Ella asked herself. She didn't believe he was. But what if she was wrong? What if he'd sent the letters, made the phone calls, left the flowers? What if pursuing her was part of his plan for vengeance?

She wouldn't see him again, wouldn't allow herself to be alone with him. He might excite her in a way no other man ever had, but he also frightened her in the same inexplicable way. No doubt about it—Reed was a dangerous man. Any smart woman would stay the hell away from him.

Cybil looked at herself in the bathroom mirror and groaned. Despite the face-lift she'd had three years ago when she turned forty-five, old age was catching up with her. Every day she noticed a new wrinkle, fine lines creeping up her neck and at the edges of her eyes. She ran her fingers through her tousled hair. If not for the monthly visit to her beautician, her black hair would be streaked with gray.

She filled a cup with water and rinsed out her mouth. The residue of one too many whiskey sours last night had left a bitter taste. At least her teeth were still good and all her own. She raked a hand down over her naked body, across her full breasts—not quite as pert as they'd once been, but not sagging either. Her hips were trim and her legs lean. She eased her hand between her thighs and rubbed her fingers over her feminine folds. Even though she'd begun menopause last year, she hadn't experienced any real problems. Her periods were erratic, but she had yet to have her first hot flash. And there were no problems with dryness. Thank God. She inserted her fingers into her body and strummed her thumb over her clitoris. Her nipples peaked. Moisture coated her inner folds.

Loud, repetitive tapping from outside her bedroom door ended her sensual musings. Damn, it was probably Judy, all fresh and cheerful. How the woman had anything to smile about, Cybil would never know. She was poor as a church mouse. She had slaved away five days a week as their housekeeper for the past twenty-odd years. She had an ex-con son who was nothing but trouble. She'd been married and widowed twice—once to a real louse who deserved killing more than anyone Cybil had ever known. In retrospect, Cybil admitted that her brief fling with Junior had been the biggest mistake of her life. Death had been too good for the likes of Junior Blalock. Someone should have tortured him for endless weeks before slitting his throat. Of course, she didn't have the stomach for torture herself. Murder, yes. Torture, no.

"Judy, just leave the tray outside and I'll get it later," Cybil called to the housekeeper.

"It isn't Judy," Jeff Henry said.

Cybil went deadly still. Her husband seldom bothered coming to her room anymore. If he came to her more often, she might not be inclined to seek out lovers elsewhere. And if Jeff Henry truly loved her, she'd swear off booze and other men altogether. But his loving her was about as sure to happen as Webb ever loving Carolyn again.

On her way out of the bathroom, she jerked a sheer black robe off the door rack and slipped into it, but didn't belt it. She opened her bedroom door to her husband, the front of her body boldly displayed for his view. He stood there with a breakfast tray in his hands. His gaze traveled the length of her, from head to toe. The expression on his face didn't alter, showing no sign of either disgust or arousal. But she detected a gleam in his eyes. He wasn't as immune to her charms as he'd like for her to believe.

"We need to talk," Jeff Henry said as he pushed past her to enter her private domain.

When was the last time he'd been in here? Hmm . . . Almost a year. She'd lured him in here on their wedding anniversary. After plying him with champagne to loosen him up a little, she had seduced him. He had been tenderly passionate. Jeff Henry was always a considerate lover.

"What could we possibly have to discuss?" she asked flippantly as she closed the bedroom door and turned to face him.

He set the tray on the writing desk by the windows overlooking the backyard. "I've been patient and understanding. I've excused your drinking binges and I've looked the other way when you've had affairs."

"How very noble of you, the poor cuckolded husband." She noticed how red his face was and thought it odd. Only when he was very hot or very angry or sexually aroused did a scarlet flush stain his face. "My goodness, something has your boxer shorts in a wad."

"I will not allow you to publicly shame yourself or me or our families." His broad, thick hands curled into fists. "We have an unspoken agreement, or at least I thought we did, that you're to keep your misconduct discreet."

"What the hell are you talking about?" Cybil sauntered across the room, lifted the silver dome from the plate, and inspected the pancakes dripping with butter and maple syrup.

Jeff Henry slapped the dome out of her hand. It hit the floor with a thud. "You're nothing but a slut."

"And just how is this news to you?"

Jeff Henry's eyes glimmered with pure rage. "I saw you yesterday. In the park, in the garden. You and that white trash grease monkey, Briley Joe Conway."

Cybil's mouth opened to a shocked oval. He'd seen her? With Briley Joe? No, no, no! They'd chosen a secluded spot, hidden behind shrubbery and a grove of trees. She'd been so sure no one could see them. "I'm sorry."

"You're sorry, all right. A sorry piece of nothing. But you know what makes it even worse? I wasn't alone when I came upon you and your lover. Ella was with me. Do you hear me? The child who means more to you than anyone in this world was with me, and she saw you screwing that low-life scum. He had you backed up against a tree, pumping into you like a jackhammer."

"Ella saw me?"

"She saw you and felt the same disgust that I did. How do you think she's going to feel about you now that she knows you'll spread your legs for any man?"

Pain washed over Cybil, drowning her with self-pity and self-loathing. The only person whose opinion still mattered to her was Ella's. She had loved her darling girl since the first moment she saw her, since the very instant she had held her in her arms.

"You, of course, told her what a slut I was, didn't you?" Cybil glowered at her husband. "You enjoyed filling her in on my legion of lovers. Did you tell her that I'd even screwed Junior Blalock?" She saw the truth in his eyes. "My God, you did, didn't you? You bastard!"

She slapped his face, anger and frustration riding her hard.

Jeff Henry grabbed her wrist and twisted her arm, painfully tugging her up against him. His nostrils flared. His eyes flashed. The red stain on his cheeks darkened even more. For the first time in a long time—not since the night Junior was killed—Cybil was afraid of her husband.

He dragged her to the bed and tossed her down atop the wrinkled satin coverlet. She watched anxiously, shocked by his actions. He unzipped his pristine khaki slacks. She shook her head in disbelief. He eased his hand inside the open zipper slit and into his boxer shorts. She scooted away from him. He jumped her, almost knocking the breath out of her. She glared up into his face, into his hard, cold eyes, and wondered who this man was. It wasn't Jeff Henry Carlisle, her well-bred Southern gentleman husband. He forced his knee between her legs and parted her thighs.

"What do you think you're doing?" she demanded.

"I'm going to fuck my wife," he told her.

Before a rational reply came to mind, he grabbed her hips, lifted her swiftly, and thrust into her, hard and deep. She moaned with unexpected pleasure. He pumped into her relentlessly, like a madman bent on breaking the spirit of the animal he rode. He lifted one hand to her breast and kneaded it roughly; then he lowered his mouth to hers and consumed her with a raging hunger.

Cybil wrapped her legs around his waist, lifting herself up to take all of him, to accept every pounding thrust. She caressed his buttocks, then slipped her hand between them and sought his scrotum. They mated wildly, passionately, Jeff Henry using her as if she'd been a whore he'd picked up for the night.

He climaxed first, jetting into her as he groaned and buried his face against her shoulder. The feel of his fluid bursting within her sent Cybil over the edge. A powerful orgasm shook her to her bones.

Without saying a word, Jeff Henry disengaged his body from hers. He lifted the edge of the satin sheet and cleaned himself with it. Then he stood, put his penis back in place, straightened his clothes, and walked toward the door.

"I'll bet that was one time you weren't thinking of my sister when you were screwing me," Cybil called after him.

He halted but didn't bother to glance back at her or respond in any way. He opened the door, went into the hall, and closed the door behind him.

Cybil lay on her back, not moving, her body still tingling as aftershocks of release rippled through her. Only one other time had she ever seen Jeff Henry so upset. Only one other time had he taken her with the same fury as he had this morning. And God help her, she'd loved it—then and now. This morning he had been angry enough to kill, just as he had been that other day. The day he'd caught her with Junior Blalock, less than eight hours before Junior had been found with his throat slit.

Chapter 14

Ella walked down Main Street, smiling and speaking to people on her short trek from the courthouse to Callahan's, three blocks away. She was meeting Dan for a farewell lunch. They had agreed that they wanted to part as friends. After all, they moved in the same social circles and were bound to run into each other on numerous occasions. And if Ella didn't miss her guess, it was only a matter of time before Heather zeroed in on Dan. Why the guy had never noticed her gorgeous redheaded friend, she didn't know. Back in high school, Heather had had a major crush on Dan. Of course, he'd been older and considered quite a catch. Dan was conservative to a fault. And Heather was liberal in the extreme. They'd probably mix like oil and water, but then again, opposites do attract. Case in point—Reed Conway and Ella Porter. Not in a million years would she ever have thought she'd be in a perpetual state of heat over a man like Reed. No, not a man *like* Reed. Just Reed.

No matter how much her body yearned for Reed, her mind warned her that he was dangerous, not to be trusted. Okay, so her instincts told her that he wasn't the person harassing her. But what if her instincts were wrong? Reed could very easily be coming on to her as part of some elaborate scheme of revenge against her father. After all, why would he want her? She couldn't possibly be his type. Even in high school, he'd gone for the flashy sexpots. She had to stay away from Reed. No good could come of getting involved with him.

She crossed the street at the red light. The restaurant was in the middle of the three-hundred block of Main Street. Checking her watch, she realized she was running five minutes late. Dan was a stickler for punctuality. She could see him now, waiting at Callahan's, his arms crossed over his chest, his right foot tapping impatiently against the floor.

As she approached the restaurant entrance, something up the street caught her attention. Reed Conway. Her stomach tightened. *He doesn't see you,* she told herself. *And if he looks this way, act as if you don't see him.* But for the life of her, she couldn't take her eyes off him. What was he doing? He reached inside the pocket of his T-shirt, pulled out a folded envelope, and spread it apart. Ella's heart caught in her throat. He went straight to the mailbox on the corner, lifted the metal flap, and dropped in the envelope.

He's mailing a letter. A letter in a white envelope. Another threatening love letter to her? *No, please, no.* Even if she couldn't surrender to the temptation and become lovers with Reed, she didn't want him to be her stalker. *Please, let him be innocent.*

Do not let your imagination run away with you. Just because Reed mailed a white envelope does not mean the content is a letter to you. It could be a bill he's paying. A letter he dropped off for his mother. A business letter of some sort for Conway's Garage.

But if she got another letter—tomorrow—she would know there was a very good chance that it had came from Reed. But why would he mail this one? The others had been hand delivered, hadn't they?

Her mind swirled with concern as she reached for the handle of Callahan's front entrance. But the door swung open, almost knocking her over.

"I was concerned that something had happened," Dan Gilmore said. "You're late."

Ella sighed deeply. So predictable. So typical of Dan. "Yes, I know and I apologize. But I'm here now."

"So you are."

When Dan slipped his arm around her waist, she started to pull away, but instead she glanced over her shoulder. Her gaze traveled down the street to where Reed Conway stood by the mailbox. Reed nodded, acknowledging that he knew she'd seen him. And then he smiled. Damn him! He actually smiled. As if he were saying, "You saw me mailing a white envelope and I don't care what you think."

Ella quickly averted her gaze and focused on Dan. "Having lunch together today was a wonderful idea. I certainly want us to remain friends."

The moment Ella Porter turned to her lunch date, the smile on Reed's face vanished. His gaze was riveted to where Dan Gilmore's arm circled Ella's waist. He wanted to walk down the street, rip her way from the man, toss her over his shoulder, and carry her off to the nearest private corner. Ever since yesterday afternoon when they'd come so close to making love in the park, he had been unable to think of anything or anyone else. He could have gone to Ivy again and worked off his desire for Ella. He could have, but he hadn't. And he wasn't going to. Screwing Ivy might ease some sexual tension, but only temporarily. The frustration would stay with him, and the moment he thought about Ella again, the desire would return. The only woman who could ease his suffering was Ella Porter herself.

Yeah, and hell will freeze over before she ever lets you get near her again!

The moment Ella and Dan disappeared inside Callahan's, Reed walked up the street and went directly behind them into the restaurant. The hostess was showing them to their table when Reed took a stool at the bar. He could see them from his vantage point, since the bar area was four steps up from the restaurant. He ordered a Coke and popped a few peanuts into his mouth. Striving to act as nonchalant as possible, he eased his sunglasses off, slipped them into his T-shirt pocket, and spied on the couple at the corner table.

He had allowed Ella to become a distraction. That wasn't good. His purpose in returning to Spring Creek rather than trying to start over in another town was to search for Junior's real killer. He'd known it wouldn't be easy, that it might even prove an impossible task. After all, Junior hadn't been a very likable guy. He'd had a lot of enemies. Just about anybody who knew him was suspect.

But someone—maybe the real killer—was running scared. He wanted Reed back in prison, not free to snoop around into the past. Without realizing it, that person was actually helping Reed. It might be impossible to solve a fifteen-year-old murder, but it should be easier to solve an ongoing harassment case.

He had to stop thinking of Ella as a desirable woman and start thinking of her as a means to an end. If he could find a way to convince her that he wasn't her stalker, he might be able to persuade her to let him help her unearth the person behind the phone calls and letters. But working together meant spending time together, and he wasn't sure he could do that and keep his hands off her.

You're jumping the gun. You don't know that she would ever agree to cooperate with you. Just look at her over there with her boyfriend. All smiles. And he's holding her hand!

Reed didn't like the feelings Ella brought out in him: a hunger that he couldn't satisfy with another woman, and a raging jealousy unlike anything he'd ever known.

What the hell was it about her? She was pretty enough, but not the most beautiful woman he'd ever known. She had a lush, full figure, but not a perfect form. She was the last woman on earth he should even think about messing with. *For pity's sake, she's Webb Porter's daughter.* And what would happen if he wound up proving that her father killed Junior? *She'd really hate you then.*

Of course, he didn't know for sure Webb had killed Junior, but Webb had always been right up there at the top of his personal list of suspects. Junior had been the one who'd told Reed that he had some information that the Porter family wouldn't want to get out. He could still hear Junior laughing.

"That family's got more than one dirty little secret and I know what those secrets are," Junior had said. "What you want to bet they'd pay through the nose to keep me quiet? With some of Webb Porter's and Jeff Henry Carlisle's money, I could move us out of this rat hole."

Had Junior been blackmailing Webb? If not Webb, then maybe Jeff Henry, or possibly Cybil. All Reed knew was that just about everyone in Ella's family might have had reason to want Junior dead.

Reed lifted his Coke from the bar and downed half of it in one long, thirsty swig. He wiped his mouth with the back of his hand, then glanced at the table where Ella sat. Dan was no longer holding her hand. She wasn't laughing. She wasn't even smiling. And she certainly wasn't gazing at Dan Gilmore as if she wanted to rip off his clothes and have her way with him. No, she wasn't looking at good old Dan the way she had looked at the town bad boy she feared, the man who made her tremble and whimper. Remembering the way Ella had come unglued in his arms yesterday was arousing him all over again.

Get the hell out of here while you can still get up and walk without showing off a prominent woody. He paid for his drink, then stood and walked over to the edge of the bar area. After a farewell glance, he started to reverse directions and head out the front door, but Ella glanced up at that precise moment and saw him. Her eyes widened. Her mouth rounded. A telltale pink flush tinged her cheeks.

She might be dating Mr. Suit-and-tie, but Reed would lay odds that he wasn't the man she'd dreamed about last night. Oh, no. Reed would bet his last dime that she'd never creamed her pants when Dan Gilmore kissed her. But she'd been dripping after he'd kissed her yesterday.

Mark paid the delivery boy and gave him a generous tip. He took the bag filled with their supper into his office, where Regina was busy clearing away the files stacked on his desk. He'd had to ask her to work overtime tonight to help him prepare for a big case that went to trial next week. She had dutifully volunteered to help him over the upcoming weekend, to assist him in any way he needed her. They had sent his secretary, Cara, home four hours ago, at five-thirty, and the two of them had been hard at it ever since. But twenty minutes ago, Regina had taken time out to order them a meal from the Spring Creek Cafe, a local fast food place that stayed open and delivered until midnight on Friday and Saturday nights.

"Just leave those books," Mark said. "I'll put them back in the case later." He laid the paper sack on his desk and nodded to the computer on Regina's desk in the adjoining room. "Did you save everything to disk?"

"I always save everything to disk. And you always ask me if I did." She opened the sack, pulled out the paper napkins and spread two of them to create place settings, then removed the wrapped food.

When Regina smiled at him, his stomach flip-flopped. She was breathtakingly beautiful. Tiny and delicate, with an air of fragility about her that made him want to wrap her in soft cotton and protect her from anything and anyone that might harm her. Lately Regina made him feel like a tongue-tied teenage boy with raging hormones. He'd been wanting to ask her for a date for months now, but hadn't worked up the courage. He knew she didn't date, so what made him think she'd make an exception for him?

"I was wondering if you think you're actually going to be able to help Reed," Regina said as she placed the sandwiches, chips and cookies on the napkins.

Slightly taken aback by her question, Mark gaped at her without responding immediately. Where had that come from? he wondered. Didn't she and Reed talk? Hadn't they discussed the situation since Reed's release from prison?

"I hope you realize that I've done everything in my power to help him," Mark told her. "My father tried his best for years. He used every legal means at his disposal to have Reed's case appealed. And he tried to persuade the powers-that-be to reopen the case."

"My mother is concerned about Reed," Regina said. "She . . . we know about the letters and the phone calls to Ella Porter. And we know that Webb Porter is convinced that Reed is the person harassing his daughter. The Porter and Carlisle families are the most powerful in this county. They can make things hard for Reed. Mama is afraid Reed will do something out of anger and wind up getting his parole revoked."

"We all know Reed isn't the person harassing Ella," Mark said. "And I think I've convinced Ella that he isn't the one."

"Are you saying that Ella Porter believes Reed is innocent?"

Mark sat down in the chair behind his desk. "I'm saying Ella has an open mind in the matter. She's willing to give Reed the benefit of the doubt."

Regina pulled up a chair to the side of Mark's desk

and reached for a sandwich. "Do you really think there's any way to prove Reed didn't kill Junior?"

"The only way to prove Reed innocent is to find the real killer." Mark ripped open his bag of potato chips.

"If the police didn't find any other suspects fifteen years ago, then how are you and Reed going to come up with any now?"

"The police didn't look for other suspects. They arrested Reed almost immediately after Junior was murdered and pretty much closed the case then and there."

"A lot of people hated Junior," Regina said, then bit into her chicken salad sandwich.

"Yeah, from my research, I'd say the list is endless."

Mark studied the expression on Regina's face. Serene. Unemotional. Totally calm. One would think that discussing Junior Blalock had no effect on her whatsoever, that he hadn't tried to rape her when she was just a child.

"I suppose Mama and I would head that list." Regina's gaze met Mark's, a soulful look in her eyes. "We had more reason to hate him than anyone. He mistreated her, you know. He'd come home drunk and hit her. He and Reed fought all the time. And Reed stayed angry with Mama because she wouldn't leave him." Regina shook her head. "For better or worse—that's what Mama would say. She believed marriage vows were sacred."

"Those must have been terrible times for you and your family."

Mark couldn't begin to imagine such horrors. He'd grown up in a fairly normal family: a father, a mother, an older sister. He supposed he'd never truly appreciated how good he'd had it growing up, or how lucky he'd been to have had a father he not only loved but respected. He missed his dad a great deal.

What would it have been like living in a household

with a drunken, abusive stepfather? Mark's own father had been a gentle, soft-spoken man who would have sooner cut off his right hand than strike his wife.

"Mama didn't kill Junior," Regina said as she laid her sandwich back on the napkin spread out atop Mark's desk. "She's not capable of murder. And even if she were, she wouldn't have let Reed go to prison for a crime she had committed."

"I've never considered your mother a suspect." Mark lifted his tuna melt sandwich and took a large bite.

"What about me? Have you ever considered me a suspect?"

Mark nearly choked on his food. He swallowed, coughed a couple of times, and stared at Regina. "You were just a kid. Only eleven."

"Junior was drunk that night and Reed had beaten him senseless. It wouldn't have taken much strength to slit his throat, not with him practically unconscious. I could easily have taken Reed's knife and—"

Mark shot to his feet, dropped his sandwich on the table and reached out to grab Regina by the shoulders. "You didn't kill Junior."

"No, I don't think I did. But I could have. I hated him enough. I wanted him dead. When he was touching me, I prayed for God to strike him dead."

Mark pulled Regina to her feet and into his arms. She made no protest, accepting his comfort willingly. "If I'd known you then, if I'd been there at the time, I'd have wanted to kill him myself. I can't bear to think about what you went through at the hands of that monster."

Regina tensed in his arms. She pulled away from him and looked at him point-blank. "A man could never be with a woman, knowing . . . knowing she'd been violated the way I was, without thinking about what had happened. Any decent man would never want me."

Mark couldn't believe what he'd heard. Was this the

way she truly felt? No wonder she never dated. Did she think that no man could see beyond the abuse she had endured to appreciate the special woman she was?

"Regina, do you consider me a decent man?"

"What?" She stared at him quizzically.

"Do you consider me—"

"Yes, of course. You're one of the most decent men I know. A good and honest man."

Even if she rejected him, Mark knew that now was the time to be honest with Regina, to admit to her how he truly felt about her. "Then I know one decent man who wants you. He wants you very much."

Her eyes rounded in large blue-centered circles. "You . . . you want me?"

Did he dare touch her again? He wanted to wrap her in his arms and hold her, keep her safe, and banish all the bad memories. He had to touch her, but only a tender caress with the back of his hand across her cheek. "I'm not quite sure when it happened, but some time in the past few months, I started falling in love with you."

"Oh, Mark. I—I . . . I don't know if I can ever . . . I might not be able to give you what a man needs from a woman. Even with all the therapy I went through when I was a teenager, I'm still not a whole person."

"All I want is for you to give me a chance. Give us a chance. Do you think you can do that? Do you even want to?" He searched her eyes for any indication of what she was thinking. "You might not feel the same way about me as I do you. If that's the case, then I understand and—"

"I do," she whispered. Tears glistened in her eyes. Her lips lifted into a soft smile. "I feel the same about you."

His heart sighed with relief. Excitement and anticipation swirled through him. Regina cared about him.

"We'll take things slow and easy. We'll start out with a first date. No pressure, no expectations. How does that sound?"

"A date?" Her smile widened. "That sounds wonderful."

"How about tomorrow night? We'll leave the office in time to go out for dinner and then a late movie. And when I take you home, it'll be up to you whether I get a good-night kiss or not."

Impulsively Regina kissed him on the cheek, then jumped back away from him. He wanted to kiss her properly. He wanted to show her what it could be like between a man and a woman who cared for each other, who truly wanted each other. But he had promised her to take their courtship one step at a time. He would keep that promise, even if it killed him. He had to hold on to the hope that someday Regina would be able to fully give herself to him. She was a prize worth waiting for, and he would wait as long as necessary. Until she came to him. In the meantime, he'd take a lot of cold showers and pray for strength.

No more letters—at least not for now—and no more breathy phone calls. Those simple tactics weren't getting the job done. Of course the green snake in the roses had been little more than a practical joke—one staged merely to lay the groundwork for the next step in the harassment of Ella Porter.

One couldn't rush these things, despite the fact that the longer Reed Conway remained a free man, the more likely the chances that the truth about Junior Blalock's murder would come out. Of course, that could not be allowed to happen. However, framing Reed couldn't be rushed, or someone might get suspicious. This had to be handled delicately, one step at a time. So far, no one had been harmed. No damage had been done. Perhaps it was time to change all that. Unsettle things a bit more. Get Reed into deeper trouble.

And what better time to escalate the harassment than while Ella's parents were out of town?

Chapter 15

Ella came home that evening as she had every evening since her parents departed for the Gulf almost a week ago, but she would spend the night—again—with her aunt and uncle next door. She'd thought it overcautious on her father's part, insisting that she not spend the nights alone at home while they were out of town. But to pacify him, she had finally agreed. She had always felt safe in the big house on East First Street, and despite the recent harassment, she still felt safe here. She owned a gun and knew how to use it. Her father had taught her as a teenager about the safe use of firearms. And the hunting dogs her father kept would wake the dead if an intruder came anywhere near the house during the night. But to make her parents happy, every night she trekked down the sidewalk and went next door to sleep at Aunt Cybil and Uncle Jeff Henry's house. Then, each morning she returned home to shower and dress for the day.

But today had been an especially tiring day, and she longed to take a long soak in her bathtub and crawl into her own bed. Maybe she'd phone her aunt and tell her that she wasn't going to stay over tonight. Surely just one night alone at home wouldn't upset her father. Actually, there was no need for him to know.

Although she had encouraged her parents to get away for a week, she missed them. Perhaps being lonely for one's parents at the ripe old age of thirty was a sure sign that you had no real life of your own. Nothing except work.

Ella hiked her briefcase under her arm, shoved back her shoulder bag, and inserted the key into the lock. After opening the front door, she stepped inside, flipped on the overhead light in the foyer and turned toward the spiral staircase. That was when she noticed the gilt-framed mirror over the eighteenth-century flame veneer commode. Large cracks spread out across the antique mirror from a circular break in the very center, as if a hard object had smashed into the glass. Or perhaps a fist. A big, strong fist.

A rumble of uneasiness spread through Ella's body. Who had broken the mirror? And when had it happened? Ordering herself to remain calm, she backed toward the closed front door, her gaze traveling in a crescent, left, front, and right, then back again. The wide expanse of foyer in front of her that spanned the depth of the entire house lay in semidarkness, as did the dining room on the left, with only a soft glow of evening twilight coming through the windows. To her left, illumination from the streetlight directly outside blended with the fading sunlight and seeped through the sheer curtains into the room. Just enough light for Ella to see that no one lay in wait for her, unless they were hiding behind a large piece of furniture.

As she glanced into the living room, she noticed the fireplace. Above the Italian blue marble mantle, the portraits of her father's parents had been defaced with hideous black X marks. A shocked cry caught in her throat. Then she noted, in quick succession, the overturned chairs, the broken vases and figurines, and the pillows tossed haphazardly over the floor, every one ripped apart. She stood frozen, unable to move as the enormity of the ransacking began to sink in. Someone had totally destroyed the living room.

Damn! Her gun was upstairs in her bedside table. Naturally, she couldn't take it to work with her. And her father's rack of hunting rifles was in the den, locked in a display case. What about Daddy's handgun? The one he kept in his desk in the library? *Forget about defending yourself if someone is in the house,* she told herself. *Your best course of action is to get out of here as quickly as possible.*

Run, dammit, Ella, run! He could still be in the house. Her heartbeat thundered inside her head as her pulse raced at breakneck speed. Fear clutched her stomach, knotting it painfully. Bitter bile rose in her throat. The fright encasing her limbs melted suddenly. She ran toward the front door. Just as her hand touched the doorknob, the loud, ferocious yapping of her father's hunting dogs in the kennel on the far side of the backyard startled her. Her briefcase dropped from under her arm and landed on the heart-of-pine foyer floor with a dull thud.

She struggled with the brass doorknob, her palms damp with sweat. It was as if her hands were covered with grease, preventing her from gripping the knob. Whoever had wreaked such havoc inside her home was undoubtedly still on the premises—in the yard. The dogs had either heard him, seen him, or sensed him. Was he running away? Or simply lying in wait?

Finally the doorknob turned. Ella flung open the door and rushed out into the humid summer night. Streaks of heat lighting flashed through the twilight sky. Ella ran down the herringbone brick sidewalk and out onto the street, glancing over her shoulder as she went. Expecting what? A demon to be chasing her? But there was no one.

She arrived on her aunt and uncle's doorstep, out of

breath, her chest aching, her nerves screaming. The moment Cybil opened the front door, Ella flung herself into her aunt's arms.

"My God, Ella, what's wrong?"

Breathless, panting, she tried to speak. "House. Break-in. Still there."

Cybil cried out, "Jeff Henry!"

Ella slung her shoulder bag around, unzipped the side pouch, and rifled the contents, searching for her cell phone. "Have to call the police."

Cybil clasped Ella's shoulders and gave her a gentle shake.

"Calm down, darling girl. You're safe."

Ella jerked her phone out of her purse, hit the instant emergency button, and placed the phone to her ear. As she listened to the ringing, her heartbeat slowed to a more normal rate. Here within the safety of her aunt's home, she tried to free herself from the fear that had overwhelmed her in her own house.

The 911 operator answered and Ella told him who she was and what had happened. She was assured a police car was on its way. Cybil yelled a second time for her husband, then put her arm around Ella's shoulder.

"Come on in the den with me. I'll get us both a drink."

Ella nodded agreement and allowed her aunt to guide her into the large antique-filled den that looked just as it had every summer of Ella's childhood. She'd always suspected that very little had been altered in Uncle Jeff Henry's lifetime. The sofa and chairs wore white cotton slipcovers for the summer, and the heavy winter drapes had been replaced with white dimity. Cabbage-rose wallpaper and a bold-print English Wilton carpet added color to the otherwise drab room.

Odd, Ella thought, what one noticed, what one's mind was able to process even in the throes of near-panic. Of course, she wasn't feeling quite as panicky as she had only a few minutes earlier.

"What in tarnation is all that screeching about?" Jeff Henry demanded as he stormed into the room. Wearing a satin smoking jacket and puffing on a pipe, he epitomized the lord-of-the-manor stereotype—an irate lord of the manor at the moment. When he saw Ella, his expression softened. "Is something wrong, my dear? You look quite pale."

"Someone broke into the house . . . my house." Ella patted her chest with her fingertips. "The living room has been ransacked, perhaps the entire house. I don't know. I didn't get any farther than the foyer before I ran."

"Dear Lord!" Jeff Henry rushed to Ella's side so that he and Cybil flanked their niece. "We must call Frank Nelson immediately."

"I've already called nine-one-one," Ella said.

"Yes, yes. Quite. But Frank should be notified. The break-in and destruction is no doubt the work of that hoodlum, Reed Conway. He's a dangerous man. We all know that he should be behind bars. Thank God you didn't encounter him. No telling what he might have done to you."

Reed? Her uncle believed that Reed was the culprit? The thought hadn't crossed her mind. But why should it? Only if she still believed him to be her stalker, the person bent on tormenting her, would she consider him a suspect.

"It isn't fair to automatically condemn Reed Conway," Ella said, and was surprised that she'd actually voiced her opinion aloud. "There's no evidence linking him to anything that's happened. Not the letters or the phone calls or the green garden snake in the roses."

"Who else would it be?" Jeff Henry led Ella over to the sofa. "Do sit down, dear."

"I'll get you some brandy." Cybil hurried to the makeshift bar set up on the antique tea caddy.

"Liquor—your aunt's solution to everything," Jeff Henry grumbled, then sat beside Ella. "All these problems started the very week that man was released from prison. He had sworn revenge against Webb. He's a murderer, capable of anything. And I well remember what a cocky, ill-mannered hellion he was as a teenager. Take my word for it, he's the person behind your harassment. And now this break-in."

Cybil held a crystal goblet. "This should soothe your nerves."

Ella grasped the glass, sniffed the liquor, and lifted the brandy to her lips. Mellow and rich. Expensive. Uncle Jeff Henry purchased only the best. A family trait for generations, or so she'd heard him say. Only the best for the Carlisles. But he had settled for second-best in a wife, Ella thought; then she shivered as the smooth brandy burned a trail down her throat and coated her stomach like a toasty-warm liquid blanket.

Jeff Henry rose to his feet. "I'll contact Frank immediately. Then I'm getting in touch with Webb—"

Ella grabbed her uncle's arm. "No, please, don't call Daddy tonight. Let him and Mother have one more night on the Gulf. We'll phone them tomorrow to let them know what happened."

"Very well," Jeff Henry agreed. "No need upsetting Carolyn at this point. She'll be heartsick as it is, but by morning Frank should have Reed Conway in jail and that will put an end to all this craziness."

Ella nodded, then glanced at her aunt. Cybil's features hardened to a pinched, pained expression at the mention of her sister. The look passed as quickly as it had appeared. Only a woman who cared about a man would be jealous. Was it possible that despite her adulterous affairs, her aunt actually loved her husband?

Although Uncle Jeff Henry insisted that he could handle matters without her, Ella insisted on going with him when the police car arrived. Before the two officers got past the foyer, Frank Nelson showed up and began issuing orders. He warned Ella and Jeff Henry to stay outside out of harm's way; then he followed his men into the house. Shortly thereafter another police car arrived and two uniformed officers—one man and one woman—began a search of the grounds. And all the while her daddy's hounds kept baying as if they'd treed something.

Had they? she wondered. No, of course not. The dogs were confined to the kennels, which were within a fenced area. Their howling chant unnerved Ella almost as much as the situation. And unbidden flashes of Reed Conway played inside her head: Reed running, chased by the police, hunted down, captured. And all the while he kept insisting he was innocent.

Ella shook her head in an effort to erase those horrific thoughts from her mind. She didn't want Reed to be the culprit. She couldn't bear the thought of him being her stalker. But she had suspected him, even if for only a moment, last week when she'd seen him mailing a plain white envelope. But she hadn't received another letter. *So there,* she told herself, *doesn't that prove that it isn't Reed?*

By the time Frank Nelson rejoined them, Cybil had walked over from next door and stood several feet away beside the tall live-oak tree in the front yard. Wearing an above-the-knee black silk robe, she all but gave the chief of police a come-hither stare. Frank looked. What man wouldn't? He cleared his throat.

"Evening, Cybil," Frank said.

Cybil saluted him with the brandy snifter in her hand, then put the glass to her lips and drank slowly, seductively. Frank hurriedly turned his attention to Ella.

"There's no one in the house," Frank said. "My people are still searching the grounds and will do a thorough check of the neighborhood." Frank turned to Ella. "I'm afraid several of the downstairs rooms were totally trashed. An act of senseless violence. The way things look, you'd think somebody just went completely berserk. From my experience, I'd say it's someone who hates your family."

"Find Reed Conway and you'll have your man," Jeff Henry said.

"We'll check the house for any kind of evidence the intruder might have inadvertently left behind, including fingerprints," Frank assured them. "And if Reed Conway—"

"*If?*" Jeff Henry's face turned red. "Good God, man, who else would have done something so despicable?"

"I can't arrest a man without evidence," Frank said. "And I know that with Reed's prison record and his publicly acknowledged hatred for Senator Porter, he's the most likely suspect."

"Even without any evidence, I'd think you could lean on the man a little, now couldn't you, Frank?"

"I can speak to him," Frank said. "Find out if he has an alibi for the approximate time of the break-in. Uh, by the way, Ella, why don't y'all have a security system?"

"A security system?" Ella sighed. "To be honest, I don't believe my parents thought a security system was necessary. After all, the crime rate in Spring Creek is very low and all the doors in the house have very secure locks. And as you know, everyone in my home carries a gun permit, even Viola." Ella directed her gaze at Frank. "How did he break in?"

"Through the French doors that lead from the living room to the side porch," Frank said. "Look, Ella, if I were you, I'd go on home with your uncle and then in the morning call your insurance agent. I assume y'all have coverage with Steve Williamson. I can even contact him for you, if you'd like."

She nodded. Of course their insurance agent was Steve Williamson. Everyone who lived on East First Street, indeed almost everyone in her parents' social circle, used the same doctor, dentist, and insurance agent. And their memberships were equally divided between two churches in town—the Presbyterian and the Methodist. There were a few Baptists and Episcopalians among her parents' friends, but only a handful.

Ella's grandfather Porter had once been a partner in Williamson and Porter, the local insurance company now operated by Steven Williamson IV. Her father retained his father's half ownership of the business, which added greatly to the Porters' yearly income.

"You'll let me know when you find the person who broke in and ransacked the house." Ella gazed at the three-story structure that had been home to several generations of Porters.

"I certainly will," Frank said. "I'll even post a man to keep watch here tonight, until the pane in the French door is fixed. And I intend to speak to Senator Porter about having a security system installed after this."

"Yes, you do that," she said. "It's obvious to me now that even here in Spring Creek decent citizens aren't safe in their own homes."

Her uncle draped his arm around her shoulders and escorted her up the sidewalk. Ella wanted to scream at the injustice of it all. She'd been on the bench for only a short period of time, but she had presided over numerous criminal cases. She saw the dregs of local society and heard their excuses for committing crimes ranging from marijuana possession to child molestation. It wasn't as if she were some naive innocent who wasn't aware of what went on in the world, even in a rural county like Bryant. But seldom did bad things happen to people in her social realm. For the most part, her parents and their peers seemed immune to the woes that plagued ordinary people. She supposed that, as their child, she, too, had subconsciously felt that she was protected.

But you aren't their child, she reminded herself. Not their biological child. Ella didn't spend much time worrying about who her natural parents were or why her mother had chosen to give her up for adoption. When she'd been in her late teens, she'd considered looking into the possibility of finding out more about the woman and man who had created her. But Carolyn had assured her that her natural parents had been "our kind."

"Your father has all the information about their medical records and education and backgrounds," Carolyn had said. "Your biological parents weren't married, and your mother—your first mother—decided it was best to allow a married couple to raise you. The adoption was handled privately, between her and us. Milton Leamon took care of everything for us. We never met the woman . . . your other mother."

"Was money exchanged?" Ella had asked, wondering if her natural mother had sold her.

"If you're asking if we bought you—if we paid your mother—the answer is no."

Cybil joined Ella and Jeff Henry on their trek back to the Carlisle house. The moment they went inside, Jeff Henry gave his wife a disapproving glance, his gaze fixed on the empty brandy snifter in her hand.

"Why don't you go on up and take a bath and get ready for bed," Jeff Henry told Ella. "You must be exhausted after all that's happened."

"Thanks. I think I will." She kissed her uncle's cheek, then went to her aunt and gave her a hug.

Cybil reciprocated. "I'm so glad you're all right, darling girl."

Practically running up the stairs, Ella left her aunt and uncle, whose voices carried so that she could hear their quarrel until she rushed into the bedroom and closed the door behind her. Even when she'd been a child, she had been aware of her aunt and uncle's arguments and had even asked her mother about them.

"You and Daddy don't ever argue," Ella had said. "Why do Aunt Cybil and Uncle Jeff Henry fuss at each other all the time?"

"Your father and I love each other and don't have anything to argue about," Carolyn had explained. "Unfortunately, your aunt and uncle aren't always nice to each other and sometimes they hurt each other's feelings. That's when they get into a fuss. If they loved each other . . ."

Ella remembered that odd, distant look in her mother's eyes when she had allowed her train of thought to wander off. Ella had always wondered why her aunt and uncle had married if they didn't love each other. She had sworn then and there that she would never marry for any other reason, that she wanted a love like her parents had. Of course, since then she had come to realize that even her parents' marriage wasn't perfect. But despite everything, they still loved each other.

Didn't they?

Cybil paced the floor in her bedroom. The grandfather clock on the landing in the center of the divided staircase chimed eleven o'clock. She gazed down into the dark amber liquid as she swirled the brandy in her glass. This was her third drink. No, maybe it was her fourth. Whichever, she'd had enough so that she felt very little pain. Actually, she felt very little of anything. And that was the way she liked it. If Ella weren't here, she'd call Briley Joe and ask him to meet her at the motel over on River Road, which was on the other side of Smithville, the closest town to Spring Creek. But she wouldn't leave, not on the off chance her niece might need her.

Her niece. Ella. The person she loved more dearly than anyone on earth.

Cybil downed the last of the brandy, set the glass on the bedside table, and then headed for the door. After opening the door, she secured the belt of her robe with unsteady fingers as she made her way down the hall. She eased open the door to Ella's room. Her niece lay curled in a ball, fast asleep, her hair spread out on the pale pink pillowcase like black silk. Moonlight washed the room with transparent gold.

Cybil tiptoed into the room, which they had called

Ella's room since the first time Ella had spent the night with them. She'd been two years old and by night's end had wound up in bed with Cybil, who had stayed awake the rest of the night just looking at the precious child. Having Ella was the closest she would ever come to motherhood.

Cybil stood at the foot of the bed and stared at her niece. If she could have given Jeff Henry a child, would he have loved her? She would never know, of course. There had never been even the slightest possibility for them.

What do you think of me, Ella, my darling girl? Cybil asked silently. *That I'm a drunk and a slut? Are you as ashamed of me as Carolyn is? As Jeff Henry is? You've never said, never implied that you were. I didn't want to disappoint you. Truly I didn't. I foolishly thought that you'd never have to know what a terrible person I am.*

Cybil sensed someone else's presence. She glanced sidelong at the shadow hovering in the doorway. She took one last look at Ella and quietly walked out of the room, passing her husband, who eased the door shut.

"Is she all right?" Jeff Henry asked.

"Yes, she's sleeping like a baby." Cybil staggered awkwardly down the hall.

Jeff Henry came up beside her and slipped his hand beneath her elbow. She looked right at him. Tears welled up in her eyes.

"She should have been ours," Cybil said, her voice a slurred whisper.

"Yes, you're right. She should have been ours."

Jeff Henry assisted Cybil to her room, helped her off with her robe and then into bed. She lay there naked, her husband only a few feet away. She held open her arms to him, inviting him. She could barely make out his face through the sheen of tears in her eyes. When she blinked the tears away, she noted the melancholy expression on his face.

He leaned over and kissed her forehead. "Get some sleep." Then he turned and walked out of the room.

Cybil flung herself over onto her stomach, grabbed her pillow, and buried her face in its softness. Sobs racked her body as she cried herself to sleep.

Chapter 16

Reed dumped his duffle bag on the floor, then took a long, hard look at the room. Nothing fancy, that was for sure, but it was four walls around him and a roof over his head. His mother had asked him not to leave, but he'd convinced her that moving out on his own was the best thing for all of them. He felt smothered living with his mother. No man his age should live with his mother. Part of being free was not having to report in to anyone, not having to tell somebody what time you'd be home and explain where you'd been or who you'd been with.

Damn lucky for him that the room above Conway's Garage was empty. There was a bathroom of sorts, with a shower that produced only cold water. For now, cold showers were okay. The weather was hot and Reed was even hotter. Hot and bothered over Ella Porter. Go figure. Of course, before winter he'd have to put in a new water heater. And by then he'd either have had Miss Ella in his bed, or he would have found another way to get her out of his system.

He'd spent the past four hours working his new place

into shape. He had swept, dusted, mopped, and aired out the fifteen-by-fifteen-foot square, and he'd scrubbed the toilet, sink, and shower stall. The only windows in the room ran the length of the back wall and overlooked an alley that separated the garage from the back wall of the building that had once housed the local theater. The hot summer air had cooled a fraction. The overhead ceiling fan, a relic from the past that whined and moaned with each rotation, whipped the warm, humid breeze and spread it throughout the room.

He'd borrowed bedding from his mother for the ancient metal bed. The tan sheets looked cool and crisp and inviting. He was bone weary after working all day and then cleaning his new abode before moving in. Living here should work out just fine. Since he didn't own a car and had to borrow one from Briley Joe whenever he couldn't get where he was going on foot, being this close to work saved him a long walk in the mornings and evenings.

Reed removed his dirty shirt and tossed it into the plastic clothes basket he'd picked up along with numerous other items at the local Dollar Store on his lunch break today. *Be it ever so humble,* he thought as he headed toward the tiny bathroom. He'd been out of prison for only a few weeks, and the heady sense of freedom still seemed new to him. In a way, he was almost afraid to rock the boat, to create any waves. But on the other hand, he felt that things were moving too slowly. Every day that passed was one more day that Junior Blalock's real killer had an opportunity to find a way to put Reed back in jail. But solving a fifteen-year-old murder wasn't an easy task. Especially not in a town like Spring Creek, where everyone believed him guilty and the police had never investigated any other suspects. Mark's father and then Mark had tried unsuccessfully to have the case reopened. And years ago, Reed's last appeal had changed nothing.

He'd gone over the possible suspects time and again,

but everyone had an alibi. Of course, considering how many people detested Junior, there was always the chance that someone with a hidden motive might have taken the opportunity to slit the semiconscious man's throat. Reed had ruled out his mother and his sister. Even though both of them had had motive and opportunity, neither would have let him go to prison. But Regina seemed to recall only bits and pieces of that horrible night. Was it possible that she'd taken Reed's knife, killed her attacker, and then couldn't remember what she'd done? If Regina were the killer, Reed knew he'd go to his grave keeping her secret.

But there were more plausible suspects, people in power who could have easily used their influence to keep the law from probing deeper into the crime. First and foremost, Webb Porter came to mind. If he hadn't killed Junior for reasons of his own, perhaps he did the deed as a service for his family. Reed suspected that Junior had tried blackmailing more than one member of the Porter and Carlisle families. There were dozens of possible scenarios. He wasn't quite sure how to go about untangling such an intricate web of lies and secrets.

Just as Reed walked into the six-by-six bathroom and unzipped his jeans, a loud, demanding series of knocks sounded on the outer door. *Who the hell?* He glanced at the old windup alarm clock he had brought from his mother's. Eleven-thirty! Who would be beating down his door at this time of night?

Reed zipped up his pants, crossed the room, and called out, "Hold your horses." When he reached the door, he hollered, "Who is it?"

"Chief Nelson. Open up, Reed. We need to talk."

Reed flung open the door. Frank Nelson appeared a bit frazzled, as if he'd had a bad day and the night wasn't looking much better.

"What could you and I possibly have to talk about?" Bracing his body by clasping either side of the door frame, Reed leaned forward and glared right at the police chief.

"Where were you tonight, let's say between seven and eight-thirty?"

"Moving into this place," Reed said. "Why? What business is it of yours?"

"Anybody with you?" Frank asked. "You got someone who can verify where you were?"

A sickening feeling of déjà vu seeped through Reed like a slow-acting poison. "Am I being accused of a crime?"

"No. I'm simply checking out a few possible suspects. Anyone with a motive to want to create problems for or harm the Porter family."

"Ah, I see. So, naturally, mine was the first name that came to mind." Reed grinned. Better to try for humor in this situation, he thought. Anger would definitely work against him. "So, what's happened now? Miss Ella get another ugly letter? Another breathy phone call?"

"Someone broke into the Porter house and ransacked the place—destroyed quite a few priceless antiques."

"Was Ella there? Was she hurt?" An irrational fear surfaced. And a possessive, protective attitude that Reed could not control. If anyone had harmed Ella, he'd take them apart piece by piece.

"Ella's fine. She came home and found the place torn apart," Frank said. "Our guess is that the culprit left just as Ella arrived."

"I haven't been anywhere near the Porter house." Reed removed his hands from the door frame, hooked his thumbs into the waistband of his jeans, and surveyed Frank from head to toe. "There's no way you could have any evidence to the contrary."

"Didn't say I had any evidence." Frank's cheeks flushed beneath the heavy cluster of freckles.

"Look, I'm getting sick and tired of every time something happens with Ella Porter, you come knocking on my door. I'm going to have to speak to my attorney about pressing harassment charges against the Spring Creek Police Department.''

Frank took a tentative step forward, the tip of his shiny black shoes touching the threshold. ''Now you listen to me, you cocky son of a bitch. I'm going to nail your ass and send you back to Donaldson if I find out that you're the one messing with the Porter family. That is, if I get the chance. Webb Porter is liable to get a-hold of you first. And whatever he does, he'll be within his rights as a father protecting his daughter.''

Reed glared at Frank Nelson, but said nothing. Anger boiled inside him like molten lava, threatening to over-flow and annihilate everything in its path. He had butted heads with the law once before and the law had won. He might have been a hotheaded fool back then, but not any longer. In fifteen years of time served, he had learned one thing if nothing else. Patience.

''Stay away from Ella Porter,'' Chief Nelson warned before he turned and walked down the wooden stairs attached to the back side of the garage.

Reed slammed the door and cursed aloud. Had Ella been the one who had sicced the police on him once again? Had she counted on the police chief's threats to keep him at arm's length?

''Sorry, babe,'' Reed said aloud. ''I don't scare off that easy.''

Everything had gone just as planned: a break-in at the Porter home; destruction throughout several rooms; executed without a hitch only moments before Ella arrived. No doubt, she'd been frightened, perhaps even terrified. No evidence to point to anyone in particular, but Reed Conway would be the chief suspect. One more nail in the man's coffin. One more step in his journey back to prison.

There was far too much to lose if the truth ever came out. That could not be allowed to happen, whatever the price, and no matter who got hurt in the process. One did what one had to do to protect oneself. If loved ones were hurt, it was regrettable. But when a person had suffered the torment of the damned for so many years, it became easier and easier to feel no sympathy for others.

After a lifetime of playing to win, there could be no compromise. All or nothing, the motto to live by. Junior Blalock had learned, the hard way, the price of going up against a superior opponent. Reed Conway would have to be taught the same lesson.

The only case on the docket for the morning had been a sentencing hearing for a recently convicted murderess, whose trial had concluded in record time. Considering the damning evidence, Ella had had no choice but to give the woman the stiffest sentence possible.

With part of the morning left free, Ella had been able to speak to Steve Williamson about insurance on the house, as well as get a report from Frank Nelson. Although the insurance would cover the cost of replacing the furniture and other items, no amount of money could restore the destroyed antiques. And to add insult to injury, the police had come up with a big fat goose egg as far as evidence. No fingerprints other than those of people who regularly frequented the Porter house. Nothing found inside or outside the house to indicate who the offender might be. And no one in the neighborhood had seen anyone suspicious that evening. Of course, what made matters worse, at least in Ella's mind, was the fact that Frank had confronted Reed again. Her feminine instincts told her that it was only a matter of time before she would be forced to face Reed's wrath. He would think she had been the one who'd instigated Frank's visit.

"I don't believe Reed Conway will bother you again,"

Frank had told her this morning. "He knows that by harassing you, he's putting his parole at risk."

But what if Reed isn't the one harassing me? She had barely stopped herself from voicing her opinion. Neither Frank Nelson nor her father wanted to look beyond the obvious, to search for someone other than Reed as a suspect. Was this what had happened fifteen years ago? Had everyone assumed Reed was guilty and therefore closed the case without a thorough investigation?

Maybe Reed is guilty. Maybe I'm wrong and everyone else is right. He could have killed Junior Blalock and he could be the person tormenting me.

The telephone rang. Ella jumped. She was a nervous wreck lately, but especially after last night.

"Judge Porter."

"Ella, are you all right?"

A silent groan reverberated inside Ella's head. "Yes, Daddy, I'm fine."

"I just got off the phone with Jeff Henry," Webb said. "Why the hell didn't someone call us last night? You just wait until I see Frank Nelson. He's going to get a piece of my mind."

"Daddy, will you stop ranting and raving. Frank didn't call you because I asked him not to. The same holds true for Uncle Jeff Henry and Aunt Cybil. You and Mother have so little time alone together. I didn't want to disrupt your last days at the beach when there's nothing you can do back here."

"Your mother and I are hardly alone. Viola is here with us."

Ella heard the displeasure in her father's voice. Neither she nor her father was overly fond of Viola, but they tolerated the woman for Carolyn's sake. Her mother depended on Viola and seemed to genuinely care for the sour-faced, unfriendly woman. And Viola was obsessively loyal to Carolyn. Sometimes Ella felt that the two women shared a symbiotic relationship, each feeding off the other.

"I haven't told Carolyn yet," Webb said. "I'm going to make some excuse for coming home early and then I'll tell her the truth right before we get there." He huffed loudly. "I knew leaving you there alone with that man on the loose was a bad idea."

"That man? I assume you mean Reed Conway."

"Who else?"

"There is no evidence that Reed was the person who broke into the house and ransacked it."

"I don't need any evidence to know he did it."

"Just the way you didn't need any evidence to convict him of killing his stepfather?"

Ella wished the words back the moment they were out of her mouth, but it was too late. A painful silence interrupted the conversation. She could hear her father's deep, agitated breathing.

"I'm sorry, Daddy," Ella said.

"Why are you defending that man?"

"I'm not defending him. I'm merely stating that there is no evidence to indicate he's done anything illegal since he was paroled several weeks ago."

"I want you to stay away from him. Do you hear me?"

"Believe me, if I never see Reed Conway again, it will suit me just fine."

Webb walked along the crowded beach, but paid no attention to anyone, not even the bathing beauties who usually caught his eye. He had to come up with a plausible reason for their leaving the Gulf a day early. He would use business—government business—as an excuse. Carolyn never questioned his excuses, no matter how feeble they might be. She tolerated a great deal from him, more than most women would endure. Her life couldn't be easy, paralyzed as she was. And being married to a man who didn't love her should have added to her unhappiness, but she didn't seem to mind so much. What mattered to Carolyn was that she remain his wife.

"I intend to be Mrs. Webb Porter as long as I live," she'd told him. "You would never divorce me, would you? Not with me in this condition? Please, Webb, promise me that you'll never leave me."

She'd been right. He would never leave her. How could he? Thirty years ago he had given her the promise she'd asked for, and in return she had agreed to adopt a child. Their marriage had become a series of compromises. Not what he wanted, but the price he had to pay. For Ella. For his political career. To ease his guilty conscience.

He didn't feel especially guilty about the other women, but he did still blame himself for the accident that had crippled Carolyn. They had been arguing. He'd asked her for a divorce. She'd gone berserk and told him that she would never give him a divorce.

She'd cursed him, saying, "If you think I'll give you up, then think again, you son of a bitch. You're my husband and you're going to stay my husband. How could you even think of leaving me for that whore?"

That was when he'd realized that Carolyn knew about his relationship with Judy Conway. He hadn't meant to fall in love with Judy. But Judy was everything that he had sadly discovered his wife was not. When he'd married Carolyn, he'd been deceived by her beauty and her genteel manners. She hadn't allowed him to touch her until their wedding night, which had, for him, been a disaster. His bride hadn't liked sex. She had endured it. He'd soon found that his genteel wife was not only cold in the bedroom, but was a bitch to anyone she considered a subordinate. He had tried to make the marriage work, but after two miserable years, he had asked for a divorce.

Fate had stepped in and dealt him an almost lethal blow. After Carolyn's accident, he had ended his love affair with Judy. Guilt ate away at him for years, and he'd tried his best to be a faithful husband. But he hadn't been able to get Judy out of his mind or out of his heart. They had come together again, years later, for one unforgettable night. Junior Blalock had known about that night and about the child Judy had conceived. If Junior had ever told Carolyn that Webb had fathered Regina Conway, only God knew what Carolyn would have done—not only to him, but to Judy. And to little Regina, the child he had never been able to claim. He supposed there was a special place in hell for men like him—men who fathered illegitimate children and never acknowledged them.

Webb suspected that the intense hatred that now existed between Reed Conway and him had actually begun all those years ago. Even as a small boy, Reed had seemed to sense that Webb was bad news for his mother. And as the years went by, Judy's son became her zealous protector. Did Reed know the truth about Regina's paternity? Was that one of the reasons that, as a teenager, he had bristled every time he'd come into contact with Webb?

Webb had questioned his own motives when he had prosecuted Reed for Junior's murder. He'd known that by not stepping down, not turning the case over to the assistant district attorney, he would sever all ties to Judy. She hadn't been able to forgive him. But that had been what he'd wanted, hadn't it? Losing Judy forever had been his punishment and, oddly enough, his atonement.

But did Reed think Webb hadn't suffered enough? Was Judy's son intent on hurting the person Webb loved most in the world—his daughter Ella?

Webb knew that he had to do whatever was necessary to protect those he loved, just as he'd always done. Even if that meant protecting them from himself.

* * *

"Miss Ella?" Roy Moses eased open the door to her office. As always, he offered her a warm smile. "I got your lunch. A small barbeque sandwich, a little bag of chips, and a diet Dr Pepper. I got your order right, didn't I?"

"Yes, Roy, thank you." Ella exchanged the sack lunch for the cost of the meal, plus a generous tip. "By eating here in my office, I can relax for a while."

"I heard about what happened at your house," Roy said, his smile wavering. "Who would do something so mean?"

"I don't know, but I hope the police catch him."

"It wasn't Reed," Roy told her. "Reed ain't a bad man. Not like people think he is."

Ella set the paper lunch sack on her desk. "No one is accusing Reed."

"Reed's my friend." Roy's smile returned, broader than before, showing off uneven rows of crooked, yellow teeth. "Me and him are fixing up an old Corvette over at the garage. He says I got a natural talent for mechanic work. And Reed, he don't never fuss at me the way Briley Joe does."

"I'm glad you've found a friend in Reed," Ella said. She really didn't want to discuss Reed Conway's virtues, not even with Roy. She didn't want to be reminded that Reed might actually be a good guy.

"You enjoy your lunch, Miss Ella. I gotta get back to work." Roy paused in his slow, plodding exit. "If you need me for anything, just have Kelly call down to the basement when she gets back from lunch."

"Yes, thank you, Roy."

As soon as he closed the door, Ella grabbed the sack off her desk, collapsed onto the leather sofa, kicked off her shoes, and sighed. An hour of peace and quiet . . . she hoped. Dealing with the police, their insurance agent, and her father all in one morning was more than enough stress. And despite the defendant's guilt in the case before her earlier today, it hadn't been easy sentencing a woman to life in prison.

She felt the door open before she actually looked up and saw Reed Conway burst into her office. He slammed the door shut, almost jarring it off the hinges. Ella sat up straight, bringing her legs around so that her bare feet hit the floor. Her lunch sack scooted off her lap and onto the sofa.

Pure rage—that's what she saw on Reed's face, in his eyes, in his tight jaw. Instinct told her to run. The old fight-or-flight mentality kicked in. With Reed, her best bet was flight. No way could she win in a fight with this man. Not when she would be fighting herself as well as him.

"Why the hell do you keep siccing Frank Nelson on me?" Reed stood just inside her office, his big body a solid block positioned between her and the only escape route.

"I didn't . . ." She cleared her throat. "I did not sic Frank Nelson on you. It isn't my fault that you're the most likely suspect."

Reed took several steps in her direction, his presence threatening. "I am not harassing you. I did not break into your home and ransack the place. What I want to do is prove that I didn't kill Junior Blalock—not commit a crime that would send me back to prison. Haven't you got enough sense to realize that?"

"You shouldn't be here." She rose to her feet, squared her shoulders, and aimed her gaze point-blank at his cold blue eyes. "I want you to leave."

"Do you?" He moved steadily toward her.

"Turn around and leave right now. If you don't, I'll be forced to call security."

He didn't seem to hear her. Or if he had heard, he chose to disregard her warning. Within seconds he came upon her. Big. Intimidating. Threatening. A man to be reckoned with.

"It's time you and I settle this thing between us," he said.

"There is nothing between us."

"Oh, yes, there is. There's this."

Before she could voice a protest, he grabbed her by the nape of her neck and took her breath away with a kiss of raw fury and unleashed desire.

Chapter 17

Stop him. Stop him now. You can't let this happen. You'll regret it. Oh, God, help me!

She struggled against him, but he held fast, and when she tried to protest verbally, he thrust his tongue into her mouth. Heady, sexual sensations burst inside her, shooting through her at the speed of light. Ella found herself responding automatically, instinctively, as if her body recognized this man as her mate.

This is wrong! This is so wrong. Think of the consequences of your actions.

She laid her hands on his chest and shoved him as hard as she could. Her effort accomplished her goal and ended the ravaging kiss. When he released her neck, he glared at her, hot passion in his eyes.

Ella's knees weakened, and for a split second she thought they might give way. Wiping the moisture of his kiss from her lips, she looked straight at him. He was, without a doubt, the most devastating man she'd ever seen in her life. All hard, masculine muscle. Totally male. Whatever softness that might have once graced his features had disappeared over the long years in prison and left behind only the strong, granite features of a tough warrior.

Their gazes locked. He was staring her down, proving his dominance, trying to intimidate her. He had to know the effect he had on her—had to have guessed by the way she'd responded to his kiss that she was hungry for him. His icy blue eyes, pale against the rich, leathery tan of his face, possessed a mesmerizing ability that drew her to him. Fighting with all the strength she possessed, she tried to resist the urge to fling herself into his powerful arms.

"Whatever you think is going to happen, it's not," she told him.

"Are you sure?"

"Yes, I'm sure."

"No, you're not," he said, his voice deep and seductive. "You're not sure of anything anymore, are you?"

"I'm very sure that I dislike you and that I want nothing to do with you. As a matter of fact, I'm beginning to hate you."

He grinned. Actually, the curve of his lips was more an amused smirk than a grin. "You don't hate me, lady. You hate yourself for wanting a man like me."

Color stained her cheeks and she cursed herself for allowing his comment to embarrass her. For pity's sake, she was thirty years old. She'd heard cruder propositions come out of other men's mouths and she'd simply been offended. Her reaction to Reed's statement came from the fact that there was some truth in what he'd said. *Some truth? Face it—you want him like crazy.*

"You're wrong," she lied.

Taking her off guard, he grabbed her chin, clamping his fingers and thumb over her cheeks. Shocked by the unexpected move and by the fierceness of his touch, Ella gasped.

She heard the sound of people passing by outside her office, feet padding along the hallway. Voices engaged in conversation. *Cry out for help. Do it now, while you still can. Otherwise, you'll be lost.*

She could tell by Reed's expression that he heard the people beyond the closed doors and he knew what she was thinking. As he held her head in place, positioning it to accept the onslaught, his mouth took hers in a hard kiss. It was all she could do not to react. She forced herself to resist temptation. Suddenly he ended the kiss and withdrew from her.

"There's the door, babe"—he nodded in that direction—"leave now or you're not going anywhere for a while."

"This is my office. If anyone is leaving, you are." She felt a certain amount of satisfaction for standing her ground. She had called his bluff.

"Last chance," he said.

Ella didn't budge.

He turned around and headed for the door. She breathed deeply, sighing with relief. And yet at the same time a wave of inexplicable disappointment washed over her. *You idiot,* she chided herself. *Count yourself lucky that he backed down, otherwise you would have done something you would regret for the rest of your life.*

Ella's relief and her disappointment were short-lived. A distinct click alerted her that Reed had locked the door. All her senses came to full alert. Reversing his stance, he faced her. She knew there would be no reprieve. She had to accept the truth. Reed hadn't been bluffing.

"There's one thing I want to know, Miss Ella. Have you ever been fucked?"

Ella gasped.

"And I don't mean made love to by one of your suitable beaus. I mean screwed by a man who wants you so bad it's eating him up inside."

"You have no right to talk to me this way. No right to think that I'd have sex with you." As she shook her head in denial, she held up her hands in a defensive measure, as if to ward him off.

He took one slow, deliberate step after another, drawing ever closer, his gaze riveted to hers. "Give me the right. You know you want to. You want it as bad as I do."

"You're wrong." Panic spread through her like an insidious disease, destroying her resistence.

Why aren't you screaming? Why aren't you running from him? There's still time.

He reached out to cradle her face with his hands. She sucked in a deep, startled breath. His touch was strong yet gentle. A shiver of fear and longing shimmied along her nerves. His lips settled over hers: warm and moist, demanding but not brutal. Female reacted to male—woman to man, recognizing her mate. Ella kissed him back with the same desperate need, and that response ignited an uncontrollable blaze within him. Keening softly, she leaned into him, her breasts pressing softly against his hard chest. He eased his hands from her cheeks, across her ears, to spear his fingers into her hair and grasp her head. He deepened the kiss, his tongue delving into her mouth and dueling with hers. She braced her open palms over his chest to balance her unsteady body. And because she needed to touch him. The kiss went on and on until they were both breathless. When he broke the bond, Ella felt momentarily bereft, as is she'd lost a part of herself. But within seconds, his lips found new territory. He nibbled at the side of her neck, then mouthed her ear.

As she licked her swollen lips, her hands moved of their own accord to tug at his short-sleeved chambray shirt. One by one, she undid the buttons to mid-chest and slid her hands inside to caress his bare chest. Her fingertips encountered swirling brown hair that spread over defined muscles, circled tiny male nipples, and descended in a thin triangle. Oh, how she loved the feel of him.

The moment he touched her, she unraveled, whimpering with longing. He unzipped the back of her sedate navy blue summer dress and dragged it to her waist, all the while his hands smoothing their way down her back. With his arms circling her and his lips pressing into the hollow of her throat, she explored his body. After tugging his shirt free of his jeans, she finished unbuttoning it and spread it apart to give her complete access to his upper torso.

Reed unhooked the back closure of her bra and eased it off her shoulders, inch by inch, slowly revealing her breasts. When he lifted the weight of each mound and flicked his thumbs across her nipples, Ella closed her eyes and allowed the painful pleasure to radiate through her body. He tormented each pebble-hard point, flicking, pinching, rubbing, until Ella was panting. Then he lowered his head and took one nipple into his mouth while his fingers continued their assault on the other. When she thought she couldn't bear another moment of such exquisite torture, Reed lifted his head and looked into her eyes. They exchanged a heated glare as their labored breaths created the only sound in the room.

Desire so intense that it was a palpable thing sucked them into the hot, dark depths, down into the irrational, primeval abyss of mating. All other considerations ceased to exist. Only one thing mattered, and that singular need outweighed all others. In that endless moment when they looked at each other, they both knew. Both understood.

Although the air conditioning in Ella's office was quite adequate, she suddenly felt hot, as if the Southern summertime heat had invaded her body. She had never felt this way, had never known such powerful sexual hunger. Had never needed a man the way she needed Reed. And he felt the same urgency, the same raging ache, riding him hard. She could see it in his eyes.

When he cupped her buttocks and pulled her up

against him, she made no protest. Indeed, she went willingly. With their gazes still connected, he inched his hand down, down, down until he could insert his hand under her dress. She clung to his shoulders, her lips becoming acquainted with his throat, his chest, his nipples. His big hands worked their way up her thighs to her hips where he encountered her silk panties.

He slid a couple of fingers beneath the leg band of her panties, running the edge of his calloused fingertips over the curly hair flattened by her underwear. She shuddered against him. He groaned as if in pain, but Ella instinctively recognized the mating call for what it was. Hurriedly he removed his fingers, then swept one arm under her hips and lifted her off her feet.

Reed tossed her onto the leather sofa. She lay there gazing up at him. While he unbuckled his belt and unzipped his jeans, he watched her, seemingly unable to take his eyes off her. Then, without a word exchanged—no request for permission or whispers of affection—he reached under her dress and dragged her panties over her hips, down her legs, and off.

All Ella could think at that very moment was how glad she was that in the hottest part of summer, she never wore pantyhose or stockings. Crazy, idiotic thought. And quite wanton. Heaven help her, she was wanton. A real hussy.

When Reed came down over her, bracing one hand on the back of the sofa and the other on the edge of the cushion just below her shoulder, he inspected his handiwork. She knew from the feel of them that her lips were red and swollen. And glancing down at her breasts, she saw her tight, distended nipples, bright pink from his suckling.

He shoved the skirt of her dress up above her hips, preparing her, then pulled his jeans and briefs down. She held her breath, shocked and yet aroused by his actions. He was big and hard and powerfully male. He was going to take her, ram himself inside her and . . .

Never had she wanted anything more. Positioning himself over her, his penis brushed across her mound. She shivered. The tip of his strong erection found the opening of her body. He inserted himself only a couple of inches. She lifted her hips, seeking more.

"I've got to fuck you, babe. I've got to have you now." He thrust his hands under her hips and lifted her up, impaling her, imbedding himself as deeply into her as possible.

She cried out. The feel of him inside her, filling her, expanding her sheath to its limits, produced a nearly orgasmic response. "Reed . . ."

"I know, babe. I know." He began moving, slowly at first, setting the pace, breaking her in gently, allowing her body to adjust to his size.

His lips and hands were everywhere. Caressing, encouraging, arousing. She was lost in a whirlwind of carnal pleasure, a new and glorious experience for her. She was no simpering virgin, but God help her if Reed didn't make her feel as if she'd never been with another man.

They went at each other like animals, wild with a bestial craving that only complete, unbridled sexual satisfaction could appease. She writhed beneath him, giving herself over completely to the carnal act. Gentleness and tenderness gave way completely to savagery. Lust controlled their every action. And with each thrust— each hard, fast lunge into her body—Reed brought her closer and closer to fulfillment. Flooding with steamy moisture, she swelled tighter and tighter, her internal movements milking his stiff penis.

Her climax was inevitable. She could feel the oncoming tide of release, and the overwhelming sensation frightened her. It had never been like this—an unbearable pleasure, an intensity that shook her to the very core of her being.

"No, babe. Don't be afraid," he murmured, as if he'd read her thoughts. "Come for me, Ella. Just for me."

Swept away completely. Shattered into a million fragments of pleasure. Her orgasm went on and on, affecting her entire mind and body, leaving no part of her untouched by the magnitude of their lovemaking.

Reed hammered into her, hard and fast. While the aftershocks of her release radiated through her, he came inside her. His ejaculation powerful, he groaned as his body jerked convulsively. As satiation claimed them, Reed kissed her and whispered her name. She reciprocated, loving the aftermath of affection that he displayed. But within minutes, reality set in, making her painfully aware of where she was and what she'd just done.

Wriggling beneath him to dislodge him, she shoved against his chest at the same time. "Please, let me get up."

He gazed down at her for a long moment, then lifted himself off her. Once his feet hit the floor, he pulled up his briefs and jeans and closed the zipper. His shirt hung open loosely at either side of his big body. He held out his hand, offering her assistance. Reluctantly, she accepted his hand. He pulled her to her feet. When her bare breasts made contact with his chest, she gasped.

She looked at him pleadingly. This shouldn't have happened. It was wrong. They had made a huge mistake. It must never happen again. All these thoughts and more came to mind, but she didn't say a word. She knew she should feel shame and remorse, yet she didn't. How could she regret something so incredibly wonderful, the most fabulous sexual experience of her life?

She'd just had sex with an ex-convict, her father's sworn enemy. A man as dangerous as any of the criminals who came through her courtroom.

Reed released her, but for just a second neither of them moved, letting the remnants of desire caress them. He stepped away first. Ella dragged the undone bodice of her dress up just enough to cover her breasts.

"I'd better go," Reed said.

She nodded.

"Ella . . ."

"Please, just go."

"Yeah, sure."

He turned around, crossed the room and unlocked the door. Glancing over his shoulder, he said, "See you around."

He opened the door, went out into the hall, and closed the door quickly behind him. Thank God Kelly was still at lunch. Ella sucked in a deep breath and released it slowly. What the hell had just happened?

The moment the telephone rang, reality hit her over the head like a sledgehammer. She scurried across the room, locked the door, and dashed back to answer the phone.

"Judge Porter." How was it possible that her voice sounded so calm when inside she was a mass of quivering jelly?

"Ella, how are you?" Cybil Carlisle asked. "I'm sorry I was still sleeping when you left this morning."

"I'm all right." A definite lie. After what had happened with Reed Conway, Ella doubted that she would ever be all right again.

"I suppose Webb and Carolyn are coming straight home."

"Yes, I'm afraid so. I tried to persuade Daddy not to cut short their vacation, but he insisted."

"I'm glad Webb's coming back to look after you. I worry about you, you know."

"I'm fine," Ella said. "I'm a big girl. I can take care of myself."

Yeah, sure you can. You can take care of yourself, all right. You just had unprotected sex with Reed Conway on the sofa in your office. Good heavens, girl, you don't have the sense the good Lord gave a billy goat!

"I couldn't bear it if anything bad ever happened to you," Cybil said, her voice catching with emotion. "I love you, darling girl."

"I love you, too."

Ella hung up the phone, then searched for her bra.
The soft, silky material lay draped over the wastebasket,
where apparently it had landed when Reed tossed it
aside. She put on the bra, thrust her arms through the
armholes of her dress, then reached around to pull up
the zipper. She found her discarded panties between
the sofa back and the seat cushion.

The moment she walked into the bathroom, she
stopped dead still as she caught a glimpse of herself
in the mirror over the sink. Merciful heavens! Anyone
seeing her right now would know, without a doubt, that
she'd just been fucked. And fucked real good.

She had to clean up, brush her hair, reapply some
makeup, and try to get that satisfied look off her face
before she went into her courtroom. It wouldn't do
for anyone to suspect that Her Honor, Judge Eleanor
Porter, had spent her lunch hour getting laid.

Chapter 18

Cybil Carlisle raced her T-bird at breakneck speed down the old country road. Her shorts were stained with Briley Joe Conway's semen and her breasts ached from his rough handling. She'd met him at the river cottage co-owned by her and her sister. This was the first time she had risked inviting her current lover to the family's weekend getaway, because five people possessed keys and used the place at various times and for various reasons. She'd often wondered if Webb ever used the place for his trysts these days, but she doubted it. After all, a U.S. senator had to be discreet about his affairs.

Lifting the bottle of vodka to her lips, she took a large gulp and coughed as the liquor set her insides on fire. Keeping one hand on the wheel, she stuck the bottle between her thighs, nestling it against her crotch. She preferred having a man between her legs, but the effects of an orgasm faded quicker than the buzz she got from drinking.

With the hot summer wind whipping her short hair about her face, she laughed, the sound lost in the breeze. She continued laughing—at herself, at Briley

Joe, at Jeff Henry, at Webb and Carolyn. And at Junior
Blalock, the sorry son of a bitch. If anyone had ever
deserved to die, he had. If he had lived, he would have
destroyed several lives, including her own. The man
had known too many secrets, had threatened too many
people.

Images of that black-haired devil flashed through her
mind. He'd been handsome in a lean, mean sort of way.
She'd been attracted to him the minute she met him.
There had been something about him that had
reminded her of Webb. The same coal-black hair and
striking good looks. The same cocky, insolent manner.
The same self-assurance with women. But where Webb
possessed a conscience and a heart, Junior had been
sadly lacking in both.

She recalled the times she and Junior had set the
sheets afire. She'd been damned and determined to
hurt and humiliate Jeff Henry. If he couldn't love her,
then by God, she had wanted him to hate her. She'd
desperately needed him to feel something, even if it was
loathing.

But Junior had threatened to make their affair public.
Jeff Henry knowing about the affair was one thing, but
the whole town knowing about it would have been different. Jeff Henry's humiliation would have been public,
and he'd have had no choice but to divorce her. She'd
warned Junior that if he dared breathe a word about
their sordid affair, she'd kill him.

She'd gone to him that night and found him lying
in a heap, bloody and bruised after Reed's beating. An
unopened pocket knife on the ground beside his body
had glistened in the moonlight. The temptation to pick
up the knife and use it had been overwhelming.

Cybil sighed deeply and shoved her foot down on the
accelerator, speeding the T-bird to ninety. She jerked
the bottle from between her legs and lifted it to her
lips. Just as her sister Carolyn intended to spend her
entire life as Mrs. Webb Porter, Cybil meant to live out

her days as Mrs. Jefferson Henry Carlisle . . . no matter what.

Jeff Henry strolled through the park. His walking cane was simply for show, as was his white Panama suit. But the Cuban cigar in his mouth was for pleasure, one of the many he could well afford. Being the descendant of one of the town's founding families, he had a reputation to uphold. As a gentleman. As a pillar of society. As an eccentric. He knew his reputation. Some envied him; some pitied him. Some believed him to be a relic of a bygone era. But everyone knew him and had a begrudging respect for his money and social standing, if not for him personally.

Despite his unhappiness because he was married to a drunken whore, he rather enjoyed his life. Although the woman he truly loved could never be his, he could see her, be with her, and lavish attention on her. And he could fulfill his duties as godfather to Carolyn's only child. Never once did he look at Ella without thinking that if circumstances had been different, she might be his daughter and not Webb's.

Other than losing Carolyn, his biggest regret was that he and Cybil hadn't had children together. Of course, if his wife had gotten pregnant, God only knew who the father would have been—someone like Briley Joe Conway or Junior Blalock. What would it have been like, being stuck with the offspring of that black-hearted bastard? Junior hadn't been merely scum of the earth; he'd been evil. Any man capable of raping a child didn't deserve to live.

A lot of people had hated Junior and had been glad to see him dead. Jeff Henry knew at least a half dozen people who'd had a motive—and the opportunity—to slit the drunken bum's throat as he lay there semiconscious on the ground. Jeff Henry could see him lying there where Reed had left him after beating the hell out of him. Reed's pocket knife, which had apparently fallen from his pocket during the fight, lay on the ground, shiny and tempting, there in the moonlight.

Killing Junior had been a good deed, not only for Junior's family, but for the Carlisles and the Porters. Hell, the killer had done the whole goddamn town a favor.

While Webb Porter watched from the doorway, Viola lifted Carolyn out of her wheelchair and placed her in the bed. What would she do without Viola? No one cared for her as much as Viola did, except perhaps Jeff Henry. And if her old beau really knew the person she had become, he might not remain so infatuated with her. But there was no reason for her sister's husband to ever know the truth.

Carolyn held out her hand to her husband, beseeching him to come to her. He didn't move, made no attempt to accommodate her request. Although he had been dutifully attentive while on vacation, he'd been in a rush to leave this morning. He had used some feeble excuse about business to explain why he was cutting their vacation short by a day. Only when they were within a few miles of Spring Creek had he told her about the break-in at the house. She was sure Ella was fine, but she could hardly have told him that her concern for their daughter didn't equal his. It wasn't that she didn't love Ella. She did. She simply wasn't obsessed with the girl the way her husband was.

Webb had been a less-than-pleasant traveling companion on the drive up from the Gulf. No doubt he had been in such a tizzy over Ella's well-being that he'd all but forgotten he had an invalid wife to consider. Hadn't he realized the fact that it was her home that had been invaded, her beautiful house ransacked, her priceless antiques destroyed? You'd have thought he could give her some sympathy and a little consideration. After all, she was his wife. And it wasn't as if Ella had been hurt.

But with each passing year, Carolyn realized more and more that if it ever came down to a choice between his wife and his daughter, Webb would choose his daughter.

"I'm going next door to speak to Jeff Henry about what happened here last night," Webb said. "Then I'll have a talk with Frank Nelson. By that time, Ella should be out of court and the three of us can have dinner together tonight."

"The house is wrecked," Carolyn said. "There are so many beautiful things that can never be replaced." A lone tear trickled down her cheek. She had learned years ago how to cry on cue, and had perfected the poor, pitiful invalid act to perfection.

"They were just things," Webb said. "All that matters to me is that Ella wasn't harmed."

"Of course, that is what's most important to me, too." Carolyn swiped the tear from her cheek and gave Webb a forlorn look. "You must have Frank do something about Reed Conway before he actually harms Ella. Apparently the man isn't going to stop with simple harassment."

"If Reed Conway is behind the break-in, then I'll—"

"What do you mean, 'if'? Who else could it possibly be?"

"I don't know," Webb admitted. "But I intend to find out."

The moment Webb disappeared down the hallway, Carolyn sat up straight in bed and listened for his footsteps as he descended the staircase. "Go make sure he leaves and that there's no one else in the house," Carolyn told Viola. "I have a few things to do and I don't want to be disturbed."

Viola, ever dutiful, obeyed instantly. Carolyn stretched her arms over her head and leaned back into the pillows stacked behind her. The downstairs area of the house had been thoroughly ransacked and several priceless antiques destroyed. The sight of the destruction had turned her stomach.

She couldn't believe Webb had the slightest doubt that Reed Conway was responsible. After all, their home had never been broken into before, and Reed was the only logical suspect, wasn't he? The man was a bad seed, a murderer. Birthed by a whore and the brother of an emotionally disturbed bastard child.

If Carolyn had her way, the entire Conway family would be wiped off the face of the earth in one fell swoop. It was unfortunate that the night Junior Blalock met his fatal end, his wife and two stepchildren couldn't have joined him in hell.

Reed tossed the wrench into the tool box, slammed the lid shut, and shoved the red metal box aside. Holding out his hands, he inspected the grease and grime covering his skin, and the thick black muck under his nails. Only hours ago those very hands had caressed Ella Porter, had explored her body and helped bring her to fulfillment. Just the thought of Ella's whimpers, of her shuddering completion, gave him a hard-on.

Cursing under his breath, he jerked a rag from his back pocket and wiped the top layer of filth from his hands, then tossed the rag into the nearby garbage pail. He'd spent the afternoon working like a madman, determined to put Ella out of his mind, but the harder he tried to dismiss what had happened, the more vivid the memories became. So he'd screwed Webb Porter's daughter. No big deal. She was just another woman, another really good lay.

If that was true, then why was he so bent out of shape? Maybe she was hot for him. Maybe she couldn't get enough of him. Maybe he had never wanted a woman quite that much before. So what?

Truth time, buddy boy. Who was it you fantasized about all

those years in prison? It hadn't been any of the girls he
had dated in high school, or any of the older women
he'd messed around with. No, it had been Ella Porter.
That plump, shy little girl who used to look at him with
those big brown eyes of hers and never say more than
hello. He had thought about her a great deal because
of those two stupid letters he'd written to her . . . and
because she was Webb Porter's daughter. He had
thought how much it would upset Webb if he screwed
Ella. He'd gotten a great deal of pleasure from that
particular daydream.

Was that why it felt so good making it with Ella Porter?
Was that why he wanted her again right now? Maybe.
Hell, he didn't know.

Reed jerked open the door to the washroom, turned
on the faucets, and covered his hands with a generous
amount of Go-Jo. After lifting the scrub brush from the
edge of the sink, he went to work removing the grease
from under his fingernails. When he touched Ella again,
he wanted his hands to be clean, as clean as the hands
of those fancy gentlemen she dated.

Staring at himself in the mirror, he asked, "What
makes you think she'll let you touch her again?" He
grinned. "Because she wants you as much as you want
her. If one time wasn't enough for you, it won't be
enough for her."

Judy opened the door of the Carlisle home to discover
Webb Porter standing there. Big. Handsome. Every time
she saw him, her stomach quivered nervously. How was
it possible that at her age, a man could still make her
feel like a giddy teenager? Perhaps because, despite
everything that had gone wrong between them, she still
cared about Webb, still loved him.

"Afternoon," he said as he entered the foyer. "I'd
like to speak to Jeff Henry and get his version of what

happened at my house last night. Damn place looks like a bomb exploded in the downstairs area.''

"I'm terribly sorry about your home being broken into and ransacked." Judy knew that the police had questioned Reed. And she knew just as surely that her son hadn't committed the crime.

Webb focused his gaze on Judy. She willed herself not to blush. She was too old to let a man's sexual perusal embarrass her.

"How is it that you're still so pretty?" he asked. "You don't look any different now than you did—"

"Mr. Jeff Henry isn't here," Judy said, squaring her shoulders as she gazed point-blank at Webb. "He's taking his afternoon stroll in the park."

"The man needs a job. But then when you inherit a sizable fortune and a penchant for laziness . . ."

Webb left the sentence unfinished, the thought incomplete, but his meaning was clear. Judy had always known that although Webb liked Jeff Henry, he had little respect for his brother-in-law.

"When do you expect him back?" Webb asked.

"His walk usually takes about an hour, but since the weather is so miserably hot, he'll probably cut it short. I'd say he'll return in about fifteen minutes."

"Then I'll wait."

"Very well, Senator Porter," Judy said. "May I get you something to drink? I made a fresh pitcher of lemonade this morning."

Webb nodded. Judy closed the front door and, with a sweep of her hand, invited him into the living room. "Make yourself at home," she told him. "I'll bring in your drink shortly."

When she turned to leave, Webb grabbed her wrist. She gasped as her gaze met his. "Please, let me go."

"Don't you feel anything?" he asked. "Don't you ever want—"

Judy jerked her wrist out of his grasp. "You're a married man. I ignored that fact in the past. I won't make that mistake ever again."

She all but ran from him, escaping down the hallway and into the kitchen. Breathless, her heart racing like mad, she leaned her head against the refrigerator and prayed for strength. From time to time over the years, Webb had made overtures, but she had always rejected him. Only God knew the strength it took to refuse the man to whom her heart had always belonged. And always would.

As she poured the lemonade into a glass, she checked the wall clock and hoped that Jeff Henry would return early today. She could hardly ask Webb to leave, but she couldn't allow herself to be alone with him for very long. *Make an excuse,* she told herself. *After all, it wouldn't be a lie to say that you have work to do.*

When she entered the living room, she found Webb still standing, obviously waiting for her return. He smiled. Memories of sweet moments in this man's arms flooded her mind. Promises had been made to each other in the aftermath of passion. Broken promises. A child born without a father. Bittersweet memories.

Webb held out his hand for the glass of lemonade, and Judy gave it to him, being careful not to allow their fingers to touch. "I'm sure Mr. Jeff Henry will be home shortly. If you'll excuse me, I have work to do."

"I suppose you know that the police questioned Reed about last night's break-in at my house," Webb called after her.

Judy froze to the spot, just inches from the doorway, only a hairbreadth from escaping. With her back to him, she replied, "Yes, I'm aware that my son is always going to be the prime suspect in any crime against you or your family."

"Reed has always hated me, even when he was a child," Webb said. "You must know that the last thing I ever wanted to do was cause you pain, and that seems to be all I've done."

Judy reversed her avoidant position to one of head-on defensiveness. She looked right at him. "His aversion to you when he was a boy was childish jealousy over his mother. But now his hatred has merit, don't you think? After all, you went after him with a vengeance when you prosecuted him for Junior's murder. You were determined to see my son convicted."

"Your son killed a man." Webb set the glass of lemonade down on a nearby Chippendale table with such force that the contents spilled over onto the highly polished wood.

Judy whipped out a cleaning cloth from her apron pocket and rushed across the room to wipe up the spill. Once that had been accomplished, she picked up the glass. "Reed didn't kill Junior. I tried every way I knew how to convince you of that fifteen years ago, but you wouldn't listen. You sent an innocent boy to prison. So if he hates you now, he has good reason."

"Do you hate me, too?" Webb asked.

Her hand trembled. She tried to move away from Webb, but her legs wouldn't cooperate. *Tell him that you hate him. Tell him that you can never forgive him.*

"No, I don't hate you," she admitted reluctantly.

Jeff Henry lifted his hat and nodded his head in a mannerly greeting when he met Regina Conway on the walkway leading to his house. Such a pretty girl. A young replica of her mother. The child's father hadn't left his mark on her, disproving the old adage that illegitimate children always resemble their fathers.

"Good afternoon, Mr. Jeff Henry."

Such a pleasant child. So sweet and friendly. How was it possible that Judy had mothered two such different children? Reed had always been sulky and insolent, and downright unfriendly. That boy had been headed for trouble all along, and everyone had turned a blind eye to his boyish high jinks because he'd been such a great athlete.

"Well, hello, Regina. Don't you look pretty today in that pale-blue suit. Pretty as a picture."

"Thank you."

The girl possessed a marvelously shy smile, as if she truly had no idea what a rare beauty she was. If he were twenty years younger . . . But no, not even then would he have approached this young lady. She might be pretty and sweet and educated, but she was the housekeeper's daughter and therefore innapropriate for any type of personal relationship. A man in his position couldn't lower his standards any more than his predecessors had. A Carlisle always chose a mate from his social stratum. It was expected. And never let it be said that Jeff Henry Carlisle didn't do the proper thing.

"Is Mama still here?" Regina asked. "I've come by to give her a ride home."

Jeff Henry glanced at the driveway and the small compact vehicle. Some sort of economy car, and not a new one from the looks of it. "As far as I know, Judy's still here. She always prepares dinner before she leaves. I think it's prime rib tonight." He walked up onto the porch and straight to the front door. "Come on in, dear." He opened the door.

"Beautiful day today," Regina said. "I heard it's supposed to rain before morning and be dreary all day tomorrow. Maybe the rain will cool things off a bit."

"More than likely it'll only add to this dreadful humidity." As if to emphasize the truth of his comment, Jeff Henry removed a white handkerchief from his pants pocket and wiped the perspiration from his face as he crossed the threshold. "Go on in the kitchen. I'm sure that's where you'll find your mother."

Regina followed him inside and closed the door behind her. Intending to go straight up to his bathroom for a shower before dinner, Jeff Henry headed toward the staircase. He glanced casually into the living room, which was to his left. He gasped loudly. *What the hell?* Before his mind could process the full implication of what he had seen, Regina cried out, "Mama?"

Webb held Judy Conway in his arms, their bodies intimately pressed together as they exchanged a heated kiss. Jeff Henry's gasp and Regina's cry alerted Webb and Judy to the fact that they were no longer alone, that someone had caught them.

Judy jerked out of Webb's arms and looked pleadingly at her daughter, who stood in the foyer staring at her, shock and dismay etched on the girl's features. "Regina, please, I can explain."

"No, you can't!" Regina ran to the door, swung it open, and fled from the house.

"Oh, Lord," Judy said, then raced after her daughter.

Jeff Henry watched as Judy caught up with Regina on the walkway, and he listened as she pleaded for understanding.

"Please, sweetie, let me explain," Judy said.

"What is there to explain? I caught you kissing a married man—and not just any married man, but Senator Porter. My God, Mother, his poor wife is an invalid! How could you?"

When Regina hurried down the sidewalk to the driveway, Judy followed. Jeff Henry closed the front door just as Regina got in her car and sped out of the driveway.

"Well, brother-in-law, that was quite a display." Jeff Henry turned and all but snarled at Carolyn's philandering husband. "How will Judy ever explain that kiss to her daughter? She can hardly say, 'Dear, it was all right that I was kissing Webb Porter. You see, he's your father.' Then again, perhaps she will tell her. How would you handle that?"

"Judy won't tell Regina," Webb said with supreme confidence.

Webb was a cocky, egotistical womanizer. He had betrayed Carolyn dozens of times over, with countless women. Just how many illegitimate children had Webb fathered? Jeff Henry wondered.

"No, she'll keep your little secret, won't she? Just the way . . . Never mind. It doesn't matter. Nothing matters except that we protect Carolyn from all this ugliness. So help me"—Jeff Henry balled his hands into fists and shook them at Webb—"if you do anything to hurt Carolyn, I'll—I'll—" Jeff Henry spluttered. Rage boiled inside him. "I thought your affair with Judy ended years ago. You swore to me that it had. You promised me that you'd keep your dalliances out of Spring Creek and protect Carolyn from any gossip. What happens if Regina tells someone what she saw here today, in my house?"

"My affair with Judy did end years ago," Webb said. "But I still have feelings for her, as she does for me. You of all people should understand what it's like to love a woman who can never be yours."

With that said, Webb stormed out of the house. Jeff Henry stood in the open doorway, a feeling of immense sadness welling up inside him. But one simply couldn't dwell on life's sorrows, could one? A gentleman bore his cross without complaining.

Searching for any sign of Judy, he saw none. Undoubtedly, she had walked home, leaving without finishing up dinner. That meant no prime rib meal tonight. Oh, well. Under the circumstances, poor Judy couldn't be held responsible for her actions. He and Cybil would just have to dine out this evening, perhaps join some friends at the country club.

Chapter 19

The moment Ella heard the knock, she jerked open her office door, grabbed Heather's arm, and dragged her inside without saying a word. After slamming the door behind them, Ella gazed at her best friend, knowing her feelings showed plainly on her face.

"What's wrong with you?" Heather asked. "You sounded frantic on the phone. Has something else happened since the break-in at your house last night? Another letter?" Ella shook her head as she released her tenacious hold on Heather. "Another phone call?" Ella shook her head again. "Then what?"

How could she tell anyone, even Heather, that she had been half out of her mind ever since she'd had sex with Reed Conway, right here in her office, less than six hours ago? Ella had amazed herself by actually presiding in the courtroom as if nothing had happened, as if she hadn't made the most monumental mistake of her life during her lunch hour today. But she had to talk to someone, and God knew she couldn't tell either of her parents what she'd done. Aunt Cybil might understand, considering her penchant for bad boys, but her aunt's advice wasn't likely to be sensible or even helpful.

And you think Heather's will be? Ella couldn't help being amused by her choice of confidantes.

"No, nothing like that," Ella said. "It's just that this has been a killer afternoon and I needed a shoulder to cry on. I had to sentence a seventy-year-old woman to thirty days in jail and I hated doing it, but she left me no choice."

"Mrs. Sherer, right? You shouldn't feel bad about locking up that nutcase. My God, her yard is an eyesore and she has refused to do anything to clean it up. This was her third time in criminal court. You simply did your duty."

"Yes, I know, but I rather like Mrs. Sherer and admire her eccentricities. She's certainly her own woman, willing to go to jail rather than give in."

"I call that being stubborn to the point of stupidity." Heather narrowed her gaze as she inspected Ella thoroughly. "Something else is going on here. More than your having a bad day in court. Come on. What gives?"

"I'm swearing you to secrecy." Ella grabbed Heather's arm, led her friend toward the leather sofa, then stopped dead in her tracks. She stared at the couch where she'd lain beneath Reed and experienced the most incredible sex of her life. Would she ever be able to sit on that sofa again?

"You're worrying me, you know that?" Heather pulled loose from Ella's tenacious hold and stared at her. "Want to tell me what the hell's going on? You're acting very peculiar."

"If you ever breathe a word of what I'm about to tell you, I'll kill you even if I have to hunt you down to do it." Ella inhaled, then exhaled slowly.

Heather lifted her eyebrows and pursed her lips. "Uh-oh, I have a nasty little feeling that I'm going to regret being privy to this information. It's about Reed Conway, isn't it?"

"How did you know?"

"My God, it is. It is about Reed. What happened? Did he kiss you?"

"Lower your voice." Ella felt the heated flush creeping up her neck and spreading across her cheeks. "Yes, it's about Reed."

"He did more than kiss you, didn't he? And don't you dare try to deny it. That bright pink blush on your face gives you away."

"My parents are home. They rushed back from the Gulf because of last night's break-in. I called the house and left a message with Bessie to tell them I'd be running a little late because something had come up here at work. I feel as if the truth is written all over my face, and the minute I enter the house and they see me, they'll know."

"They'll know what?" Heather asked.

"That Reed and I . . . that we . . . today . . . here . . ." she glanced meaningfully at the sofa. "I don't know what happened." Ella shook her head frantically. "Scratch that! I do know what happened. I lost my mind. I did something so stupid, so incredibly stupid."

Heather fell into the nearest chair, her mouth agape and her eyes wide. "You and Reed . . . on the sofa?" She gazed at the tufted-backed, burgundy leather couch. "Well, I'll be damned."

"No," Ella corrected, *"I'll* be damned. Lord help me, I am damned. I had sex with a convicted murderer, a man who hates my father—and vice versa—a man who is little more than a stranger to me, who has been out of prison only a few weeks and—"

"So how was it?"

"What?"

"How was the sex?"

"Oh, God!"

"That good, huh?" Heather grinned.

"Unprotected sex," Ella said.

Heather let out a long, low whistle. "Well, I'll say this

for you: when you decide to walk on the wild side, you don't do it by half measures. You risked it all, didn't you?''

"I have never, in my entire life, done anything I'm ashamed of, nothing that was illogical or unreasonable or . . .'' Ella groaned. "What am I going to do? What if he tells someone? You know how men are about their conquests. He's bound to tell his cousin Briley Joe and Lord only knows who else.''

"You can always deny it,'' Heather suggested. "After all, who would believe him? The proper and dignified Judge Eleanor Porter doing the nasty with Reed Conway.'' Heather's lips twitched as if she were on the verge of smiling. "Tell me something. Have you fallen in love with him?''

"What? Heavens, no!'' How could Heather ask her such a thing. In love with Reed Conway? Ridiculous. She didn't even like the guy.

"Mm . . . So, are you going to see him again?'' Heather's mouth finally burst into a smile. "I mean, if the sex was great and—''

"I didn't say the . . . No, I hope I never see him again, but since this is a small town, I'm sure we'll see each other occasionally. When he left, he said that he'd see me around.''

"You're angry with him for that comment, aren't you,'' Heather said. "When it was all over, he didn't say or do anything romantic and you were offended.''

"I was not offended,'' Ella said. "I'm glad he didn't try to get all mushy and romantic on me. After all, it was just sex.''

"Was it? Are you sure?''

"Yes, I'm sure.'' But that was what bothered her the most—she wasn't sure. Yes, it had been sex. Great sex. But it had been more, hadn't it? At least for her. "Do you think I should contact him and ask him not to say anything about what happened?''

"If you're serious about not wanting more of what

you got today, then you'd better stay the hell away from him." Heather rose from the chair, then went over and put her arm around Ella's shoulders. "Remember that the spirit is willing, but the flesh is weak. If you go talk to him, you're liable to wind up flat on your back again."

"Ooh ... If my father ever found out about what happened, he'd go ballistic."

"Let's hope that Reed isn't the type to kiss and tell."

The insistent ring of the doorbell buzzed through the house, alerting Mark, who'd just taken off his coat and tie, that someone was eager to see him. As he made his way from the bedroom, he undid the top two buttons of his shirt. He hoped whoever was so determined to disturb him wasn't a client or business associate. He'd had a long, hard day, and all he wanted was to fix himself a bite of supper, watch some mindless show on TV, and go to bed early.

Through the sheer-curtained French door, he saw a woman's outline, and by the time he reached for the doorknob, he realized it was Regina. The minute he opened the door, she rushed toward him. He instinctively spread his arms wide and engulfed her in a tender embrace. Tears streamed down her cheeks. She quickly buried her face against his shoulder. He patted her on the back.

"Regina, honey, what's wrong?"

She clung to him, and he had to admit he rather liked holding her. What he didn't like was the way she kept crying. Something or someone had upset her.

"Oh, Mark, I—I still can't believe what I saw," she said.

Continuing his comforting caresses, he asked, "What did you see?"

She lifted her head and looked directly at him. Her face was blotchy from crying, her nose pink, and her eyes slightly swollen. "Since I got off work early today,

I went by the Carlisles' house to surprise Mama with a ride home. But I'm the one who got the surprise. Oh, Mark . . ." Regina burst into fresh tears.

He wrapped his arm around her waist, kicked the door closed, and led her down the hall to the living room. "Come on over here and sit down. Then I want you tell me what's upset you so much."

She followed without protest, clinging to his hand and sitting as he instructed, but she never released her hold on him. "Mr. Jeff Henry and I walked in on Mama and Senator Porter kissing. Right there in the Carlisles' house."

Mark felt as if he should shake his head or pop his ears to improve his hearing. Surely he had misunderstood Regina. "Say that again, please."

Regina tilted her head to one side and glared at Mark. "Senator Porter and my mother were kissing. And I don't mean a peck on the cheek. I mean a passionate man-woman kiss."

"What did they say when y'all walked in on them?"

"Mama said she could explain. But she can't. How could she ever explain kissing a married man?"

"I take it that you didn't give her a chance to explain."

"No, I didn't. I just got in my car and drove away. I came here, to you. I didn't know where else to go or what to do."

Mark cupped her chin in the hollow between his thumb and forefinger. "I'm glad you came to me. I hope you know that you can always count on me. But honey, sooner or later you're going to have to talk to your mother."

"I know, but just not now. Not tonight. I can't."

He skimmed his fingertips over the side of her face. "Then stay here as long as you'd like. I'll fix us some supper and then later, if you'd like, you can go home and see what your mother has to say."

She clasped Mark's hand tightly in hers. "You know that I'm illegitimate, don't you?"

"Regina . . ."

"I have no idea who my father is. My mother has refused to discuss the circumstances of my birth with me. I thought"—Regina took a deep breath, then released it.—"that her affair with my father had been a one-time thing, that they had loved each other and for some reason simply couldn't get married. But now, after seeing Mama with Senator Porter, I wonder how many men there have been. How many affairs has she had? Is she having an affair with Senator Porter?"

"You won't know the answers to these questions until you talk to Judy," Mark said. "But don't assume the worst about your mother and don't judge her so harshly. You don't have all the facts."

"I don't have any of the facts."

Mark brought Regina's hand to his lips, kissed her, and said, "Come into the kitchen with me. We'll grill some chicken, toss a salad, and spoon up some sherbet. Helping me with supper might take your mind off things, at least for a little while."

Regina nodded. A tentative smile played at the corners of her mouth. "You're wonderful. Thank you for being so good to me."

How he loved this woman! This beautiful, emotionally fragile doll. "I'm glad you think I'm wonderful, but honey, you don't ever have to thank me for being good to you."

Mark led her into the kitchen, removed her jacket, tied an apron around her waist, and lined the ceramic tile counter with various items. "Why don't you marinate the chicken while I run to the bedroom and change clothes?"

She nodded and quickly set to work. Mark rushed to his bedroom, stripped off his suit trousers and starched white shirt, and replaced them with a pair of khaki slacks and a navy blue cotton pullover shirt. Then he picked up the phone, dialed, and waited.

"Hello," the woman's voice said.

"Judy, this is Mark Leamon. I thought you'd want to know that Regina is here with me. She's going to stay for dinner and then I'll see that she gets home safely."

"Is she all right?"

"Look, I'll be honest with you. She told me what she saw this evening."

"Mark, I can explain."

"You don't owe me any explanations," he said. "But you do need to be honest with Regina. I don't know why you've never told her who her father is, but—"

"I couldn't tell her. I still can't."

"Then I'm afraid you're going to have a problem." Mark paused to consider what he was about to say. "Regina has suffered a great deal in her life, and although she's a survivor, she isn't emotionally strong. You know that probably better than anyone. From now on, I'm not going to let anyone hurt her again. Not even you."

Silence. A long, painful pause. "You love my daughter."

"More than anything."

"Then help her, Mark, because I can't."

Ella had forced herself to eat a few bites of the delicious meal Bessie had prepared, but everything had tasted like cardboard. She was eaten alive with guilt. She never kept secrets from her father. Although she didn't discuss her love life with him, he'd always been aware when there was someone special in her life. From the time she'd first started dating, she had turned to her father for his approval or disapproval of her boyfriends. A thumbs-down from Daddy had meant she didn't see the guy again.

You aren't dating Reed Conway, she reminded herself. *No, you skipped the dating stage and went straight to the . . . Stop this, right now! You're driving yourself crazy. Act normal or Daddy will figure out that something is wrong.*

Since the dining room remained in utter chaos, the family had eaten dinner in the kitchen. Her mother had complained and her father had promised a speedy repair to the destruction in the dining and living rooms. Bessie had spent the better part of the afternoon cleaning up the kitchen, which had received only minor damage. Broken dishes, scattered items, and spray paint on the back door.

"Frank tells me that there's nothing more he can do," Webb said as he paced the floor in the den, the one downstairs room that had been left unscathed by the intruder. "There is no evidence against Reed, so he can't arrest him. And Frank has tried warning him, but that doesn't seem to do any good."

"I'm afraid of that man." Carolyn wrung her hands nervously. "What if he doesn't stop at just breaking into our home?"

"Since there is no evidence against him, how can you be so sure that Reed Conway is the one who broke in and—" Ella said.

"How can there be any doubt?" Carolyn glared at Ella. "When Jeff Henry came over to see me the moment I arrived home, we discussed this very thing and agreed that there is no one else it could be. No one has ever broken into our house. This family hasn't had any problems—not until Reed Conway was released from prison. Jeff Henry said he didn't think it was a coincidence, and neither do I."

"But you're condemning a man without evidence," Ella said.

"Why are you defending him?" Webb demanded.

"I'm not defending him," Ella replied. "I'm simply pointing out the facts, which y'all seem perfectly willing to overlook."

"There's circumstantial evidence." Webb stomped across the room to the liquor cabinet, flung it open, and pulled out a bottle of bourbon. "As a good lawyer and now a judge, you should know that sometimes circumstantial evidence is enough to convict."

"Only when the person's guilt has been proven beyond a reasonable doubt."

Carolyn clapped her hands together. "Enough. Enough. I hate it when the two of you argue." She looked beseechingly at Ella. "Dear, you mustn't be fooled by any sob stories you hear about that young man from either his mother or his sister. Is that it, Ella? Have you been listening to Judy or Regina professing Reed's innocence?"

"No, Mother, I haven't been listening to anyone," Ella said. "And I didn't mean to argue with Daddy. I was simply pointing out what Frank Nelson had already explained—that he cannot arrest a man without evidence, and there is none in this case."

"Oh, dear me. All this talk of guilt and innocence is wearing me to a frazzle." Carolyn sighed dramatically. "Ella, call Viola to come take me upstairs. Then I want you and your father to kiss and make up. Do it for me."

Ella leaned down, placed her hand on her mother's shoulder, kissed her on the cheek, and said, "I'm sorry if I upset you."

Carolyn patted Ella's hand. "You're my good girl, aren't you? You've always been so considerate of my feelings."

Carolyn gave Webb a meaningful glance and Ella understood that look. She'd seen it before, more times that she could count. When she'd been younger, that forlorn, melancholy look her mother often gave her father had puzzled Ella. But in her late teens, she had finally figured out the meaning. It was Carolyn's subtle, nonverbal way of chastising her husband, of letting him know that he was not being considerate, understanding, or attentive enough to suit her.

Ignoring his wife's silent reprimand, Webb poured himself a glass of bourbon. Ella released the catch on her mother's wheelchair, grabbed the handles, and pivoted her mother around toward the door.

"I'll call Viola for you," Ella said. "Of course, if you'd like, I can come up with you and help you."

"No, dear, you stay and see if you can improve your father's mood. He's been a real bear ever since he heard about the break-in. He's terribly worried about you." Carolyn choked back her tears. "And so am I. If anything ever happened to you . . ."

"Nothing is going to happen to me."

Before Ella had the chance to say more or to give her mother a hug, Viola appeared at the top of the stairs. "Are you ready to come up for the night, Miss Carolyn?"

"Yes, please, Viola. I'm weary after that long drive from the Gulf."

Viola descended the stairs with quick, heavy footsteps. Ella stood aside and watched while Viola lifted Carolyn from the wheelchair and placed her in the chairlift that had been built into the stairs shortly after Carolyn's accident.

As the lift began moving, Carolyn waved and smiled, then called out, "Go talk to your father."

Ella released a heavy breath. Now, to face Webb Porter's displeasure.

Just as she started to reenter the den, she met her father coming out the door. "Let's take a walk, princess," Webb said. "I haven't looked in on Beau and Stonewall and Lee since I got home. I want to take them some treats."

Ella nodded, a sense of relief inching its way through her body. Webb had given her a reprieve, perhaps deciding that Reed Conway wasn't worth continuing the argument with her. Whatever the reason that her father had decided to cease and desist, she was grateful. She never seemed to win a battle with him.

"There's rain in the air." Webb took a deep breath upon entering the back porch, then reached down to a sack of dog treats he kept there, removed two handfuls, and stuffed them in his pockets.

Ella sighed contentedly when her father took her arm

and draped it through his as they went down the steps that led to the patio. The aroma of honeysuckle wafted about them, mixing with the heady scent of roses from the garden.

"Did you and Mother enjoy your vacation?" Ella asked.

"We had a pleasant time," Webb said. "Your mother always enjoys having my undivided attention."

"You two should get away together more often. I know Mother would like that."

"Hm."

"Daddy, is something wrong—other than concern about me and the break-in? You seem distracted."

He caressed her arm. "Nothing for you to worry about. Just some old business that won't go away."

Ella loved these moments alone with her father. Throughout her childhood, he had taken time for her. To talk. To listen. Showing a genuine interest in her life. She did so adore her father and had always strived to please him.

He certainly wouldn't be very pleased if he knew you'd had sex with Reed Conway.

Twilight shadows fell across the backyard. The hum of nighttime insects began to stir to life. During the daylight hours, sleepy Southern towns often looked old, tired, and sometimes shabby. Hybrid creatures, a blend of a bygone era with touches of progress here and there. But come sundown and towns like Spring Creek took on a magical quality. Like faded beauties, faded towns appeared their best by candlelight or moonlight. Behind the closed doors of the stately old mansions, the modern houses in new neighborhoods, and the rundown homes in need of repair, people lived and loved and died. Some with dignity. Some with passion. Others with cruel intentions.

"The boys are quiet tonight," Webb said as they approached the kennels. "They're usually boisterous when they hear me coming."

Ella flipped the switch that turned on the lights surrounding the kennel area. All three dogs seemed to be asleep. They were stretched out on the ground just inside the fence. An oddly unnerving feeling rippled along Ella's nerve endings.

Webb whistled and then called out, "Get up, you lazy hounds." He pulled out a handful of treats. "I've got some goodies for you. Come on, Lee. Get up, Beau. Stonewall—"

Webb broke into a run, unlatched the gate, and hurried inside the enclosure. He tossed aside the treats he'd brought with him.

"Daddy, what's wrong?" Ella cried out as she raced after him.

Webb knelt down and ran his hand over the unmoving Stonewall. When Ella approached, she knew before her father said a word. Knew that her daddy's hunting dogs—animals he dearly loved—were dead.

Chapter 20

Regina helped Mark fill the dishwasher and clean up the kitchen after their meal. Her boss had a lovely old house that had belonged to his parents. Odd, she thought, how much at home she felt here, in this house with Mark. But then she supposed she'd feel the same way no matter where she was, as long as she was with the man she loved. He had been kind and caring since the moment she rushed into his arms after fleeing from the Carlisle home hours ago. He had listened to her rant and rave and cry. But not once had he been judgmental of her mother or Webb Porter. After she'd vented her initial frustration, she had calmed down enough to enjoy the meal with Mark, and it was while they were eating orange sherbet that he'd told her he had telephoned her mother earlier, so that she wouldn't worry.

"Would you like to sit outside in the swing for a while?" Mark asked. "Since the sun has set, it should be a lot cooler."

She nodded and gave him a fragile smile. He took her hand in his and led her from the kitchen, through the house, and onto the side porch, which was secluded from the street and the neighboring house by a tall, white fence. They sat side by side, letting the warm night air caress their skin. Mark lifted his arm and draped it across the back of the swing. Regina scooted closer to him and laid her head on his shoulder.

"I think it's going to rain," he said, then leaned over and brushed his lips against hers. "Feeling better?"

Regina sighed. "Yes, some. Thank you."

"Are you ready to go home and talk to your mother?"

She shook her head. "Not tonight." She glanced at him in the semidarkness, the moonlight and streetlight creating the only illumination in the dark night except for an occasional burst of heat lighting off in the distance. "Could I stay here with you tonight?"

After clearing his throat, Mark swallowed hard. "I know you aren't telling me that you want to sleep with me, but if you stay the night, people are bound to talk. Will you mind if my neighbors think we're having an affair?"

"I wish we were having an affair," Regina said. "I wish we could make love tonight and every night. You can't imagine how inadequate I feel not being able to give myself to you the way any other woman could."

Mark kissed her again, softly, nondemanding. He didn't touch her, and his gentle approach allowed Regina to respond without feeling threatened. She knew she was safe with Mark. He would never ask more of her than she was willing to give. She opened up to him, allowing him to ease his tongue inside her mouth and explore with leisurely tenderness. A shiver of sexual longing fluttered inside her stomach, and of their own accord, her arms lifted and her hands flattened against his chest. He deepened the kiss. She loved the feelings bursting inside her. A tightening sensation. A tingling awareness. Then suddenly Mark cupped the nape of her neck. *No, don't*, she cried silently. Junior had held her neck, forcing her to lie still so that he could kiss her. His breath had smelled of beer and cigarettes. He had trapped her beneath him, pinning her to the ground. And while he'd ravaged her mouth, he had rammed his hand inside her panties and . . .

Regina jerked free, jumped up, and gulped in deep, nervous breaths. Mark rose to his feet, but didn't touch her.

"I'm sorry, honey. What did I do that upset you?"

"My neck," she said, between quick, harsh breaths. "Junior held my neck and . . . and . . . Oh, Mark!" She swerved around and flung herself at him. "Hold me. Please hold me."

He engulfed her in his big, strong arms and pressed comforting kisses along the side of her face. "It's all right, Regina. Oh, honey, it's all right."

Burying her face against his chest, she clung to him, shivering, but not crying. Regina wasn't sure how long he held her like that, but she was fully aware of his erection pressing against her. And strangely enough, the feel of his arousal didn't frighten her.

Because you trust Mark totally.

Mark released her, then grasped her shoulders and said, "Let's try something that will give you complete control over the situation."

She stared at him, puzzled by his suggestion. "What do you mean?"

"We care about each other, and I think you want me as much as I want you, but you're not ready for us to make love. I understand and I accept the fact that I'll have to be patient with you."

"I'm not worth—"

He pressed his index finger over her lips. "Shush. Don't ever say you're not worth the wait. You, my sweet Regina, are well worth the wait." He took her hands in his and laid them on his chest. "Why don't you touch me, kiss me, do whatever you want to me, and I won't touch you unless you ask me to."

"What?"

"We can start out here, in the swing, or we can go inside. It's your call. You're the one in charge."

"Mark?"

"What, honey?"

Regina's voice trembled. "What if I don't . . . can't—"

"Hey, kiss me, touch me, tickle me, strip me naked. Whatever you want. I'm putty in your hands."

She eyed the swing. The porch was totally secluded. Here they had complete privacy. Even though she wasn't sure why, somehow she felt safer outside than she would in the house.

Did she have the courage to do as Mark had requested? To take charge, be in control, do with him as she wished?

With trembling hands, she undid the buttons on his shirt, all the way to his waist. He stood perfectly still, his arms hanging limp and his hands curled into loose fists. Regina spread apart Mark's shirt. Her breath caught in her throat. He was stocky built, with a broad, thick chest, but she'd never realized how muscular he was. She touched him, tentatively at first, smoothing only her fingertips over his hard, masculine flesh. However, that wasn't enough for her. She curled a lock of chest hair around an index finger, then sought out his small male nipples. When she circled one and then the other with the tip of her finger, Mark drew in a deep breath.

Regina glanced up, looking directly into his eyes. He smiled. She returned the smile. And without thinking, she stood on tiptoe and kissed him on the mouth. He didn't move a muscle. She kissed him again and when he responded, she inched her tongue inside his mouth and was rewarded with a sensual moan erupting from his throat.

Her lips moved down his neck and over his exposed shoulder blades. Mark shivered. She painted damp kisses over his chest, stopping to lave each nipple. He blew out a shuddering breath.

"Would you let me see you naked?" she asked. "Even if I leave on my clothes?"

"If that's what you want, yes."

"Maybe we should go inside now ... to your bedroom."

"Are you sure?"

"As long as I'm in charge."

"You're in charge. I promise."

She took his hand and led him inside, where he indicated with a nod of his head in which direction they should go. Mark's bedroom was magnificently masculine, but decorated with the flair and style that Regina associated with the man himself. Honey-toned paneling graced the walls of the large room, and various shades of tan, beige, brown, and gold dominated the area. Bookshelves flanked the fireplace, and a trio of oil paintings of thoroughbred horses hung above the mantel.

Tugging on his hand, she drew him across the room and over to the king-size bed with a woven straw headboard. The tan-and-brown striped spread had been turned down to reveal crisp beige linens. Moonlight streamed through the tall windows that spread across one wall.

Regina unbuckled Mark's belt, then undid his slacks and unzipped them. "Would you ... please ... take off your clothes?"

Casually, as if he had all the time in the world and undressing before her was an everyday occurrence, Mark removed his shirt and tossed it on the five-foot square tufted ottoman at the foot of the bed. While Regina looked on, her gaze glued to his body, he bent down, took off his shoes and socks, and then slid his slacks down and off, placing them alongside his discarded shirt. He stood before her wearing only his navy blue boxer shorts. The bulge of his erection strained against the fly front.

"Do you want me to leave these on"—he tweaked the elastic waistband of his shorts—"or take them off?"

She wanted to see all of him, every rock hard inch of his thick, stocky body. She longed to run her hands over his hair-roughened chest and arms and legs. And he would let her do whatever she wanted to do and ask nothing in return.

"Please . . ." She hesitated, frightened by her own bold thoughts. "Take them off."

He obeyed her request, turned his back, bent at the waist and pulled down his shorts, then kicked them aside. Regina sucked in her breath at the sight of his tight buttocks and the glimpse of his scrotum. When he straightened to his full height, he didn't turn and face her, so she rushed to him and wrapped her arms around his naked waist. Hurriedly, as if her lips were on fire and his bare back provided the only cooling balm, she spread kisses from his shoulders to his spine. He trembled.

Inch by slow, torturous inch, she crept her fingers over his belly and downward until she encountered his penis, which stood at full alert.

For a split second, unbidden memories of Junior taking her hand and forcing her to touch him ceased her exploration of Mark's body. *This isn't Junior,* she reminded herself. *You would never have willingly touched him. This is Mark. The man you love. The man who loves you.*

She circled his penis with her hand. He groaned. She released her hold on him. Grasping his shoulder, she turned him around, but kept her gaze on his face as she marched him backward toward the bed. With a heady feeling of power, she gave him a shove and toppled him onto the bed. He lay there, spread out, waiting for whatever she chose to do next. He didn't move, didn't say a word. But he gazed at her with such undeniable passion that Regina swayed toward him, drawn by the sexual undercurrent passing between them.

Still fully clothed, she crawled into bed with him, straddling him. She covered his body with kisses, stopping only when she reached his bulging sex. She wanted to put her mouth on him, to taste, to lick, to suck.

"I want to . . ." she couldn't bring herself to say the words aloud.

"Do it," he said, his voice hoarse with desire.

She nuzzled him with her nose first. The musky scent of him excited her, but she was unable to go further, to actually touch him with her mouth. She lifted her head, sat up, and scooted away from him.

"I'm sorry," she said. "I can't."

"It's all right," he told her.

"I don't know why you want me." She shook her head as tears gathered in her eyes. "I'm of no use to you. Not the way a woman should be to a man."

Lying there, flat on his back, Mark held out his hand to her. When she placed her hand in his, he drew her toward him, then laid her hand over his penis. She sighed. Her fingers curled around him. He encompassed her hand with his and began moving her hand up and down. Within seconds she relaxed and became one with the rhythm he set, so that when he removed his hand, she continued the caress.

"I'm fixing to come, honey," he groaned the admission.

Nodding her understanding, she accelerated the rhythm.

Clutching the bedding tightly on either side of his hips, Mark groaned and jerked spasmodically as his semen jetted out, covering Regina's hand. She watched his face, the expression akin to pain. But it wasn't pain, it was ecstasy. Suddenly she realized that she had given him this wonderful pleasure. He lay there for quite some time, but she continued to hold on to his penis, although she could feel his erection subsiding. Still breathing raggedly, he sat up, circled her wrist and removed her hand. He scooted off the bed and took her with him, then guided her into the adjoining bathroom, where he washed her hands before cleaning himself.

She couldn't take her eyes off him and wondered if all women in love felt so utterly, completely insane about the man they adored.

As Mark dried himself with a towel, he said, "I could give you the same pleasure, without our having sex."

Yes, her body screamed. *Yes!* She ached with the need for release. But she didn't want to undress, to lay herself bare and vulnerable, even knowing that Mark would not invade her body.

"I can't take off my clothes," she said, her voice a mere whisper. "I'm sorry, but I just can't."

He pulled her into his arms. "Remember, honey, you don't have to do anything you don't want to do."

She sighed. "I'd like to lie in your arms and have you kiss me and . . . and touch me."

Mark scooped her up in his arms. Surprised by his sudden move, she yelped softly, but quickly adjusted and threw her arm around his neck. He laid her on the bed and came down beside her. He was a big, powerful man. But he wasn't Junior Blalock. Mark would never hurt her. She relaxed. He kissed her, and as he deepened the kiss, he ran his hands over her body, caressing her through her clothes. The soft silk blouse, the wrinkled blue skirt, the confining panty hose. When he lifted his head and gazed into her eyes, she saw the love he felt for her.

"If I do anything you don't want me to do, tell me immediately and I'll stop," he said.

She nodded.

"May I take off your panty hose?"

"Just my panty hose. Nothing else."

"All right."

He slid his hands under her skirt, grasped the waistband of her panty hose, and slowly, carefully tugged them over her hips and down her legs. After tossing aside the sheer hose, he massaged her feet. Regina shivered with apprehension. Was she ready for this?

When Mark eased up beside her and lowered his mouth to her breast, she tensed. But the moment his lips suckled her through her blouse and bra, her femininity tightened and a wild sensation shot from her breasts to the center of her body. She whimpered as he sucked at one breast and rubbed the other with his fingers.

Moisture flooded between her legs. Her body clenched and unclenched. Mark unzipped her skirt. She drew in a deep breath, preparing to protest, but when he slid his hand beneath the skirt and under her panties, she simply shivered with anticipation.

"Is it all right for me to touch you?" he asked.

Was it? Could she enjoy Mark's erotic caresses without panicking? "Yes. But if I say stop, then—"

"I'll stop immediately."

He touched her there, in the most intimate of places. Hesitantly at first, and then more boldly. While his fingers worked magic between the swollen feminine lips, his mouth covered hers and kissed her until she was breathless.

"Mark!" she cried out, aware that release was close. So close.

"Let it happen, honey. Please, just let it happen."

Her orgasm rocketed through her, an explosion of immense satisfaction that went on and on and on. When she bucked up against his hand, he moved his fingers harder and faster. She cried and whimpered and finally fell apart.

When the aftershocks subsided, Mark removed his hand from her panties and pulled her into his arms. She cuddled against him, sighing his name over and over again. Regina had never known anything so wonderful. There were many ways to make love, she realized. Only with Mark could this have happened. Because she loved him. Because she trusted him. And because he didn't ask more of her than she was capable of giving.

* * *

"Thanks for getting here so quickly and for keeping it quiet." Webb shook hands with Frank Nelson. "I'd rather Carolyn didn't know about this tonight. She's been upset enough by the break-in. I'm afraid if she knows someone poisoned my dogs, Viola would have to give her a sedative."

Ella couldn't believe this had happened. That those big, lovable hounds of her father's were dead. They were assuming the dogs had been poisoned because there was no evidence of wounds on them anywhere.

"I'll get the dogs to Doc Hambry and tell him we need autopsies right way," Frank said. "I've sent Wilkes and Bankhead to inspect the kennels and go over the grounds for any evidence."

"My guess is that they won't find anything." Webb paced back and forth on the patio. "I'd say my dogs ate all the evidence."

"Poisoned meat." Frank nodded. "Easiest way to kill an animal. But dammit all, Webb, who'd kill a man's hunting dogs?"

"Someone who hated him. Someone who wanted to hurt him."

"You're thinking Reed Conway, and I'm telling you that there's no way I can accuse the man of this crime without some evidence." Frank removed his hat and scratched his head. "I've come darn close to harassing Reed more than once these past few weeks. If I step over the line again, he'll be bringing me up on charges."

"Then it's time I had a talk with Reed," Webb said. "I've a good mind to go over to Judy's right now and have it out with him."

"Now, don't you go doing something you're going to regret," Frank told him. "Remember, you're a senator and whatever you do can wind up front page headlines. Besides, Reed isn't living with his mama anymore. He's moved into the room above Conway's garage."

Webb slammed his right fist into the palm of his left hand. The smack reverberated in the nighttime stillness. Ella jumped. Her father was fighting mad, and all his anger was directed at Reed. As much as she wanted to believe Reed incapable of such an inhumane act, she, like her father, could think of no one else who truly hated her family, and Webb in particular. Had Reed's years in prison dehumanized him to the extent that he could ruthlessly murder innocent dogs?

Tears gathered in the corners of her eyes. She remembered Stonewall, Lee, and Beau as pups: boisterous, rambunctious, yelping and playing. And the first time her father had taken them hunting, he'd come back with tales of what fine beasts he'd raised.

"As soon as Doc Hambry finishes up those autopsies, I want my animals back," Webb said. "I plan on burying them in the coon dog cemetery. They were fine hunting dogs. They deserve a place of honor for their final rest."

Ella heard the slight catch in her father's voice and noted the fine mist covering his eyes. She could still see the image of him hunkered down over Stonewall, his favorite of the three, stroking the dead dog's slightly swollen body. Tears had trickled down his cheeks, but he'd wiped them away quickly before he stood and moved on to check Lee and Beau.

"You and Ella might as well go on to bed," Frank said. "Nothing else y'all can do tonight. I'll give you a call tomorrow morning, if we find anything out here. And I'll let you know as soon as I hear back from Doc Hambry."

Webb nodded. "Yeah, I suppose you're right." He glanced at Ella. "You ready to go in, princess?"

"You go ahead, Daddy. I think I'll stay out here for a while. I couldn't sleep even if I went to bed."

"I'm going inside to pour myself some bourbon and toast those three fine animals." Webb grabbed Ella around the shoulders and hugged her to his side. "Don't stay out too long." He glanced up at the night sky. Streaks of summer lightning drew closer and closer.

"I'll come in before it starts raining," she promised.

The moment her father was out of earshot, Frank Nelson said, "Webb sure did think a heap of those animals, didn't he?"

"Yes, he did."

"Miss Ella, do you believe Reed Conway poisoned your daddy's hounds?"

"I don't know."

"The way I look at it, if Reed's the one behind your harassment and behind the break-in and now killing Webb's dogs, then it's only a matter of time before he targets one of y'all for some real harm. You. Your daddy. Your mama."

Ella shivered. "No, I . . . I can't believe that. You're saying he'll kill again, aren't you? Do you think he truly hates my father that much, that he'd risk spending the rest of his life in prison? He keeps professing that he didn't murder Junior Blalock, that all he wants is to prove who the real killer is and clear his name. If that's true—"

"You shouldn't be listening to anything Reed Conway has to say. Nothing would please him more than for you and your daddy to be on opposite sides, you believing Reed innocent after your daddy prosecuted him for murder."

Ella didn't know how to respond, so she said nothing. Frank tipped his hat and went to catch up with the two men inspecting the kennels. She glanced up at her mother's room and wondered if Carolyn was asleep. She hoped so. The last thing her mother needed was to be upset more than she already was. And what about her father? He might have let things go for tonight, but come morning, he might confront Reed. She couldn't let him do that. There was no telling what her father might do. Or what Reed might do.

And just who are you worried about, your father or Reed?

There was only one way to prevent a confrontation between the two men. She had to see Reed herself. If he had been the one to slaughter her father's hunting dogs, she would know the truth the moment she looked into those cold blue eyes of his.

Having satisfactorily rationalized her behavior to herself, Ella went upstairs, changed from her navy linen dress to a casual cotton dress, and replaced her heels with sandals. She grabbed her purse, picked up her car keys and slipped down the back stairs. Her mother's bedroom door had been closed and so had her father's, so neither had any idea that she wasn't safe and sound in her bed. She hoped that if anyone heard the roar of the Jag's motor, they would think it came from next door or across the street.

The trip to Conway's Garage took all of ten minutes. She eased her car around to the back of the building, killed the engine, and got out. Was she crazy for coming here? Was she asking for trouble? What if Reed was as bad as people thought he was? What if he was a murderer? He could snap her neck like a twig with his big, brutal hands.

A shiver of apprehension zinged up her spine. She glanced at the wooden stairs that led up to the second floor. Only a dim light shone through the window that she could see from this angle. Did that mean Reed was still awake? Of course, there was a chance he wasn't even home, that this trip had been for nothing.

A jagged streak of heat lightning crackled across the sky, followed by a loud boom of thunder. The storm was getting closer. She took a deep breath, garnered her courage and started climbing the outside staircase. When she reached the halfway point, she heard the soft, sweet strands of a mellow jazz tune. Her heart skipped a beat. Reed was home. He was listening to music.

Another blaze of lightning flashed. An earth-shattering rumble of thunder announced that the storm was fast approaching. Ella hesitated when she reached the door. *Either you confront Reed or your father will.*

She lifted her hand and knocked. No reply. She knocked again. Harder. Repeatedly. Suddenly the door swung open. There stood Reed. Big and broad, his shoulders filling the doorway. His blond hair was tousled, as if he'd been raking his fingers through it. She surveyed him and noted he was barefoot and wore nothing but a pair of unsnapped jeans. He stared at her, narrowing his gaze until his eyes were mere slits. Ella swallowed her fear.

"As I live and breathe, if it isn't Judge Eleanor Porter come knocking at my door." Reed's mouth curved into the cocky grin that was capable of turning her stomach inside out. "What are you doing here, babe? Come for some more of what I gave you this afternoon?"

Without any conscious thought, acting purely on instinct, Ella drew back her hand and slapped Reed's face. She gasped when she realized what she'd done. She'd never struck another person in her entire life.

Still grinning, Reed rubbed his cheek. That deadly stare of his pinned her to the spot. *Run, damn it, run!* she told herself. Reed grabbed her wrist and jerked her up against him. For just a second she couldn't breathe, couldn't think, couldn't respond. When she finally tried to pull free, he held fast.

Placing his mouth over her ear, he whispered, "I'm going to give you what you came here for."

Chapter 21

Reed hauled her into his apartment, kicked the door shut with his bare foot, and gripped the back of her neck with his big hand. Fear raced through her body, like the white streaks of lightning racing across the black sky that she could see through the windows facing the alley. Her heartbeat accelerated alarmingly. Perspiration trickled down her spine and between her breasts. The room was warm and humid, like the weather outside. An ancient ceiling fan spun overhead, creaking with each rotation as it blew the tepid air around the room. Even if consciously Ella didn't realize that Reed's place had no air conditioning, her damp, flushed body recognized the fact.

The scent of a man permeated the air. Remnants of cleanliness left by an unscented soap. Heat-induced perspiration. A unique muskiness, as personally identifiable as fingerprints. She could not only see Reed, rawly masculine and sexy as hell, but she could smell him, smell the very essence of his masculinity. Her fingers itched to touch him, to comb over his chest, to tease and tempt and entice. Powerless to resist, she gave in

to the urge to look him over from head to toe. Her gaze
traveled the length of his six-three body, lingering over
the wide shoulders and powerful, deeply tanned arms.
His jeans were undone and the zipper only halfway up,
revealing the tautness of his belly and exposing the
pencil-thin line of brown hair that disappeared behind
the closure of the zipper. His growing erection swelled,
telling her without words that simply touching her
turned him on.

The mournful saxophone wail wove around Ella, like
unseen, sensual hands caressing her. The cool jazz mel-
ody whispered with bass and drums and piano, but gave
center stage to the provocative sax. She felt the heat
within her as well as the sweltering external temperature
that embedded itself in Spring Creek every summer.

Bringing her inspection upward, her glare met
Reed's—the determined, daring gazes of two strong-
willed people, neither willing to give an inch. She tried
to twist her neck and free herself from his hold. He
refused to release her. Her breathing quickened. Reed's
gaze dropped to her breasts, compelling her to watch
the rapid rise and fall of her chest—and the peaks
of her tight nipples pressing against the cotton dress.
Realizing how he was looking at her, and why he was
staring so intently, stimulated clenching sensations
between her thighs, in the very core of her body.

*I don't want to feel this way. How is it possible that every
time I'm near Reed Conway, I get hot and bothered? Why do
I want this man in a way I've never wanted another?*

With his hand secure at the nape of her neck, he
drew her toward him, slowly, taking his time, never
breaking eye contact, as if their melded gazes connected
them physically and emotionally. His cold blue eyes no
longer appeared so cold. A white heat burned in their
depths.

Don't be fooled, she cautioned herself. *You know Reed
isn't emotionally involved. It's only sex for him. Nothing more.
He wants you the way he'd want any other willing female.*

Damn! Was he right? Had she actually come here to see if they could repeat this afternoon's incredible experience? Had she persuaded herself that she'd come here to demand the truth—had he or had he not poisoned her father's hunting dogs?—when all along she'd come to him for more earth shattering sex? What sort of woman was she that she had allowed Reed to reduce her to a smoldering mass of sexual needs?

Reeling her in, he snaked out his other hand and grasped the side of her waist; then when the gap between their bodies closed, he wrapped his arm around her. She knew she should struggle more, try harder to get away from him, but she didn't. When her breasts pressed against his bare chest, he speared his fingers into her hair and jerked her head back, preparing her for his attack.

"Noooo . . ." she moaned as his mouth covered hers.

The moment their lips touched, she was lost and she knew it. There was a brutality about him that wasn't akin to cruelty. He was primitive man driven by basic needs. And he made her feel those same primeval desires. Nothing mattered except appeasing those hungers. He didn't push for entry, instead he ravaged first the upper lip and then the lower. And all the while one of his massive hands held her head in place while the other clutched one of her buttocks. His actions claimed her, a preliminary possession that informed her without words that she was his.

With a desperation felt deep inside, she tried to resist, pleaded with herself to stop before things got completely out of hand. *Remember why you came here. If Reed killed Daddy's dogs . . .* But he didn't. Somehow she knew he hadn't harmed Beau and Stonewall and Lee. *And if you're wrong?* she asked herself.

Suddenly, when she felt his stiff erection throbbing against her thighs, rational thought ceased to exist. Her body recalled the pleasure of being with this man. And it wanted more. His mouth moved over her chin and down her throat. She gulped in deep breaths. He buried his face against her neck and licked softly. Tiny flicks, damp and arousing, sending shivers dancing throughout her body.

Don't touch him! Keep your hands off him and maybe you can still resist. But it was already too late. Her arms lifted up, up, up. . . . Her hands curved over his wide, muscular shoulders. She sighed. Ah, the feel of him.

His hand on her butt pushed her harder and harder against him, until she whimpered and automatically rubbed her mound against his sex. She clamped her hands tighter on his shoulders, her short nails biting into his naked flesh. He groaned, then suddenly released his hold on her head to seek the zipper at the back of her dress. Before she realized what was happening, Reed undid the zipper and lifted her arms to free the dress. The cotton garment slid over her hips, down her legs, and pooled around her feet. She stood before him in only her pink floral panties. As his gaze scorched her bare breasts, she knew why she hadn't bothered to put on her bra when she'd changed clothes. Heaven help her, she had come to Reed for this. Her father's dead hunting dogs had been nothing but the feeble excuse she'd given herself for doing what she'd longed to do. Go to Reed.

When he grabbed her, the sensation of hard bare chest against naked feminine breasts took her breath away. At that very moment, she felt as if she'd been born for this. Born to be Reed Conway's woman. Who he was and who she was didn't matter. Whatever past history existed between their families was unimportant. Any shame or scandal that resulted from their affair seemed a small price to pay for such indescribable ecstasy.

Reed walked her slowly backward as he kissed her. She made no attempt to resist. The back of her legs encountered the edge of the bed. They ended the kiss. Breathlessly, they stared at each other. She wrapped her arms around his neck. With a gentle shove, he toppled her onto the rumpled bed, and with her arms clinging to him, she brought him down with her. He was big and heavy at first, but he quickly braced himself with his elbows and straddled her, stationing his knees on either side of her hips.

"What the hell is it about you, Ella Porter? I can't seem to keep my hands off you."

His hot gaze traveled from her face to her breasts, then lingered. Her nipples tightened even more. The bluesy moan of trumpet and the tinkling chime of the piano played around inside her head, lulling her, seducing her as surely as Reed's passionate inspection.

He lifted her hand to his crotch and laid it over his erection. She knew what he wanted. While looking at him point-blank, she finished unzipping his jeans and in the process dragged them down his hips just a fraction. His sex sprang free. Impressively large. Undeniably rock hard. He was fully aroused and ready.

"This time I want us both naked," he said as he proceeded to remove his jeans.

He hovered over her for just a moment before he reached down and grasped the waistband of her panties. She lifted her hips to help him remove the scanty garment. As she lay beneath him, totally naked, every inch of her body revealed to him, her insecurities came into play. Would he find her unattractive? She wasn't a small, slender woman, no delicate hothouse flower. Would he find her full curves uninviting? Would he think her fat? It had never mattered this much that a man think she was beautiful.

He eased downward, setting one knee between hers to urge her legs apart. She held her breath as he lowered his body by slow degrees until his penis rubbed against the thatch of dark hair that covered her mound. He lowered his lips to her breasts, his breath warm and stimulating against her already pebble-hard nipples. *Touch me there*, she pleaded silently, but he seemed in no hurry to do as she wished. He rubbed against her, sending waves of longing through her; then, before she had a chance to pull him completely down on top of her, he slid to her side and flipped her over and onto her stomach. She gasped in surprise, completely startled by his actions. When she tried to turn over, he laid his hand in the center of her back and held her in place.

"I want to look at you . . . all over," he said, his voice a raspy whisper. "And then I want to touch you and kiss you and lick you until you think you'll go mad if I don't take you. I want you begging for it."

I'm close to that point right now, she felt like shouting. But instead she lay there . . . waiting. His calloused hands began a sensual survey, caressing her from neck to heels, then returning to cup and fondle her buttocks. While his hand slipped between her legs, he lowered his mouth to her shoulders, his lips warm and tender, his tongue wet. His teeth nipped, then his tongue soothed. She moaned with pleasure. But then he moved his attention to her hips, to her butt, and just when she thought she couldn't bear anymore, he moved down the back of her legs and on to her feet.

His fingers sought and found her core, then began a repetitive stroking that soon produced a flood of moisture. Preparation for when he fulfilled his promise to take her. *But only after you're begging for it,* she reminded herself. Her feminine lips swelled, folding around his fingers, as if trying to trap the feel of him.

"Please, Reed," she whimpered.

"Please what?" He taunted her with his question, and by suddenly withholding his touch as he eased away from her.

She lay on her stomach, her cheek resting against the pillow. He was going to make her say it. Damn him! She turned over, her movements deliberately leisurely, as if an urgent sexual fire weren't burning her alive. Avoiding any eye contact with Reed, she lifted her arms over her head and rested them on the pillow, the act thrusting her breasts forward. In her peripheral vision she noted that he watched her like a hawk circling its prey, ready to pounce when the time was right.

"Do you want me?" Ella boldly brought her hand down over her throat, letting her own fingers caress her skin. She looked straight at Reed and saw him swallow hard. "Do you really want me?" She ran her hand over her right breast and nearly cried out when her palm grazed her erect nipple.

"I want you, all right," he said, his lips twitching with an almost-grin. "But if you think playing this little game is going to force me into taking you before you do a little more begging, then you'd better think again."

A tremor of apprehension jarred her already crumbling composure. "I want you," she admitted.

He simply stared at her.

"I want you so very much," she rephrased.

He continued staring.

"Please, Reed, I need you."

"Then tell me exactly what you want, babe, and I'll give it to you." He leaned over and nuzzled her mound, then kissed her intimately.

Ella thought she might unravel completely. Of their own volition, her thighs separated slightly, just enough for Reed to notice.

"You want that, too?" he asked, grinning. "Say the words, Ella, and I'll go down on you first."

The spot between her thighs throbbed unbearably. She reached out and grabbed his shoulders, her gaze focused on his blue, blue eyes. "Damn you. I want you to fuck me. Now."

With a self-satisfied smile on his face, he parted her legs and slipped between them. He put his mouth on her and flicked out his tongue to tease and taste. She shivered. He slid one hand up her belly and to her breast. His fingers closed around her nipple, and when she moaned, he began moving back and forth from one breast to the other, giving each nipple equal attention.

And all the while his mouth and tongue sucked and stroked. Pure sensation took control. She clutched the sheet on either side of her hips, bracing herself for the inevitable.

"I've never . . . this . . ." She gasped. "This is the first time . . . anyone . . ." His tongue worked harder and faster. She moaned. "Ah . . . ah . . . ah . . ." She clutched his head with both hands, keeping him in place, steadying his movements until he burrowed his tongue deeper and deeper.

She cried out when she climaxed, and the world exploded around her in a series of multi-colored lights. While she still shuddered with release, Reed came up and over her, lifted her hips and rammed into her. She took all of him fully and completely into her body, into the hot, wet depths.

His thrusts were deep and hard, driven by pure, frenzied need. She clung to him, moving against him, urging him on. He lunged and retreated, lunged and retreated. Repeating the process, the speed quickly increasing until he was jackhammering into her. Sensation returned to her feminine nub, and once again she felt the tightening that was a prelude to orgasm.

"I've never had two," she murmured as she rose up to kiss his neck. "Oh, Reed . . ."

He was beyond speech, capable only of beastly grunts. His climax hit him hard. The sounds coming from his mouth were those of an alpha male, roaring to the pack that he had just made this female his personal property. As he jetted inside her, she fell apart, her second release even more profound than the first. She held on tight, her body milking his, draining his fluid while she shook with unparalleled pleasure.

He eased off her, slid to her side, and brought her close, confining her within his sheltering arms. Perspiration coated their flesh.

"Reed?"

"No postmortem, babe."

She shook her head, then cuddled against him, a myriad of feelings bombarding her. She cared about this man—cared more than was good for either of them.

He kissed her temple, then draped his arm possessively over her belly. "Get some sleep. We both need a little rest before we go at it again."

"I shouldn't stay. I should go." But actions didn't follow her words. She lay cocooned in his arms, sated and safe.

How odd that she should feel so utterly, completely safe lying naked in the arms of a convicted murderer.

He woke with a start. The tape player he'd borrowed from Briley Joe had kicked off, ending the sexy jazz tunes. But a heavy rain beat down on the metal roof and thunder rumbled overhead. The lights he hadn't bothered to turn off hurt his eyes. He eased out of bed and walked across the room to switch off the overhead light and the lamp, then closed the bathroom door more than halfway, so that only a two-foot panel of light spread across the floor. He reached down in the plastic cooler, retrieved a beer from the melting ice, and popped open the can. He sipped on the cold liquid as he headed back across the room. Then he sat on the side of the bed and drank his beer while he watched Ella sleep.

He'd had her twice, but he still wanted her. Maybe more now than ever. He didn't understand this craving for such rare pussy. Why wouldn't Ivy or somebody like her do just as well? Any woman should do—any willing female who would spread her legs for him. But that wasn't the case. He wanted Ella. Only Ella. He wanted her every way a man could want a woman and then some. He'd nearly lost it when she told him that he was the first man who'd ever gone down on her. That confession made him want to give her more pleasure than she'd ever known. And her admission that no man had ever brought her to a second orgasm had given him a heady sense of power and pride.

He reached out, lifted a lock of her silky black hair, and curled it about his index finger. Ella was one fine-looking woman, and responsive to his every touch—as if he and he alone had the ability to bring her to life.

They were as wrong for each other as two people could be. The judge and the ex-convict. The housekeeper's son and the senator's daughter. If the truth hadn't been so sadly, pathetically true, he would laugh.

Ella's eyelids flickered. When she awoke, would she leave? Would she look at him with regret in her eyes? He didn't want her to go. Not until he'd slacked his desire for her. She opened her eyes and looked up at him, then smiled.

He loved her smile.

"Reed?"

"Yeah?"

"You didn't poison my daddy's three hunting dogs last night, did you?"

Chapter 22

"What the hell are you talking about?" Reed drew back, moving away from her, a wounded look in his eyes—eyes that only moments ago had been gazing at her so tenderly.

She realized instantly that he was innocent, that he honestly didn't know anything about the deaths of her father's beloved dogs. "Reed, I—"

He shot up off the bed, gloriously naked. "Don't bother." He snapped the words. "I take it that somebody killed Webb Porter's hunting dogs, and of course, I'm the number one suspect." He glared at her. "Is that why you came here—to accuse me? What happened, honey, did you get a little sidetracked by your lust for my body?"

"Don't do this. Please, let's don't say things that we'll regret later." She started to rise from the bed, but became acutely aware of her nudity. What the hell? He'd not only seen every inch of her, he was personally acquainted with the territory. She crawled out of bed, stark naked.

Reed's facial muscles tightened, giving him the look

of a dangerous predator. "Lady, the only thing I regret is screwing you twice."

She couldn't endure his cold, unemotional stare. The man who knew her body better than she knew it herself had instantly become a stranger—a frightening stranger.

"I'm sorry." She reached over and laid her hand on his chest.

He jerked away from her. "Not as a sorry as you will be if you come up pregnant." His sudden smile mocked her. "I didn't use a condom again tonight, Miss Ella. Now, wouldn't that be something if I knocked you up?"

"Go ahead and lash out at me," she told him. "If it makes you feel any better. I suppose I deserve it. But I just wish you'd listen to me. I'm sorry I asked about Daddy's hunting dogs." Her fingers itched to touch him, to grab him and pull him to her. But she didn't dare touch him. Fury radiated from him. Strong and deadly. "I realize now that when I decided to come here tonight I told myself I needed to know the truth, that I had to come here and confront you personally about the dogs. But that was just a lie I told myself. The truth is . . . the truth is—"

"You want to know what the truth is?" He grabbed her upper arms, his fingers pressing hard enough to hurt. When she winced, he instantly loosened his hold. "The honest to God truth is that I did not kill Junior Blalock. I haven't written you any letters or made any threatening phone calls or sent you flowers with green snakes. And I sure as hell didn't kill Webb's hunting dogs."

"I believe you. And I'm sorry I asked about the dogs. It's just that I loved Beau and Stonewall and Lee, and I needed to be sure that the man I . . . that you hadn't poisoned them."

"God damn it, I'd never hurt innocent animals."

Tears gathered in the corners of her eyes. She nodded. "Someone did. Someone poisoned those wonderful dogs. Daddy and I raised them from puppies." Tears trickled down her cheeks. "I loved them almost as much as Daddy did. Stonewall was the runt of his mama's litter and I bottle-fed him." Ella swallowed her tears.

Reed stared at her. She could barely see the blurry outline of his body through her tears. When he touched her, she jumped.

"Don't cry, babe."

"Reed . . ."

He encompassed her in his embrace, his strong arms comforting her. She loved the feel of him, the power of his big body. While she wept against his chest, he cradled her buttocks and lifted her upward until they touched intimately.

"I'm an insensitive asshole," Reed said. "About those things I said a couple of minutes ago—"

She kissed him, then pulled back and smiled at him, her face damp with tears. "You were trying to hurt me because I had hurt you. I understand."

He kissed her forehead, her cheeks, her chin, then licked the teardrops from her eyelashes. "I don't want to hurt you. Not ever. What I want is to protect you from anything and anyone who would harm you. Looks like I'd better start with myself."

"I don't want to hurt you either," she said. "If you'll let me, I'll help you find out who really killed Junior Blalock. Will you let me help you?"

He grinned, but this time there was no anger or sarcasm associated with the smile. "Your folks aren't going to like the idea of their little girl getting involved with a man like me."

"I'm not a little girl." She rubbed herself against him. "I'm a woman."

"You sure are," Reed agreed.

His penis swelled to life between them. Ella sighed, loving the feel of him. When he took her hand and led her toward the bed, she hesitated when she noticed the time glowing brightly on the small digital alarm clock sitting on the floor beside the bed. It would be daylight soon. She had spent the night with Reed.

"I should go home," she told him.

"Want to sneak in before anyone realizes you've been gone all night?"

"Can you understand?"

"Yeah, I can understand," he said. "Just tell me something, Ella. Are you ashamed that you spent the night with me."

"No!"

"But you wouldn't want the whole town to know, would you?"

She sighed. He had her dead to rights. No, she didn't want people to know about her involvement with Reed. "I'm sorry, but—"

"You're a Porter, a circuit court judge and a lady." He poked her shoulder repeatedly, inching her backward until he toppled her onto the bed. "You can stay another thirty minutes, can't you?"

"Yes."

Her compliance signaled Reed to take action. Within seconds he had joined her on the bed, lifted her up to straddle him, and impaled her with his stiff sex.

"Come on, babe, one last wild ride for the road."

Ella unlocked the back door, then moved through the kitchen as quietly as possible, hoping she wouldn't awaken anyone. Bessie never arrived before six o'clock, and there was no reason why the rest of the household wouldn't still be asleep. As she headed upward, the back stairs creaked slightly, the whine echoing in the stillness of the dawn hour. When she reached the top of the stairs, she sighed. Just a short walk down the hall to her room and she was home free. No one need ever know that she'd stayed out all night.

Her hand hovered on the crystal doorknob to her bedroom door, but before she grasped it, she heard footsteps behind her. Glancing over her shoulder, she saw her father coming toward her. Uh-oh! She knew how she looked—as if she'd spent the night making mad, passionate love. Wrinkled. Mussed. Tired. Sated. And if she could smell sex on herself, then her father would, too. Her heart sank. She supposed she could lie to him and tell him she'd been with Dan, but her father would know better. And she'd never lied to her father, not once in her entire life. She wasn't about to start now.

"You look like hell," Webb said.

"I'm a grown woman, and if choose to stay out all night, it's nobody's business," she told him.

"Agreed." His gaze traveled over her. "You'd better get a shower and change clothes. You wouldn't want your mother to see you looking like that."

Ella nodded, relief flooding through her. "Thanks, Daddy. For not asking any questions."

"None of my business, remember?" But there was no warm smile, no twinkle of devilment in his eyes.

"You know, don't you?" The sudden realization that her father was probably aware of where she'd spent the night, and with whom, unnerved her.

"Is it more than sex?" he asked.

Ella swallowed. "I honestly don't know."

"I don't approve."

"I know."

"You're playing a dangerous game with a dangerous man. You could get hurt. I can't let that happen."

"Daddy, please—"

"Take your shower."

"We'll talk later, okay?"

He nodded, then turned and went back to his room. Ella opened the door and went straight through to the bathroom. As she stripped off her clothes, she encountered the strong scent of Reed Conway, as if it were embedded in her skin. She tossed her dress and panties in the laundry hamper, turned on the shower, and stepped under the lukewarm spray. As she began to scrub her body, she recalled the feel of Reed's hands, the touch of his mouth and tongue, the power of having him deep inside her.

"Is it more than sex?" her father had asked.

She didn't want it to be more. If it were only sex between Reed and her, it would simplify this untenable predicament she was in. But if she were totally honest with herself, she would have to admit that she truly feared that it *was* more than sex. Much more. Heaven help her.

Judy Conway sat at her kitchen table, a cup of strong coffee in her hand. She hadn't slept more than a couple of hours all night. Even though she trusted Mark Leamon and knew he would never do anything to hurt Regina, Judy couldn't help wondering what had happened between Regina and her boss last night. Her daughter had been upset and angry when she'd run away from the Carlisle house yesterday. And Regina had every right to be outraged at seeing her mother sharing a passionate kiss with a married man.

What could she say to Regina? How could she ever explain without being totally honest? She had sworn to herself that she would never reveal the identity of Regina's father to anyone, not even Regina herself. Too many lives could be destroyed if the truth ever came out. Poor Carolyn Porter would be devastated. And Webb's political career would be ruined.

When Judy heard two cars drive up outside, she set her cup on the table, jumped to her feet, and raced to the door. Glancing through the glass panes in the kitchen door, she watched Mark get out of his car and rush to open the driver's door of Regina's Honda. Then he took Regina's hand in his. The two of them looked into each other's eyes, exchanging a lovers' glance. Suddenly Judy felt like a voyeur, inappropriately glimpsing a very private moment. She opened the door, walked out onto the back porch, and waited as the couple approached.

"Good morning," Judy said, trying to make her voice sound cheerful.

"Good morning," Mark replied.

Judy noted that he still held Regina's hand and couldn't help wondering if Regina held on to him so tightly because she felt that Mark was her lifeline. "I've got coffee. And if y'all are hungry, I can fix breakfast."

"Thanks, but we've already eaten," Mark told her as he and Regina stepped up on the porch. "I made my specialty—ham-and-cheese omelets."

Judy tried to avoid eye contact with her daughter, afraid of what she might see in her child's eyes. Hatred? Condemnation? But as Judy allowed her gaze to casually glimpse Regina, she became even more convinced that something of a sexual nature had transpired between Regina and Mark. Her daughter's suit was wrinkled, her hair slightly untidy, and her face devoid of makeup.

"I think you should know that I didn't want to come home this morning," Regina finally said. "But Mark convinced me that I should give you a chance to explain what I saw at the Carlisle house yesterday."

When Judy exchanged a glance with Mark, she saw sympathy in his eyes. "Thank you, Mark. I appreciate your being there for Regina last night. I knew you'd take care of her."

"I think you should know that I love Regina," Mark said.

"And I love him, too," Regina informed her mother.

"I couldn't be happier for both of you." Judy longed to put her arms around her child, to hug her and kiss her. She, better than anyone, knew how much Regina longed to love and be loved, to be capable of a normal relationship with a man. Had Mark and Regina made love last night? Judy wondered. Was the dark, damaging sexual fear buried deep in her daughter's soul now vanquished?

"Judy, I think this morning would be a good time to explain everything to Regina," Mark said.

"Yes, you're right. Come on inside." The couple followed her into the kitchen. She took a deep breath. "I'm not a promiscuous woman. I've had sex outside of marriage with only one man"—she glanced meaningfully at Regina—"with your father, whom I loved with all my heart."

Regina opened her mouth to speak, but Judy spoke first. "I made a vow to never reveal his identity, and I intend to keep that vow. I'm sorry. But I can tell you this about what you saw yesterday. I'm not having an affair with Webb Porter. He and I dated years ago, when I was in high school. When his family disapproved of him dating a girl from the wrong side of town, we broke up and I married Reed's father, and later on Webb married Carolyn. But we've always had . . . feelings for each other. I'm afraid that yesterday, we let those feelings get out of hand."

"But why, Mama?" Regina asked. "I don't understand. How could you care about the man who prosecuted Reed, the man most responsible for my brother having to spend fifteen years in prison?"

"I don't know exactly how it happened," Judy admitted. "One minute Webb and I were talking, and the next thing I knew . . . It was a terrible mistake, and I am so very sorry that you saw what happened."

"I don't know if I believe you or not," Regina said. "I've spent my entire life defending you—to myself and anyone who dared say anything against you. I want to believe that my father was your one and only illicit lover, that you haven't been with countless men. That you aren't the whore Junior told me you were the night he tried to rape me."

"Oh, Regina." Emotion lodged in Judy's throat, almost choking her. The pain of knowing that she had brought Junior Blalock into their lives, that she had allowed herself to be seduced by his good looks and boyish charm, made her sick to her stomach. She had unleashed a monster on her children, and to this day, both Reed and Regina were paying for her monumental mistake.

"I knew he was lying. I knew when he said that I'd turn out to be a whore just like my mama that he had to be lying." Regina turned to Mark, who opened his arms to her.

Tears welled up in Judy's eyes. "Junior Blalock was a mean, worthless piece of trash who nearly destroyed us. I didn't have the courage to leave him because I was terribly afraid of him. I'd give my life if I could go back and undo the things he did. If I had it to do over again, I wouldn't have married him."

Regina glanced up from where she had her face buried against Mark's chest. She sobbed softly, then eased out of Mark's embrace and went to her mother, stopping when only inches separated their bodies.

"I'm not a whore," Judy said. "I've been with only three men in my entire life. Reed's father, who was my first husband. Your father, whom I loved. And Junior." At the mention of her former husband's name, a cold numbness set in deep within Judy.

"Is Webb Porter my father?" Regina asked.

Judy couldn't breathe. She thought that perhaps her heart had stopped beating. It was as if a two-ton weight sat squarely on her chest. She couldn't speak.

"Does he know?" Regina asked. "Has he always known?"

Webb Porter parked his Mercedes in front of Conway's Garage. He assumed that Reed would be at work. After all, it was shortly after nine, and Webb assumed that most service stations and garages opened early. He'd been forced to sit through breakfast with a chattering Carolyn, still griping about the ransacked condition of the house and the fact that Reed Conway didn't deserve to be walking the streets a free man. Ella had been her usual sweet, dignified self, but all the while she chatted with her mother, smiling warmly and agreeing with whatever Carolyn said, Webb had been tormented by the fact that his daughter had all but confessed to him that she'd spent the night with Reed.

The six gas pumps at the garage held three customers filling up their tanks this morning. The two men and the woman standing by their vehicles waved, nodded, and spoke to Webb. He vaguely recognized the woman, had known one of the men all his life, and knew the other man, too, even though he couldn't recall his name. Of course, all three knew who he was—the curse of being a local politician.

Webb headed toward the garage. As he drew nearer, he saw Reed behind the counter at the cash register, waiting on another customer. Webb entered the building. Reed glanced over at him, no emotion showing on his face; then he returned his attention to the customer, Waylan McGuire, who owned the only pawn shop in Spring Creek.

"Morning, Senator," Waylan said. "Already hot and humid out there, isn't it? Going to be another scorcher."

"Seems that way," Webb agreed.

Reed handed Waylan change from two twenties. "Come back and see us, Mr. McGuire."

The minute Waylan closed the glass door behind him, Reed shut the cash register and met Webb's glare head-on. "What can I do for you this morning, Senator?"

You can stop screwing my daughter, that's what you can do.

"You can stay the hell away from my family," Webb said, just barely controlling his rage.

Reed came out from behind the counter and walked right up to Webb, totally unafraid. Webb wasn't used to that. He was the type of man who normally put the fear of God into other men. But not Reed Conway. Not now. Not fifteen years ago when Reed had been an eighteen-year-old. And not even when Reed had been just a kid, warning Webb to stay away from Judy. Was having an affair with Ella Reed's way of exacting revenge for more than just Webb having prosecuted him for Junior's murder? Was Reed telling him that if Webb could screw around with his mother, then he could screw around with Webb's daughter?

"You need to be more specific," Reed said.

"I don't know what kind of game you're playing, but I'm warning you to stay away from Ella."

"I'd say that's up to Ella."

Webb grabbed Reed's arm, clamping his hand over Reed's biceps. "You stay away from her or I'll make you sorry you're not back in Donaldson. I protect what's mine. Do I make myself clear?"

"Something we have in common, Senator. I protect what's mine, too. And as of last night, your daughter falls into that category."

Webb swung at Reed, his fist just barely connecting with Reed's body because Reed had seen the blow coming and sidestepped to avoid a direct hit. Reeling slightly backward, Reed glared at Webb. He rubbed his bruised jaw.

"I won't beat the hell out of you, you son of a bitch, no matter how much satisfaction it would give me," Reed said. "I won't even hit you. Because you're Ella's father."

Webb stared at Reed Conway, not sure what to think of this man. Hearing a sound from behind him, Webb glanced over his shoulder and realized that they had an audience. One man stood in the open doorway. The other man and woman stood outside, looking in through the glass storefront. Outside, two other customers watched.

Mustering up as much dignity as possible, Webb turned and faced the small crowd. He nodded to each as he passed them, but didn't bother honoring them with his politician's smile. Once he sat down behind the wheel of his Mercedes, he took a deep, tortured breath and asked himself for the first time in many years if it were possible he'd been wrong about Reed Conway. Wrong in believing he had killed Junior Blalock fifteen years ago. Wrong in assuming that the man didn't care anything about Ella and was only using her.

Chapter 23

Reed pulled the truck up in the parking lot across the street from the courthouse. Ella saw him from the window in her office, where she'd been watching for him, and her heart did a silly little lurch. She shrugged off her robe and tossed it on the sofa, then hoisted the straps of her bag over her shoulder and rushed out of her office. By the time she had raced up the hall, out the side door, and across the street, she was breathless with anticipation. Reed kept the motor of the old truck idling as he waited. The minute he saw her, he leaned over the seat and flung open the door on the passenger side. Ella climbed into the truck's cab, and before she got her seat belt buckled, Reed shifted gears and swung out into the light traffic along Cotton Street.

"Sandwiches and chips in that bag." Reed nodded to the brown paper sack on the seat between them. "And there's bottled water in the glove compartment."

"When you called and asked me for lunch—"

"I thought you'd turn me down," he said as he headed the truck down the one-way street that led into

Spring Creek Park. "You're being very daring riding through town with me."

"I figure if I'm going to help you search for Junior Blalock's murderer, people are bound to talk anyway. Besides, there's no way anyone will know how involved we are on a personal level."

"All anyone would have to do is take a good look at my face whenever I'm around you and they'd know," Reed said. "I have a feeling no one could miss seeing the lust in my eyes."

Ella smiled. "I called Mark this morning and told him that I intend to discuss the case and your trial with my father and with Frank Nelson."

Reed pulled the truck off the road that circled the park and drove onto a dirt path that ended several yards away under two huge live oaks with high, intertwining branches. After killing the engine, he opened the driver's door, then leaned across Ella and opened the passenger's door.

"We need to get a little cross-ventilation going," he said, then lifted his head to kiss her.

"Not here. People might see us."

He laughed. "There's nobody around on this side of the park. Besides, trying to keep your reputation intact while fooling around with me might prove impossible."

"Why do you say that? Do you know something I don't?" she asked.

Reed popped open the glove compartment, pulled out two sweating bottles of water, unscrewed the lid on one and handed it to Ella, then placed the second between his thighs. "Briley Joe told me that he overheard some guys talking."

"What guys?"

"Just some guys. But you should know that somebody saw your car parked behind the garage early this morning. And these guys know that I moved into the room upstairs yesterday."

"I see."

Reed lifted the paper sack off the seat, opened it, pulled out a wrapped sandwich, and offered it to Ella. She took it, unwrapped it, and sat there staring at the corned beef on rye.

"I suppose I could say that I left my car overnight at the garage because something or other needed to be fixed." She took a large bite of the sandwich.

Reed removed the second sandwich and laid it on his lap, then unscrewed the cap on his water bottle. "Yeah, you could, but I doubt anybody's going to ask you. They'd rather talk behind your back."

"I can't risk coming to your room again," Ella said. "And there's no way you can come to the house."

"We can meet in the park. Tonight. Right here. Not many people come to this side of the park, and the odds are that no one will see us." Reed took a huge gulp of water, then wiped his mouth with the back of his hand.

"Tonight? But we were together all last night and again this morning."

"Are you saying you got enough, that you don't want any more?"

She glared at him. The shock in her eyes quickly turned to fury when he laughed again.

"Damn you, Reed. You just love to aggravate me, don't you?"

His hand shot out, grabbed her around the neck, and pulled her close. He covered her mouth with his, kissing her hard and fast, then releasing her just as quickly. "I love making love to you more than anything else."

"Reed?"

"Eat up, babe. I've got to get back to the garage. I only get a forty-five minute lunch break."

"You shouldn't be wasting your time working in Briley Joe's garage. Mark told me you earned a college degree while you were in prison. I'm going to check into finding you more suitable work."

"Just help me prove that I didn't murder Junior,"

Reed said. "Once my name is cleared, I'll be able to find a better job without any help from you. A job somewhere far away from Spring Creek."

"You're not going to stay here?"

"No way in hell."

"But your mother and sister are here."

"They can go with me or they can visit me."

"But what about . . ."

She let her sentence trail off without completing it, but apparently Reed knew what she'd been about to ask.

"You can come visit me, too," he said.

When she saw him grinning, she socked him playfully on the arm. "All the girls in high school had big crushes on you. Did you know that?"

He shrugged. "What about you, Miss Ella, did you have a crush on me?"

She shook her head. "No, not really. But I found you interesting and intriguing. Especially after you went to prison and sent me those letters."

"Those were some letters, huh? Bet they scared the heck out of you, didn't they?"

"In a way, I suppose they did, but . . . they also awakened something in me. A true curiosity about sex."

"Meet me here tonight," he said. "If it doesn't rain again, we can spread a blanket out under the stars."

"What time?"

"I'll leave the garage about sundown."

"I'm hoping that before I see you tonight, I will have convinced my father that he's wrong about you. If we could enlist his help in trying to get Junior's murder case reopened, it will make things much easier for us."

Reed didn't have the heart to tell her about his confrontation with Webb this morning. She'd hear about it sooner or later. Rumors and gossip abounded in Spring Creek. Everybody seemed to know a little bit about everyone else's personal business. "Don't count on any help from your old man."

"And don't you be so sure that my father can't admit when he's wrong," she said. "Daddy trusts my judgment. If I can convince him that I believe in your innocence, then I think there's a good chance he will at least give you the benefit of the doubt."

"Damn it, girl, don't you know that man's using you?" Webb paced back and forth in the gazebo. "Now I know why you said you wanted some privacy for our conversation, why you insisted on our coming out here."

"I thought you'd be more reasonable about this," Ella said.

"Be reasonable about my daughter having an affair with a convicted murderer. A man I prosecuted. A man who swore revenge against me. Can't you see that the best form of revenge, even better than harming you, is him making you care about him and believe in him?"

Ella shuddered. Her father was wrong, dead wrong. He had to be. Of course, the same suspicious thoughts had crossed her mind, but she had dismissed them. Reed wasn't faking the passion, of that she was certain. He made love to her as if she were the only woman in the world.

"Haven't you ever had one single doubt about Reed's guilt? Now or in the past?" Ella laid her hand on her father's back and felt him tense.

Webb hung his head. "Do you think I wanted that boy to be guilty? Well, I didn't." He turned to face her, inadvertently knocking her hand off his back. "I can't even say that I blame him for what he did. Junior deserved killing. He deserved worse for the hell he put Judy through, for the beatings he gave her and Reed. And for the things he tried to do to Regina."

"If you've always felt this way, then why—"

"If he'd beaten Junior to death, it would have been one thing—legally as well as in my mind, too. But Reed went back after he'd beaten Junior, when Junior was unconscious and couldn't defend himself, and slit the man's throat. That's murder, Ella, any way you look at it. And you know it."

"Someone else killed Junior Blalock."

"Reed had motive, opportunity, and the murder weapon belonged to him."

"But he wasn't the only one who had opportunity and motive, was he?" Ella moved closer to stand side by side with her father as he gazed out over the backyard flower garden. "There were others who hated Junior enough to kill him. Why did the investigation end with Reed's arrest?"

"The police were certain they had their man. And I was certain." Webb shoved his hands into the front pockets of his slacks. "I was so sure. Back then, I didn't have a doubt in my mind."

"And now?"

"And now, I have a few doubts," Webb admitted. "I still think Reed killed Junior, but . . . Did he tell you that I stopped by the garage this morning?"

"No, he didn't."

"I wanted to rip him limb from limb." Webb stepped down from the gazebo and looked up at the early evening sky. "I warned him to stay away from you."

"What did he say?"

"He told me you could make your own decisions."

"He's right. I can."

Webb breathed deeply, then looked directly at her. "I hit him."

"Oh, Daddy, you didn't."

"He wouldn't hit me back," Webb told her. "And you know why he wouldn't hit me?"

"Why?"

"He said he wouldn't hit me because I was your father."

Instantly tears stung her eyes. "I can't believe he said that. He tries so hard to be tough, to never let anyone see that he has feelings, that he cares about anything or anyone."

"If I agree to talk to Frank Nelson about reopening Reed's case, will you promise me to stay away from him?"

"Oh, Daddy, you know I can't make that kind of promise."

"You've fallen in love with him, haven't you?"

Ella followed her father out into the garden, and when he paused, she wrapped her arms around his waist and hugged him. "I don't know if it's love or . . . or . . . All I know is that I care about him and I want to help him."

"I'll give Frank a call in the morning. I hope for your sake that I *did* convict an innocent man fifteen years ago."

By early afternoon almost half the town had heard about the confrontation between Webb Porter and Reed Conway. Some said it was the old quarrel—that Reed still claimed innocence in Junior Blalock's murder and blamed Webb for his murder conviction. Others were saying that the good senator was accusing Reed of being the perpetrator in the recent harassment of his daughter and the death of his hunting dogs last night. But by evening, there were a few whispered innuendos floating around that something was going on between Reed Conway and Judge Eleanor Porter. Reed had been seen going into Miss Ella's office yesterday and staying for quite some time behind locked doors. And someone thought they saw the judge's car parked behind Conway's Garage at dawn this morning. And then another somebody had spotted Ella getting into a beat-up old truck with Reed around noon today.

Believing the worst about Ella was difficult, but hearing with one's own ears was proof positive. Eavesdropping sometimes paid off royally. Learning that Webb was actually going to help Reed Conway, that he planned to suggest to Frank Nelson that he reopen a fifteen-year-old murder case, came as quite a surprise.

Things were going to have to progress a little faster, get a little more deadly. Reed Conway had to return to prison before the truth about Junior's murder was revealed. And the only way to get rid of Reed was to see to it that he committed another crime. Another murder, maybe, or at least an attempted murder.

Getting hold of the gun that Briley Joe kept in his desk at the garage shouldn't prove too difficult, not for someone very clever. Half of Spring Creek knew Briley Joe kept the old Sauer & Sohn .308—the weapon his father had taken off a dead German soldier in World War II—loaded and in his unlocked desk. He liked to bring the pistol out from time to time, wave it around, show it off, and threaten to blow to smithereens any thieves who might be foolish enough to try to rob him. There probably wouldn't be any way to get Reed's fingerprints on the gun, but as long as no one's fingerprints other than Briley Joe's were on it, the plan might work.

Time was running out. Drastic action needed to be taken—tonight.

A sense of excitement radiated through Ella as she eased her Jag up beside the old truck Reed had once again borrowed from his cousin. She wondered if he'd told Briley Joe that he had a late evening rendezvous with a lady judge. She'd like to think that Reed wouldn't discuss the personal aspects of their relationship with anyone, that what transpired between them was sacred.

A giddy ripple of laughter emerged from her throat. *Sacred? Get a grip, Ella. This isn't a love affair, not some grand passion. At least not for Reed. Not for you either. You know what this is—it's sex, pure and simple.* But that was just it. There was nothing pure or simple about her feelings for Reed. If she had a lick of sense, she wouldn't be here right now. She'd be home—safe and secure, and as far away from Reed as she could get.

She heard his truck door slam shut. Her heartbeat accelerated. *You can start the Jag's engine, back up, and drive away,* she told herself. *Escape before it's too late.* But it was already too late and she knew it. She wanted to be with Reed. To lie in his arms tonight and look up at the starry sky. She wanted to make love with him again.

He pecked on her closed window and motioned for her to get out. The sun had disappeared beyond the horizon, leaving streaks of multicolored light spreading across the sky. At sundown the world took on a hazy, golden glow, a surreal beauty that masked the ugliness so clearly seen in the bright light of day.

She looked out the window. He carried a blanket draped over his arm and a small tape player in his hand. More cool jazz? she wondered. As long as she lived, whenever she heard a saxophone's sweet moan, she'd think of Reed and the night she'd spent in his arms. Hurriedly she unlocked her door, stuffed her keys into the pocket of her shorts, and got out of the car. Before she had a chance to close the door, Reed draped his free arm around her waist and dragged her up against him. He kissed her thoroughly, taking her breath away in the process. How was it possible that when this man touched her, she lost every ounce of common sense she possessed?

"Come on, babe, let's find a perfect spot to spread this blanket."

She closed her car door, clasped Reed's hand, and followed where he led. Off behind the huge live oaks and into a clearing close to where the winding stream joined the nearby creek. A train's horn blew in the distance. The railroad tracks spanned a nearby bridge. Here with Reed, on the back side of the park, she had indeed crossed over from the right side of the tracks to the wrong side. Streets lined with houses that were little more than shacks lay on the other side of this hidden grove. Reed had grown up in one of those houses. His mother and sister still lived there.

Reed spread the blanket on the ground, then set the tape player to the side and pushed the "Play" button. Soft and low, a jazz tune began, a sweet reminder of last night.

Why was she so nervous? It wasn't as if she and Reed hadn't been together before. They had been—yesterday, last night, and again early this morning.

"I spoke to Daddy, and he's agreed to talk to Frank Nelson about reopening the Blalock murder case," Ella said.

"You're kidding," Reed laughed.

"No, I'm not kidding." Ella sat on the blanket, crossing her legs at the ankles. "When I saw you earlier today, you didn't mention that my father paid you a visit this morning."

"I'm surprised he mentioned it to you." Reed lay flat on his back and crossed his arms behind his head.

"He said that when he hit you, you didn't hit him back. I think by showing him that you could control your temper, you impressed Daddy."

"I seriously doubt that I impressed Webb Porter," Reed said. "He's just pacifying you, Ella, if he's told you that he'll help me."

Ella stretched out beside Reed and looked up at the sky. With sundown, nighttime hurried to take charge, darkening the sky and cooling the temperature. The moon appeared, pale and almost transparent.

"Think what you will," she said. "But I know my father. If he said he'll speak to Frank Nelson, he will."

"Whatever you say, babe." He eased up, bracing himself on one elbow as he leaned over her. "Right now, I don't want to talk about the chief of police or your daddy."

"What do you want to do?" she asked, her body already tightening with anticipation.

"I want to kiss you, Miss Ella," he told her.

"Is that all you want to do, just kiss me?"

"That will be enough to start with; then I'm sure we'll think of what to do next."

"I'm sure we will."

Webb Porter sat alone in his den, a bottle of bourbon resting beside his chair, and an empty glass in his hand. The armchair stood near the window, positioned with one arm to the window and the other to the room. There had been a time when harming Webb would never have been an option. But that time had long since passed. Perhaps, by being very careful and taking precise aim, the shot wouldn't kill him but only severely wound him. Reed Conway had been alone in the room above the garage less than twenty minutes ago, so it stood to reason he was still there. Alone. Without an alibi. Whether the bullet killed Webb or merely wounded him, the mission would be accomplished. Reed would be charged with a crime and sent back to prison, thus ending any chances of having the old Blalock murder case reopened.

I must be very careful. Can't let Webb see a shadow outside the window. Wait for the right moment . . . when he turns this way. I must make the shot count. I can't risk two shots. Webb might see me. And if he lives, he could identify me. Take a deep breath. Count to ten, then aim and pull the trigger. This close, I can't miss.

Something was wrong. Horribly wrong. The moment Ella saw the flashing lights of the police cars in her driveway, her heart caught in her throat. Oh, God, please, let everyone be all right.

She whizzed her Jag around the corner, then came to a screeching halt at the edge of the sidewalk. Frank Nelson stood on the front porch talking to two uniformed policemen. The moment he saw Ella jump out of her car, he came down the front steps and onto the brick walkway to meet her.

"What's happened?" she asked.

Frank grasped her shoulders. "It's bad. I won't try to kid you. Your father's been shot, but he's alive."

Ella gasped. Tears lodged in her throat. "How? When? Who?"

"About an hour ago," Frank said. "Your mother and Viola heard the shot and Miss Carolyn sent Viola downstairs to see what had happened. Viola found Webb and called nine-one-one immediately."

"You said it was bad—how bad?"

"He got hit in the chest, pretty close to his heart," Frank told her. "They rushed him straight to Bryant County Hospital. One of my boys can drive you over there right now."

"Thank you, Frank."

He nodded, then released her.

"Oh, Lord," Ella cried. "Mother! She must be out of her mind with worry. I'll have to see her before I leave."

"Viola has taken Miss Carolyn to the hospital," Frank said. "She insisted on going. She's upset, but holding it together pretty good. You know what a strong woman your mother is."

Ella nodded again.

"Goodman!" Frank called out, and a dark-haired policeman in his mid-twenties came running.

"Yes sir, Chief?"

"I want you to drive Judge Porter to Bryant County Hospital."

"Yes, sir." Officer Goodman turned to Ella. "Ready whenever you are, ma'am."

She followed the officer to his patrol car. When he opened the door, she slid onto the front seat. He eased the vehicle out into the street and headed toward downtown Spring Creek. None of this seemed real. But it was real. Someone had shot her father. But who? And why?

Please, God, don't let him die. The very thought was unbearable. Since her earliest memories, Webb Porter had been the center of her world—a doting father, who called her "princess" and made her feel like one.

She wished she could phone Reed and tell him that she needed him desperately. Odd that he was the one person she wanted at a time like this. But even if he would be willing to come to the hospital and hold her hand—which she doubted he would—he would hardly be welcomed by her family. They'd probably even accuse him of shooting her father. But they'd be wrong. No one knew better than she that this was one crime Reed Conway most definitely hadn't committed.

Chapter 24

After taking a hefty swig, Reed set his beer bottle on the bar. He would have liked nothing better than for Ella to have spent the night in his arms, but that wasn't possible. She had a reputation to uphold, and for now, their affair had to remain a secret. He was willing to accept her terms. Hell, he'd accept her on any terms, take her any way he could get her. Chuckling to himself, he shook his head. He'd gone and done something really stupid. He had let himself get emotionally involved with Webb Porter's daughter. Why her, of all the women in the world? She wasn't the most beautiful, didn't have a built-like-a-brick-shithouse body, and wasn't even the sexiest. But there was something about her that gave him a hard-on just thinking about her. She had the blackest, silkiest hair, the kindest brown eyes, the softest, sweetest lips, and a luscious, tempting body. And when he touched her, he set her on fire. He could tell by the way she looked at him that she was crazy about him. And God help him if he wasn't just as crazy about her.

The bartender scowled at a group of particularly

rowdy customers at the far end of the bar. "Hey, there, you guys keep it down for a minute, will you? I'm trying to listen to this news bulletin." He turned up the sound on the wall-mounted television.

Reed glanced at the screen just as a picture of Webb Porter appeared. He lifted his beer and moved down the bar, getting closer to the TV.

"Tonight at approximately nine o'clock, Senator Webb Porter was critically wounded. At this time details are sketchy, but Spring Creek Police Chief Frank Nelson, informed us that there was a single gunshot wound to the chest and that the shooter stood outside the senator's den window and shot him from no more than ten feet away. The senator was rushed to Bryant County Hospital, where at this time the family and close friends are holding a prayer vigil."

Reed laid a five-dollar bill on the bar beside his half-finished beer and headed for the door. His first instinct was to rush to the hospital, to see how Ella was doing. Had she gone home and found her father? Had the police already been there when she arrived? She had to be half out of her mind with worry. Ella loved her daddy better than anything.

As he walked outside, the warm evening air clung to him, heavy with moisture and heat. Sweat broke out on his face immediately. He wiped his forehead with his hand and headed toward his truck. He unlocked the door, opened it, then hopped up and slid behind the wheel. Sitting inside the truck, with the door open and his crossed arms resting on the steering wheel, he gave his jumbled thoughts time to separate and settle into something vaguely resembling logic. Should he rush to the hospital to comfort Ella? Would she even want him there? Or should he drive over to his mother's place and see if she'd heard the news. He wasn't sure just what his mother's relationship with Webb Porter had been, whether he was Regina's father or not, but he knew his mother had cared about the man. Maybe she still did.

After slamming the door, he stuck the key in the switch and started the engine. Still considering his options, he pulled out of the parking lot. *Go see your mother first,* he told himself. That would give him more time to make the right decision. He could always just call the hospital and ask to speak to Ella.

Within five minutes, he pulled the truck to a stop in his mother's driveway. The lights were on in the house, so that meant she was still up. He got out and headed straight for the porch. When he knocked on the closed front door, Regina answered.

"Reed, come on in," his sister said. "Have you heard the news about Senator Porter?"

"Yeah, that's the reason I dropped by. I wanted to find out if y'all had heard."

"Mama and I were listening to the ten o'clock news." Regina grasped Reed's shirtfront and whispered, "She's awfully upset. I haven't seen her this torn apart since . . . I think she loves Webb Porter. She's gone to the bathroom to wash her face. She's been crying."

"What do you know about Mama and the senator?" Reed asked.

"Nothing really. But I saw them kissing, only yesterday. Tell me the truth, Reed, is Webb Porter my father?"

Damn! He'd never understood why his mother hadn't just told Regina who her father was, why she'd protected the guy who'd gotten her pregnant and never claimed his child. For years, he'd wondered if Webb Porter was Regina's father, and he'd even considered the possibility that Jeff Henry Carlisle might be. And when his mother had married Junior Blalock, he'd even thought that maybe Junior was Regina's father.

"I honestly don't know," Reed said. "I think there's a possibility that Webb is your father, but I've got no proof, and Mama's never breathed a word to me."

"I know you were just a little kid when I was born, but don't you remember if there was a man she was seeing?"

"Haven't we had this conversation before? The only men Mama was around on a regular basis in the months before you were born were Jeff Henry Carlisle and Webb Porter. And that was because she worked for the Carlisles then, just as she does now."

Regina nodded, a look of resignation on her face. "I'll go tell Mama you're here."

But Judy entered the living room at that precise moment, her eyes swollen and red-rimmed. "Reed?"

"Yes, Mama."

"Have you heard about Webb?"

"Yeah, I heard."

"Who would do such a terrible thing?"

"A man in politics is bound to have enemies," Reed said. Then he had a sobering thought. Hell, he was one of those enemies. *Yeah, you are, buddy boy, and sooner or later, if they don't find their shooter, the police are going to come knocking on your door.* But this time there would be no weapon with his fingerprints on it, no weapon with which he could be connected. Besides, he had an alibi. Scratch the alibi. No way would Ella Porter publicly admit that she'd been screwing him in the park when somebody shot her father. But other than no alibi, there was nothing to link him to this crime. What about motive? The police would believe he had a motive, wouldn't they?

And if Mark's theory was correct—that Junior's real killer was trying to get him sent back to prison—then it wasn't beyond the realm of possibility that he could get framed for Webb's shooting.

"The police will question you," Judy said. "I know you didn't shoot Webb, but I hope you have an alibi."

"Don't worry about me. I was with a friend."

"Good." Judy took a tissue from the pocket of her

slacks and blew her nose. "I wish I could go to the hospital and find out how Webb is doing, but—"

"Why can't you go?" Reed asked. "You've been a family friend for years, haven't you? I'll bet there are dozens of people there, people who don't know the Porters half as well as you do."

"I couldn't go," Judy replied. "What would people think?"

"I'm going over there," Reed said. "You could go with me."

"What?" Judy's eyes widened. "Why would you go to the hospital to check on Webb? You hate the man. Besides, you know you wouldn't be welcome there."

"I'm going because despite how I feel about Webb Porter, he's Ella's father."

"I don't understand," Judy said, a puzzled look in her eyes.

"Ella Porter was the friend I was with tonight."

Regina gasped. "You and Eleanor Porter? I don't believe it. When did this happen?"

"Recently," Reed admitted. "Very recently."

"You can't mean that you and Ella are . . . are . . . You're seeing her socially?" Judy asked.

Reed laughed. "Let's just say that we're involved, and leave it at that."

"Don't go to the hospital tonight," Judy said. "No matter what's going on between you and Ella, those people aren't going to want you there with them. They'll tell you to leave."

"I don't care what they tell me to do. I just want to make sure Ella's okay and that she knows . . . well, that she knows I don't want her father to die."

"You actually care about her, don't you?" Judy stared at him.

"I wouldn't go that far. . . . Okay. Yeah, I care about her, just like you used to care about Webb."

Gasping loudly, Judy glanced at Regina. "Perhaps we

should all go to the hospital. Just drop by to let the family know that we care.''

"You go with Reed," Regina said. "I'm not going."

"Come on, Mama." Reed grabbed her wrist. "Nobody is going to question your being there, and if anybody gets huffy about me being with you, we'll tell them I'm there only because I drove you to the hospital."

Nodding agreement, Judy slipped her hand into his. Reed didn't know if Webb was Regina's father. But he knew one thing—his mother still loved the man.

The surgery waiting area on the second floor at Bryant County Hospital was filled to capacity. And there had been a steady stream of concerned friends in and out for the past hour. Ella stood just outside the door, taking a breather in the hallway, which was itself fairly crowded. She could keep an eye on her mother from this vantage point and still give herself room to maneuver. She had begun to feel smothered. And every time someone new spoke to her and mentioned what a fine man her father was, she broke into fresh tears. People were already talking about him as if he were dead.

She wouldn't let these people count him out. Her father was a fighter. He was going to fight and win this battle. He had to. She couldn't imagine her life without him.

As always, she found herself astonished by her mother's strength and composure. Carolyn sat in her wheelchair in the middle of the room, holding court, the composed, weepy wife of Senator Webb Porter. Ella never doubted her mother's love for her father, and she realized that not knowing if her husband would live or die had to be excruciating for Carolyn. How did she do it? Ella wondered. How could her mother remain so calm when she herself was practically a basket case?

Suddenly, she felt arms wrap around her waist and

pull her backward against another body. Glancing over her shoulder and seeing a face she dearly loved, Ella smiled.

"He's going to live, darling girl," Cybil said. "I don't know a stronger, tougher man than Webb Porter."

Ella laid her hands over her aunt's where they met at the front of her waist. "Why would anyone want to shoot Daddy?"

"Before he became a senator, your father was a lawyer, a DA, and a judge. A man in his line of business makes enemies."

"It wasn't Reed," Ella said. She knew some people thought that Reed was the most likely suspect. Of course, she knew better.

"Nobody said it was Reed." Cybil loosened her hold about Ella's waist, then grabbed her hand and tugged. "Let's go get some coffee."

"No, I can't leave. Mother might need me, or there could be word on Daddy."

"Okay, I won't press you to go to the coffee shop. But why don't we take a walk, just up and down the corridor. We won't get out of sight of the waiting room."

Ella nodded. They walked. When they passed the elevators several minutes later, the doors swung open and there stood Reed Conway and his mother. Ella's breath caught in her throat. Her gaze connected instantly with Reed's. He cupped his mother's elbow and led her out of the elevator.

"How is Webb?" Judy asked, looking directly at Cybil.

"He's still in surgery," Cybil said. "They're giving him a fifty-fifty chance."

Judy's mouth rounded into an oval as she gasped silently. Tears glistened in her eyes. Cybil reached out and took Judy's hand, then led her down the hall several feet away. Ella watched her aunt with her housekeeper, the two women huddled together, whispering. It didn't seem at all odd that Aunt Cybil and Judy would comfort each other. Even though Uncle Jeff Henry was a bit of a snob and treated Judy like nothing more than a servant, Aunt Cybil had always considered her not only a valued employee, but also a friend.

Ella glanced back at Reed. He was close. No more than a few feet away. She wished she could rush into his arms and seek comfort. She desperately needed his strength right now. He just stood there, looking at her, not saying anything. Ella felt like screaming.

"My mother was concerned," Reed finally said. "I'm here because I drove her to the hospital."

Tears lodged in Ella's throat and spilled over and out of her eyes. Suddenly she began trembling. *Please, Reed, hold me. Even if for just a minute.*

"Ah, babe, don't. Your father is going to be all right."

Reed instantly closed the gap between them and pulled her into his arms. She went without a thought of what anyone would think. Right this minute, she didn't give a damn. Her father was in surgery and might be dying. She needed to be held and comforted by the man she loved. As Ella clung to Reed, she buried her face against his chest and wept as if her heart was breaking.

He held her tight, stroking her back tenderly and whispering, "He'll be all right" over and over again.

"What the hell is this!" Jeff Henry demanded as he came storming down the hallway.

"Lower your voice," Cybil told him as she hurried up the corridor.

"Eleanor Porter, get away from that man." Jeff Henry headed toward Ella, his hand outstretched to grab her.

Cybil ran in front of him, effectively cutting off his attack. "Don't make a scene. People can see us from the waiting room. You wouldn't want to upset Carolyn, would you?"

"If she sees her daughter in that man's arms, she'll have a stroke," Jeff Henry said. "Hasn't Carolyn been through enough tonight? What the hell is he doing here, anyway?"

"My son drove me here to the hospital," Judy said

as she approached her employers. "I was concerned about Senator Porter."

"Ella!" Jeff Henry ignored both his wife and his housekeeper, shoving past both women, who had tried to block his path.

Ella took a deep breath, eased out of Reed's arms, and turned to face her uncle's wrath. Reed stood at her side. She longed to hang on to to him for support. But she didn't.

"What's that man doing here? And how dare you allow him to touch you." Jeff Henry's round, full face was splotched, and his eyes were wild with rage. "For all we know he's the one who shot Webb."

"Don't be ridiculous," Ella said. "Reed didn't shoot Daddy."

"You seem mighty friendly with this ex-convict, a man your own daddy prosecuted for murder."

Jeff Henry glowered at Reed, as if he thought he could make the younger man back down. Ella could sense the tension in Reed's big body, and she knew how much control he was exerting not to tell her uncle to go to hell. Didn't Uncle Jeff Henry realize that Reed Conway was not the kind of man who would back down from a fight, that he couldn't be bluffed or bullied?

"I think you should know that just today, Daddy and I had a long talk and he agreed that he's going to speak to Frank Nelson about reopening the Blalock murder case," Ella said."

"You can't be serious!" Jeff Henry clutched his chest. "Good Lord, girl, have you lost your mind? I can't imagine what you could have said to Webb to make him even consider that he and the jury were wrong about Reed."

"I told Daddy that I believed Reed was innocent."

Jeff Henry glanced at Ella, then at Reed, and then back to Ella. "He's hoodooed you. You know that, don't you? Reed always did have a way with the ladies, but I figured you were too smart to fall for his line of bull."

Her uncle grasped her hands in his. "Don't you see that he's using you?"

"Uncle Jeff Henry, you're wrong about Reed. He's not—"

"Save your breath, Ella," Reed said. "Nobody can convince this pompous ass of anything. He's just like the rest of his kind, only too willing to condemn the housekeeper's son."

Before Jeff Henry had a chance to reply, the elevator doors swung open and out stepped Frank Nelson. He glanced around the hallway, from Judy to Cybil to Jeff Henry to Ella and finally to Reed. He scratched his head, clearly puzzled by the assembly.

"How's Webb?" Frank asked.

"Fifty-fifty chance," Jeff Henry said. "He's still in surgery."

Frank looked directly at Reed. "What are you doing here?"

"He brought me." Judy moved toward the police chief.

"Was Reed with you tonight?" Frank directed his gaze at Judy.

"Why do you ask?" Judy glanced hurriedly at Reed and then back to Frank.

"Your boy needs an alibi," Frank said.

"Why does Reed need an alibi?" Ella asked.

"We found the murder weapon," Frank told her. "We got an anonymous call. Somebody said they saw a man throw a gun in the trash Dumpster over at Conway's Garage."

"Damn," Reed cursed under his breath.

"What does that prove?" Cybil draped her arm around Judy's shoulder.

"The gun belongs to Briley Joe." Frank rubbed his chin. "I recognized it the minute I saw it. It's either that old Sauer & Sohn .308 that Briley Joe's daddy brought back from Germany or a gun just like it."

"That still doesn't prove anything," Ella said.

"It proves Webb was shot with Reed's cousin's gun, which he could have easily gotten hold of," Frank said. "And the whole town knows Reed's got a motive, so if he doesn't have an alibi—"

"He does," Ella said.

"If he does, then I want to hear it." Frank looked point-blank at Reed, who didn't say a word.

Ella reached down and took Reed's hand in hers. "Reed was with me. We were in Spring Creek Park. I met him a little before eight-thirty and I didn't leave him until about nine-thirty."

"What the devil were you doing alone in the park with—" When the realization hit the police chief, he stopped talking mid-sentence. "Are you willing to swear to that, Miss Ella?"

"Yes, Frank, I'm willing to swear on a bible in front of the whole world."

Reed squeezed Ella's hand. She had never been prouder of herself than she was at that very minute.

Chapter 25

For the past ten days, Spring Creek had been abuzz with rumors about who shot Webb Porter and why. Gossipmongers were having a heyday. Not only were they picking apart every detail they'd heard about Webb's shooting, but they were reveling in speculation about an especially juicy tidbit—Reed Conway's alibi. The socially prominent citizens were shocked and appalled by Eleanor Porter's association with such a man, but even they were talking about the affair, albeit behind closed doors.

How could such a thing have happened? The girl had been raised with high moral standards, taught her place in this world and shown by her mother's example what a lady should be. To think that she had given herself to the likes of Reed Conway. The very thought was enough to turn a person's stomach. It would be impossible to look at Ella without knowing she was now contaminated. Such disappointment. It broke one's heart to think that someone so dear could turn out so badly. But of course, she was adopted, which meant her bloodlines might not be pure.

The perfect plan to shoot Webb and frame Reed hadn't been so perfect after all. But how could anyone have known that Reed would not only have an alibi, but his alibi would be that he'd been having sex with Webb's daughter at the time. This kind of mistake couldn't be made again. With Webb home from the hospital only today, he was already pushing Frank Nelson to reopen the Junior Blalock murder case. Finally the police were listening to Mark Leamon's insistence that Junior's real murderer was trying to frame Reed. Of course, most people didn't believe a word in Reed's defense, but most people weren't the problem. The problem was that Webb now had serious doubts about Reed's guilt.

Before Frank reopened the Blalock case, another crime must be be committed—one in which Reed would be implicated. And there couldn't be any mistakes. Everything had to be carefully planned down to the last detail. There was no time to waste. Spring Creek was about to have one of their most prominent, well-liked citizens murdered. Brutally killed by Reed Conway.

"I won't have that man in my house!" Carolyn's face contorted with rage. "I absolutely forbid it."

"Calm yourself," Webb said, his tone impatient. "If seeing Reed will upset you, then go upstairs to your room and stay there. I've invited him here, along with Mark and Frank Nelson. If I helped convict an innocent man fifteen years ago, then I think it's high time I corrected that mistake."

"Just because Ella has forsaken everything for which this family stands, it doesn't mean that you have to do an about-face when it comes to Reed Conway." Carolyn wheeled herself to her husband's side, where he reclined on the sofa in his den. "Just because Reed didn't shoot you doesn't mean he didn't kill Junior Blalock. And it certainly doesn't mean there's a conspiracy to frame Reed."

"Carolyn, I know that you're upset about Ella's involvement with Reed, but—"

"I don't want her name spoken. I can't bear to think of how she has disgraced us. She's as bad as Cybil. But at least my sister has had the decency not to publicly announce that she's been sleeping with white trash." Carolyn sighed. "I shall never be able to forgive her."

"You don't have a maternal bone in your body, do you?" Webb glared at his wife. "I despise you for the way you've treated Ella since the night I was shot and you found out about her affair with Reed. He wouldn't be my choice of a man for her either, but by God, there's nothing that girl could ever do that would make me stop loving her."

"I've never understood why it has always been so easy for you to love her, a child that isn't even ours, when you can't love me, your own wife."

"Is that what this is really all about?" Webb readjusted himself to a more comfortable position on the sofa. His wound was healing nicely, but he was still in some pain. "I've tried to convince myself for years now that even you couldn't be jealous of your own child, but you are. You resent Ella because you know how much I love her."

"I've been a devoted mother to that child." Carolyn curled her hands into tight fists and held them in her lap. "And I have loved her. But now . . ."

"Now what?" Webb bellowed his question. "Now that she's done something that displeases you, you've disowned her, kicked her out of our house, told her that unless she ends her relationship with Reed, you'll never speak to her again."

Heat rose up Webb's neck and suffused his face. There had been numerous times during the years he had been trapped in this farce of a marriage that he'd wanted to strangle Carolyn, but never more than at that precise moment.

Webb leaned toward Carolyn, stared at her, and

grasped the arms of her wheelchair. "When Ella and Reed come here today, I want you to welcome our daughter with open arms."

"I can't do that."

"Then get yourself upstairs and stay there until my guests have left." Webb glowered at his wife—his poor, pitiful, crippled wife. What had he ever done to deserve a life sentence, chained to Carolyn for as long as he lived? "And I'm warning you, woman, if my daughter isn't welcome here, then neither am I. Is that what you want—to be left alone in this house, with only Viola to keep you company?"

"What I want is a loving husband and a dutiful child," Carolyn said. "I thought at least I had the dutiful child, but it seems I was wrong on that count."

Carolyn met Webb's stare, and the two gazes locked in mortal combat. Finally Carolyn glanced down at Webb's hands, still clutching the arms of her wheelchair. "If you'd be so good as to release me, I'll leave you to wait for you guests."

The minute Webb released his hold on the wheelchair, Carolyn glided toward the door, but stopped abruptly. Without glancing back, she said, "Please, tell Ella that I would like for her to come home."

Webb cursed under his breath as he watched his wife disappear into the hallway. Damned infuriating woman. Why didn't Carolyn appreciate how fortunate she was to have a daughter like Ella, who had been a dutiful child all her life? Until recently Ella had always bent over backward to please Carolyn, as well as to please him. And now he felt a bit guilty at having allowed Ella to devote so much of herself to Carolyn and him, as if she thought it her duty to repay them for having adopted her. If she knew the truth about her parentage, she would realize that he was the one who owed her. He had loved her the first moment he held her in his arms, and over the years, she had come to mean everything to him. She had been the joy of his life and had made him so proud when she decided to follow in his footsteps and become a lawyer.

There was nothing Ella could ever do that could make him stop loving her—not even having an affair with Reed Conway. As an elected official, the fact that his daughter was embroiled in a public scandal certainly created reelection problems. As a father, he worried that Ella would wind up hurt and disappointed. Webb felt certain that Reed was simply using Ella—using her to not only punish Webb, but to help himself by getting Ella to rally the local powers-that-be to prove he wasn't Junior Blalock's murderer. His baby girl was in danger of getting her heart broken and there wasn't a damn thing he could do about it. If he thought threatening Reed would do any good, then he'd have warned him off. But if there was one thing he'd learned about Reed Conway, it was that the man couldn't be intimidated.

"Will you please stand still?" Ella said. "I'll never get this thing tied right."

Reed pulled away, snatched off the silk tie, and tossed it on the bed. "I'm not a suit-and-tie man. You're wasting your time trying to make a silk purse out of this"—he tapped his index finger on his chest—"sow's ear."

"Today is very important. I think you should look your best."

"Babe, no matter what you do to improve my appearance, your daddy isn't going to approve of me." Reed grasped Ella's shoulders. He glanced down at the tan dress slacks and navy blue button-down shirt. "That's what this makeover is all about, isn't it? You want me to make a favorable impression on your old man."

"My father is willing to meet you halfway. The least you can do is—"

"I'm meeting him halfway, too. I'm willing to put aside the fact that he's the man who prosecuted me for Junior's murder, the man who convinced a jury that I was guilty." Reed tightened his hold on Ella. "Back then, I was convinced that he had killed Junior and that was the reason he was so damned and determined to put me away."

Ella stared at him in disbelief. "You can't mean that you actually thought my father killed Junior. Why? What reason would he have had?"

Reed realized that he couldn't tell Ella about his suspicions—that his mother and her father had once had an affair and that his sister Regina was Webb's biological child.

Reed shook his head. "He hated Junior, just like everybody who knew the son of a bitch."

"I understand," Ella said. "At one time, I wondered if perhaps your mother had killed him, but then I realized Judy wouldn't have let you go to prison for a crime she'd committed. No mother would do something so terrible to her own child."

Reed pulled her into his arms. "You're thinking about your mother now, aren't you?" He stroked her back. "Ah, babe, I never meant to be the cause of a rift between you and your mother. But I guess we should have known that finding out about us would put her in a tailspin. She's got to be embarrassed that you announced to the whole world that we were together when Webb was shot. But I can't believe she kicked you out of your own home or that your father let her."

"Daddy told me to stay, but I couldn't, not with Mother feeling the way she does. Besides, I've always had my own room over at Aunt Cybil and Uncle Jeff Henry's. It's no problem for me to stay with them until Mother cools off. I'll deal with her and her embarrassment later. For now, my main concern is convincing Frank Nelson you're innocent and that he must find out who really killed Junior."

Ella looked at Reed, her gaze soft and loving. Every time she gazed at him that way, all hell broke loose inside him. The woman did crazy things to him. He wanted to take her to bed again and make love to her until they were both exhausted. Every male instinct within him wanted to possess her completely, but at the same time was determined to protect her.

"Whoever killed Junior is dangerous," Reed said. "Not just to me, but to anyone who gets in the way. Maybe, for the time being, until this person is caught, you should stay away from me."

Ella kissed him. "You might as well ask me to stop breathing. If you haven't figured it out by now, Reed Conway, I'm hopelessly in love with you."

"Ah, Ella . . . babe . . ." His mouth devoured hers as her confession echoed inside his head. *I'm hopelessly in love with you.* He didn't deserve this woman, but he couldn't give her up. Not even for her own good.

A rapping at the door gained their attention. They broke apart instantly, each breathless and smiling.

When he opened the door, he discovered his lawyer standing there. Mark looked him up and down, inspecting his new clothes that Ella had bought for him.

"Good choice in attire," Mark said. "Needs a tie, though."

"Come on in," Reed said. "We're almost ready."

Mark followed Reed into the one-room apartment over the garage; then, when he saw Ella, he nodded and smiled. Reed went over to the bed, picked up the striped tie, put it around his neck, and stuffed it under his collar.

"Want to give tying this thing another try?"

"It would be my pleasure," Ella replied.

"Roy, I've got to go over to Hopewell and pick up some parts from the junkyard there," Briley Joe said. "Think you can hold down the fort while I'm gone?"

"Sure thing," Roy said, pleased that Briley Joe trusted him to take care of business on Saturday evening, a busy time at the garage.

"If you run into any trouble, call me on my cell phone. The number is written down on that yellow pad on the desk in the office. Otherwise, I'll see you in a couple of hours."

"Don't you worry none about me." Roy grinned.

Roy strutted around, proud as a peacock that Briley Joe trusted him to run things all by himself. Once the boss left, he met each new customer with a grin. He washed windshields, filled up gas tanks, and even checked the oil for one nice lady. And he made correct change for the people who paid cash, not making one mistake. By sunset things had begun to settle down enough so that he felt he could stop working long enough to drink a Coke. He rummaged around in his overalls pocket for some quarters to use in the cola machine.

Briley Joe should be back soon, sometime in the next thirty minutes. He'd take over then and tell Roy he could go on home. Of course, if Reed was here, he would brag on Roy and tell him what a good job he'd done. Briley Joe was okay, but Reed was a nicer man. He actually took the time to talk to Roy, to make him feel like he mattered. Not many people did that.

He knew he was slow and that some people made fun of him. But Miss Ella had told him once that those people were the ones to be pitied because they were just plain ignorant. He sure did like Miss Ella. She was the finest, bestest person in the world.

People were talking about Reed and her, some of them saying ugly things. But the way Roy figured it, Reed and Miss Ella belonged together. They were both his friends and he sure hoped they'd invite him to their wedding.

Roy inserted the coins into the cola machine, and just as he grasped his canned drink, he heard something in the garage, back in the work station. Briley Joe had closed up before he left, but he hadn't locked the side door, in case Roy needed to get in there for some reason.

Was it possible Reed was back already? He'd figured that the big meeting over at Senator Porter's would take longer than this, but who else would be pilfering around in the garage.

Roy thought he'd better check and see, just in case some kids had gotten inside and planned to steal something. Of course, it might be a stray dog or cat. If that was the case, then he'd have to find the poor thing something to eat. He still had part of a sandwich left in his lunch box.

Roy walked around to the side door, which was open just a crack. It had been shut earlier, when Briley Joe left, hadn't it? Maybe not. He opened the door, but couldn't see a darn thing. Whoever or whatever was in there was feeling their way around in the dark. Must be a dog or a cat hunting for food.

But suddenly Roy saw a small light in the far corner, near the row of red tool boxes. It had to be a flashlight. That meant it wasn't an animal. Probably kids looking to steal something. He'd just scare them off. No need to call the police and get anybody in trouble.

"Hey, you in there," Roy called loudly as he stepped inside the garage. "I know you're there, so you'd better come on out. If you don't give me no problems, I won't call the police."

The flashlight went out, but no one answered. Roy could hear somebody moving around and he saw a shadow. He moved farther inside, then turned halfway around, searching for the wall switch.

"I'm going to turn on the light," Roy warned. "You'd best be hightailing it out of here before I see you." He'd just keep his back turned and give the kid a chance to leave on his own.

Roy heard a rattling sound, as if whoever was in there with him had gotten into one of the tool boxes. "You'd best not be stealing nothing." Roy hated to do it, but he didn't have much choice. He'd have to turn on the light and expose the thief.

He reached for the switch, but before his finger made contact, somebody hit him on the head. Hard. His head throbbed something awful. When Roy lifted his hand to rub his head, he felt something sticky. He was bleeding.

A second blow followed the first, then a third. The big, stupid retard fell to his knees, crying. A fourth blow knocked him out. Just one more to be sure he doesn't get up.

It was regrettable that Roy Moses had heard something and come to investigate. If he'd stayed out front where he belonged, it wouldn't have been necessary to resort to violence. Maybe he wasn't dead. But of course, it didn't really matter. The man was an inferior creature. Mentally deficient.

Drop the wrench. You're wearing gloves so there will be no fingerprints except Briley Joe's and Reed's. Too bad Reed has an alibi.

Hurry. Get what you came here for and leave. No one saw you on the walk over here, and even if they did, they wouldn't know it was you. With the big meeting at the Porter house going on right now, you don't have time to waste. Once the Blalock case is reopened, it's only a matter of time until the truth comes out. You can't let that happen. Do what you must do to protect yourself.

Chapter 26

"It's not going to be easy investigating a murder that happened fifteen years ago," Frank Nelson said. "Some of Junior's buddies are either dead or in the pen." Frank cut his eyes toward Reed, giving him a quick glance, then refocused his attention on Webb. "And let's face it, half this town had reason to hate Junior."

"Including members of my family," Webb admitted.

"Are you sure you want to—"

Webb interrupted Frank mid-sentence. "No, I don't want to go there, but if we're going to prove Reed didn't murder his stepfather, then a lot of ugly truths are bound to come out—some secrets that I'd rather stay hidden."

"Daddy, what are you talking about?" Ella glanced up from her seat on the sofa beside Reed and stared at Webb.

The last thing he wanted was for Ella to know that he had feet of clay, that the father she idolized was a mere mortal, a man who had committed more than his share of sins. But if there was any hope of finding out who, if not Reed, killed Junior Blalock, then Webb had to be honest—not only with Frank Nelson, but with Ella.

"Unless it becomes necessary, I'd rather Carolyn not know about this." Webb paced back and forth in front of the fireplace, nervous tension propelling his movements. "If it becomes public knowledge, I'll tell her myself."

Ella rose from the sofa, walked over to Webb, and put her arm around his waist. "Are you saying that someone in our family—"

"Yes, I'm saying that several people in the family had motives."

"Who?" Ella asked.

"Me, for one," Webb admitted. "Jeff Henry for another. And even Cybil."

Ella's gasp pierced him like an arrow, causing deep pain. She slipped her arm from around his waist and stepped in front of him, her gaze directed at his face. "But you didn't kill Junior, and I can't believe that—"

"No, I didn't kill Junior, but I wanted to," Webb said. "I wanted to do what Reed did—beat Junior half to death. That son of a bitch made Judy's life a living hell. And if I'd known he tried to rape Regina . . ." Webb slammed his right fist into the palm of his left hand.

Ella stared at her father and he at her. Webb realized that his daughter had never seen this side of him, a man capable of violence. She eased backward, several feet away from him.

"What about Uncle Jeff Henry and Aunt Cybil? Why would they have a reason to kill Junior?"

Reed shot up off the sofa. "Isn't there some other way to do this?"

Reed hadn't said, "without hurting Ella," but the implication was there. Webb understood only too well the desire to protect her. But it seemed rather odd for another man to be as protective of his daughter as he was. However, if Reed truly cared about Ella, then it would be only natural.

Webb shook his head. "Cybil had an affair with Junior and Jeff Henry knew about it. And I knew about it."

Ella closed her eyes, as if trying to blot out the truth. Reed went to her and put his arm around her. She opened her eyes and looked at Reed. Webb glanced away. He'd seen the look of love in his daughter's eyes.

"Why didn't you mention this to the police fifteen years ago?" Mark Leamon, who sat in the leather chair beside the bookshelves, glanced from Webb to Frank Nelson.

"I don't think Jeff Henry or Cybil is capable of murder," Webb said. "Besides, fifteen years ago I was convinced that Reed killed Junior."

"What motive did *you* have to kill Junior?" Mark asked. "Was it because of Judy?"

Webb nodded.

"Why did you care so much about what was happening to your in-laws' housekeeper and her daughter?" Mark stood as he spoke, and when Webb didn't respond immediately, Mark questioned him further. "Were you personally involved with Judy Conway?"

"Yes." Webb couldn't look at anyone in the room. He stared down at the floor. What would Ella think of him when she knew the truth? "Judy and I had an affair years ago."

With his arm still securely around Ella's waist, Reed glared at Webb. "Are you Regina's father?"

Ella gasped silently, but the expression on her face said it all. Webb looked at her, hoping she could forgive him. "Yes."

"Daddy!"

"Damn son of a bitch!" Reed cursed under his breath.

"How could you have fathered a child and never claimed her?" Ella asked. "Couldn't you have at least acknowledged her?"

"No, of course he couldn't," Reed said. "Admitting that he had fathered an illegitimate child would have ruined his reputation and ended his political career."

"The decision was Judy's as well as mine," Webb told them. "She knew that I couldn't leave Carolyn—not ever. Judy loved me enough to want to protect me, and fool that I was, I let her."

"You're not the man I thought you were if you were capable of abandoning your own child." Ella pulled away from Reed and went to her father, her presence demanding that he look at her. "Tell me that you've done something over the years to take care of Regina."

"I have," Webb said. "But not enough. Nothing I've done could even begin to make it up to her for growing up without a father and for having endured a stepfather like Junior Blalock."

"Just what have you done for Regina?" Reed demanded.

"He got her a job with me, for one thing," Mark Leamon said. "And I suspect that he arranged the college scholarship Regina received. Am I right?"

"I did everything that Judy would allow me to do," Webb said, then reached out for Ella. He sighed with relief when she allowed him to take her hand. "I would have liked for you to have grown up with your sister, for the two of you to have lived together. My greatest regret is that she couldn't be a part of our family. But Judy and I did what we thought was best for everyone."

"Oh, Daddy, how terrible for both of you." Ella wrapped her arms around her father.

Suddenly, a ringing noise distracted Webb, and for a few seconds he didn't recognize the sound. Then, when he heard Frank Nelson talking, he realized that Frank had received a call on his cell phone.

Webb smiled weakly at Ella. "There are things about my marriage to your mother that—"

Ella placed her index finger over her father's lips. "I know you and Mother love each other, but I understand that Mother's paralysis has been as difficult for you as for her."

Frank cleared his throat. "Sorry to interrupt, but there's something y'all need to know."

Four sets of eyes focused on Spring Creek's chief of police. Webb's gut instincts told him that the news wasn't good.

"What's wrong?" Webb asked.

"There's been a murder," Frank said. He looked directly at Reed. "Over at Conway's Garage."

"Briley Joe?" The color drained from Reed's face.

"Nope," Frank said. "Briley Joe found the body. Seems he'd left Roy Moses at the garage to tend to things while he went over to the junkyard in Hopewell, and when he got back about fifteen minutes ago, he discovered Roy's body in the garage."

"Roy's dead?" Ella grasped her father's hand tightly.

"Seems that way." Frank shook his head. "Poor old fellow. Somebody beat him repeatedly in the head with a twelve-inch Crescent wrench."

"Oh, Lord!" Tears glistened in Ella's eyes.

"Who would want to hurt Roy?" Reed asked.

"I've got to get on over there," Frank said. "We think we may have a witness who saw somebody leaving the garage about half an hour before Briley Joe got back."

"I should go with you," Reed said. "Briley Joe's bound to be pretty shook up."

"Let us know what you find out," Webb said. "I was rather fond of Roy. Simple-minded fellow, but a real sweet man. Anybody who'd hurt him would have to be downright mean."

Her father had asked her to stay, to come home to live, but Ella had declined, saying she'd rather give her mother a while longer to come to terms with her relationship with Reed. She had fixed coffee for them and shared two cups of Irish Creme decaf while they'd discussed Roy Moses's murder. Neither could believe that anyone would hurt such a dear, kind man.

Ella stood at the back door with her father. She leaned over and kissed him. "I'll tell Uncle Jeff Henry and

Aunt Cybil about Roy. Call me if Frank lets you know anything tonight.''

Webb clamped his hand down on her shoulder. "We need to talk more about my relationship with Judy, and about the fact that Regina is my child.''

"Yes, we do," she agreed. "But not tonight." She felt as sorry for her father as she did for Judy and Regina. And her poor mother. "You do realize that sooner or later, you'll have to tell Mother.''

Webb nodded. "Ella, about your mother . . .''

"You don't have to tell me that you love her. I know—''

"No, you don't know. That's the problem. I've let you believe that Carolyn and I are devoted to each other, but that's not true. I haven't loved your mother in a long time. The truth is that I had asked her for a divorce the very day she had her riding accident.''

"You don't love Mother?" Ella couldn't believe what she'd just heard. All her life her parents had presented a picture of marital happiness. She didn't think she'd ever heard them arguing, at least not about anything serious. And all this time, her father hadn't loved her mother.

"The only woman I've ever truly loved is Judy Conway," Webb said. "We dated when she was in high school, but I broke up with her because my parents didn't approve of her. By the time I realized how much she meant to me, she was already married to Reed's father.''

Ella wondered why she wasn't more shocked, why this revelation hadn't been a total surprise. Perhaps it was because on some instinctive level, she had known that something wasn't right in her parents' marriage, that despite their shows of affection and devotion, there had been no passion between them. As their child, she had seen only what she wanted to see, believed only what she wanted to believe.

"You still love Judy, don't you? All these years, you've

stayed with Mother because of her paralysis, because you weren't the kind of man who would desert his crippled wife."

Webb hung his head. "I won't ever leave Carolyn. She needs me too much. And if I hadn't argued with her that afternoon about a divorce, she would never have ridden off in a huff the way she did and—"

Ella grabbed her father, hugged him fiercely, and spoke softly, emotion tightening her throat. "I love you, Daddy. And whatever happens, I'll be right at your side."

Webb returned her hug, then released her and kissed her on the forehead. "You go on. I need to look in on Carolyn. I'll call you if Frank phones me tonight."

Ella hesitated, then smiled, turned around, and went out the back door. The night sky was alive with stars— diamond specks glittering in the black heavens. A slight breeze rustled through the treetops, but the wind was warm and saturated with moisture. She hurried along through their backyard into her aunt and uncle's yard next door. Before she reached the back porch, she removed the key from her pocket. Once inside the kitchen, she heard voices. Two male voices. Uncle Jeff Henry and . . . and Frank Nelson!

Following the voices, Ella rushed out of the kitchen and down the hall. She found the two men in the living room. Frank had the look of a funeral mourner, as if the news he bore was tragic. Uncle Jeff Henry's face was red-splotched, the way it got when he was very angry. She paused in the doorway, listening, realizing that neither man was aware of her presence.

"I don't give a damn what Jim Pendleton thinks he saw. I'm telling you that Cybil wouldn't have been anywhere near Conway's Garage tonight." Jeff Henry stomped back and forth between the two sofas facing each other in the center of the room.

"I'm not accusing Cybil of anything," Frank said. "But if she was there, she might have seen or heard something. All I want to do is see her for a few minutes and ask her a couple of questions.''

Jeff Henry halted abruptly, narrowed his gaze, and glowered at the police chief. "And I told you that she had a sick headache and went on to bed early. I absolutely refuse to bother her with this nonsense.''

"If there hadn't been a murder, I wouldn't be so insistent. But damnation, Jeff Henry, this town's going to be in a panic when word gets out. The shooting of a U.S. senator was bad enough, but now we've got this mess—the murder of a sweet, harmless guy like Roy. Things like this don't happen in Spring Creek. If Cybil was there, like Jim Pendleton says, then I've got to talk to her. Tonight.''

"You might as well leave," Jeff Henry said. "Unless you have a warrant to arrest Cybil, then—''

"Frank, what's this all about?'' Ella entered the room. "You can't honestly believe that my aunt was in any way involved in Roy's death.''

The moment he turned and saw Ella, Jeff Henry's face lit up and a fragile smile played at the corners of his lips. "Oh, my dear, thank goodness. You must talk sense to our police chief. That idiot, Jim Pendleton, thinks he saw your aunt near Conway's Garage tonight.'' Jeff Henry looked at her pleadingly. "I've assured Frank that it's not possible. Cybil has been here with me tonight, and she's upstairs asleep right this minute.''

"Frank, is it absolutely necessary for you to speak to Aunt Cybil tonight?'' Ella asked. "Couldn't she come down to the station and answer your questions in the morning?''

"If this weren't a murder case, then—''

Ella heard the noise the moment Frank did. Jeff Henry tensed. Someone had just come in the front door. Footsteps—high-heeled footsteps—clicked across the foyer floor. Within a minute, a tipsy Cybil appeared in the doorway. She clutched the door frame as she glanced around the room.

"What's going on?" she asked, her speech slightly slurred. "Are we having a party and nobody told me?"

Frank looked point-blank at Jeff Henry. "I thought you said Cybil had been with you all evening and was upstairs asleep."

"What?" Cybil laughed, a rather throaty, almost gurgling sound. "I don't know why he'd tell you such a thing."

"Mrs. Carlisle, would you mind telling me where you've been tonight?" Frank asked.

"Don't answer that, Cybil!" Jeff Henry rushed to his wife's side.

"I think perhaps we need to call Mark Leamon or one of your lawyers, Uncle Jeff Henry," Ella said.

"Why do we need to call a lawyer?" Cybil asked, puzzlement in her voice. "And Frank, why so formal? You don't have to call me Mrs. Carlisle."

"Aunt Cybil, Roy Moses was murdered tonight at Conway's Garage," Ella said. "Someone thinks they saw you at the garage about half an hour before Briley Joe found Roy's body."

"Oh!" Cybil moaned, then stuck her fist up to her mouth. "Poor Roy," she mumbled. "Poor, dear man."

"See," Ella told Frank. "She doesn't know anything about Roy's murder. She had no idea he was dead."

"Is that true?" Frank asked. "You weren't at Conway's Garage tonight?"

Cybil lifted her head. Her eyes seemed incapable of focusing as she glanced around the room; then suddenly she looked right at Jeff Henry. "I—I stopped by the garage earlier tonight, looking for Briley Joe."

Ella's heart sank. Jeff Henry released his inebriated wife, squared his shoulders and turned his back on her.

"Cybil, do you remember what time you stopped by?" Frank asked.

She held up her slender wrist. "Never wear a watch."

"Jim Pendleton told us he saw you about thirty minutes before the time Briley Joe says he returned to the garage. That would have been around eight-thirty."

"I thought it was earlier," Cybil said. "I don't think it was dark. I saw Roy and he told me Briley Joe wasn't there, so I left and drove over to Smithville and . . ." She glanced at Jeff Henry, who stood facing the windows, his back to her. "I met up with some friends and had a few drinks."

"All right," Frank said. "While you were at Conway's Garage, did you see anybody else around—anybody who looked the least bit suspicious?"

"There wasn't anyone else there. Just Roy."

Frank nodded. "Thanks. That's all the information I need for now. Sorry to have bothered you folks. I hope you understand that I was just doing my job."

"We understand," Ella said.

"I'll show myself out." Frank nodded to Ella, then left the room.

"Poor old Roy," Cybil said. "Who would kill a sweet guy like that?

Chapter 27

Now was the time to move forward, to rush into action, but only after careful planning. The weapon with Reed's fingerprints had been easy enough to obtain. The plan had been to steal a tool that could be used as a weapon from one of the toolboxes at the garage, but as luck would have it, Reed had left his lunch box there—and what had been discovered inside was an even better choice. A fork, a spoon and a knife—a sharp paring knife, something suitable for peeling apples, halving sandwiches, and slitting throats. Careless of him to leave such an appropriate weapon so handy. The man had been convicted once before of killing with a knife. How interesting that he would choose the same type of weapon for another murder.

With the town in an uproar over that idiot Roy Moses's death, people were distracted, even members of the Carlisle and Porter families. It was unbelievable that not only had Webb and Ella attended Roy's funeral, but that Webb had actually paid for it. Of course, Webb was known for his generosity. One of his more noble attributes.

Tonight would be the night. Regrettable choice of a victim, but necessary. Once a second murder had been blamed on Reed Conway, no one would even consider reopening the Blalock case. And once Reed was in prison again—this time for the rest of his life—things could return to normal. There would be a proper time of bereavement, of course, but eventually everyone would move on. And no one would ever know the truth. Only the two of them. And they would take the secret to their graves.

"I won't go if you need me to stay here." Ella patted her aunt's unsteady hand. "I know Uncle Jeff Henry is terribly upset about your admitting to Frank that you had stopped by Conway's Garage looking for Briley Joe."

"I was too drunk to think straight that night," Cybil admitted. "But even if I'd been completely sober, I would have had no choice but to tell Frank the truth. My heavens, he was actually considering me a suspect in Roy's murder."

"I don't think he actually believed you'd killed Roy."

"Maybe not." Cybil squeezed Ella's hand. "Don't you worry about me. Unfortunately, your uncle and I have been through this sort of thing before and survived."

"You do know that Daddy told Frank about your affair with Junior Blalock."

Cybil caressed Ella's cheek. "Yes, I know. I understand he also confessed a few of his own sins."

Ella nodded.

"He told me that you didn't judge him too harshly." Cybil leaned forward and kissed Ella's cheek. "You have such a generous and forgiving heart. And so understanding. How much would you be willing to forgive, darling girl? Would you forgive Webb and me for almost anything?"

"I love you, Aunt Cybil. Almost as much as I love Daddy. Of course I could forgive you for anything."

"Remember that promise." Cybil rose from where she'd been sitting on the edge of Ella's bed, then tapped the top of Ella's closed suitcase. "You and Reed need a weekend away after the hellacious week we've all had. A couple of days and nights down at the river cabin will be good for you."

"I hate leaving with things in such a turmoil." Ella stood, then lifted her small suitcase and set it on the floor. "With Roy's murder unsolved, Frank won't have any time to reopen the Blalock murder case for a while. And as long as Reed is a convicted murderer, Mother will never accept him."

Cybil laughed, the sound a mockery of real humor. "Don't kid yourself. Carolyn will never accept Reed Conway as your significant other. His mother is not only a housekeeper, but she gave birth to one of Webb's daughters. Once Carolyn knows about Regina, she'll despise the entire Conway family."

"Mother accepting Reed is only a minor consideration at this point," Ella said. "Reed deserves to be exonerated. He didn't kill Junior."

"You love him very much, don't you?"

Ella sighed. "It's quite obvious, isn't it?"

"Yes. To those of us who know you well and love you dearly."

"I don't understand why it happened or how it could have happened so quickly. At first I tried to convince myself that it was only sex, but . . . I have never felt anything like this in my entire life. I ache with wanting him. He's my first thought every morning and my last thought every night. No matter how much I'm with him, it's never enough."

"I know." Cybil glanced past Ella at the wall, a faraway look in her eyes. "I was in love like that once."

"Were you?"

"Mmm . . ."

"With whom?" Ella asked.

"You wouldn't believe me if I told you."

"Try me."

"With Jeff Henry Carlisle. That silly fool." Tears misted Cybil's eyes. "But he was in love with Carolyn. When he couldn't have her, he settled for me. I was a substitute for my sister. At the time, I thought I could make him love me. Oh, how wrong I was."

"Aunt Cybil . . ."

When Ella reached out to embrace Cybil, she grasped Ella's shoulders. "Don't you feel sorry for me. I made my own bed and I've been lying quite uncomfortably in it for years. But you don't have to settle for anything less than the love and passion of the man you want. Everybody may think Reed is all wrong for you, but if y'all love each other and he makes you happy, then don't let anyone come between you."

Ella hugged Cybil. "I'll be back Sunday night. And I suppose I'll continue to impose on you and Uncle Jeff Henry for a while longer. If Mother doesn't come around soon, I'll probably have to find a place of my own."

"You know you're welcome here for as long as you want to stay."

Ella released her aunt, turned, and lifted her suitcase. "If Reed should call for any reason, tell him . . . well, just tell him to hurry."

"Why aren't y'all going to the cabin together?" Cybil asked.

"It's his Friday night to close up at the garage. He's promised to be at the cabin by nine," Ella said. "Briley Joe had already made plans that he couldn't or wouldn't change. He left yesterday for a long weekend in Tunica. Reed says his cousin loves to go to the casinos and try to strike it rich. And I think he needed to get away. Finding Roy's body shook him up badly."

"I imagine he's taking some woman with him." Cybil grinned. "Don't think that I care. What I had with Briley

Joe was just sex and that I can find with a dozen other men.''

''Aunt Cybil?''

''Don't ask. You would have had to live my life to even begin to understand why I do the things I do.''

Ella nodded, then opened the bedroom door and walked out into the hall. For the next forty-eight hours, she and Reed would be alone together at the family's riverfront cabin. They could, if only for a short time, escape from reality and lose themselves in each other's arms.

Reed had been watching the clock for two hours, wishing time would pass faster. Only one more hour and he could close up the garage, hop in Briley Joe's old pickup, and head for the river. The only other time in his life he'd been this eager for something was the day he was released from prison. The thought of spending forty-eight hours of uninterrupted time with Ella was enough to give him a permanent hard-on. When she'd first suggested they spend the weekend at her family's cabin on the river, he'd been surprised. But then, Ella was a surprise—a very pleasant surprise. She seemed totally at ease with him around other people now, and all the stares directed at them whenever they were in public together didn't seem to bother her at all. He didn't know what the hell he'd done to deserve a woman like Eleanor Porter, but he thanked God for her.

That's just it, he told himself. *The reality of the situation is that you don't deserve Ella and you know it. And she damn well deserves better than the likes of you.*

The customer at the self-serve pump entered the garage and handed Reed a twenty, the exact amount of his fill-up.

''Thanks,'' Reed said.

Grinning, the guy nodded before he headed for the

door. Just as he left, the telephone rang. Reed lifted the receiver. "Conway's Garage."

"Reed?"

"Yes."

"Oh, I'm so glad I caught you before you left for the cabin. This is Cybil Carlisle," the woman said. "Ella asked me to call you and tell you that she can't meet you at the cabin until late, around eleven. She's terribly sorry, but something came up at the last minute. It has to do with a court case. She said she'd explain everything when she sees you tonight."

"All right. Thanks. Does she want me to just go on up to the cabin and wait on her?" Reed asked.

"No, she has the key, doesn't she? You don't have one, so she said to meet her at eleven. She's sure she'll be able to be there by then."

"Okay. Thanks, Mrs. Carlisle."

Reed glanced at the clock again. No need counting the minutes until closing time. Briley Joe had told him to close up at eight instead of staying open until nine, but now there was no reason to close early. No big deal. A few more hours wouldn't make that much difference. He and Ella would still have the whole weekend alone together.

Ella pulled her Jag into the gravel drive at the back of the cabin. After locking her car, she undid the trunk and lifted two bags of groceries into her arms. She'd bought steaks to grill tomorrow, baking potatoes, red and white wine, and a carton of Tennessee tea. Also ice cream, which needed to be refrigerated immediately. She had stopped at a roadside stand on the drive from Spring Creek and bought fresh strawberries, peaches and a cantaloupe.

Moonlight washed the cabin and the nearby river with gold. Soft, creamy, translucent gold. Here and there, scattered about in the black sky, several stars winked at her. Ella sighed happily. She'd never looked forward to anything as much as she did this weekend with Reed. Only three things were lacking in order for her life to be just about perfect: one, Reed being exonerated in Junior Blalock's murder; two, her mother's acceptance of Reed in her life; three, for Reed to tell her that he loved her.

When Ella reached the front door, she placed both brown sacks on the porch and inserted the key in the lock. Once she got inside, she would open the windows, turn on the ceiling fans, and cool the place off before Reed arrived. After opening the door, she reached inside and felt along the wall until her hand encountered a switch plate. She flipped on the light, lifted the groceries and walked into the cabin. As she headed toward the kitchen area to the back of the huge combination living room and dining room, she checked her wristwatch. It was already nine. She'd taken more time at the grocery store than she'd intended, and the stop at the roadside stand had taken another fifteen minutes. She had planned to be here at least thirty minutes before Reed arrived, but he was sure to get here any minute now. After all, it took less than half an hour to drive here from town.

She set the sacks on the counter, then quickly stored the perishable items in the refrigerator and put away the other groceries. Her small suitcase was still in the car, but she wanted to open windows and turn on fans before going back to get it. And maybe she should change the bed linen. The sheets were clean, but they'd been unused for at least two months.

Ella busied herself opening the windows in all four rooms and setting the ceiling fans in motion. Just as she reentered the living room, she heard someone on the porch. Odd, she thought, that she hadn't heard Reed drive up. That old rattletrap truck usually made a heck of a noise. She rushed toward the partially open door.

"Reed?"

Suddenly a shadow appeared in the doorway. Not Reed, she realized. The person wasn't tall enough to be Reed. Ella halted her mad rush, then gasped when the person stepped over the threshold.

"What are you doing here?"

The woman smiled, her face half shadowed.

"Is something wrong?" Ella asked. "Has something bad happened?"

She shook her head.

"Is it Reed?"

She shook her head again.

"Daddy?"

"Nothing is wrong with Webb or Reed," she told Ella. "And nothing bad has happened. Not yet. But it's going to."

"I don't understand."

The woman's smile widened.

Ella's stomach lurched. This wasn't possible. Was she hallucinating? Seeing things that weren't there? No, this was quite real. The woman standing only a few feet away from her wasn't the person she had first thought it was.

Reed searched the aisles in the state liquor store on Fourth Street. He wished he knew more about wines. He wanted to choose something nice, something just right, for his weekend with Ella. He supposed he could ask the cashier, but he doubted she knew any more about the wines she sold than he did. Since it was only nine-fifteen, he had more than enough time to choose a wine, go back to his room above the garage, and take a shower before he headed up to the cabin. Ella had said it wouldn't take thirty minutes to get there. So that meant he could leave at ten-thirty. Hell, he had nearly two hours to kill. Maybe he'd run by his mother's for a while.

Just as Reed reached out for a bottle of California

Merlot, he caught a glimpse of Cybil Carlisle at the other end of the aisle. He picked up the wine bottle and headed in her direction. Maybe Ella's aunt could tell him if this wine was a good choice.

"Evening, Mrs. Carlisle," Reed said as he approached her.

"Reed?"

He could tell by her expression that she was surprised to see him.

"Yes, ma'am."

"You're running a bit late, aren't you?" Cybil asked. "I thought you were supposed to meet Ella at the cabin around nine."

"What? I don't understand. You called me and told me that . . ."

She stared at him oddly, obviously confused by what he'd said.

"You didn't call me earlier tonight?"

"No," she replied. "What made you think I'd called?"

Cybil Carlisle hadn't called him. Then who had impersonated her and why? Adrenalin rushed through Reed's body. Fear consumed him.

"What's wrong?" Cybil asked.

Reed grabbed her shoulders. "Ella's in trouble. Call Frank Nelson and tell him to meet me at the cabin. Tell him to hurry. It could be a matter of life or death."

Chapter 28

"Surprised to see me, dear?" Leaving the door open behind her, Carolyn Porter moved toward Ella. "Your uncle Jeff Henry mentioned that you were coming to the cabin for a weekend tryst with Reed."

Carolyn was attired in a pair of pink cotton slacks and a matching short-sleeved summer sweater. Over her shoulder hung a small straw purse with pink roses embroidered on the flap.

"Mother? I—I don't understand. You're walking!" Ella stared dumbfounded as her mother walked toward her slowly, steadily, without any hesitation. And no sign of even the slightest limp.

"Yes, I am, aren't I." Carolyn smiled that same glowing smile that had always mesmerized her admirers and intimidated her underlings.

"When did this happen?" Ella felt overjoyed. Undoubtedly, this miracle had occurred recently. How marvelous that her mother would come to her to tell her the incredible news. "Is Daddy with you? Did he drive you up here?"

"No, dear, Daddy doesn't know anything about this,"

Carolyn said as she stopped right in front of Ella. "Viola drove me up here. She's outside on the porch. If I need her to help me, I'll just call her."

Ella grabbed her mother's hands. "Shouldn't you sit down? You mustn't overexert yourself. Not until you're accustomed to walking."

"How sweet of you to worry so about me." Carolyn tenaciously gripped Ella's right wrist. "But I'm perfectly all right. And I'm quite accustomed to walking."

"I don't understand. What do you mean you're . . ."

Carolyn's warm smile widened, darkened, and suddenly became cold and menacing. Ella shook her head to dislodge such a silly thought. This was her mother, the woman who had raised her from infancy and loved her dearly.

"I've loved you as if you were my own daughter," Carolyn said. "For such a long time. It meant so much to Webb for us to have a child. I agreed to adopt you for his sake, you know. I would have done anything to have held on to him, to have kept him married to me."

"Mother, I know. Daddy told me recently about the day you had your accident."

"Did he tell you that guilt and pity are the only reasons he has stayed married to me?"

"No, Mother, I know he cares—"

"He doesn't love me. He loves Judy Conway. He always did. But it doesn't matter." Carolyn's fingernails bit into the soft flesh of Ella's wrist. "You see, I don't love him anymore. But I'll never let him go. No matter how many women he has in his life—mistresses, one-night stands—he will remain married to me as long as we live."

An odd feeling of apprehension settled in Ella's stomach. A foreboding sense of doom. She'd never seen her mother act like this, never heard her talk this way. Why now, when she could finally walk, did she seem like a stranger to Ella?

Carolyn peered deeply into Ella's eyes. "You were a

comfort to me at first. Such a good baby and an adorable
little girl. But I soon realized that Webb loved you more
and more each day. And he gave you so much attention.
By then, it was too late to send you back, to get rid of
you, so I made the best of it. I did everything I could
for you. I was a good and loving mother, wasn't I? But
all the while I've resented you terribly, my dear.''

Ella tugged on her wrist. Her mother held fast. Their
gazes locked in a heated glare. Ella's heartbeat accelerated at an alarming speed. *Who was this woman, this
stranger who had possessed her mother's body?*

"Webb has never appreciated having a wife who
would do anything to keep him and is willing to go to
any lengths to protect his reputation,'' Carolyn said.
"I've looked the other way, ignoring his lady friends. I
even forgave him for fathering Judy Conway's bastard
child.''

"You know about Regina?''

"Yes, I've known for years.''

"But why—''

"During those first few years after my accident, I
wanted Webb to remain my husband because I loved
him so much, but later that love turned to hatred and
I kept him tied to me to punish him.''

"How long have you been able to walk?'' Ella asked,
although she was afraid to hear the answer.

"For quite some time,'' Carolyn admitted. "After all
the surgeries, the feeling in my lower body came back
gradually. Viola worked with me tirelessly, and finally,
about eighteen years ago, I was able to stand on my
own. But it wasn't until about fifteen years ago that I
regained full use of my legs.''

"Why keep it a secret for fifteen years? Why punish
yourself as well as Daddy?''

"Oh, my dear, by that time, I thoroughly enjoyed
playing the invalid. Everyone around me, including you
and your father, jumped to do my bidding. I wasn't

fool enough to give that up. Besides, if your father had
known, he would have asked me for a divorce.''

"So you've hidden the fact you can walk for fifteen
years."

"Hmm . . . I can see the wheels in your head turning,
Ella. Are you finally figuring it out?'' Carolyn suddenly
released her death grip on Ella's wrist.

The vicious thoughts swirling about in her mind tormented Ella with a truth too horrendous to accept. ''I
can't believe that you would—''

"Believe it.'' Carolyn moved right up in Ella's face.
"Junior Blalock was a vile, worthless man and he
deserved to die. And Judy Conway deserved to suffer.
My husband loved her. He fathered her child. What
better way to punish them both than to have Webb
prosecute her son for a murder he hadn't committed?''

"You're not making sense. Are you saying that—''

"I killed Junior Blalock.''

"No!''

"Yes." Carolyn took a step back, putting a few inches
between Ella and her. "That good-for-nothing bastard
found out my secret. He caught me walking on my own,
and when I tried to pretend that I was Cybil, he didn't
buy it. At that time I had no idea, of course, that he
was one of Cybil's lovers."

Ella started backing away from Carolyn, who immediately followed her, until Carolyn had Ella shoved against
the bar that separated the living and dining room from
the kitchen area.

"Such a stroke of luck, my finding Reed's pocket
knife where he dropped it when he was beating the hell
out of Junior." Carolyn's eyes brightened with each
word as she related the events of that fateful night fifteen
years ago. "I went there that night to meet Junior to
pay him blackmail money, but to my surprise I found
his stepson knocking him senseless. After Reed left
Junior lying there on the ground, half unconscious, I
realized fate had given me a golden opportunity."

"You slit Junior Blalock's throat with Reed's pocket knife? But only Reed's fingerprints were found on the weapon."

"I was wearing gloves that night," Carolyn said. "A lady always wears gloves when she goes out, especially if she doesn't want her fingerprints to show up on anything she might touch."

Ella watched with morbid fascination as Carolyn removed a pair of white cotton gloves from the pocket of her slacks, then slipped them over her hands. Suddenly, before Ella could take a deep breath, Carolyn reached inside her small shoulder bag and pulled out a paring knife. Ella tensed.

"As much as I hate having to do this, you see, Ella, you've become expendable. You've disgraced your family by having sex with that white trash ex-convict. I can only imagine the damage that's done to your Daddy's career. Of course, when Reed kills you, the entire state will sympathize with Webb and me. Our poor, misguided daughter, killed by her lover."

"Mother, you can't . . . you wouldn't . . . I'm you're daughter. You love me. And Daddy. Daddy loves me. If anything happens to me, it will break his heart."

"Yes, I know. Of course, that's simply an added bonus. I shall greatly enjoy seeing Webb distraught over your death. Who knows, he might even kill Reed with his bare hands."

Ella simply couldn't comprehend what was happening here. Her mother could walk—had been able to walk for fifteen years. Her mother had murdered Junior Blalock and framed Reed. And her mother was going to kill her. *By God, not if I can help it!* Ella tried to sidestep Carolyn, but Carolyn moved quickly, brandishing the knife.

"Mother, please, don't do this." Her heart simply would not accept the possibility that her mother was capable of following through and actually killing her.

"Ah . . ." Carolyn's mouth rounded into a sad oval.

"I tried other things, but nothing worked. The letters and phone calls to you. The roses and the snake. And Viola hired someone to break into the house while your father and I were in Gulf Shores. But because I couldn't conjure up proof that Reed was guilty, things had to take a more deadly turn. All I wanted was for them to send that man back to prison so he couldn't stir up a stink about Junior's murder."

"Oh, dear God, you shot Daddy!"

"Hmm . . . Viola was able to steal Briley Joe's gun from the garage for me and the rest was rather simple. I just had to wait for the right moment, pull the trigger, and then slip back into the house and up the stairs."

"You could have killed Daddy."

"Yes, I realize I might have hit something vital, but I did try to only wound him."

"And Roy Moses? Who killed him, you or Viola?"

"I did," Carolyn said. "That fool Jim Pendleton was driving by and saw me, but he thought I was Cybil."

Ella could deny the truth no longer. Her mother was insane. There could be no other explanation. And crazy people did crazy things—like kill their own daughters.

"Reed will be arriving any minute now," Ella said. "He'll find you and Viola here and he'll—"

Carolyn's laughter sent a chill up Ella's spine. "Reed has been delayed. I called him and pretended to be Cybil. I told him to meet you here at eleven. He won't arrive until you're already dead. But he's going to be found with your body. And the murder weapon will have his fingerprints on it."

"No one will believe Reed would kill me. We're lovers."

"Ah, but you see, I'll have to confess to the police that, in confidence, you told me you realized Reed was only using you and you asked him to meet you at the cabin so you could break things off with him. Of course, in a rage over being rejected, Reed killed you."

"You've thought of everything, haven't you?"

"I believe I have."

This is going to happen if you don't do something, Ella told herself. *You can't just stand here and not put up a fight. You're bigger than your mother. You should be able to overpower her.* But Carolyn had a weapon, and an accomplice waited patiently to come to her assistance if necessary. Ella knew her best bet was to escape. But could she? She tried again to get away from Carolyn, but once again Carolyn outmaneuvered her. *You're going to have to run,* Ella told herself. *Go out the back door as fast as you can and try to get to the car.* No, no, she couldn't do that. The keys were lying on the kitchen counter. No way to get to them. She could run down to the pier. Her father's motorboat was moored there. If she could get to the boat and start the engine, she could escape.

"You're trying to think of a way to escape, aren't you?" Carolyn shook the knife at Ella in the way a teacher would shake her finger at a naughty child. "If you run, Viola and I will come after you. You can't get away from both of us. Two against one isn't fair, I know, but then I always prefer the odds to be in my favor."

Ella glanced toward the open door. There stood Viola, the loyal, obedient servant. She had never liked her mother's nursemaid, and now she realized that even as a child she had sensed an innate evil in the woman. If only her instincts had warned her against her own mother.

"See, you can't get out the front door, not with Viola waiting there," Carolyn said.

"I don't see Viola," Ella lied.

Carolyn glanced over her shoulder quickly, but that hasty look gave Ella the opportunity she needed. She scurried past her mother and headed toward the back door, which opened onto a screened porch facing the river.

"Stop! You fool, you can't escape," Carolyn called as she ran after Ella.

Ella grasped the doorknob, twisting and turning it.

The door was locked. Hurriedly, she undid the bolt and turned the knob again. Just as she swung open the door, Carolyn came hurtling toward her, reaching out for her. The knife in Carolyn's hand sliced through the back of Ella's dress, directly above her waist. The sting of the blade ripping across her flesh halted Ella in her tracks, but only for a moment. Intense pain radiated through her body. She had no idea how badly she'd been cut, but she didn't have time to worry about it now. She had to keep moving. Her only hope of escape was not to slow down, not to give her mother a chance to plunge the knife into her back.

Ella ran out onto the porch, flung open the screen door, and rushed down the steps. Carolyn came after her, all the while screaming for Viola to hurry to the back of the house and head Ella off.

Run. Run. Run. No matter how much your back hurts, keep running. Don't slow down.

Ella headed for the pier, but immediately saw that Viola had somehow managed to get there first. Viola blocked the path to the boat—so much for an alternate means of escape.

Just hold on, Ella told herself. *Find a way to hide from them. Reed should be here any minute now and . . .* Reed wasn't coming. Not until eleven. Unless she was able to get away, she would be dead long before then.

Ella headed straight for the wooded area that flanked the cabin. She could find a place to hide. Carolyn and Viola wouldn't be able to see her shrouded in darkness, surrounded by trees and brush. She ran until she was breathless and the pain in her back overwhelmed her. She stopped, braced one hand against a tall pine tree, and breathed deeply. Folding her left arm at the elbow, she slid her hand across her back. Her fingers encountered the tear in her dress and the wet stickiness of her own blood.

"Come out, come out, wherever you are," Carolyn said, her voice a maddening sing-song chirp.

Keep moving. Damn it, you cannot let her catch you. The sound of footsteps crunching over dried leaves and rotting underbrush alerted Ella that Carolyn and Viola were coming after her. Gulping in air, she shoved herself away from the tree and started running again. Farther into the woods. Deeper into the darkness.

Reed zoomed Cybil Carlisle's T-bird into the driveway behind Ella's Jag. He'd driven a hundred miles an hour all the way from Spring Creek. Sitting at his side, Cybil had used her cellular phone to call the police, alerting them that Ella was in danger. Reed didn't know what to expect when he jumped out of the T-bird and rushed toward the open cabin door. Once inside, he scanned the vast room and saw no sign of Ella and no indication of a struggle. The back door stood wide open. Reed's heart thumped wildly. When he reached the porch, he surveyed every inch of the screened area. Large dots of a dark substance marred the weathered surface of the porch floor. In the semidarkness he couldn't make out exactly what it was. Just as he knelt and ran his finger across one of the spots, Cybil came barreling through the back door.

"What is it?" she asked.

Reed brought his finger to his nose and sniffed, then he put his finger to his lips and tasted. "Blood," he said.

"Ella! Where is she?"

"We'll search the house and if we don't find her—"

A voice calling Ella's name came from somewhere to their left, off in the wooded area that ran along the riverbank. Cybil grabbed Reed's arm.

"Yeah, I heard," he whispered.

"That voice . . ."

"A woman's voice," Reed said.

"That's Carolyn's voice."

"What?"

"Carolyn. My sister Carolyn. What is she doing here?"

"Your sister must have been the one who phoned me pretending to be you. She's the one who—"

A piercing scream rent the stillness of the humid summer night. Reed and Cybil ran down the porch steps and out into the woods, following the lingering echo of that terrified scream.

Chapter 29

Viola Mull blocked Reed's path. Stupid woman. Did she think she could stop him? As he drew closer, the moonlight reflected off the gun in Viola's hand. *Damn!*

"Stop right there, Reed Conway," Viola instructed.

"Where's Ella?" Reed asked as he crept, inch by inch, closer and closer to Carolyn Porter's companion.

"It's unfortunate that you arrived so early," Viola told him. "But no matter, we will simply have to readjust our plans. Perhaps we can arrange it so that it looks as if Ella was able to shoot you before she died."

"Where is she?"

"Don't come any closer," Viola said. "If you do, I'll be forced to shoot you right now."

"You're going to shoot me regardless," Reed said just before he rushed her.

Taken off guard by Reed's bold move, Viola didn't get off a shot before Reed tackled her. They struggled on the ground, the gun held tightly in Viola's hand between them. Suddenly the gun went off. Reed heard the shot echo inside his head. He rolled Viola off him and over onto the ground. She stared up at the night sky with sightless eyes. With only the moonlight for illumination, Reed could see her dimly, but well enough to believe she was dead. He felt for a pulse. There was none.

Cybil ran toward Reed. He rose to his feet just in time to put his hand over her mouth.

"Don't say anything," Reed whispered.

Cybil nodded.

And then they heard the voice again. "Ella, did you hear that gunshot? Viola just killed someone. Do you think perhaps Reed showed up earlier than he should have?"

Cybil's eyes rounded with shock. "It's Carolyn's voice," she murmured. "How is it possible that my sister is out there in her wheelchair in the woods with Ella?"

If Ella was still alive, that meant he had to get to her, had to save her from her own mother. "Viola is the one who's dead," Reed shouted.

"Reed!" Ella screamed.

Reed plowed through the dark woods, heading straight toward the sound of Ella's voice. But if he could follow her voice, so could Carolyn. How the hell was the woman maneuvering in a wheelchair? The explanation hit him about two seconds before he came upon Ella struggling with her mother, both women standing upright.

"Get away from her," Reed said as he zeroed in on the two.

Ella shoved Carolyn, who just barely managed to remain on her feet. Ella slumped to the ground. Reed rushed Carolyn, but before he could overpower her, she stabbed him in the shoulder. Instinctively Reed grabbed his injured shoulder, and when he did, Carolyn whirled around and lifted her knife, bringing it down toward Ella.

Reed lunged for Carolyn, but before his body made contact with hers, a gunshot blasted from behind him. Carolyn went limp when the bullet struck her in the back of her head. She crumpled into a heap as her life's blood drained from her. Reed didn't glance backward. He rushed to Ella, lifting her up onto her feet. When she fell against him, he swept her up into his arms.

Cybil, still tenaciously grasping Viola's gun in her hand, walked toward Reed. "Are you two all right?"

"Yeah, thanks to you," Reed said.

Cybil reached out and tenderly ran her fingertips over the wound in Ella's back. "We have to get her to a hospital. And, you, too."

"Mother . . . Mother . . ." Ella moaned.

"God!" Cybil glanced down at her sister's lifeless body. "She could walk. She wasn't paralyzed."

"She killed Junior," Ella whispered, then started coughing.

"Hush, darling girl." Cybil caressed Ella's cheek. "Time enough for explanations later. We have to get you to the hospital right away."

As Reed carried Ella toward the cabin, Cybil followed, the gun still clutched in her hand. Off in the distance, the sound of sirens grew louder and louder.

Carolyn Walker Porter was laid to rest in the family plot at Spring Creek Cemetery directly following a brief private service. Only her husband, her daughter, her sister, and brother-in-law attended. Carolyn's funeral had been delayed at Ella's request. She had asked her father to wait until she was released from the hospital— four days after her mother had tried to kill her. Viola Mull's body had been cremated, as her will had requested, and her ashes left for the funeral home to dispose of as they saw fit.

When the black limousine pulled up in the driveway at the Porter house, a police entourage kept the reporters and sightseers at a distance. Reed, who waited on the porch, came out to meet Ella. The moment she saw him, she rushed into his arms. He led her up the walkway toward her home. Her father, aunt, and uncle followed, keeping their backs to the press and ignoring the shouted media questions.

Little had been said among the family members at Carolyn's funeral. Indeed, what was there to say? In the emergency room that night after the incident at the cabin, both Cybil and Reed had told Frank Nelson what had happened, and Ella had given a statement the following morning. The Junior Blalock murder case had been officially reopened, and it was only a matter of time before Reed was exonerated of all charges and given a full pardon.

As she started to enter the living room, Ella caught a glimpse, in her peripheral vision, of Judy Conway standing at the end of the hallway, near the entrance to the kitchen. Regina was at her side. Ella stopped, turned slowly, and headed down the corridor toward Reed's mother and sister. Reed went with her, but before they reached their destination, Webb Porter called out to them.

"Ella, I asked Judy and Regina to come here today," Webb said.

Ella approached Reed's mother and sister.

"I'm very sorry about Carolyn," Judy said. "She must have been truly sick in her mind to have been capable of doing the things she did. But if it is any comfort to you, I know that she once loved you very much."

Ella reached out and grasped Judy's hand. "Thank you. I appreciate your being so kind, especially considering how destructive my mother—Carolyn was to you and your children. She tried to ruin all your lives."

Reed tightened his hold around Ella's waist. "This could have waited." Reed glanced back at Webb, his gaze accusatory, then looked straight at his mother. "Why did you agree to come here, today of all days?"

"Your mother and sister are here at my insistence," Webb said. "I realize we could wait, but I see no point in continuing the lies one day longer. It's past time for the truth to be told—the whole truth."

"I think we know the truth, don't we?" Ella felt certain that she knew all the hard, cold facts about her parents and about her own life. Her mother had been a murderer, a woman who had hated her enough to kill her. The father she had always worshiped had a biological daughter that he could now claim. No matter how much Webb Porter loved Ella, wasn't it possible that Regina would now take her place in his heart? All she had was Reed, to whom she clung. But even her relationship with Reed wasn't something she could count on. He had made her no promises, made no plans with her about a future together.

"Mark Leamon is waiting in the den for us," Webb said. "Please, if all of you will bear with me, I'm prepared to put an end to a lifetime of lies."

When Webb held out his hand, it wasn't to Judy Conway, as Ella had expected. Instead it was to her aunt Cybil, who gave her husband a sad, forlorn glance, then walked to Webb's side and accepted his outstretched hand. Together they entered the den, followed slowly by a puzzled Ella, who still depended upon Reed's comforting support. Within minutes the den was filled to capacity. Webb seated Cybil at his desk and took his place behind her, his hands resting on her shoulders. Mark Leamon nodded a greeting to the others as they filtered into the room, then motioned for Regina to come to him, which she did instantly. Judy Conway gazed at Webb, a wealth of love and sympathy plainly visible in her eyes. Ella searched for her uncle and found him standing in the doorway. Their gazes met. He smiled at her. Tears misted his eyes.

A knot of anxiety tightened in Ella's stomach. Reed guided her toward the sofa, but she shook her head when he tried to help her sit. "I'll stand," she told him.

"Whatever Webb has to tell us, we'll deal with it together," Reed told her.

She nodded, then turned her attention to her father, who cleared his throat several times before he spoke.

"I believe everyone here knows that I've been in love with Judy Conway most of my life." Webb gazed at Judy for just a moment, then visibly tightened his hold on Cybil's shoulders. "And I think everyone knows that she and I had an affair that resulted in a child." Webb looked at Regina, who tilted her chin and stared straight at her father. "I intend to publicly acknowledge Regina as my child, and she, along with my older daughter, Ella, will become my legal heirs. Regina, I don't know if you can ever forgive me for not claiming you long before now, but your mother and I thought we were doing the right thing for everyone involved, considering the circumstances."

"I don't know what you want me to say," Regina told her father. "I'm really not sure how I feel about you."

"Fair enough," Webb said. "All I ask is that you give me a chance to be a father to you . . . because you see"— he looked at Judy again—"when a decent amount of time has passed, I'm going to ask your mother to marry me."

Ella gasped. Reed squeezed her hand. Ella felt as if her entire life were evaporating before her very eyes, as if she had never truly existed. Her mother was gone— a mother who had wanted to kill her. And her father had a child who was truly his. And one day soon he would marry Reed's mother and build a new life with her and their child.

"I don't understand why this family meeting was necessary," Ella said. "All of us already knew everything you've told us."

"There's more," Webb said.

"Perhaps I should explain." Cybil took a deep breath, then released it slowly. "Thirty-one years ago, Webb found himself trapped in a marriage to my sister. She'd been paralyzed in a riding accident and Webb wouldn't leave her." Cybil looked point-blank at Jeff Henry. "I was young and foolishly in love—with a man who loved my sister.''

Ella watched the play of emotions on Jeff Henry's face. Shock. Disbelief. Amazement.

Cybil continued. "After Carolyn's accident, Jeff Henry thought that perhaps he had a chance with Carolyn. Even then, he still wanted her." Cybil breathed in and out through her nose as she clenched her teeth, obviously in an effort not to cry. "I hated Jeff Henry because he couldn't love me, and I hated Carolyn because she toyed with Jeff Henry, keeping him emotionally on a string, not wanting him, but never letting him go. So I decided to seduce Carolyn's husband." Cybil laughed, the sound hollow and sad. So very sad. "This happened a little over a year before I married Jeff Henry. I was only seventeen."

Ella's gaze traveled around the room, studying the faces of the principal players in this game of absolute truth. She could tell by the expressions on their faces that whatever her aunt Cybil was about to reveal wasn't news to either Judy or Jeff Henry.

"Webb and I were both miserable. He loved Judy. I loved Jeff Henry. We couldn't be with the ones we loved, so we turned to each other for solace—once and only once." Tears misted Cybil's eyes.

"Let me take over from here." Webb tenderly patted Cybil's shoulders. "Cybil came to me a couple of months later, after our one night together, and told me she was pregnant."

Both Ella and Regina gasped. Reed glowered at Webb but never released his tight grip on Ella's hand.

"I concocted what I thought was a brilliant plan," Webb told them. "I spoke to Carolyn about our adopting a child, and to my surprise, she agreed. Cybil moved away, supposedly to college, until after the baby was born. Then my lawyer, Milton Leamon, arranged a private adoption. Carolyn never knew the baby girl we adopted was my biological daughter. Mine and Cybil's.''

Ella felt as if the world were spinning out of control. She heard every word of what her father was saying, and on some level, she understood. However, the reality that Webb was truly her father and that Cybil was her mother seemed impossible to believe:

"I don't think any man could have screwed up his personal life more than I did," Webb admitted. "I've lived most of the past thirty years lying about everything that was important to me. Ella, honey, can you ever forgive me?"

"Can you ever forgive us?" Cybil asked.

What could she say? "I don't believe this." But she did believe them. It made perfect sense, didn't it? This was the reason she'd always felt so close to her aunt Cybil, why she'd always felt as if her aunt and uncle were like a second set of parents. And this was the reason that she was so much like Webb, why they thought a great deal alike. And why she'd often thought she actually resembled her adoptive parents.

Ella glanced at her uncle. "You knew, didn't you?"

"Yes, Cybil told me once, years ago, when she was drinking and crying and calling for her baby," Jeff Henry said. "You were about three years old at the time." Jeff Henry came forward, moving directly toward his wife. He hovered at the edge of the desk. "Why didn't you ever tell me that you loved me? All these years, I've thought you loved Webb."

"You silly, stupid jackass." Tears streamed down Cybil's face.

Jeff Henry turned to Ella. "She loves you more than anything. You must know that. And you must understand why she did what she did. It was for you, so that you could grow up as part of our family without the shame of illegitimacy hovering over you like a dark cloud."

Cybil rose from the chair. "Ella? Darling girl?"

Ella jerked her hand out of Reed's and met Cybil as she rounded the edge of the desk and held out her arms.

Ella went into her mother's arms—her real mother. By the time mother and daughter had hugged and cried and hugged some more, they both noticed they were alone in the den. Everyone had disappeared.

"I know I'll never win an award for Mother of the Year," Cybil said. "I'm no prize. But I love you. I've always loved you. And I tried to be as big a part of your life as I could."

"I know."

Cybil clutched Ella's chin in the curve between her thumb and index finger. "You mustn't let Reed get away. If you love him, then tell him. Don't waste one more day of your life without making a commitment to each other."

"But—"

"No buts." Cybil turned Ella around and headed her toward the door. "All this past history can be sorted out in the weeks, months, and years ahead. What's important right this minute is your happiness."

Ella found Reed in the gazebo, standing alone with his back to her. "Reed?"

He turned slowly and faced her. "Are you okay?"

She nodded. A weak smile hovered on her lips. "I will be."

"So, what now? Things won't ever be the same for you once the whole town knows all the family secrets."

"I don't care about the family secrets being revealed," Ella said as she stepped up and into the gazebo. "Don't you think it's apparent that what people think of me isn't that important. After all, I've already ruined my reputation by having a love affair with you."

Reed grinned. "So you have."

Ella draped her arms around Reed's neck and pressed her body to his. "What about you? What are you planning on doing with the rest of your life?"

Reed cupped her buttocks and pressed her against

his erection. "I'm not sure what I want to do with the rest of my life, but I thought that after our honeymoon, you could help me decide."

"What did you say?"

"I said that after our honeymoon—"

"You haven't asked me to marry you."

"Oh, you're right," Reed said. "Just an oversight, I can assure you." He kissed her quite thoroughly, then ended the kiss when they both were breathless. "Ella Porter, will you marry me?"

"No candlelight and soft music? No diamond engagement ring?"

"Nope. Sorry. All I have to offer is myself."

"Well, it just so happens that that's all I want."

Epilogue

Two years later . . .

Reed Conway walked his mother down the aisle. Waiting for her at the altar was her groom, Webb Porter. At Webb's side stood his son-in-law, Mark Leamon, the best man. The wedding was a small affair and the guest list kept to only family and close friends, like the newlyweds Heather and Dan Gilmore. An intimate ceremony suited the recently retired senator and his bride, who wanted a more private lifestyle in the future.

Ella thought her father looked handsome as always in his black suit. And Judy, whom Ella had grown to love dearly in the eighteen months she'd been married to Reed, looked beautiful in her pale ivory suit. But no one could outshine her husband. Reed was utterly, devastatingly gorgeous. She knew that as soon as the reception was over, he'd divest himself of his tie immediately. Even in his job as a teacher at the local community college, Reed never wore a tie.

Ella watched as Judy handed her bridal bouquet to Regina, then leaned over and kissed her daughter. The huge arrangement of cream roses and baby's breath almost covered all of Regina's protruding belly. She was due to deliver her first child in approximately six weeks—a daughter.

Judy then walked past Regina and went to Ella, who was acting as her second matron of honor. Ella accepted her mother-in-law's kiss and gave her a hug, her own rather large belly getting in the way. She and Reed were expecting their first child any day now—a son.

While the minister spoke the words uniting Webb Porter and Judy Conway, Ella glanced to the front pew. There sat Cybil and Jeff Henry, their hands clasped together. Her mother had been sober for almost two years now, ever since she underwent treatment at a rehabilitation center. Not only had Cybil given up liquor, but she'd given up other men, too. Jeff Henry had become besotted with his wife, and it was rather sweet to watch the two lovebirds together.

As the minister pronounced Webb and Judy husband and wife, they turned to each other and shared a tender kiss. And then, as if on cue, Reed, who stood at Mark's side, came to Ella, took her in his arms, and kissed her. Mark followed suit and kissed his wife. Then, together the three couples marched down the aisle and out to the waiting limousine that would take them to the country club, to the gala reception hosted by Cybil and Jeff Henry Carlisle.

CLOSE ENOUGH TO TOUCH . . .

He's their secret admirer, wooing them with phone calls, love letters, and special gifts. From a distance, he admires them. Desires them. Despises them. And when he gets close enough, he kills them all.

CLOSE ENOUGH TO KISS . . .

Adams County, Alabama, is a small, friendly place where everyone knows each other—but not well enough, it seems, because Sheriff Bernie Granger has a serial killer on her hands, a total psycho who first romances, then stalks, kidnaps, and kills his victims. It's Bernie's first big case, a chance for her to prove herself to her new partner, Memphis police detective Jim Norton, but it won't be easy. This killer is uncannily smart. It's as if he knows what Bernie is thinking. And his next move is more than shocking—it's chillingly personal.

. . . CLOSE ENOUGH TO KILL.

A terrifying game is underway. A desperate hunt has begun. Bernie is determined to stop a twisted serial killer at all costs. But is she getting nearer to catching him—or being drawn ever deeper into his deadly web?

Please turn the page for an exciting sneak peek of Beverly Barton's CLOSE ENOUGH TO KILL coming in July 2006!

Chapter 1

Please, dear God, let him kill me.

Stephanie Preston lay on the narrow cot, listening to the rapid beat of her heart. Staring up at the ceiling in the small, dark room, she tried to pretend she was somewhere else. At home, with Kyle. Or at work, surrounded by people she knew and trusted. Perhaps at church, where she sang in the choir. Anywhere but here. With anyone but him.

As hard as she tried to mentally remove herself from the reality of this moment, from where she was and what was happening to her, she could not fully escape into her mind.

Try harder. Think about last Christmas. About how surprised you were when Kyle proposed, on bended knee, right there in front of your parents and your sisters.

Just as the image of her smiling parents flashed through her mind, the man on top of her rammed into her again, harder this time. With more fury. And his fingers dug into her hips as he forced her body upward to meet his savage thrust. As he accelerated the harshness and speed of his deep lunges, he voiced his need, as he did every time he raped her.

"Tell me." He growled the words. "Say it. You know what I want to hear."

No, I won't. Not this time. I can't. I can't.

She lay beneath him, silent and unmoving, longing for death, knowing what was going to happen next.

He slowed, then stopped and lifted himself enough to gaze down into her face. She closed her eyes, not wanting to look at him. Not wanting to see the face of terror.

He grabbed her, clutching her chin between his index finger and thumb, pressing painfully into her cheeks. "Open your eyes, bitch. Open your eyes and look at me."

Her eyelids flickered. *Don't obey him. Not this time. Be strong.*

"Why are you being so stubborn?" he asked, a tone of genuine puzzlement in his voice. "You know that I can force you to do whatever I want. Why make it so hard on yourself? You know that, in the end, you'll obey me."

"Please . . ." She opened her eyes and looked at him through a mist of tears.

"Please, what?"

Tears pooled in her eyes despite her determination not to cry. He liked it when she cried. "Just finish it."

"If you want me to finish with you, then tell me what I want to hear. Otherwise, I'll punish you. I'll make it last a long time." Lowering his head to her breast, he opened his mouth and bared his teeth. Before she could respond, he clamped down on her nipple and bit.

She cried out in pain. He thrust into her several times. Harder each time.

When he moved his mouth to the other breast, she gasped, then cried out hurriedly, "I love you. I want you more than I've ever wanted anyone. Please, darling, make love to me."

He smiled. God, how she hated his smile.

"That's a good girl. Since you asked so nicely, I'll give you what you want."

She lay there beneath him and endured the rape, hating every moment, despising him and loathing herself for having given in to him yet again.

This can't go on forever. Sooner or later, he'll kill me.

I hope it's soon. I hope it's very soon.

He stood across the street, on the corner, and watched her get out of her car and walk up the sidewalk to her front porch. She was lovely. He would enjoy sketching her, but before he could begin, he would need to see her up close. When he created the pictures of her, he wanted to get every detail correct. The slant of her eyes. The curve of her nose. The fullness of her lips. Her neck was long and slender; her body nicely rounded, neither skinny nor fat. Just right.

The first thing he would do was call her. Just to say hello. To make contact. He would be able to tell by the sound of her voice if she would be receptive to his overtures. He wouldn't listen to what she said. Women so often lied— unless you forced them to tell the truth. But he could always tell when a woman was interested just by the way she spoke to him.

"Thomasina, Thomasina. Such a lovely name for a lovely lady."

The thought of their courtship excited him. He reveled in the days leading up to the moment before a woman became his completely. It was the prelude to the mating dance that intensified the pleasure, those incredibly delicious events that prepared them for the inevitable.

However, he couldn't begin pursuing Thomasina in earnest until he ended his current relationship. He'd been keeping tabs on her, learning everything he could about her—but from afar. He wasn't the kind of man who would betray one woman with another. It wasn't his style. It wouldn't be easy ending things with his current lover. She was very much in love with him. He had been wild about her in the beginning, when she had posed a challenge to him, when she had led him on a merry chase. And the first time they'd made love had been good, although not all he had hoped it would be. He was certain that she knew their relationship was coming to an end, that they both needed to be free. And soon.

Perhaps tonight he'd tell her.

She would cry, of course. She cried a great deal. And she would beg him, plead with him, offer to do anything he wanted her to do.

Poor darling. It was simply going to kill her when he told her that their love affair was over.

Sheriff Bernie Granger removed her jacket, hung it on the hall tree in the mudroom, then took off her holstered gun and hung the strap over her coat. Every muscle in her body ached. She hadn't slept in nearly thirty-six hours, hadn't eaten in twelve, and needed more than the whore's baths she'd taken in the restroom sink yesterday and today. This had been the third search she'd headed up during the past two weeks, each time following a lead that ended nowhere. Trying to stay optimistic and give hope to a family who had all but given up wasn't easy. But damn it all, she wasn't willing to throw in the towel and admit defeat. During the two and a half years she had been the sheriff of Adams County, Alabama, she'd been lucky. Only one murder had occurred in her county while she was in office, and the killer was now serving a life sentence in Donaldson. She'd had to handle four missing persons' cases. The first had ended within twenty-four hours, when they'd found the elderly Alzheimer's patient who'd walked away from home and gotten lost in the woods. The second case had been rough on everyone involved. A missing three-year-old. When they'd found the little boy two days later in a deep ravine, his tiny body bloody and bruised from the fall, she had walked away, found a solitary spot, and cried. In private. Where none of her deputies could see her. She was one of only a handful of women in local law enforcement, so she had to be tough as nails in order to survive. Thankfully, the third missing person's case had turned out to be nothing more than a woman leaving her husband for another man.

And now Bernie was dealing with the fourth missing person's case. Stephanie Preston, a young bride of five months, had been missing for two weeks after last being seen leaving Adams County Junior College, where she attended night classes two evenings a week. Technically, this was an Adams County case, since the woman was last seen in this county and the college campus was not within the city limits of Adams Landing. But the Jackson County Sheriff's Department was also involved since Stephanie lived in Scottsboro, and Sheriff Mays over there was Stephanie's uncle.

"You look like hell," Robyn said when Bernie entered the kitchen.

She glanced at her younger sister and grinned. "I feel like hell."

She and Robyn were as different as night and day. Robyn was tall, model-thin, and possessed a mane of curly black hair. At twenty-eight, she was still single and liked it that way. She had left college without graduating and had flitted from one job to another, one boyfriend to another, for the past eight years. She had finally come home to Adams Landing a year ago and, with some financial help from their parents, opened up a small fitness center that was, surprisingly, doing quite well.

Bernie, on the other hand, was tall, large boned, and sturdily built. She wore her plain brown hair in an easy-to-care-for ponytail most of the time, or she occasionally pulled it into a neat bun. She'd gotten married straight out of high school to her childhood sweetheart and they'd gone off to college together. After four years of marriage, two miscarriages for Bernie, and at least three affairs for Ryan, they had parted ways. Bernie had come home to Adams Landing, gotten a job as a deputy, and then almost three years ago was elected sheriff when her dad retired from the job, which he'd held for nearly thirty years.

Robyn lived at home with their mom and dad, but occasionally she'd spend a few days at Bernie's. This time, when she'd shown up on the doorstep, suitcase in hand, she'd told Bernie that she had to find a place of her own and soon. Being an old-fashioned, church-going Southern lady, Brenda Granger didn't approve of Robyn sleeping around, and when she'd caught Robyn's latest lover sneaking out of the house at five in the morning, Brenda had exploded in motherly outrage.

"Mom has called me every couple of hours to check on you," Robyn said. "She's worried about you."

"That's old news. Mom's always worried about me and about you. We're both single and childless."

Robyn grinned. "Yeah, you'd think the only reason she had us was so we could give her grandchildren."

Bernie trekked across the kitchen, opened a cupboard, and removed a bag of preground coffee. "Have you and Mom talked about things? Have you settled your differences?" Bernie removed the glass pot from the coffee-maker, walked over to the sink, and filled it with cool water.

"You know how it is with Mom—she doesn't talk with

you, just to you. And no, we have not settled our differences and we probably never will. Good God, she was living in the fifties when she was a kid, not in the twenty-first century. Do you know what she said to me about having sex outside marriage?"

Bernie clicked her tongue against the roof of her mouth. "Hmm . . . let me guess. Could it have been the old tried-and-true adage about a man not buying a cow if the milk is free?"

Robyn chuckled. "You'd think she'd at least come up with some new material, wouldn't you?"

Bernie emptied the water into the coffeemaker, turned it on, and removed a cup from the cupboard. "Want some?"

"Huh?"

"Coffee. It's decaf. Want some?"

"No, thanks. I'm heading out any minute now. Paul Landon is taking me to Huntsville for dinner."

Paul Landon? Lord help us! Robyn could do a lot better than Paul. Good looks was about all the guy had going for him. That and a rich daddy. The man had been married and divorced twice, was rumored to have a drinking problem, and the general consensus was that he wasn't worth shooting.

But she supposed it wouldn't hurt for Robyn to date the guy, as long as she didn't get serious about him, and that wasn't likely to happen. After all, it wasn't as if Adams County was running over with eligible bachelors. Bernie's last date had been four months ago with Steve Banyan, a widower with three kids, a receding hairline, and the beginnings of a beer belly. They'd had a total of four dates over a period of a month. She liked the guy well enough, but they had little in common. He was a pharmacist, fifteen years Bernie's senior, and considering how much he talked about his deceased wife, Carol Anne, was probably still in love with her.

"Look, if you two wind up spending the night here, then either the two of you be very, very quiet or just go rent a motel room," Bernie said. "I'm dead on my feet and I've got to have a decent night's sleep."

"This is our first date," Robyn said. "It's highly unlikely I'll let him get in my pants so soon. Despite what Mom thinks, I do have my standards."

Bernie's lips curved into a weak grin. God, she was tired. All she wanted was a cup of coffee and a sandwich, followed by a long, hot bath. Then about ten hours of sleep. She'd be lucky if she got six. She'd have to be at the office early tomorrow morning, ready to meet her new employee. Bill Palmer had retired several months ago, after a heart attack and bypass surgery, leaving her without a chief deputy, someone qualified to head up the criminal investigative division. Originally, she'd thought about promoting from within the ranks, but that would have been a difficult call since she had two equally qualified deputies in that division, each with approximately the same seniority. She'd gone to her dad for advice, as she often did, and he had suggested looking outside the local force.

"You never know when a highly qualified person might be looking for a change," R.B. Granger had said. In her opinion, Robert Bernard Granger was the best darn law enforcement officer who'd ever lived. "I've still got contacts in Alabama, Tennessee and Georgia. Why don't I make a few phone calls and see what I come up with? In the meantime, you do the same. Check around. Could be you can bring somebody in from Huntsville or even Chattanooga. One of those big-city guys might want to move to a place where the pace is a little slower."

"Or a gal."

"Huh?"

"A guy or a gal, Dad. Or have you forgotten that the

sheriff of Adams County is female?" she'd asked, only halfway joking. Since her little brother, Bobby, had drowned in the river on a Boy Scout picnic when he was twelve, Bernie had been the closest thing her dad had to a son. She'd been the one who had played high school basketball, soccer, and softball. And she'd played sports more for her dad's sake than because she loved the games herself. She was the one who sat around and watched football games on TV with him, went fishing with him, and even went hunting with him once each year.

Bob Granger had put his arm around Bernie's shoulders and said, "You know how proud I am of you, don't you? You're carrying on a family tradition. You're the third generation of Granger to be sheriff of Adams County."

A car horn honked, bringing Bernie out of her thoughts and back to the present moment, here in her kitchen.

"That'll be Paul," Robyn said.

"Quite the gentleman, isn't he, honking for you instead of coming to the front door."

Robyn groaned. "Now you sound like Mom." She rushed over, gave Bernie a quick kiss on the cheek and flew out of the kitchen, calling loudly as she left, "I love you, sis. Don't wait up for me."

Bernie heard her sister giggling just before she slammed the front door. The moment Bernie was alone, she sighed, leaned her head back and stretched her aching muscles. Just as she eyed the coffeepot, intending to pour herself a cup before she prepared a sandwich, the telephone rang. Her heart leaped into her throat. She had left several of her deputies, along with Adams Landing police officers and several volunteers from Jackson County, still scouring Craggy Point, the area where an eyewitness swore he saw a woman fitting Stephanie's description arguing with a burly black man at the roadside park.

"Sheriff Granger." Her hand clutched the phone with white-knuckled pressure; then she glanced down at the caller ID and groaned.

"Good, you're home," Brenda Granger said. "Have you eaten supper? Taken a bath? Do you need me to come over and fix you something to eat? Or I could bring some leftovers. Dad and I had pot roast for supper and—"

"I'm fine, Mom. I was just fixing to make a sandwich."

"A sandwich? What kind?"

"Peanut butter and jelly." Bernie said the first thing that popped into her head.

"You don't eat right," Brenda said. "That's the reason you can't ever get rid of those ten extra pounds around your hips."

"Mom, I'm really tired. Could we discuss my eating habits and my weight problems another time?"

"Of course." Brenda paused for half a minute. "I'd like for you and Robyn to come to dinner on Sunday."

"All right. I'll be there, if I can. And I'll mention it to Robyn when—"

"Isn't she there?"

Thinking fast on her feet and telling a white lie to avoid further explanations, Bernie said, "She's in the shower. I'll tell her when she gets out, and I'm sure she'll be able to make it for Sunday dinner."

"Good. I've invited the new preacher. He's not married. And I've also invited Helen and her son Raymond. Raymond's divorce is final, you know. Helen and I agree that it's high time he started dating again."

"Good night, Mom. See you Sunday."

"Yes, dear, good night."

Bernie hung up the phone. When she told Robyn that their mother expected them for Sunday dinner, and that she was providing each of them with a potential husband, Robyn would throw a hissy fit. But in the end, she, like Bernie, would go to dinner and endure yet another matchmaking scheme concocted by a desperate grandmother wannabe.

Jim Norton unlocked the front door of his rental duplex on Washington Street. While driving through town, he'd noticed that a great many of the streets in Adams Landing were named for presidents. Washington, Jefferson, Madison, Monroe. Before entering the house, he reached inside and felt for a light switch, which he quickly found. He had rented this place, sight unseen, fully furnished and move-in ready. He stepped inside, dropped his suitcase to the carpeted floor, then closed and locked the door behind himself.

Scanning the living room, he noted the place looked like most furnished rentals. Clean and neat. Furniture, drapes, and carpets slightly worn. Not a home, just a place for a guy to hang his hat. He hadn't had a real home in a long time. Not since he and Mary Lee divorced. He could have bought a house or even rented a nicer place and furnished it himself, but what was the point? While working as a lieutenant on the Memphis police force, he hadn't spent much time at home. Slept and bathed there. And occasionally ate there. If he'd been given joint custody of Kevin, he probably would have bought a house, but Mary Lee had been given full custody and he'd gotten squat. Just visitation rights—and those visits were under Mary Lee's supervision.

He'd driven straight from Memphis this evening,

across northern Mississippi and northern Alabama, taking Highway 72 all the way. Adams County was a small county nestled in the northeastern corner of Alabama, a stone's throw from both the Tennessee and Georgia state lines, and the Tennessee River divided the county seat, Adams Landing, from its nearest neighbor, Pine Bluff.

Jim's neck was stiff and his bad knees hurt like hell. He'd made only one pit stop on his journey from his past to his future. His bleak future. Not that his future on the Memphis force had looked all that bright—not since he'd fallen from grace and an air of suspicion had surrounded him ever since.

Jim left his suitcase there by the front door as he walked through the duplex, turning lights on and off as he went from the living room into the small efficiency kitchen. Then he backtracked and went into first one bedroom and then another. The bath was small, but clean, with a shower/tub combination. He'd rented a two-bedroom place despite the added expense because he wanted Kevin to have his own room when he came to visit.

Leaving the bathroom light on, Jim went over to the bed and sat down. He should at least brush his teeth before turning in, but he thought maybe, just this once, he'd forgo his usual routine. After removing his shoes and socks and stripping down to his briefs, Jim flipped back the covers and crawled into bed.

He lay there for several minutes, thinking he'd go right to sleep. But the longer he lay there, the more he realized that until he took something for the pain in his knees, he'd never go to sleep. He had two choices. Both were in his suitcase: either whiskey or the painkillers the doctor had given him. He chose the prescription medicine. After bringing his suitcase into the bedroom and digging through his shave kit for the plastic bottle, he took one pill and went back to bed. He gazed up at the shadows flickering across the white popcorn ceiling. He had left the bathroom light on and closed the door almost shut. He hated the darkness, especially when he was in a strange place.

He wished the pill would take effect soon. Not just to relieve the pain, but to knock him out. Otherwise, he'd think too much. Thinking about Mary Lee and Kevin and why he was here in this one-horse town was a useless exercise in torment.

He'd met and fallen madly in love with Mary Lee at the University of Tennessee; then they'd married right after he graduated. There had been some good years. They'd been happy. For a while. Kevin's birth had been the greatest day of Jim's life. He'd never known you could love someone the way he loved his son. Back then, Jim had thought he had the world by the tail. Despite knee injuries destroying his dream of playing pro football, he had found a new and satisfying career as a Memphis police officer. He'd made detective fairly young and life had been good. Until his cockiness and stupid arrogance had cost his partner his life. After that, everything fell apart, including his marriage. When he'd found Mary Lee in bed with another man, he had wanted to kill them both. And he almost had. Almost.

He had walked out of his house that day and filed for a divorce two weeks later. Forgiveness wasn't a word in his vocabulary, because as far as he was concerned, some sins were unforgivable.

For the past seven years, Mary Lee had made his life as miserable as possible, at first trying to turn Kevin against him, then later jerking him around about his visitation rights. So it hadn't actually come as a great surprise to him when, after remarrying six months ago, she'd told him that she was moving with her new husband to Huntsville. Kevin's stepdad had recently been transferred to the Rocket City.

"You can drive to Huntsville a couple of times a year to see Kevin," Mary Lee had said. "And he can come stay with you a week every summer."

"No way in hell!"

He had known that going back to court wouldn't do any good. Despite being a whore, Mary Lee wasn't a bad mother. And Jim had proved by his actions years ago that he wasn't such a good father. So he'd realized he had only one choice if he wanted to see his son on a regular basis. He had to move closer to Huntsville. It had taken him six months to find a job—the right job. One that paid him enough to live on and stay current with his child support payments. Being a chief deputy in Podunk was a demotion from being a lieutenant on the Memphis police force, and his yearly salary dropped by over twenty thousand. But he figured he'd do okay since the cost of living here was slightly less than in the big city.

The only thing that mattered to Jim was that he'd now be living less than an hour away from his son.

Stephanie wondered when he would return. Without a calendar or a clock, she had no way of knowing what day it was or what time. It could be twelve noon or twelve midnight. There were no windows in this room and the only light was a bare bulb hanging from the ceiling, too high for her to reach without a ladder. Those first few days after he had abducted her, she had tried everything to escape, but soon realized that there was no way out except the way she'd come in, the single door at the top of the stairs through which he had dragged her. A week ago? Two weeks ago? To her, it seemed a lifetime ago.

He didn't keep her shackled any longer. She was free to roam about in the twelve-by-twelve room, which she felt certain was a partial basement, under either a house or a building of some kind. In the corner, surrounded by a four-foot cinder block stall, was a shower, commode, and sink, as if someone had once planned to turn this area into a spare bedroom and bath. The block walls had been painted yellow, which over time had faded to a dirty cream.

The smell of mildew and mustiness permeated the entire room and everything in it, which wasn't much. A metal bed, a chair, and a desk. He made her sit at the desk to eat when he brought her food, which he did almost every day. At first she had refused to eat; but then he had punished her, telling her that he would not allow her to starve herself to death.

The first time he raped her, she'd fought him, but she soon learned that the harder she fought, the more severe the punishment. He never tortured her to the point where she passed out. At least not yet. Just enough to derive pleasure from her screams. Sometimes he would rape her with a bottle or a wooden phallus before climbing on top of her. And he liked to bite her. She had his teeth prints all over her body, as well as dozens of small burns from where he'd pressed lighted cigarettes on her skin. Most of the burns were on her buttocks and breasts.

He had raped her so many times, tortured her so often, that there was nothing else in her mind, no room to remember her life before this madman had kidnapped her. It wasn't that she had given up easily or that she hadn't hoped and prayed to escape. She had climbed those stairs leading to the outside world numerous times, beaten on the door and cried for help. But there was no help for her. No hope of being rescued. There was nothing ahead for her except more of the same.

She wanted to die. Longed to die. It was the only way she would ever be free of him. But there was nothing in this room she could use to aid herself in committing suicide, so all she could do was hope that he would tire of her soon and kill her.

The lock on the door clicked. Stephanie's body tensed and her mind screamed silently as she stood there, frozen to the spot, knowing the monster would open the door and come down the steps.

Listening, her eyes focused on the bottom of the wooden staircase, she heard his footsteps. Slow and steady. Not rushing. Taking his time.

"Good evening, Stephanie," he said, a self-satisfied smile on his face.

"Is it evening?"

"Yes, it's nearly eleven o'clock."

He gazed at her, studying her from the top of her disheveled hair to the tips of her bare toes. Without being told, she knew what he expected, what he demanded of her. She was allowed to wear nothing except a black silk robe, and only when he wasn't there. With numb, trembling fingers, she undid the tie belt and peeled the robe from her shoulders. It fell to her feet, puddling on the floor like a soft, black cloud.

"My lovely Stephanie."

He came to her, took her by the hand and led her to the bed. Without being told, she lay down, parted her thighs and held her arms open to him.

"Always so willing to please," he said. "I love that about you."

"I love you." She told him what she knew he wanted to hear. "I want you more than I've ever wanted anyone. Please, darling, make love to me."

He quickly shed his clothing, as always very eager. What would he do to her first? He had to inflict some type of pain before he could become aroused enough to rape her.

But apparently not this time. When he stood over her, his eyes wild and his breathing hard, she saw that his penis was already erect.

"Turn over," he told her.

Knowing what he intended and that it was useless to protest, she turned over onto her stomach. She waited for the first blow, but there was none. Instead, his hand caressed her buttocks. Tenderly. And then she felt him as he crawled on top of her. She held her breath. He rammed into her. She whimpered in pain. He rode her with a fury, coming within minutes. Still embedded inside her, he kissed her shoulder, then grasped her hair and jerked her head up off the pillow.

He'd never done this before so she didn't know what to expect next. Suddenly, she felt something pressing against her neck, just below her chin.

"Do you want me to set you free, my darling?" he asked.

And then she realized that he held a knife to her throat.

No, please don't kill me, a part of her begged silently. That tiny part of her consciousness that longed to live, longed to believe that there was still hope. But the terrified, tormented part of her who couldn't bear to suffer any longer said aloud, "Yes, please. Please set me free."

And with one quick, deep slice of the sharp blade, he ended their relationship.

Please turn the page for an exciting sneak peek at
Beverly Barton's romantic suspense thriller
KILLING HER SOFTLY
available wherever books are sold.

Prologue

Lulu Vanderley was rich, blond and beautiful. Women envied her. Men wanted her. She had it all. Everything. Except . . . There was one thing she wanted that could never truly be hers. Quinn Cortez. And knowing she couldn't have him made her want him all the more.

They'd been lovers for several months, ever since they'd met through mutual acquaintances in Vail months ago. In the beginning, a hot affair had been enough for both of them. He'd made it clear from their very first date that he was a no-strings-attached kind of guy. And she'd been well aware of his love 'em and leave 'em reputation. But that was before she fell in love with the gorgeous hunk, before she'd decided that she wanted to become Mrs. Quinn Cortez. And as a general rule, Lulu got what Lulu wanted.

She stared at her reflection in the mirror and smiled devilishly. No man had ever been able to resist her. And that was one reason she and Quinn were perfect for each other. They were two peas in a pod—a couple of gorgeous, irresistible philanderers.

Tonight she would spring the trap, the age-old trap that had caught many a poor fool. Quinn wasn't invulnerable. He was as susceptible as any man to feminine wiles and little white lies. She'd weep and swear she didn't know how it could have happened. She'd told him the first time they had sex that she'd been on the pill for years, and since he'd also used a condom every time, convincing him she was pregnant might not be easy. But all he had to do was talk to her doctor. Lulu was definitely six weeks along.

Running her hands over her tall, slender body, from waist to narrow hips, she studied her image. Her beauty had always gotten her whatever her family's wealth couldn't buy. But neither could give her what she wanted most.

Quinn might be a womanizer, but he wasn't a heartless cad. If he believed she was carrying his child, then there was a good chance he'd do the honorable thing and marry her.

And if he doesn't, what will you do?

She'd get an abortion, of course. No way in hell did she want to get tied down with a squalling baby unless the little brat served some purpose.

The mantel clock struck the hour, reminding her that Quinn would be arriving soon. Her stomach tightened. Lulu laughed. It wasn't like her to be nervous.

Everything was ready. A bottle of champagne was chilling. A second bottle. She'd already drunk three glasses from the first bottle in an effort to steel her nerves and lull herself into a tranquil haze. Not good for the baby, she supposed, but what the hell. The silk bed linens were turned down, soft music was playing and she was wearing her most alluring sheer black teddy.

Quinn had just won another high profile case, this time involving country singer Terry McBryar. The Nashville jury had come back with a not guilty verdict in the case against McBryar, who had been accused of murdering his manager. Of course, this victory was only one in a long line for Quinn Cortez, who was one of the most highly acclaimed trial lawyers in the United States.

The fact that Quinn had a reputation for being ruthless excited Lulu. She'd always been fascinated by bad boys.

When she had telephoned him earlier today to congratulate him on his big win, she'd heard reluctance in his voice the minute she invited him to drive over to Memphis this evening so they could celebrate together. But in the end, she had persuaded him. Telling him that she'd be waiting in her bedroom, wearing only a teddy, and eager to suck his dick had given him all the incentive he needed.

"I can get there by eight," he'd told her. "Is your extra house key in the usual place?"

"Right where it always is," she'd said. "Just let yourself in. I'll be waiting."

Thinking about the night ahead, Lulu shivered with excitement. She'd had dozens of lovers, but none compared to Quinn. The guy was a real stud, in every sense of the word. She'd give him a blow job, and then they'd drink champagne and cuddle by the fireplace here in her bedroom. After he was relaxed and mellow, she'd spring her big surprise.

Guess what, Quinn; you're going to be a daddy.

Laughing, pleased with her almost foolproof plan to trap her man, Lulu twirled around the room.

She heard a noise. Someone had just opened the front door. Her heartbeat accelerated. Quinn was here. He'd arrived early. He must have broken every speed limit between Nashville and Memphis. That had to mean he was eager to see her.

Hurriedly she turned off all the lights and lit the candles she had arranged on top of the sleek, modern cherry dresser. Only the candlelight and the glow from the flickering blaze in the fireplace illuminated the room. The right ambience was so important.

"Quinn? Darling, I'm back here waiting for you."

His footsteps tapped quietly over the hardwood floors in the foyer and down the hall.

"You got here early, didn't you?" She licked her lips. Why wasn't he answering her?

She scratched her long fingernails over her nipples, hardening them instantly. "Come on back here, big boy. I've got just what you need."

She stood by the fireplace, primed and ready, eager for what lay ahead. When she saw him standing in the doorway, her heart caught in her throat. She did love this man, loved him to distraction. He stood there in the shadows, a tall, dark silhouette. Broad shouldered, lean hipped. Six-one. And every inch a man.

She held open her arms. "Come to Mama. Let me take good care of you."

He took several steps toward her. His blue-black hair glistened in the firelight. God, he was handsome. Ruggedly handsome in that exotic way only men of mixed heritages were. Quinn was a delicious mixture of Mexican and Irish.

As he neared her, she thought how incredibly young and sexy he looked tonight. Apparently even men looked better by candlelight. At forty, he possessed a body any twenty-year-old would envy. And she knew from personal experience that he had the stamina of a man half his age.

"Hello, Lulu," he said and she thought there was an

odd tone to his voice. He didn't sound quite like himself.

She took a tentative step toward him, closing the gap between them. When she looked up into his piercing black eyes, she gasped. "Quinn?"

"Were you expecting someone else?" he asked. "Another lover?"

"No, I wasn't expecting anyone else." She felt a sudden sense of unease. What was wrong with him? He was acting so strangely.

Maybe the problem wasn't with him. After all, she had drunk three glasses of champagne. Perhaps she was picking up on strange vibes where there were none.

He reached out and grasped her shoulders. She quivered.

"What's wrong? You're shivering," he said.

She stared directly at him, studying his tense features, as his big hands bit painfully into her shoulders. *Oh, God, how could this be?* She didn't understand what was going on.

"You're acting as if you're afraid of me."

"I—I am." She tried to pull away, but he held her in his strong grip. "Let go of me." When she struggled against him, he pushed her backward, his dark eyes boring into her with unadulterated hatred. "I don't understand . . . what . . . how . . ."

She felt addled, her thoughts fuzzy, her mind playing tricks on her.

As he shoved her backward, she somehow managed to escape his tenacious grasp. She had to get away from him before he hurt her, and her gut instincts warned her that he was definitely dangerous. She turned and ran, intending to lock herself in the bathroom and use the telephone in there to call for help. But before she reached the bathroom door, he caught her by the wrist, whirled her around and flipped her over and onto the bed.

The satin sheets felt cold and clammy against her bare arms and legs. The menacing shadow hovered over her. Shock waves jangled her nerves. Why hadn't she realized sooner that something wasn't quite right?

Because you drank too much champagne.

He came down over her, bracing his knees on either side of her hips, trapping her beneath him. She opened her mouth in a silent scream, her voice paralyzed by fear.

Don't panic. Maybe he just wants to play rough. Maybe he isn't going to hurt you.

"You're a fool, Lulu," he said in that strange, unfamiliar tone of voice. "And I don't suffer fools gladly."

"What—what are you talking about? Please—"

"Do you know what I do to foolish women?"

He reached over and picked up one of the king-size pillows from the head of the bed. She tried to shove him off her, but without success. He was too big, too strong. He lifted his knee and pressed it against her belly, effectively holding her in place and enabling him to use both hands to maneuver the pillow.

"I kill foolish women," he told her. "I kill them softly . . . tenderly . . . and put them out of their misery."

"No!" She managed to scream once before he covered her face with the huge pillow. Oh, God, he really was going to kill her. Smother her.

Help me, please, dear God, help me.

She wriggled and squirmed, thrashing her head about, seeking air, but he kept the pillow securely in place. With what little strength she had left, she grasped his wrists, but the effort proved useless. He pressed the pillow down and held it tightly. Within seconds her hands loosened. Her arms dropped languidly to either side of her still body. Her chest ached. Swirling gray circles appeared in the blackness behind her closed eyelids.

Lulu had one final coherent thought.

I can't breathe. I can't breathe!

Romantic Suspense From
Lisa Jackson

More Nail-Biting Suspense From Your Favorite Thriller Authors